Dickens and
the Despised Mother

Dickens and
the Despised Mother

A Critical Reading of
Three Autobiographical Novels

SHALE PRESTON

McFarland & Company, Inc., Publishers
Jefferson, North Carolina, and London

LIBRARY OF CONGRESS CATALOGUING-IN-PUBLICATION DATA

Preston, Shale.
Dickens and the despised mother : a critical reading of three autobiographical novels / Shale Preston.
p.   cm.
Includes bibliographical references and index.

ISBN 978-0-7864-7139-3

1. Dickens, Charles, 1812–1870 — Family.   2. Dickens, Charles, 1812–1870 — Criticism and interpretation.   I. Title.
PR4582.P74 2013
823'.8 — dc23   2012044135

BRITISH LIBRARY CATALOGUING DATA ARE AVAILABLE

Front cover images: Woodcut of woman pointing with border (clipart.com)

Manufactured in the United States of America

McFarland & Company, Inc., Publishers
Box 611, Jefferson, North Carolina 28640
www.mcfarlandpub.com

I dedicate this book to my mother,
Erica Corinna Smith

Acknowledgments

I would like to express my great appreciation to Professor Virginia Blain who consistently gave me her excellent, incisive advice and whose comments on the manuscript led to important changes. Special thanks to Associate Professor Jennifer Gribble for confidently suggesting that I could write a book on Charles Dickens. Without this nudge, I would never have embarked on this difficult but fascinating journey.

I am particularly grateful to Sue Felix for her meticulous proof-reading.

My abiding gratitude is extended to Dr. Elizabeth Parry who insisted that I must finish this project when I had all but given up. My sincere appreciation is also extended to Sarah Parry for her encouragement over the course of this project.

Immeasurable thanks to my mother, Erica Corinna Smith, who fostered my love of literature and helped me from a young age to develop my writing skills.

Some of the contents of this study have appeared elsewhere in different forms. Material from Chapter 3 appeared in "Dirty Davy and the Domestic Sublime," in Jeanne-Pierre Naugrette, coord., *Réussir l'épreuve de littérature: David Copperfield*, C.A.P.E.S./Agrégation Anglais, Paris: Editions Ellipses, 1996, 128–36, and "True Romance? Dirty Davy and the Domestic Sublime: From the Alps to the Abject in *David Copperfield*," *Australasian Victorian Studies Journal* 3:2 (1998): 59–69. Material from Chapter 6 appeared in "Beating Foucault to the Punch: Dickens, Death, Limit Experience and the Pleasure of Killing Nancy," *Australasian Victorian Studies Journal* 4 (1998): 88–97.

Table of Contents

"But he had — as most men who grow up to be great and good are generally found to have had — an excellent mother."
— Charles Dickens, *A Child's History of England*

Preface

This book offers new pathways into the novels of Charles Dickens which contain extended first-person narratives (*David Copperfield, Bleak House* and *Great Expectations*) with reference to the only piece of autobiographical writing that Dickens is known to have produced. This manuscript, which covers the early years of Dickens's life, has not survived and is something of a mystery. As John Bowen notes: "We do not know for certain when it was written, how long it was, or how much of Dickens's life it treated."[1] Nevertheless, it would appear that it was written around 1847 and regardless of its length and scope, it clearly expresses Dickens's anguish at having been put to work as a child in the Warren's Blacking warehouse after his father was arrested for debt and taken to the Marshalsea Prison. Originally intended to form part of an autobiography, the piece (now known as the autobiographical fragment) was instead put to use in a transmuted form in Dickens's novel *David Copperfield* and, much later after Dickens's death, was incorporated in John Forster's *The Life of Charles Dickens*.

Dating from the publication of Edmund Wilson's seminal article "Dickens: The Two Scrooges"[2] in 1941, critics have turned to the autobiographical fragment to produce a range of psycho-biographical trauma thesis readings of Dickens's fiction, but in more recent years some critics have actively questioned this line of approach and have sought instead to produce other, less trauma-focused readings of Dickens's work. While appreciating the reasons behind such a critical shift, I cannot help but share Lawrence J. Clipper's view (albeit expressed in 1981) that "the exegesis of Dickens's works from this biographical perspective has not gone far enough."[3] Indeed, what could arguably be described as one of the most important aspects of the autobiographical fragment — the rhetoric of implicit disgust which underlies the depiction of Dickens's mother, Elizabeth Dickens — has largely been overlooked. Accordingly, this book will seek to tease out this aspect of the autobiographical fragment and will suggest that the rhetoric of implicit disgust which underpins the portrait of Elizabeth Dickens is actually replicated in the portraits of the protagonists' mothers within Dickens's autobiographical novels. The rhetorical link between the portraits is interrogated through close textual analysis which draws upon the etiology of disgust. Whilst a range of writers within different fields have sought to understand the affect of disgust, this study will show that Mary Douglas's anthropological understanding of pollution and Julia Kristeva's psychoanalytic concept of abjection provide the most profitable exegetic tools to explore the anti-maternal rhetoric within Dickens's autobiographical novels.

To my knowledge there has been no sustained study of the mother in Dickens's fiction, let alone one that employs biographical criticism as a key feature of its exegetic framework. Most scholars note that Dickens was highly dismissive towards his mother and that the garrulous Mrs. Nickleby was probably based on her, but beyond this they do not delve much further into the relationship. Further, they do not seek to explore whether this had any significance in relation to the representation of the mothers in his fictional output. There have been some specific treatments of the mother characters in Dickens's work. Natalie McKnight's *Suffering Mothers in Mid-Victorian Novels* (New York: St. Martin's Press, 1997) devotes a chapter to the subject, and Carolyn Dever's *Death and the Mother from Dickens to Freud: Victorian Fiction and the Anxiety of Origins* (Cambridge: Cambridge University Press, 1998) examines Dickens's treatment of the mother in one of his novels, *Bleak House*. Patricia Ingham has also examined some of the mothers in his work in her book *Dickens, Women and Language* (New York: Harvester Wheatsheaf, 1992) and so too has Michael Slater in his seminal work *Dickens and Women* (Stanford: Stanford University Press, 1983). However, as a specific field of interest, there has been no sustained study of the mother in Dickens's fiction.

It is also important to note that there are surprisingly few book-length works of feminist literary criticism on Charles Dickens and of these, Patricia Ingham's *Dickens, Women and Language* is probably the best known. While this study is valuable, it rather reductively heaps all of Dickens's women characters into taxonomical categories: nubile girls, fallen girls, excessive females, passionate women and true mothers. In addition, the chapter entitled "True Mothers" explores the characters in Dickens's work that evinced "the capacity to 'mother' or nurture" and this capacity, as Ingham claims, is typically "not found in those who have actually given birth and who have the societal status of mother. Such women are excluded as monsters of selfishness, unless death made them defect from duty."[4] I believe that my analysis of Dickens's mother characters (both biological and adoptive) offers a more nuanced reading, and it has the advantage of being informed by the compelling "self-oriented" models of disgust that are put forward by Mary Douglas and Julia Kristeva.

On a personal note, when I first decided to write a book on Charles Dickens I don't think I had any idea what I was getting into. I had no idea, for instance, that it would consume years of my life and occupy most of my waking thoughts. This is ironic, in light of the fact that I can't say that I ever had a burning passion to write about Dickens! It was only because I mentioned to Associate Professor Jennifer Gribble (at Sydney University) that I had enjoyed reading Peter Ackroyd's biography *Dickens* that the subject even suggested itself. "Why don't you do a study on Dickens?" Jenny said. "I'm sure you could do something interesting with Dickens." Just two sentences but they changed my life. Following this, I went away and read everything that I could on and by Dickens, and in the process I came to understand how mountaineers must feel when they are faced with what seems like an insurmountable prospect. The sheer scale of Dickens's work is enormous (let alone all of the scholarship that has followed). It is not without good reason that Dickens's body of work has actually been characterized as sublime.[5] Many, many times I felt like giving up, but *always* something led me on, and I now know it was more than the need for closure.

If I didn't know, at the beginning, what I was getting into, I also didn't know what I wanted to write about Dickens. Initially, I decided that I was going to write a work called *Dickens and Philosophy.* That idea, however, despite yielding a couple of journal articles, just didn't and wouldn't come together. After this, I decided to write a work called *Dickens and Dirt.* Again, the idea, fittingly enough, just never took shape. There was always something that kept getting in the way and that something, in retrospect, was Dickens's mother, Elizabeth Dickens. No matter which way I turned with Dickens, it was always his relationship with his mother that seemed to be behind his work and even behind the meaning of his life. In a nutshell, this is why *Dickens and the Despised Mother: A Critical Reading of Three Autobiographical Novels* has made its way into the world, more than two hundred years after Elizabeth Dickens gave birth to Charles Dickens.

CHAPTER ONE

The Autobiographical Fragment

The mothers (biological and adoptive) of the protagonists in the novels of Charles Dickens which contain major fictional autobiographies—*David Copperfield*, *Bleak House* and *Great Expectations*—have not to my knowledge been subject to exegetic analysis as a distinct category or semantic field. In all of these autobiographical novels,[1] the protagonists effectively have two mothers. In *David Copperfield*, David Copperfield's biological mother is Clara Copperfield, and sometime after her death, his great-aunt, Betsey Trotwood, becomes his adoptive mother. In *Bleak House*, Esther Summerson's biological mother is eventually revealed to be Lady Dedlock and her foster mother is her aunt, Miss Barbary (although she is known to Esther, while alive, as her godmother). In *Great Expectations*, Pip's biological mother is the deceased Georgiana Pirrip and his foster mother is his much older sister, the termagant Mrs. Joe. Certainly this bifurcated approach to the protagonists' maternal relations in the major fictional autobiographies is noteworthy enough in itself, but perhaps more noteworthy is the fact that in each fictional autobiography the rhetorical techniques of implicit condemnation, structural antithesis, and negation are used to render the mothers (extant and deceased) as objects of disgust. In *David Copperfield*, the eponymous narrator implicitly depicts his biological mother, Clara, as worldly, foolish, vain, selfish, sexually alluring, indulgent and willful. He also juxtaposes the actions of his mother with the actions of her good and faithful servant, Peggotty, and, in doing so, highlights his mother's deficiencies. As to his adoptive mother, Aunt Betsey, he subtly works to show that she is maternally bankrupt. Indeed, without a good man at her side her judgment concerning her young nephew is completely wanting. Even a man "all out of his mind"[2] (Mr. Dick) is ironically more "well meaning" towards "the fatherless little stranger"[3] than Aunt Betsey. Compounding this, David Copperfield rhetorically constructs his eventual wife, the awesomely good and pure Agnes, as the natural object through which he can achieve sublimity and an illusion of self-creation. Accordingly, he further underscores the flawed natures of his biological and adoptive mothers and effectively negates their maternal roles in the text. In *Bleak House*, the protagonist, Esther Summerson, depicts her godmother, Miss Barbary, as severe, cruel, dismissive, unapproachable and guilt-inducing. She also implicitly juxtaposes her godmother with her much-loved doll. Ironically, this inanimate object possesses all of the qualities — kindness, patience, attentiveness and receptiveness — that Miss Barbary lacks. These qualities, albeit projected, nevertheless serve to indict Miss Barbary as unfit to be a mother. Esther also implicitly condemns her biological mother, Lady Dedlock, as arrogant, cold and abandoning and pointedly highlights Lady Dedlock's derelict nature by focusing on the absolute love and devotion that Ada Clare displays towards her. Furthermore, as I will contend, just as the omniscient narrator in *Bleak House* burns the iniquitous Court of Chancery in effigy through the spontaneous combustion demise of Krook, the masochistic and self-loathing Esther burns her mothers in effigy through "accidentally" contracting a feverish and disfiguring disease. As to *Great Expectations*, Pip implicitly depicts his deceased biological mother, Georgiana Pirrip, as a dangerously anomalous member of the Pirrip family and even (in a structural sense) holds her responsible for the deaths of his father and five brothers. Pip also depicts his older sister and foster mother, Mrs. Joe, as unjust, cruel and abusive; implicitly juxtaposes her with her apparently gentle and innocent husband Joe Gargery; and even years after her death does not credit her with any redeeming features. Why does Dickens adopt this insidious and revulsion-fueled approach to maternal representation in the works which contain his major fictional autobiographies? The answer, I believe, can be found in "Dickens's most ostensibly personal writing,"[4] the highly rhetorical piece of self-narrative now known as the autobiographical fragment.

The autobiographical fragment,[5] written, it seems, around 1847,[6] has received consistent critical attention since Edmund Wilson's seminal article of 1941, "Dickens: The Two Scrooges." In this article, Wilson asserted that the autobiographical fragment (which chiefly expresses Dickens's anguish at being put to work as a child in the Warren's Blacking warehouse after his father is arrested for debt and taken to the Marshalsea Prison) is the key to understanding Dickens's entire oeuvre:

> The work of Dickens's whole career was an attempt to digest these early shocks and hardships, to explain them to himself, to justify himself in relation to them, to give an intelligible and tolerable picture of a world in which such things could occur.[7]

Writing in 1981, Lawrence J. Clipper observed that this argument "lies at the heart of almost all that has been written about Dickens and his novels." Nevertheless, Clipper maintained, "My own view is that the exegesis of Dickens's works from this biographical perspective has not gone far enough."[8] By contrast, a later critic, Alexander Welsh, vigorously argues against using the traumatic events described in the autobiographical fragment to explain aspects of Dickens's work. Welsh rather uncharitably or "irreverently"[9] speculates that Dickens might have retrospectively believed that he was traumatized:

> We do not know when Dickens discovered or decided that his experience in the blacking warehouse was traumatic. A reasonable assumption is that he did not recognize it as such before the writing of his autobiographical fragment and of *Copperfield*.[10]

In such a way, Welsh almost accuses Dickens of having worked himself into a trauma for his own purposes in much the same way that Mrs. Joe in *Great Expectations* "deliberately took extraordinary pains"[11] to work herself into a fury. Furthermore, Welsh contends that a trauma in childhood does not provide "the best ground for biographical criticism"[12] and proposes instead that Erik Erikson's notion of "moratoria" may be used to interpret three novels that Dickens produced around the time that he wrote his autobiographical fragment: *Martin Chuzzlewit*, *Dombey & Son*, and *David Copperfield*. A moratorium, as Welsh understands it, is a period of "marking time" before "a person with a particular historical contribution to make"[13] commits to his or her respective purpose or course of action. In Dickens's case, Welsh believes, his moratorium occurred between early 1842 and late 1846, a restless period in which Dickens traveled to America, flirted with different careers upon his return, and wrote the Christmas books which variously explore the concept of starting one's life afresh.[14] Robert Newsom is somewhat skeptical about applying the term *moratorium* to this period in Dickens's life:

> Of course, in the case of a writer as energetic as Dickens, the term *moratorium* is relative, for during this interval he publishes not only *Martin Chuzzlewit* and *American Notes* but also *Pictures from Italy* and the first four Christmas books (the *Carol*, *The Chimes*, *The Cricket on the Hearth*, and *The Battle of Life*), and he founds a newspaper (the *Daily News*).[15]

Linda M. Shires is even less persuaded by Welsh's argument. For Shires, Dickens's so-called moratorium is not "fundamentally different in its emotional resonances from the painful warehouse incident"[16] described in Dickens's autobiographical fragment. So, too, Rosemarie Bodenheimer, while acknowledging Welsh's attempt to protest against the "long biographical and critical tradition of representing Warren's as an originary trauma"[17] claims that Dickens's Warren's Blacking memories were "of a piece"[18] with the emotions that he experienced during his ostensible "moratorium." I concur with Shires and Bodenheimer, and while I can appreciate that Dickens may have "marked time" before he reaffirmed his vocation as a writer, I do not feel that the concept of moratoria offers a sufficiently compelling reason to turn away in an exegetic sense from the childhood trauma described in the autobiographical fragment. Perhaps the most credible challenge to Edmund Wilson's trauma thesis has been mounted by John Drew. Drew concedes:

> The tendencies of Wilson's psycho-biographical reading retain a potent hold today. Yet a recent discovery at the British Newspaper Library threatens to undermine the legend, or at least to question whether it tells the whole story. Dickens wrote that fragment of autobiography in 1847, more than 20 years after leaving the blacking factory, and there is no doubt that by then the memory loomed large in his perspective on his life. But now there is room to claim that much earlier on in his career, Dickens's feelings of revulsion were much less vehement — to the extent, in fact, that he was prepared to write not just one but possibly a whole series of comic poems — early advertising jingles — blithely eulogising Warren's boot blacking.[19]

The discovery that Drew speaks of is a poem which appeared on the front page of the *True Sun* on March 13, 1832. This humorous poem, called "The Turtle Dove," is an advertisement for Warren's Blacking, as Drew writes: "All through the 1820s and early 1830s, London newspapers regularly carried poetic tributes to Warren's Blacking in their advertisement pages."[20] Dickens has not been directly linked to these "puff-verses" because it is generally accepted that his first published work was a December 1833 magazine tale called "A Dinner at Poplar Walk." However, according to Drew there is an entry in "an obscure diary of events for the year 1833"[21] by the leading journalist for the *Morning Chronicle*, John Payne Collier, that points to Dickens as the author of this particular comic poem. In *Old Man's Diary*, published in 1872,[22] Collier relates that Dickens's maternal uncle John Henry Barrow, in attempting to obtain a permanent job for the young Dickens at the *Morning Chronicle*, told Collier that Dickens had written puff-verses for Warren's Blacking and cited "The Turtle Dove" as an example of his nephew's literary prowess. Admiring the clever and Pindaric nature of the poem, Collier agreed to meet with Dickens, and this resulted in his employment at the *Morning Chronicle* which in turn led to Dickens's sketches of London (later collected as *Sketches by Boz*). Owing to this diary entry and the similarities between "The Turtle Dove" and other poems by Dickens (both published and unpublished), Drew confidently claims it is "almost certain that 'The Turtle Dove' (and possibly the nine other rhyming advertisements which followed it at roughly fortnightly intervals in the *True Sun*) constitutes Dickens's first published work in any genre."[23] Moreover, he believes that these poems put into question Edmund Wilson's assertion that the trauma of Dickens's blacking warehouse experience constitutes the wound that lies behind his extraordinary body of work:

> In their witty superficiality, the image of Dickens at a previously obscure period of his career is clearly reflected. Rather than the world-famous author and Victorian paterfamilias, agonising over the secret shame of boyhood bondage, they show an inventive parodist, down-at-heel and self-ironic, prepared to coin the

forms of both popular culture and his own private experience into shiny new currency.[24]

Drew's argument is compelling. However, if we give credence to Drew's assertion that Dickens is the author of one or more of these amusing Warren's Blacking advertisements, it does not necessarily follow that "Wilson's psychobiographical reading" is undermined. Rather, it shows that "an impecunious Dickens,"[25] as Drew puts it, was prepared to draw upon his experiences to good and remunerative effect. His feelings of revulsion in relation to his time in the blacking warehouse may still have been every bit as real and catalytic in terms of his art, but these feelings could be put aside in the interests of earning a living. To question the depth of his feeling because he may have produced a string of commercial poems is unfair and does a disservice to the complexity of his work. Furthermore, even if Dickens recognized his pain only much later, Wilson's trauma thesis is still not rendered invalid, as Rosemarie Bodenheimer explains: "Parodic verse would, however, be just the response to trauma one might expect from the young Dickens; the fact that early pain is recognized in retrospect conforms to a 'normal' trajectory of traumatic experience."[26] Moreover, Bodenheimer, by way of reference to work on the interface between literature and psychoanalysis, astutely points to the haunting nature of trauma: "Trauma is recognizable ... in the repetitive returns of memory fragments. There is no way to count the variety of metaphors, moods, or tones through which such fragments could be evoked by a writer like Dickens."[27]

Doubtless, the autobiographical fragment has frequently been used to explain aspects of Dickens's work, including: the dark side of his fiction primarily manifest in his imaginative identification with criminals and rebels[28]; his frequent focus on abandoned children; his fairy-tale plots[29]; the "continual preoccupation with food" in his fiction[30]; the "vein of self-pity"[31] that pervades so many of his novels; the "traces of shame" that persist throughout his oeuvre[32]; and the largely unconscious motifs that run throughout his work of aggression against parental figures along with the guilt that this induces.[33] However, it is timely to consider how it might also help to explain the disgust that underlies his depiction of the protagonists' mothers in the novels which contain Dickens's major first-person narratives.

The autobiographical fragment, as I will seek to show, is shot through with the disgust that Dickens felt towards his mother, Elizabeth Dickens. Through subtle rhetoric, Dickens effectively represents his mother as the original perpetrator of injustice in his life. Accordingly, unlike the obvious "Swiftian savagery of [Dickens's] depiction of old Mrs. Skewton"[34] in his novel *Dombey and Son*, the disgust that Dickens directs at his mother operates at a largely subterranean level. Indeed, the fragment contains what can only be described as implicit, disingenuous disgust, but this form of disgust is no less devastating in terms of

its effects. Furthermore and significantly, this particular form of disgust is replicated in the treatment of the mothers of the protagonists in the novels which
contain Dickens's major fictional autobiographies. Certainly, each protagonist
has two mother figures, unlike Dickens, but this would appear to be yet another
rhetorical strategy. Indeed, by giving each protagonist two mothers, Dickens
effectively gave himself more leverage to explore the areas of maternal transgression that concerned him. Certainly, Dickens's fiction is rarely deemed to
have an underside. As Steven O'Connor writes:

> It is hard to think of an art that is less secretive than Dickens's; perhaps the uncom-
> fortable thing about his writing is not its sense of hidden depths, but its inexplicable
> and monstrous (in its earliest etymological sense) *ostension*. Unlike other writers,
> Dickens keeps his underside clearly and flagrantly on display.[35]

While this may be the case for much of Dickens's art, I believe that this particular
area of his work seriously brings this assessment into question.

In her work *Dickens, Women and Language*, Patricia Ingham argues:

> It is appropriate for feminists concerned with the construction of gender in the
> nineteenth-century novel to address themselves to language, not directly to social
> conditions. Specifically, this means in the first instance considering what can be
> called the semantic field relating to women: all those groupings of women under
> linguistic signs (with their characteristic significances) that can be distinguished
> in Dickens's novels. A parallel would be the anthropologist's consideration of the
> linguistic terms for kinship (and their significances) in a given social group. In
> both these fields the critic is confronted by referents (or physical entities) and the
> linguistic signs to which they relate. But the relationship is not a simple one in
> which the referent is to be regarded as the meaning of the sign.[36]

Ingham goes on to consider the range of signs deployed by Dickens in his rep-
resentations of women by classifying his women characters into different categories:
nubile girls, fallen girls, excessive females, passionate women and true mothers.
Ingham is clearly critical of biographical criticism (specifically John Carey's *The
Violent Effigy* and Michael Slater's *Dickens and Women*[37]) that seeks to explain
Dickens's women characters in terms of the actual women in Dickens's life:

> The approach offered here differs radically from Carey's and Slater's. It gives a
> coherent account of the women in Dickens's novels through an examination of the
> language in which they are constructed, that common medium for the ideologies
> of class and gender which inform and evaluate them. This relocates such figures
> where they belong: in the text, not in some specious hinterland behind it. Each
> instance of a stereotype can then be shown to be the particular exponent of an
> abstraction; such images are like examples of a literary genre which never occur in
> a pure and unmodified form. To write of a work as "a courtly love lyric" or "a
> medieval romance" is to refer to individual modifications of an assumed norm.
> Similarly, each example of a female stereotype is a variation on it; and its multiple
> forms turn into a site for possible linguistic change. This kind of change always
> starts with an individual whose idiosyncratic variants create flux not stasis.[38]

In backing up her argument, Ingham provides a postscript wherein she includes excerpts from Dickens's letters to demonstrate that the accounts that Dickens gave of real women were as much literary constructs as those of the fictional women within his novels. For Ingham, while the women in Dickens's novels "interact" with the women in Dickens's life, "it is more appropriate to deal with the interaction in terms of life imitating art; of life *as* literary art."[39] If one examines Ingham's own language, it is interesting to note that while Ingham professes to be interested in linguistic flux and change, she nonetheless restricts herself and others to what she regards as "appropriate." Whether or not it is appropriate for feminists concerned with the construction of gender in the nineteenth-century novel to address themselves to language as opposed to social conditions or whether or not it is appropriate to examine life as literary art as opposed to art imitating life are moot points. Certainly it is important to consider the language in which Dickens's women characters are presented, just as it is important to consider the language in which Dickens described the actual women that he knew or met. However, while Ingham attempts to privilege linguistic criticism over biographical criticism and life *as* literary art over art imitating life; I would like in this study to draw the various fields together and in doing so hopefully tease out new meanings and frames of reference. Accordingly, I will parallel the subtle rhetorical disgust that Dickens employed in the autobiographical fragment to depict his mother with the equally subtle rhetorical disgust that he used to portray the central mother characters in the novels that he wrote which contain major first person narratives.

It should be said from the outset that I am interested in the disgust that underlies Dickens's depiction of characters (in this case the central mother characters in the major first-person narratives) as opposed to the *content* in his work which elicits disgust in readers. This is an important distinction to make because my work takes an entirely different direction to that of Annette R. Federico, who appears to be the first critic to explicitly link Dickens to disgust. In her journal article "Dickens and Disgust," published in 2000, Federico claims that "Dickens was a genius at generating images, including images of bodies which some of his contemporaries found disgusting, despite his moral intentions, social satire, or low comedy."[40] For Federico, "slime, ooze, and viscosity"[41] are the primary sources of disgust for Victorian readers of Dickens's novels and his "graphic descriptions of the body's excretions, excrescences, and explosions"[42] are particularly offensive. Drawing on Mary Douglas's anthropological work on pollution, Federico examines a number of repellent episodes in Dickens's novels, the chief of these being Krook's spontaneous-combustion death in *Bleak House.* However, while Victorian readers may have found such images disgusting, Federico takes the view that Dickens progressively worked to challenge traditional systems of knowledge: "Dickens should be understood then, as an agent for change, a celebrator of disproportion and anomalousness in a culture that cherishes order and symmetry."[43] Federico's argument is interesting, but as I am concerned with the disgust that underlies Dickens's depictions of the central mother figures in his autobiographical novels, my view is, of necessity, not nearly as sanguine as Federico's. Prior to Federico's article, when critics have considered disgust in Dickens's work, the novel that they have invariably focused on is *Our Mutual Friend*. To be sure, this is the novel which most obviously conveys Dickens's disgust towards the prevailing societal drive for "filthy lucre." Jack Lindsay, for instance, observes:

> The notion of wealth as a foul dust-heap, over which men spent their time struggling, stirred [Dickens's] deepest ironies. The equation of money and filth or dung goes far down in the psyche, as dream analysis has shown. In using the dust-heap as the emblem of the great prize for which men were fighting, Dickens starts off with a fantasy-image which fitly utters his contempt and hatred.[44]

Earl Davis is also keenly aware of Dickens's revulsion at the universal struggle for wealth. For Davis, *Our Mutual Friend* displays "exquisite and sustained disgust"[45] and it is Dickens's "sardonic disgust which gives his last great novel its character and tone."[46] Michael Steig, however, points out that Dickens's disgust is not confined to *Our Mutual Friend* because Dickens, like Jonathan Swift, possessed "an excremental vision" and this is evident "in such disparate works as *A Christmas Carol* and *Bleak House*."[47] According to Steig, if Jonathan Swift "seems torn between disgust at and acceptance of the psychological and biological facts about man, Dickens' vision of his own society is equally sweeping and equally ambivalent."[48] Added to this, Steig believes that Dickens emphasized cleanliness and order as the answer to his negative view of society, and in *Bleak House* this was embodied in the "virtual sexlessness of Esther and the law-and-order of Bucket."[49]

Steig's position is impressively developed by Jeremy Tambling. For Tambling, Dickens represents "the fascinated spirit of excess" that writes about "and hence produces" the excremental but at the same time rejects it.[50] Tambling shows how Dickens links filth with people. Not only does Dickens name characters in relation to sewage and scum (i.e., Murdstone, Turveydrop and Mr. Merdle) but he links mud to affective disorders and infection to rapacious practices. Furthermore, Tambling is sensitive to the ways in which Dickens associates the mother with filth and refuse. According to Tambling, a number of dominant places and symbols in Dickens's novels (i.e., Jacob's Island in *Oliver Twist*; Tom-all-Alone's and the Chancery in *Bleak House*; the river and the dust mounds in *Our Mutual Friend*) might be connected "with that which is imaged as the mother."[51] In making this contention, Tambling cites Julia Kristeva's theory of abjection:

The association of the mother with filth and refuse, with that which must be repudiated, corresponds in Julia Kristeva's *Powers of Horror* to abjection, which is the violent state of denial of the mother, a rejection of her body being essential for the establishment of borders, for the creation of the narcissistically complete ego (which, in Bataille's terms, would belong to the homogeneous). Kristeva places such a denial of the mother outside the Oedipal struggle with the father: however, this abjection of the mother, where she is seen as split, divided rather than as whole, produces the melancholy subject that is "abject" as well, not certain of its boundaries, neither constituted singly as a subject, nor part of the object, the mother.[52]

Tambling stresses that examining the abjection of the mother in Dickens's work does not necessarily mean that one should examine Dickens's relationship with his own mother. Rather, for Tambling, "the rejection of the mother is systemic, though the contradictions it produces in Dickens show up on every page in the violence of the writings."[53] Tambling's work is of particular interest in terms of exploring disgust and the mothers of the protagonists in the novels which contain major fictional autobiographies. His observations with reference to Kristeva's concept of abjection are also cogent. However, while I can appreciate Tambling's point that the rejection of the mother in Dickens's work is systemic, I believe that Dickens's work (particularly in the novels which contain major "first person" narratives) reveals such a profound and complex underlying repudiation of the mother that one *cannot* ignore Dickens's relationship with his own mother. Accordingly, it is important to examine the fragment that, of all Dickens's writing, gives us the best insight into how he felt towards his mother.

The Autobiographical Fragment

In March or April of 1847,[54] John Forster, Dickens's closest friend and later biographer, put to Dickens a question: "I asked if he remembered ever having seen in his boyhood our friend the elder Mr. Dilke, his father's acquaintance and contemporary."[55] Dickens said that "he recollected seeing him at a house ... where his uncle Barrow lodged during an illness, and Mr. Dilke had visited him. Never at any other time."[56] John Forster expressed surprise because Mr. Dilke had specifically spoken of having "accidentally" come upon the young Dickens working in a warehouse near the Strand. At the time of this unexpected meeting he had given Dickens "the gift of a half-crown" and Dickens had responded with a "very low bow."[57]

Forster's revelatory pronouncement apparently rendered Dickens speechless. "He was silent for several minutes. I felt that I had unintentionally touched a painful place in his memory."[58] "Some weeks later,"[59] however, Dickens affirmed that the recollection had hit a raw nerve in that it had referred to a time which he could never forget and which had always haunted him and filled him with misery. He then revealed to Forster chiefly through the means of a fragment of rhetorical writing the details of his traumatic childhood. Forster states:

> It had all been written, as fact, before he thought of any other use for it; and it was not until several months later, when the fancy of *David Copperfield*, itself suggested by what he had so written of his early troubles, began to take shape in his mind, that he abandoned his first intention of writing his own life.[60]

It is worthwhile here to present the most salient details of Dickens's childhood. At the age of nine, owing to his father's feckless nature and monetary mismanagement, Dickens was forced to discontinue his schooling. As Dickens put it:

> I know my father to be as kindhearted and generous a man as ever lived in the world. Everything that I can remember of his conduct to his wife, or children, or friends, in sickness or affliction, is beyond all praise.... But, in the ease of his temper, and the straightness of his means, he appeared to have utterly lost at this time the idea of educating me at all, and to have utterly put from him the notion that I had any claim upon him, in that regard whatever. So I degenerated into cleaning his boots of a morning, and my own; and making myself useful in the work of the little house; and looking after my younger brothers and sisters (we were now six in all); and going on such poor errands as arose out of our poor way of living.[61]

Worse was yet to come, however. When Dickens was approximately twelve years of age, his father was arrested for debt and taken to Marshalsea Prison.[62] According to John Forster, "The last words said to [Dickens] by his father before he was finally carried to the Marshalsea, were to the effect that the sun was set upon him for ever."[63] Upon hearing these words, Dickens was devastated: "I really believed at the time," said Dickens to Forster, "that they had broken my heart."[64] A short time later, it seems that Dickens's mother was forced to pawn virtually all of the family belongings.[65] Notably, there is nothing in the autobiographical fragment which directly states that Elizabeth Dickens systematically arranged to sell the family's possessions. Forster, in one of his linking paragraphs, writes:

> Then, at home, came many miserable daily struggles that seemed to last an immense time, yet did not perhaps cover many weeks. Almost everything by degrees was sold or pawned, little Charles being the principal agent in those sorrowful transactions.[66]

Significantly, Forster mentions:

> Such of the books as had been brought from Chatham, *Peregrine Pickle*, *Roderick Random*, *Tom Jones*, *Humphrey Clinker*, and all the rest, went first. They were carried off from the little chiffonier, which his father called the library, to a bookseller in the Hampstead Road, the same that David Copperfield describes as in the City Road.[67]

Earlier, in Forster's *Life of Dickens* it is made clear that these were the books that the young Dickens had loved and esteemed in his childhood. Indeed, Forster speaks of how Dickens "made the acquaintance of" these books and read them "over and over" to the point where they represented "a host of friends."[68] Dickens, then, was made to be the "principal agent" in selling his "friends." He was also made to be responsible for gradually selling the household furniture until "there was nothing left except a few chairs, a kitchen table and some beds." After this, the family "encamped as it were, in the two parlours of the emptied house, and lived there night and day."[69] Forster does not state that Elizabeth Dickens appointed the young Dickens as the family's "principal" selling agent but the implication is certainly there. He also doesn't state that it was insensitive of her to get Dickens to *immediately* sell off the books that he loved, but again, the text obliquely hints at this. In Forster's account, Elizabeth Dickens's name might be elided, but with her husband in prison, these humiliating and "sorrowful" transactions would, of necessity, have been instigated by her. Through no fault of her own then, she would have been associated in Dickens's mind with selling off not just the things he held dear but parts of his identity. In addition, she would have been associated with negatively altering the face of his childhood home.

These points are of particular importance when considering the actions of Clara Copperfield in *David Copperfield* and Mrs. Joe in *Great Expectations*. Indeed, as I will discuss later, both of these characters not only appear to engage in selling off their child or aspects of their child's identity but they are also associated with negatively altering their respective domestic spaces. Clara Copperfield, it appears, sells off her son's caul and introduces the contaminating Murdstone into the family home. As to Mrs. Joe, she seems keen to sell Pip off to the highest bidder in her insistence that he should go and play at the wealthy Miss Havisham's house; and she is directly charged in Pip's narrative with unacceptable levels of domestic discomfort: "[she] had an exquisite art of making her cleanliness more uncomfortable and unacceptable than dirt itself."[70]

In a bid to help the family, a relative[71] and chief manager of a blacking warehouse, James Lamert, proposed that the young Dickens should work in his establishment at a salary of six shillings a week.[72] Both of Dickens's parents readily agreed to this offer, as Edgar Johnson writes:

> No doubt his harassed parents were thankful enough for James Lamert's well-meant and kindly offer, but they were hardly apt to look upon it or any other aspect of their plight with complacency. Their income was entirely devoured in the endeavour to deal with their debts; and, besides Charles and Fanny, there were four helpless younger children in the family, from Leticia, who was eight, down to two-year-old Alfred Lamert.[73]

Dickens, however was filled with dismay. For him, Lamert's proposal constituted nothing less than "an evil hour for me, as I often bitterly thought."[74] The warehouse, by the river at Old Hungerford Stairs, was dirty, decayed and infested with rats. Dickens wrote:

> Its wainscotted rooms and its rotten floors and staircase, and the old grey rats swarming down in the cellars, and the sound of their squeaking and scuffling coming up the stairs at all times, and the dirt and decay of the place, rise up visibly before me, as if I were there again.[75]

Dickens worked there for a debatable period. In the autobiographical fragment Dickens states: "I have no idea how long it lasted; whether for a year, or much more or less."[76] The estimates of commentators vary. Una Pope-Hennessy writes that the period was only "six weeks."[77] Clipper maintains that "at a maximum [Dickens's] ordeal lasted about four months and three weeks."[78] Johnson, relying on the accounts of Robert Langton and Gladys Storey, believes the period "can have been little over four months, five at most."[79] Christopher Hibbert asserts: "In fact it lasted for less than six months."[80] Edmund Wilson assumes the period was for six months.[81] So, too, does Hesketh Pearson.[82] Fred Kaplan does not make a numerical estimate but opines "the months he had spent at Warren's Blacking were like years."[83] Michael Allen, in his book *Charles Dickens' Childhood*, significantly, believes the period extends to "twelve or thirteen months,"[84] from February 1824 to March 1825. Claire Tomalin, citing and commending Allen's research, writes: "How long he remained pasting and labeling is unsure, not least because he could not remember himself. It seems to have lasted for a little over a year, from February 1824, when he was twelve, to March 1825, when he was thirteen."[85] Recently, however, Michael Allen claimed, based on new evidence, that the period extended from September 1823 to either September or October 1824 (so while the period is still twelve or thirteen months, there is the difference that Dickens may have commenced work at the age of eleven rather than twelve).[86] Peter Ackroyd does not hazard a guess but comments, "The real point is that the young boy did not know how long he was likely to remain in that employment. He might, as far as he could see, be thrown away for ever."[87] Ackroyd's view echoes Edgar Johnson's position. For Johnson, the amount of time that Dickens worked in the blacking warehouse "had nothing to do with what it seemed to the child, or with the lasting impression it made upon the man. The boy had no way of knowing when his bondage would ever end, or *if* it would ever end, and he was in a state of absolute despair."[88] Certainly, the length of time appears minor in comparison to Dickens's profound sense of displacement and shock at the actions of those around him:

> It is wonderful to me how I could have been so easily cast away at such an age. It is wonderful to me that, even after my descent into the poor little drudge I had been since we came to London, no one had compassion enough on me — a child of singular abilities: quick, eager, delicate, and soon hurt, bodily or mentally —

to suggest that something might have been spared, as certainly it might have been, to place me at any common school. Our friends, I take it, were tired out. No one made any sign. My father and mother were quite satisfied. They could hardly have been more so, if I had been twenty years of age, distinguished at a grammar-school, and going to Cambridge.[89]

It was another matter, however, for Dickens's sister Fanny. Just before Dickens was "cast away" to work in a rotten blacking warehouse "from morning to night, with common men and boys,"[90] Fanny had been elected as a pupil to the Royal Academy of Music. Forster writes:

> What a stab to [Dickens's] heart it was, thinking of his own disregarded condition, to see her go away to begin her education, amid the tearful good wishes of everybody in the house.[91]

While Dickens's mother is not specifically mentioned here, in all probability the majority of these "happy tears" would have been shed by her. Perhaps Dickens stressed that *everybody* in the house was tearful because he wished to underscore his own misfortune. Perhaps he was reluctant to state that his mother openly wept with joy because the stark contrast between her ability to emote over his sister's good fortune and her complete obliviousness to his own unfortunate condition reflected very badly upon him.

Whatever the case, even if *everybody* in the house had shed joyful tears, the tears that Dickens would have *most* noticed would have been those of his mother. Indeed, his mother's response would have operated as the barometer by which he could determine his own value within the household unit. Accordingly, it is not unreasonable to speculate that Dickens might have felt thrown away by his mother, as Gwen Watkins comments:

> Charles may well have felt himself actually rejected, since his sister Fanny was being educated by means of a scholarship at the Royal Academy of Music, while he himself was merely a household drudge.[92]

Further, he might have come to believe that his proud and delighted mother had always favored his sister and indeed the female sex in general. After all, she showed no apparent concern at his deterioration into a "poor little drudge" but was manifestly euphoric at his sister's success.

So, too, Dickens's observation of his mother's reaction, might have led him to question his place in the family. If his sister had won the right to an education and by virtue of her success had elicited such sheer joy, was he of no consequence? Was he a failure to his sex? Was he superfluous? Was he even expendable? Perhaps the blacking warehouse was all he was good for?

Certainly, there is enough evidence in Dickens's fiction to demonstrate that Dickens was very preoccupied with issues of gender favoritism and ontological displacement. In terms of gender favoritism, Florence, the central character in *Dombey and Son*, is rejected by her father because of her sex. In *David Copperfield*, David, owing to his sex, is rejected at birth by his Aunt Betsey. He is also treated unfavorably because of his sex by Miss Murdstone, the sister of his stepfather. In *Bleak House*, Lady Dedlock is extremely kind to her pretty servant Rosa but she is thoroughly rejecting towards the dirty crossing sweeper, Jo (who, ironically, was treated with paternal kindness by her former lover). In *Little Dorrit* it is clear that Miss Wade prefers the female sex and wishes to take a girl, Tattycoram, under her wing. In *Great Expectations*, Mrs. Joe has complete contempt for her husband, Joe, and her younger brother, Pip, and is physically abusive towards them. Finally, Miss Havisham in the same novel is literally consumed by her wish to take revenge on the entire male sex; and she trains her adopted daughter, Estella, to treat Pip and all males with absolute contempt.

In terms of ontological displacement, Florence in *Dombey and Son* is treated as so much waste by her father:

> Mr Dombey ... had no issue.—To speak of; none worth mentioning. There had been a girl some six years before, and the child, who had stolen into the chamber unobserved, was now crouching timidly, in a corner whence she could see her mother's face. But what was a girl to Dombey and Son! In the capital of the House's name and dignity, such a child was merely a piece of base coin that couldn't be invested—a bad Boy—nothing more.[93]

Mrs. Nipper, explaining Florence's unenviable domestic position to Mrs. Richards, also states:

> "Her Pa's a deal too wrapped up in somebody else, and before there was a somebody else to be wrapped up in she never was a favourite, girls are thrown away in this house, Mrs Richards, *I* assure you."[94]

In *David Copperfield*, following his mother's marriage to the hard-hearted Murdstone, David feels profoundly displaced:

> What meals I had in silence and embarrassment, always feeling that there were a knife and fork too many, and that mine; and appetite too many, and that mine; a plate and chair too many, and those mine; a somebody too many, and that I![95]

Indeed, he is so displaced that he does not even feel like he is a person: "What a blank space I seemed, which everybody overlooked, and yet was in everybody's way."[96]

In *Bleak House*, Esther Summerson is made to feel even worse. According to her godmother she is a complete waste of space: "It would have been far better, little Esther, that you had had no birthday; that you had never been born!"[97] In *Hard Times* the Gradgrind children are so displaced that they view the family home as a "Jaundiced Jail" and the disaffected Tom Gradgrind tells his sister Louisa: "I am sick of my life, Loo. I hate it altogether, and I hate everybody except you."[98] In addition, Dickens is not above taking up the theme of ontological displacement through the voice of a hypocrite. The odious Bounderby, boastfully lying about his past, claims that he became a justifiably abused vagabond because his mother abandoned him and his grandmother abused him:

> I became a young vagabond; and instead of one old woman knocking me about and starving me, everybody of all ages knocked me about and starved me. They were right; they had no business to do anything else. I was a nuisance, an incumbrance, and a pest. I know that, very well.[99]

Turning to *Little Dorrit*, there is no doubt that Arthur Clennam suffers ontological displacement. His childhood was to all intents and purposes merely an exercise in alienation:

> [His mother] and his father had been at variance from his earliest remembrance. To sit speechless himself in the midst of rigid silence, glancing in dread from the one averted face to the other; had been the peacefullest occupation of his childhood.[100]

In addition, the eponymous character Little Dorrit barely occupies a space in Mrs. Clennam's estimation, as Affery Flintwinch remarks: "She? Little Dorrit? She's nothing; she's a whim of— hers."[101]

As for *Great Expectations*, Pip has no sense of his place in the world other than his fanciful imaginings in relation to the graves of his parents and five brothers. Certainly, while he is growing up he has a home with his sister and her husband, but his sister's brutality is such that he can never feel "at home":

> My sister, Mrs Joe Gargery, was more than twenty years older than I, and had established a great reputation with herself and the neighbours because she had brought me up "by hand." Having at that time to find out for myself what the expression meant, and knowing her to have a hard and heavy hand, and to be much in the habit of laying it upon her husband as well as upon me, I supposed that Joe Gargery and I were both brought up by hand.[102]

The examples of gender favoritism and ontological displacement above are by no means exhaustive but they do serve to show that these concerns were very much at the forefront of Dickens's psyche and for the reasons stated, I believe these concerns were very much bound up in Dickens's notions of his mother. Certainly, both parents might have unwittingly been responsible for his anxiety around gender favoritism and ontological displacement. However, prevailing gender prescriptions would have strongly helped to shape Dickens's expectations of his mother. As a woman and as a mother, she was the one who was "naturally" equipped to provide the most emotional support, and her failings in this regard would have weighed far more heavily against her in Dickens's mind that any failings on his father's part.

Ironically, while his parents were seemingly oblivious to Dickens's out-of-place condition, it was abundantly clear to all of his coworkers that he did not fit in:

> Though perfectly familiar with [the warehouse boys], my conduct and manners were different enough from theirs to place a space between us. They, and the men, always spoke of me as "the young gentleman."[103]

It was also clear to the manager of the warehouse, James Lamert, that Dickens did not fit in:

> My relative at the counting-house did what a man so occupied, and dealing with a thing so anomalous, could, to treat me as one upon a different footing from the rest...[104]

Interestingly, before becoming the manager of the blacking warehouse, James Lamert had been educated at Sandhurst and, although much older than Dickens, he had been his "chief ally and encourager."[105] Apparently, he had taken Dickens to the theater at "the very tenderest age," and as "he had a turn for private theatricals"[106] had helped to develop Dickens's comic singing abilities and theatrical talents. He had also made and painted a little theater for him. However, while obviously aware of Dickens's potential, this was not uppermost in his mind when he proposed that Dickens could come to work in the blacking warehouse. What is more, when the blacking warehouse relocated to Covent Garden, he was apparently unconcerned when workplace conditions resulted in his former protégé acquiring an entirely unwished-for audience:

> We worked, for the light's sake, near the second window as you come from Bedford Street; and we were so brisk at it, that the people used to stop and look in. Sometimes there would be quite a little crowd there. I saw my father coming in at the door one day when we were very busy, and I wondered how he could bear it.[107]

This passage is particularly revealing. Here we have Dickens's exquisite mortification; his inability to reconcile his father's absence of shame (or lack of sensitivity); and an indirect indictment of his mother. John Forster specifically notes: "[Dickens's] mother had been in the blacking warehouse many times; his father not more than once or twice."[108] At no point, however, in the autobiographical fragment does Dickens wonder, like he does about his father, how she could have borne his anomalous state (exhibited or otherwise). Accordingly, one surmises that the young Dickens was used to her insensitivity and indeed expected it, as Gwen Watkins speculates: "Was she a frequent and uncaring witness to his humiliation[?]"[109]

His father was another matter. Dickens was clearly amazed at his father's acceptance of the situation. This fact alone suggests that Dickens believed that his father had superior sensibilities or that his father cared more about him than his mother. This is ironic in light of the fact that before seeing his son in the warehouse window, John Dickens, thanks to the acquisition of a "considerable"[110] legacy, had been released from Marshalsea Prison. Even so, he had done nothing to remedy the "out of place" situation of his son and, ironically, it seems he could not even identify with his son's predicament, as Watkins writes:

> When [John Dickens] was released from the Marshalsea through the slow procedures of the Insolvency Act in May 1824, it seems not to have occurred to him to release his child ... from a much more terrible servitude.[111]

Perhaps, however, Dickens's apparent faith in his father's sensibilities was not entirely misplaced because "at last"[112] according to Dickens, he wrote to James Lamert an angry letter that immediately resulted in the insulted warehouse manager terminating his son's employment. At this, the young Dickens though upset, experienced "a relief so strange that it was like oppression."[113] But this relief was to be supplanted by terminal bitterness because his mother took it upon herself to restore him to his former anomalous state:

> My mother set herself to accommodate the quarrel, and did so the next day. She brought home a request for me to return next morning, and a high character of me, which I am very sure I deserved. My father said I should go back no more, and should go to school. I do not write resentfully or angrily: for I know how all these things have worked together to make me what I am: but I never afterwards forgot, I never shall forget, I never can forget, that my mother was warm for my being sent back.[114]

Of this passage Jeffrey Berman insightfully remarks:

> The intensity of the rhetoric, the insistence upon never forgetting his mother's actions, captures Dickens' outrage. The word *warm* carries ironic connotations; far from being a warm, nurturing mother, Mrs Dickens stands condemned for abandonment, even betrayal. In a letter to Washington Irving, Dickens described himself as a "very small and not-over-particularly-taken-care-of boy" ... and this is the way he portrays himself throughout the autobiographical fragment.[115]

It is useful at this point to include a description of Elizabeth Dickens which Michael Slater claims is "the most detailed character-sketch of Elizabeth that we have."[116] According to Mrs. Davey, the wife of the London doctor under whose care and home Dickens placed his father, John Dickens, from the time he became seriously ill in 1850 to the time he died in 1851,[117] Mrs. Dickens was a very likable, charming, entertaining, acutely observant and highly talented woman. Mrs. Davey expressed this opinion publicly in the form of a letter to the editor of *Lippincott's Magazine of Popular Literature and Science*. Notably, this letter was published in June 1874, some 23 years after John Dickens's death and four years after Charles Dickens's death. Mrs. Davey writes:

> Mrs Dickens was a little woman, who had been very nice looking in her youth. She had very bright eyes, and was as thoroughly good-natured, easy-going, companionable a body as one would wish to meet with. The likeness between her and Mrs Nickleby is simply the exaggeration of some slight peculiarities. She possessed

> an extraordinary sense of the ludicrous, and her power of imitation was something quite astonishing. On entering a room she almost unconsciously took an inventory of its contents, and if anything happened to strike her as out of place or ridiculous, she would afterwards describe it in the quaintest possible manner. In like manner she noted personal peculiarities of her friends and acquaintances. She had also a fine vein of pathos, and could bring tears to the eyes of her listeners when narrating some sad event ... I am of the opinion that a great deal of Dickens's genius was inherited from his mother. He possessed from her a keen appreciation of the droll and the pathetic, as also considerable dramatic talent. Mrs Dickens has often sent my sisters and myself into uncontrollable fits of laughter by her funny sayings and inimitable mimicry. Charles was decidedly fond of her.[118]

What an illuminating passage this is. In the opinion of Mrs. Davey at least, Charles was not simply fond of his mother but "a great deal of [his] genius" was inherited from her. These are two extremely important points. In the autobiographical fragment, the most memorable aspect of Elizabeth Dickens is her desire to have Dickens sent back to his demeaning position in the blacking warehouse, and if he feels fondness for her it is barely detectable. In terms of her contribution to his "genius" there is next to nothing about her acute sense of the ridiculous; her powers of observation, narration and mimicry; her eye for pathos; her sense of humor; her comedic abilities; and her "considerable dramatic talent." Only at *one* "blink and you'll miss it" point is there any recognition of Elizabeth Dickens's gifted nature. According to John Forster, Dickens's father, while in the Marshalsea Prison, drew up a petition requesting that the prisoners be given the right to drink to "His Majesty's health on His Majesty's forthcoming birthday."[119] Interestingly, Dickens writes:

> I mention the circumstance because it illustrates, to me, my early interest in observing people. When I went to the Marshalsea of a night, I was always delighted to hear from my mother what she knew about the histories of the different debtors in the prison; and when I heard of this approaching ceremony, I was so anxious to see them all come in, one after another ... that I got leave of absence on purpose, and established myself in a corner.[120]

Dickens mentions his repeated delight in hearing his mother's observations but, tellingly, he does not credit her with awakening his interest in observing people. Instead, Dickens, not unlike "that remarkable man and self-made Humbug, Josiah Bounderby"[121] in *Hard Times*, virtually denies the influence of his mother and convinces himself that he alone is responsible for his extraordinary and enduring powers of perception:

> Whatever was comical in this scene, and whatever was pathetic, I sincerely believe I perceived in my corner, whether I demonstrated or not, quite as well as I should perceive it now. I made out my own little character and story for every man who put his name to the sheet of paper. I might be able to do that now, more truly: not more earnestly, or with a closer interest. Their different peculiarities of dress of face, of gait, of manner, were written indelibly upon my memory. I would rather

have seen it than the best play ever played; and I thought about it afterwards, over the pots of paste-blacking, often and often.[122]

In all likelihood, Dickens's mother with her "fine vein of pathos" and "inimitable mimicry" made much of the Marshalsea petition incident, but Dickens, intent as he was on underscoring his abandonment and "singular abilities,"[123] chose to omit such a memory. He was also selective with the truth in terms of recording any affection that he felt towards his mother. In passing, he could state that her knowledge of the prisoners "delighted" him but any acknowledgment of fondness or love was apparently out of the question. Dickens's wounded pride, it seems, prevented him from recalling any such feeling. It was also, no doubt, behind his inability to empathize with her predicament when she desperately attempted to get the family out of its straitened circumstances. Forster, referring to Dickens's autobiographical fragment, writes:

> [Dickens's] father's resources were so low, and all his expedients so thoroughly exhausted, that trial was to be made whether his mother might not come to the rescue. The time was arrived for her to exert herself, she said; and she "must do something." The godfather down at Limehouse was reported to have an Indian connection. People in the East Indies always sent their children home to be educated. She would set up a school. They would all grow rich by it. And then, thought the sick boy, "perhaps even I might go to school myself."
>
> A house was soon found at number four, Gower Street North; a large brass plate on the door announced MRS. DICKENS'S ESTABLISHMENT; and the result I can give in the exact words of the then small actor in the comedy, whose hopes it had raised so high. "I left, at a great many other doors, a great many circulars calling attention to the merits of the establishment. Yet nobody ever came to the school, nor do I recollect that anybody ever proposed to come, or that the least preparation was made to receive anybody. But I know that we got on very badly with the butcher and the baker; that very often we had not too much for dinner; and that at last my father was arrested."[124]

In just three sweeping sentences, Elizabeth Dickens's attempts to "come to the rescue" are linked to unrealistic expectations; disorganization; failure; commercial hostility; domestic mismanagement and the arrest of her husband. Examining this passage, and considering the assessment of another critic, Michael Slater writes:

> Angus Wilson perceptively notes that "the details of this attack on his mother's ill-thought out scheme [not *so* 'ill-thought-out' either'] deserve careful attention, for he directly connects it to the failure of household management (which is only partly logical) and to the imprisonment of his father (which is quite illogical)."[125]

Careful attention also must be paid to Dickens's unwillingness to acknowledge his mother's good qualities. His words convey no acknowledgment of her enterprising nature; no admiration for her resourcefulness; and no recognition of her teaching skills. Significantly, Gwen Watkins notes:

Dickens told Forster that his mother had taught him the rudiments of English and Latin "thoroughly well," so that when he referred contemptuously to her plans for Mrs Dickens' Establishment, it was not her teaching abilities that he despised.[126]

However, while he may not have despised her teaching abilities, he elides them in this passage and shows no sympathy for her when the enterprise fails. As a result, her efforts are made to look ridiculous and she seems the source of all evil. This damning portrayal is reinforced when Dickens outlines an instance of a complete stranger's maternal actions towards him. Apparently, one day, Dickens, describing himself as "such a little fellow, with my poor white hat, little jacket, and corduroy trowsers" went into a public-house and because it was a festive occasion (probably his birthday) asked for a glass of "the VERY best".[127] The landlord, bemused by the little boy and his very adult request, called his wife:

> Here we stand, all three, before me now, in my study in Devonshire Terrace. The landlord, in his shirt-sleeves, leaning against the bar window-frame; his wife, look-ing over the little half-door; and I, in some confusion, looking up at them from outside the partition. They asked me a good many questions, as what my name was, how old I was, where I lived, how I was employed, etc. To all of which, that I might commit nobody, I invented appropriate answers. They served me with the ale, though I suspect it was not the strongest on the premises; and the landlord's wife, opening the little half-door and bending down, gave me a kiss that was half-admiring and half-compassionate, but all womanly and good, I am sure.[128]

The words that Dickens uses to describe this woman, so tangential to his life, are far more effusive than any words that he uses in his autobiographical frag-ment to describe his mother. Dickens is absolutely convinced that this woman is "all womanly and good." Could this be an example of the "splitting" tendency that Natalie J. McKnight identified within Dickens?:

> Dickens's tendency to see mothers as all good or all bad can be seen as a symptom of what psychoanalysts call "splitting," a tendency that exists in most people but can be exaggerated in some. In one form of splitting, the child cannot assimilate the negative aspects of its mother into its sense of self or its sense of her and there-fore "splits" them off.... Although most people have a tendency toward splitting, the tendency would likely be strong in Victorians because the predominance of the ideal-mother myth did not encourage realistic expectations of mothers.[129]

Certainly, Dickens's wholly affirmative depiction of the landlord's wife and accompanying withering depiction of his own mother within the autobiograph-ical fragment may be viewed as representative of Dickens's tendency to divide external objects into "all good" or "all bad." Or could his hyperbolic assessment of the landlord's wife simply be put down to the fact that she displays the two feelings that Dickens most wanted to elicit in his mother — admiration and compassion? Dickens at least knew that his father admired him to some degree:

"He was proud of me, in his way, and had a great admiration of the comic singing."[130] Perhaps this explains why Dickens could engage in a similar encomium when considering the actions of his father: "I know my father to be as kindhearted and generous a man as ever lived in the world."[131] Nothing in the autobiographical fragment, however, points to any admiration that Elizabeth Dickens might have felt for her son. According to Watkins:

> It is obvious that although both parents made use of him and neglected him, there was some warmth and appreciation of his son in the father, even if only intermittently and even if only appreciation of an object useful or entertaining to himself, that made it possible for Charles to come to terms with the bitterness and pain he must have felt about his father's treatment of him.[132]

So, too, nothing in the autobiographical fragment points to any compassion that Elizabeth Dickens might have displayed towards her son during a time in which he was extremely distressed. By contrast, the landlord's wife, in her brief encounter with Dickens, steps out from behind a door and comes down to his level to give him a kiss. At a symbolic level then, she "goes out of her way" to make contact with Dickens and she shows him that while she may know nothing of his life she is nonetheless intensely aware of his vulnerable "out of place" condition. Accordingly, the caring landlord's wife stands in sharp relief to Dickens's apparently uncaring mother.

Aside, then, from the central outburst against his mother, Dickens in the autobiographical fragment employs a number of different ways to express his disgust towards her. Firstly, through omission he indelibly negates the profoundly positive influence that she had on his life and he refuses to acknowledge any love that he felt towards her. From the autobiographical fragment one could never form the opinion, like Mrs. Davey, that "a great deal" of Dickens's "genius" was inherited from his mother. Equally, one could never come to the conclusion that Dickens was "decidedly fond" of his mother. Secondly, through a rolling "this happened and then this happened" style of discourse which foregrounds his mental state rather than the deictic elements of place and time, Dickens sets his mother up as the chief agent of domestic chaos and his father's "fall." Thirdly, through pointed contrast or structural antithesis, he eulogizes a woman who momentarily crosses his path and concomitantly suggests that his mother lacks basic maternal responses and therefore cannot be deemed "all womanly and good."

Dangerous Liaisons

In his autobiographical fragment, Dickens explains that initially he was segregated from the other boys employed in the blacking warehouse. Apparently he covered the pots of paste-blacking in a recessed area in the counting house on the first floor and "Two or three other boys were kept at a similar duty downstairs on similar wages." On his first day one of the boys came up dressed in "a ragged apron and a paper cap" and showed Dickens how to use the string and tie the knot. As Dickens remarks: "His name was Bob Fagin; and I took the liberty of using his name, long afterwards, in *Oliver Twist*."[133]

Dickens was also initially set apart from the other blacking warehouse boys because the blacking warehouse manager James Lamert arranged to set aside an hour every day to teach him something. However, this arrangement was soon abandoned, as Dickens states:

> An arrangement so incompatible with counting-house business soon died away, from no fault of his or mine; and for the same reason, my small work-table, and my grosses of pots, my papers, string, scissors, paste-pot and labels, by little and little, vanished out of the recess in the counting-house, and kept company with the other small work-tables, grosses of pots, papers, string, scissors and paste-pots downstairs. It was not long before Bob Fagin and I, and another boy whose name was Paul Green ... worked generally, side by side.[134]

For Dickens, sharing close quarters with the other blacking warehouse boys was far from a blessing:

> No words can express the secret agony of my soul as I sunk into this companionship; compared these everyday associates with those of my happier childhood; and felt my early hopes of growing up to be a learned and distinguished man crushed in my breast.[135]

As Bob Fagin was the boy who first crossed the threshold (so to speak) in the blacking warehouse and inducted Dickens into the ways of the warehouse, he looms large as a threatening presence in the autobiographical fragment. Effectively, Fagin's action, albeit helpful, endangered the young Dickens. It is as if once Dickens had made contact with Fagin he became contaminated. Indeed, soon after making Fagin's acquaintance, Dickens underwent a considerable diminution in terms of stature in the warehouse. His sequestered and privileged existence came to an end and he was demoted to a lower level in the warehouse, which was devoid of opportunities for intellectual growth (however slight). Compounding this, by taking the young Dickens under his wing, Fagin effectively threatened Dickens's tenuous grip on his sense of superiority. Clearly, it was very important for Dickens to feel that he was "a cut above" the other boys. On no account did he want to be thought of as one of them. As Peter Ackroyd explains:

> Here one senses some imitation of his father's own projection of a genteel persona (it is clear enough how John Dickens's fear, stemming from the fact that he was so perilously hovering between classes, was transmitted to the son). It also tells us much about his instinctive reaction to the labouring poor, although it is one that

would have been widely shared in his lifetime; the "working classes" were in a very real sense a race apart, a substratum of society which bred in those above them a fear of disease, a horror of uncleanliness and of course the dread of some kind of social revolution if ever these individual Fagins and Greens became a "mob." For Dickens, the boy who had hopes "of growing up to be a learned and distinguished man," such close contact and the resultant fear of contamination must have been appalling.[136]

Interestingly, Fagin was zealous in helping Dickens to maintain this superior stature in the blacking warehouse. Indeed, he defended Dickens when others objected to his higher caste. Dickens states: "Poll Green uprose once, and rebelled against the 'young-gentleman' usage; but Bob Fagin settled him speedily."[137]

Ironically, however, Fagin's protectiveness was a double-edged sword, for, on another occasion, it threatened to completely obliterate Dickens's sense of self-worth. One day, after nursing Dickens back to health when he was taken ill at the warehouse, Fagin insisted on walking Dickens home. Unfortunately for Dickens, this meant that Fagin very nearly uncovered his guilty secret — the fact that he lived alone in a boarding house and the rest of his family lived in the Marshalsea Prison:

> Bob (who was much bigger and older than I) did not like the idea of my going home alone, and took me under his protection. I was too proud to let him know about the prison; and after making several efforts to get rid of him, to all of which Bob Fagin in his goodness was deaf, shook hands with him on the steps of a house near Southwark Bridge on the Surrey side, making believe that I lived there. As a finishing piece of reality in case of his looking back, I knocked at the door, I recollect, and asked, when the woman opened it, if that was Mr. Robert Fagin's house.[138]

Steven Marcus usefully makes an analogy between this incident and *Oliver Twist*:

> Oliver Twist, the workhouse boy, is the son of a gentleman; and it is Fagin's task to prevent him from discovering that secret and entering upon that salvation. In life, young Charles Dickens was the son of a gentleman who was at the time inhabiting comfortable but close apartments in the Marshalsea prison; and it is *he* who keeps the secret from Fagin. The shame of admitting this secret is, in part, transformed in the novel into Oliver's incorruptibility and innocence, his instinctive repugnance for lying or stealing: so strangely are some of our virtues derived. In both instances, however, the danger is connected with a companionship or affection which is at once needed and intolerable; Bob Fagin's protectiveness is transformed into Fagin's treacherous maternal care.[139]

The much bigger and older Fagin, then, significantly endangered the young Dickens. Albeit well-intentioned, Fagin's quasi-maternal help[140] indirectly diminished Dickens's profile in the blacking warehouse; sounded the death knell to his further education; threatened to uncover his degraded circumstances; menaced him with the horrors of absorption into a lower stratum of society;

and very nearly enabled him to come to terms with the wrongs that had been done to him. Michael Slater, again citing *Oliver Twist*, recognizes the enormous shadow that Fagin cast:

> Fagin ... was the name of the boy who befriended and protected the child Dickens in the blacking-factory. For this presumption and for the appalling danger his kindliness represented, that the child might be lulled into some sort of acceptance of the outrage that had been perpetrated against him, Bob Fagin was punished by the extraordinary artist that his little protégé grew up to be. Dickens's off-hand comment on the matter, "I took the liberty of using his name, long afterwards, in *Oliver Twist*" (as though Fagin were just any character) is tantalizing; just how aware was he of what it was in him that was generating the imaginative power manifested in *Oliver*?[141]

Some of Dickens's critics have dealt rather harshly with the feelings that Dickens expresses in the autobiographical fragment. These critics "routinely"[142] point out that it was not unusual in the nineteenth century for a twelve-year-old child to be sent to work[143] and to receive no further schooling. In addition, they take the line that Dickens indulged in excessive self-pity.[144] Trevor Blount, for instance, claims that Dickens's feelings were "out of all proportion to the extent of his hardship,"[145] and Jack Lindsay writes, "we cannot but be struck by the extreme overvaluation of his misfortune — or rather disproportion between the external causes and the anguish that he undoubtedly experienced."[146] Robert Newsom rightly believes that this kind of criticism is misplaced:

> There is a profound irony in the fact that people who have been taught by Dickens what a living hell the life of the urban poor was in the nineteenth century should be so ungenerous as to deny their teacher the personal (as opposed to the artistic) feeling and expression of that horror.[147]

As to Dickens's acute sense of shame, Newsom asserts:

> It is important to recall ... that this really is a *twelve*-year-old boy we are discussing and that if there is one sense that is exquisitely sensitive at that age it is ... the sense of shame.[148]

Whether or not Dickens's feelings were acceptable, they were most certainly very important in the scheme of his life. As John Forster tellingly asserts, Dickens found nothing less than "the explanation of himself in those early trials."[149] Such a statement should not be taken lightly. Added to this, it is not hard to justify Dickens's feelings. As Edmund Wilson points out:

> one must realize that during those months he was in a state of complete despair. For the adult in desperate straits, it is almost always possible to imagine, if not to contrive, some way out; for the child, from whom love and freedom have inexplicably been taken away, no relief or release can be projected.[150]

Christopher Hibbert corroborates this:

since while he was there, overwhelmed by a sense of deprivation, degradation, loneliness and despair, he had no idea when, if ever, he would be released from his bondage, it seemed to the child interminable.[151]

It should also not be forgotten that at the time of his ordeal, Dickens was only about twelve years old and thereby just entering puberty. Granted, as Albert D. Hutter cautions, that a trauma at this age cannot, within psychoanalytic terms, be given "the status of a *formative* trauma"[152] (trauma that is limited to the first few months and years of a child's life); it was nonetheless a profound trauma that occurred at a critical age. This is more than demonstrated by its lasting effect on Dickens. As Dickens writes:

> The deep remembrance of the sense I had of being utterly neglected and hopeless; of the shame I felt in my position; of the misery it was to my young heart to believe that, day by day, what I had learned, and thought, and delighted in, and raised my fancy and my emulation up by, was passing away from me, never to be brought back any more; cannot be written. My whole nature was so penetrated with the grief and humiliation ... that even now, famous and caressed and happy, I often forget in my dreams that I have a dear wife and children; even that I am a man; and wander desolately back to that time of my life.[153]

Further, as Jeffrey Berman points out, it is not strictly correct to claim that formative trauma only relates to one's earliest years:

> And yet we know from recent history that formative traumas may occur later in life. The prevalence of post-traumatic stress disorder confirms this. The traumatic event can be reexperienced in a number of ways, and, according to *DSM-III*, the disorder can occur at any age. A formative trauma, then, is not limited to childhood. Just as Vietnam veterans are at greater risk in developing post-traumatic stress disorder if they or their families are unable to talk about the severity of the war experience, so might Dickens have been more vulnerable by his inability to discuss his experience at Warren's Blacking with his family and friends.[154]

The trauma that Dickens suffered (formative or not) was by any terms significant. In his psychoanalytic reading of the autobiographical fragment, Albert D. Hutter claims that the memory of his trial "rendered [Dickens] helpless and childlike; to use the appropriate Victorian expression, it 'unmanned him.'"[155] However, Hutter is also alert to the empowering side of the experience: "We need to see Warren's both as something that happened to Dickens and as something he did to himself, something that he used positively in his own self-development."[156] Jeffrey Berman is of a similar opinion: "We need to view Dickens' experience as a traumatic and triumphant event: traumatic in that it forever shattered the boy's conception of the world, triumphant in that it demonstrated his own inner resources."[157] Whilst I do not dispute either of these assessments, I believe the experience was far more traumatic than triumphant and am therefore more inclined to emphasize the soul-destroying nature of the experience. It is as if something in Dickens *died* at that point in his life. He may have gone on to replace his domestic situation and to achieve great success, but all of that pales into insignificance when he recalls the overwhelming pain that he experienced as a twelve-year-old boy. The memories contained in the auto-biographical fragment are therefore so potent that they can at times obliterate all of the subsequent years of his life.

The Polluting Person

Mary Douglas's classic 1966 anthropological work *Purity and Danger* is particularly useful in terms of understanding the autobiographical fragment. According to Douglas:

> If we can abstract pathogenicity and hygiene from our notion of dirt, we are left with the old definition of dirt as matter out of place. This is a very suggestive approach. It implies two conditions: a set of ordered relations and a contravention of that order. Dirt then, is never a unique, isolated event. Where there is dirt there is a system. Dirt is the by-product of a systematic ordering and classification of matter, in so far as ordering involves rejecting inappropriate elements.[158]

At base, dirt, as Douglas explains, is matter that is schematically incorrect or anomalous:

> Shoes are not dirty in themselves, but it is dirty to place them on the dining table; food is not dirty in itself, but it is dirty to leave cooking utensils in the bedroom, or food bespattered on clothing; similarly, bathroom equipment in the drawing room; clothing lying on chairs; out-door things in-doors; upstairs things down-stairs; under-clothing appearing where over-clothing should be, and so on. In short, our pollution behaviour is the reaction which condemns any object or idea likely to confuse or contradict cherished classifications.[159]

Importantly, paralleling out-of-place inanimate matter, Douglas asserts that it is also apparently conceivable for humans to step out of their perceived place and be thought of as disturbingly unclean:

> A polluting person is always in the wrong. He has developed some wrong condition or simply crossed some line which should not have been crossed and this displace-ment unleashes danger for someone.[160]

Interestingly, Douglas does not speak of a dirty person but rather a pol-luting person. For Douglas, out-of-place inanimate matter may be labeled dirty, but out-of-place animate matter in the shape of a human may be perceived as polluting. Polluting is one step further along than being dirty. If something is thought of as dirty it may exist on its own as unclean matter, but to be polluting is of another order entirely. Polluting as a verb carries the connotation of gen-erating real harm because to pollute is to *make* unclean, impure, or corrupt. An out-of-place person, then, for Douglas, unlike an out-of-place inanimate object, is an active form of dirt. As she puts it: "Bringing pollution ... is a capacity which men share with animals."[161] Bringing pollution is most likely to occur when a human does not fit in with or conform to commonly held ideas or ideals. As Douglas states:

> Power in the universe is ultimately hitched to society.... But there are other dangers to be reckoned with which persons may set off knowingly or unknowingly.... These are pollution powers which inhere in the structure of ideas itself and which punish a symbolic breaking of that which should be joined or joining of that which should be separate. It follows from this that pollution is a type of danger which is not likely to occur except where the lines of structure, cosmic or social, are clearly defined.[162]

Douglas's hypothesis thereby hinges on the fact that when people take on the ontological status of polluting it is because they have in some way transgressed or broken away from clearly defined boundaries or value systems. It does not matter whether they *intentionally* flouted such lines of structure or whether they did it inadvertently because, as noted, the result is the same — "displacement unleashes danger for someone."[163]

If one views Dickens's time in the blacking warehouse in the light of Mary Douglas's hypothesis, Dickens's profound reaction makes perfect sense. If one accepts the premise that a polluting person crosses some line which should not have been crossed and thereby unleashes danger for someone else, then Dickens could most definitely be viewed as the victim of polluting agents. Firstly, he was the victim of his father because his improvidence and willingness to engage his son in the blacking warehouse effectively endangered his son's chances in life. Secondly, he was the victim of the manager of the blacking warehouse, James Lamert, because his offer and conditions of employment endangered Dickens's social standing. Thirdly, he was the victim of his well-meaning blacking warehouse co-worker Fagin because his friendship endangered Dickens's sense of superiority. However, in Dickens's mind, his mother is the *chief* polluting agent because, had she been successful in reinstating him to his former drudgery, his *destiny* would have been entirely different. In all likelihood, he might have remained "a common labouring hind"[164] and the world would never have known the famous writer that he was later to become. Peter Ackroyd writes:

> It is interesting to speculate what he would have become, what kind of man this genius would have turned into, if he had remained at Warren's for the formative years of his development. There are occasions in his fiction when Dickens himself seems to be speculating, seems to be *imagining*, what it would have been like to have been left at the factory — particularly in his evocations of those children or young people whom nobody notices, who slink through the streets, who live without a kind word addressed to them. In little Dick who dies in the workhouse from which Oliver Twist is removed, in Jo from *Bleak House*, in Smike from *Nicholas Nickleby*, and in a host of others, it is almost as if Dickens were populating his fiction with images of his own potentially lost self.[165]

Such a hopeless prospect would have been horrifying to Dickens. This is no doubt why Dickens was haunted by his mother's actions: "I never afterwards forgot, I never shall forget, I never can forget, that my mother was warm for my being sent back."[166] The tone here is utter incredulous disgust. According to Michael Slater:

> "Resentment" and "anger" are indeed terms too mild for the emotions that must lie behind such rhetoric as this. An enduring sense of horrified dismay and ultimate betrayal — such feelings as these must, at the deepest level, have been those of Dickens towards his mother for the rest of his life.[167]

Slater is right — Dickens probably felt "horrified dismay" — but as I will argue later, horror, within Kristevan terms, is simply the most intense form of disgust. Accordingly, disgust would appear to be the predominant emotion that Dickens felt towards his mother. Behind his rhetoric also lies a series of questions: How could she do this to *me*— the boy who was destined to become the most popular writer of the age? How could she have thrown me —*her child*— away as so much dirt? How could she have been oblivious to my degradation? How could she have been so completely unaware of my extraordinary potential? How could she have been so selfish, insensitive, uncaring, unnatural, negligent and downright dangerous? Clearly, in Dickens's mind, his mother is associated with dirt, decay, displacement, degradation, paste-blacking, rats, common people, neglect, negation, servitude, and hopelessness. Indeed, for Dickens, the blacking warehouse would have stood as a symbol of his mother's abandonment.

Obviously Dickens's father was a highly irresponsible man. As Hesketh Pearson asserts, John Dickens's

> easy temper, gregarious disposition, and tendency to lavish hospitality on all and sundry, produced want and misery for his family, alienated his wife's relations, who refused to go on making gifts of cash which it pleased him to describe as loans, and deprived his eldest son of education and the companions of his class.[168]

Dickens, however, was apparently able to excuse the fact that his father's improvidence had directly led to his wretched appointment in the blacking warehouse and the premature cessation of his education. He was also able to overlook his father's other questionable actions: the fact that as the head of the family he readily agreed to his son's degrading appointment; the fact that he did not make immediate arrangements to remove his son from the warehouse after his release from the Marshalsea Prison; and the fact that the insulting letter he wrote to Lamert was probably more about his wounded pride than concern for his son, as Fred Kaplan states:

> Perhaps his pride had been offended by his son working in the window to full public gaze. John Dickens seemed more concerned about himself than his son, and his anger, the substance of which was communicated in a letter that Charles

was forced to deliver, conveniently expressed itself only after his release from prison and his awareness of the coming legacy.[169]

In addition, Jack Lindsay comments: "John Dickens, it would seem, didn't mind his son tying up pots, but he wouldn't have people knowing about it."[170] Dickens, seemingly, could excuse all of these things but, as is clear from the autobiographical fragment, he could *never* excuse the fact that his mother tried to reinstate him after his father had brought about the termination of his employment. Dickens's obdurate stance in this regard is mirrored by his lack of sympathy for his mother's predicament. Indeed, as Jack Lindsay notes:

> In all his comments on the situation Charles shows not the least inkling of the way in which his mother must have been at her wit's end; he has much sympathy for his father, who is ignoring the whole problem, but none for his mother's gallant efforts to grapple with things.[171]

Whether or not Dickens's mother was gallant, her attempt to reinstate her son came to nothing: "My father said I should go back no more, and should go to school." This position, self-serving or not, meant that Dickens Junior never returned to face another day at the dreaded blacking warehouse, and in time he went on to more than fulfill his early hopes of becoming a "learned and distinguished man." Indeed, the word *distinguished* does not even do justice to the esteem that the public held him in, as Claire Tomalin points out:

> Dickens wished to be, and was, generally worshipped — the word is not too strong for a person who evoked comparison with Christ at the time of his death — as a man of unblemished character, the incarnation of broad Christian virtue and at the same time of domestic harmony and conviviality.[172]

Nevertheless, not even extreme public endorsement could ever erase the fact that his mother, of her own volition, sought to continue his demeaning employment in a rat-infested blacking warehouse.

Black Nemesis

If there is one thing that the autobiographical fragment reveals, it is that Elizabeth Dickens crossed a line in her son's mind that should *not* have been crossed. In working to reinstate her son, it appears that she did not consider her husband's wishes or if she did, she dismissed them. As to her son's wishes, there is little evidence in the fragment that she even took these into account. Ensuring the continuation of her son's meager salary is what seems to have motivated her and every other consideration was cast aside. Obviously, Elizabeth Dickens would have had her reasons for doing this. Perhaps she feared, not unrealistically, that her husband would recklessly go through his newly acquired legacy. Accordingly, in the interests of having something to fall back on she wanted her son to remain gainfully employed. However, owing to Dickens's profound sense of abandonment it appears that he was incapable of understanding her position. Consequently and regrettably, all the reader is left with is the knowledge is that Elizabeth Dickens took it upon herself to ensure that her son did not lose his place in the blacking warehouse and that her son was enduringly affected (if not to say psychologically scarred) by her actions.

Within the terms of Dickens's autobiographical fragment, it is also clear that the boundary-breaking Elizabeth Dickens was powerful. In pursuing her own course of action, she did a number of things. Firstly, she usurped her husband's "rightful" place as head of the family and thereby contravened prevailing notions of feminine propriety; secondly, she placated the insulted blacking warehouse manager Lamert to the point where he was able to send a request for Dickens to return to work; and thirdly, she very nearly changed the course of Dickens's life. Indeed, if she had got her way Dickens may have found himself indefinitely stuck in a dead-end menial position with "common" associates and no hope of any further education. There is no doubt that Dickens would have been aware of his mother's power, if only because he would have been under no illusion that his life would have been quite different had her actions not been overridden. Indeed, it is a measure of Elizabeth Dickens's power that her independent actions are what he remembers (or chooses to remember) most about her.

A completely "out of line" woman who very nearly derailed his life — this is how Dickens sees his mother and this is what defines her as nothing less than his nemesis. Dickens may express only one distinct harsh statement about his mother in the autobiographical fragment but, as I have shown, the fragment produces extra levels of meaning which suggest that Elizabeth Dickens was the chief polluting agent within his life and therefore the supreme object of his disgust.

Cultural constraints in relation to filial duty would, no doubt, have prevented Dickens from actually confronting his mother with the pain that he felt over her actions. Certainly, there are characters in Dickens's fiction that get beyond such constraints and take the brave step of confronting a harmful parent. Edith Dombey (*Dombey and Son*) and Louisa Gradgrind (*Hard Times*) both openly confront their respective dysfunctional parents, and Louisa's confrontation with Gradgrind is particularly poignant and memorable. It appears though, that Dickens was never able to do this himself. In his autobiographical fragment he makes it clear that his parents seemingly whitewashed the whole blacking warehouse episode from their minds:

> From that hour, until this, my father and my mother have been stricken dumb upon it. I have never heard the least allusion to it, however far off and remote, from either of them.[173]

There is also nothing to suggest that he ever challenged them about the episode. Indeed, it seems that there was never a moment where he even disturbed their equilibrium. As Michael Slater observes: "Evidently, neither Elizabeth herself nor anyone in the immediate family saw Charles as anything but an exemplary devoted son."[174] In addition, Slater notes:

> We find little direct evidence in his surviving letters, or in reminiscences of him by others, of that undying bitterness he felt towards [his mother] which emerges so unmistakably in the autobiographical fragment.[175]

While there may not be any *direct* archival evidence of the undying bitterness that Dickens felt towards his mother, the major "first person" narratives that Dickens produced more than testify to it. In all of these works, Dickens deploys a similar range of rhetorical techniques to those used in the autobiographical fragment to depict the mothers of the protagonists in terms of the idiom of disgust. Similarly, just as Dickens constructs his mother in the autobiographical fragment as the original agent of pollution in his life, the protagonists in the autobiographical novels rhetorically construct their biological and adoptive mothers as the primary agents of pollution in their lives. Finally, and most significantly, all three novels were written after Dickens produced his autobiographical fragment; and even more compellingly, *David Copperfield* incorporates a transmuted version of Dickens's autobiographical fragment.

When one reads accounts of Dickens's autobiographical fragment, the polluting power that Elizabeth Dickens wielded is not emphasized. This is lamentable because the autobiographical fragment goes a long way towards explaining why Dickens, in the absence of an honest interchange with his mother, employed a subtle range of rhetorical techniques to depict the mothers of the protagonists in his autobiographical novels as primary objects of disgust.

CHAPTER TWO

The Etiology of Disgust

David Trotter, in *Cooking with Mud: The Idea of Mess in Nineteenth-Century Art and Fiction*, is (as his title suggests) more interested in the "idea" of mess than the meaning of mess:

> I want to give some standing, in discussions of the history of modern culture, to the "idea" of mess. By "idea," I mean something at once less distinct than a concept and more distinct than an experience: a phenomenology, a way of thinking and feeling, an emergent self-awareness. Writers and artists tend not to say what they understand by mess, or why they value it, or disvalue it. But there is an understanding and an evaluation at work in the idea they have of it which could be conceived, as Georges Bataille conceived formlessness (*l'informe*), in terms of a specific activity of mind and body. Writers and artists think *with* mess as well as *about* it. This idea or activity is, in Steven Connor's phrase, "experience becoming explanation."[1]

While reluctant to examine the meaning of mess, Trotter reveals that his main interest in mess, however, is its association with chance.[2] This is no doubt why the examples that he provides of mess randomly range from mud and stains to "bad behaviour" and "bad luck."[3] In terms of Dickens's work, Trotter asserts that one of Dickens's "most vivid apprehension[s] of mess" is a scene in *Great Expectations* when Pip, traveling by coach, finds himself in "chance company" with two convicts. Not only do the men crack nuts and spit the shells about but one of them breathes like "searching acid" on the back of Pip's head. Trotter claims that the acid breath and nutshells provoke disgust (as opposed to horror, anger or pity) and disgust helps Dickens "to understand mess as contingency's signature."[4] Trotter, mirroring his treatment of mess, has no interest in defining disgust:

> Disgust-in-general seems to me a topic of considerable import for enquiries into the history of modern (and indeed ancient) experience. The main difference between the approach I shall take here and the approach taken by commentators

like [William Ian] Miller is that I am not concerned with aetiology. The writers and painters whose work I shall discuss knew, or thought they knew, all they needed to know about disgust. Their aim was not to trace a specific feeling back to its origin in the body or in cultural convention, but rather to use its roughly calculable effect as a means of characterizing a person or a milieu. From their point of view, the advantage of disgust was precisely that it did not need to be defined.[5]

While I can appreciate this open-ended approach, it is quite different from my own. The etiology of disgust is, I believe, very important and I do not feel that one can adequately tackle the topic of disgust without at least addressing this issue. Accordingly, before analyzing Dickens's treatment of the protagonist's mothers in his autobiographical novels, I would like to provide a rough outline of various models of disgust and to state my position in relation to these models. Ultimately, I favor the model of disgust that is adumbrated in Mary Douglas's anthropological analysis of pollution and taboo and then later developed by Julia Kristeva in her psychoanalytic and semiotic theory of abjection, but I do not wish to proceed without seeking to situate their work within the broader field.

Disgust is a relatively recent field of enquiry. In fact in terms of scientific research so little has been done that it has been called "the forgotten emotion of psychiatry."[6] In addition, according to the social historian William Ian Miller: "Disgust has elicited little attention in any of the disciplines that claim an interest in the emotions: psychology, philosophy, anthropology."[7] In relation to psychology, Paul Rozin and April E. Fallon state:

> It is surprising that disgust is hardly mentioned in introductory psychology texts or texts on social psychology or motivation. No doubt this is because, apart from the study of the characteristic facial expression, there has been very little research on disgust.[8]

Accordingly, as late as 2004, Susan B. Miller was forced to conclude that "with a few notable exceptions, disgust has been shunned as a subject of serious inquiry, no doubt in part because its unsociable stink threatens to transfer to those who study it."[9] Notwithstanding this "unsociable stink" there have been a number of theories put forward to explain disgust. These theories, as Susan B. Miller contends, may broadly be divided into "biological" and "self-oriented" understandings of disgust.[10] Biological disgust theorists posit that disgust operates "as an instinctive response genetically maintained because of its protective value for the body: it makes us want to cease smelling, ingesting, or touching whatever substance arouses it."[11] However, such theorists differ in terms of emphasis. There are those who stress protection from germs; those who emphasize the risk of contact with human or animal waste; and those who focus on oral intake.

The work of hygiene researchers Valerie Curtis and Adam Biran falls under the first area of emphasis. For Curtis and Biran, disgust "can best be understood as a mechanism for defense against infectious disease."[12] As to the second area of emphasis, Andras Angyal, a psychoanalytic theorist of disgust, argues, "disgust is a specific reaction towards the waste products of the human and animal body."[13] Apparently, the strength of disgust depends upon the degree of intimacy of contact. As Angyal states:

> There is already some degree of unpleasantness in having disgusting objects in one's immediate surroundings, and more so if they soil one's clothes. It is even more disgusting to touch them with one's bare skin, and very much more so to take them into the mouth, not to mention ingesting them.[14]

For this reason, Angyal contends, "the main threat against which disgust is directed, is the oral incorporation of certain substances."[15] For William Ian Miller, Angyal's "disgust is richly cognitive and social, not some primitive hard-wired reflex."[16] However, while Angyal may take into account the cognitive and social aspects of disgust, his analysis of disgust seems to be based on a central question that would, no doubt, have elicited "hard-wired reflex" reactions. Angyal writes: "On asking people to name the first disgusting object which occurs to them, one obtains almost invariably some reference to excreta, especially to faeces."[17] One cannot help but think that another, more open question (e.g., What do you find disgusting?) might have elicited altogether different, more "richly cognitive and social" responses.

Whilst Angyal's analysis of disgust emphasized the risk of contact with human or animal waste, it nevertheless corroborated Charles Darwin's "oral intake" understanding of disgust. Darwin, it should be noted, was something of a pioneer in terms of the study of disgust. For William Ian Miller, "Charles Darwin was the first to risk studying disgust in its own right."[18] However, as Miller notes, he "limited his risk by keeping the discussion very brief, not even five pages."[19] For Darwin: "The term 'disgust,' in its simplest sense, means something offensive to the taste."[20] Nearly a century later, psychologist Silvan Tomkins, bolstered this position. For Tomkins, disgust "is primarily an auxiliary response to the hunger drive designed to prevent the ingestion of noxious material or to achieve its total rejection and regurgitation if it has been ingested."[21] Paul Rozin and April E. Fallon, writing in 1987, defined disgust in much the same way: "revulsion at the prospect of (oral) incorporation of an offensive object."[22] However, thirteen years later, Rozin (in association with other colleagues) sought to develop this notion of "core disgust"[23] because he had come to believe that the elicitors and meaning of disgust had substantially expanded.[24] Accordingly, he wrote:

> We have suggested that disgust originated as a rejection response to bad tastes, and then evolved into a much more abstract and ideational emotion. In this evolution

the function of disgust shifted: A mechanism for avoiding harm to the body became a mechanism for avoiding harm to the soul.[25]

William Ian Miller questions theories of disgust that support or build upon Darwin's emphasis on the sense of taste:

> Darwin is right about the etymology of disgust. It means unpleasant to the taste. But one wonders whether taste would figure so crucially in Darwin's account if the etymology hadn't suggested it. The German *Ekel*, for instance, bears no easily discernible connection to taste. Did that make it easier for Freud to link disgust as readily with the anal and genital as with the oral zone?[26]

Susan B. Miller, for quite different reasons, also questions the assumption that disgust is fundamentally connected to the sense of taste:

> To suppose a developmental line from early distaste for food to true disgust need not imply that, without distaste, disgust would never develop. We cannot assume, for example, that an infant who is tube-fed and hence lacks the experience of early food rejection would fail to develop later disgust toward food or other unacceptable contacts. Likely, the internal structures that promote so fundamental a category of emotional life as disgust are quite robust and will manifest even if particular experiences are missed. In addition to early ingestive experience, unpleasant nonoral contacts of infancy (e.g., being held too tightly) are also likely contributors to the development of disgust. Interestingly, a study of feral humans showed that people lacking *social* interactions, not ingestive experience, failed to develop disgust.[27]

Turning to "self-oriented" theories of disgust, self-protection rather than bodily protection is emphasized. As Susan B. Miller states:

> It is the self, not the body per se, whose vulnerability to invasion and degradation is at issue when disgust arises. The self is vulnerable to agents as diverse as foodstuffs, faeces, slimy messes that touch the skin, disturbing ideas and visions, immoral acts, and repellent people.[28]

"Animal reminder," moral-legal, structural and psychoanalytic understandings of disgust perhaps most obviously fit the self-oriented model[29] and, of these, I believe the latter two models are the most useful in terms of analyzing Dickens's treatment of the protagonists' mothers in his autobiographical novels.

The "animal reminder" model of disgust evolved from Rozin's biological notion of "core disgust," but it can also stand on its own as a self-oriented theory of disgust. Essentially, this theory posits that whatever reminds us that we are animals elicits disgust. Disgust, under this rubric, serves to protect our belief that we are superior to animals.[30] William Ian Miller has put forward a strong argument against this theory of disgust:

> Surely we do not need the example of the animals to remind us that our bodies generate, fornicate, excrete, suppurate, die, and rot.... Our bodies and our souls are the prime generators of the disgusting. What the animals remind us of, the ones that disgust us — insects, slugs, worms, rats, bats, newts, centipedes — is life,

oozy, slimy, viscous, teeming, messy, uncanny life. We needn't have recourse to the animals for that reminder; all we need is a mirror.[31]

As to the moral-legal model of disgust, this is premised on the view that disgust is primarily "a moral and social sentiment"[32] which serves an important regulatory function within society. As William Ian Miller writes:

> Disgust signals our being appalled, signals the fact that we are paying more than lip-service; its presence lets us know we are truly in the grip of the norm whose violation we are witnessing or imagining. To articulate one's disgust is to do more than state a preference or simply reveal a sensation in our bodies. Even if we are only using the diction of disgust as a fashion of talking, that is, independent of the feeling, we are still stating most emphatically the belief that the norms being referenced by our expression of disgust should be the sort that hold us in their grip.[33]

For Robert Rawdon Wilson, there are a number of limitations to this understanding of disgust:

> It cannot directly deal with the problem of origins (why do only adult human beings, but neither animals nor small children, experience disgust?) without appealing to one or another religious doctrine. Nor can it deal with distribution. Many things that have no social content whatsoever are found by some people to be disgusting.... A moral account of disgust cannot deal at all with transgressive art or with personal treks across social boundaries for self-fashioning or enlightenment.[34]

Added to this, Martha Nussbaum cogently argues that disgust should largely be distrusted concerning matters of the law:

> Because disgust embodies a shrinking from contamination that is associated with the human desire to be nonanimal, it is frequently hooked up with various forms of shady social practice, in which the discomfort people feel over the fact of having an animal body is projected outwards onto vulnerable people and groups. These reactions are irrational, in the normative sense, both because they embody an aspiration to be a kind of being that one is not, and because, in the process of pursuing that aspiration, they target others for gross harms.
>
> Where law is concerned, it is especially important that a pluralistic democratic society protect itself against such projection-reactions, which have been at the root of gross evils throughout history, prominently including misogyny, anti–Semitism, and loathing of homosexuals. Thus while the law may rightly admit the relevance of indignation, as a moral response appropriate to good citizens and based upon reasons that can be publicly shared, it will do well to cast disgust onto the garbage heap where it would like to cast so many of us.[35]

Nussbaum here attributes disgust to anxieties about our animal origins. Whilst I do not agree with this position, I nonetheless believe that disgust "embodies a shrinking from contamination" and is "at the root of gross evils throughout history" including misogyny. I also support her argument that the disgust-reaction should not be given credence in matters of the law.

The structural model of disgust is chiefly represented by the work of Jean-Paul Sartre and Mary Douglas. Under this model, as Wilson puts it, "Disgust arises when something is seen to have slipped into a disapprobative category: to have fallen within the boundaries of the prohibited, the taboo, the loathed."[36] Sartre expounded this model of disgust in his work *Being and Nothingness*. Analyzing the state of viscosity, Sartre maintained that slime is

> essentially ambiguous because its fluidity exists in slow motion; there is a sticky thickness in its liquidity; it represents in itself a dawning triumph of the solid over the liquid.... Slime is the agony of water.[37]

Slime apparently appears in many different shapes: "A handshake, a smile, a thought, a feeling can be slimy."[38] It presents as "a deflation ... and as *display*—like the flattening out of the full breasts of a woman who is lying on her back."[39] It is a "soft yielding action, a moist and feminine sucking"[40] and is "the revenge of the In-itself. A sickly sweet, feminine revenge which will be symbolized on another level by the quality 'sugary.'"[41] As is obvious, the trouble with Sartre's structural analysis is that it is uncritically caught up in what Nussbaum would describe as the "projection-reaction" of misogyny.[42] Accordingly, Mary Douglas's analysis of pollution and taboo offers a more promising, if not to say rational, structural model of disgust. For Douglas (as noted in the first chapter), pollution occurs (and by extension disgust arises) when one encounters category violation or slippage. When Douglas (below) discusses "pollution-worthy"[43] biological processes, for example, the natural corollary is that such processes may be viewed as disgusting:

> If I can fervently drink his tears, wrote Jean Genet, why not the so limpid drop on the end of his nose? To this we can reply: first that nasal secretions are not so limpid as tears. They are more like treacle than water. When a thick rheum oozes from the eye it is no more apt for poetry than nasal rheum. But ... clear, fast-running tears are the stuff of romantic poetry: they do not defile.[44]

Quite obviously, disgust would have no small part to play in Genet's reluctance to consume the products of his lover's nose. It is not mentioned because Douglas is concerned with outlining a theory of pollution and purity rather than a theory of disgust. Similarly, when Douglas speaks of witches, she, by extension, speaks of the disgust they may evoke:

> Witches are social equivalents of beetles and spiders who live in the cracks of the walls and wainscoting. They attract the fears and dislikes which other ambiguities and contradictions attract in other thought structures, and the kind of powers attributed to them symbolise their ambiguous, inarticulate status.[45]

The word disgust may not be stated but the implication is certainly there. At other times, Douglas is more overt. Referring to the "Hindoo caste system"[46] she writes:

the revulsion from touching corpses and excreta does not merely express the order of caste in the system as a whole. The anxiety about bodily margins expresses danger to group survival.[47]

As can be seen, Douglas is not overly concerned with the actual emotion of disgust that arises from touching corpses and excreta. Instead, she is interested in the attendant danger of touching corpses and excreta. Douglas then does not *directly* deal with disgust, but it is implicit throughout her thesis. Unfortunately, however, this has led some recent commentators of disgust to dismiss her work. William Ian Miller, for instance, states:

> Douglas's account, it should be said, remains strangely unmotivated. Disgust barely appears. It is all cold structure and its consequences. Inner states of individual actors are not her concern and so committed is she to her anti-psychological account that she does not simply ignore the emotions but seems to suggest they have no role at all in maintaining the structures of purity and pollution.[48]

Martha Nussbaum is also critical:

> The theory has a number of defects that make it problematic as an account of *disgust*, however insightful it may be about the operation of taboos and prohibitions. First of all, it runs together the idea of purity and the idea of disgust, two very different concepts. It is obvious that an item may be impure without being disgusting. Second, Douglas tends to assimilate disgust and danger: thus sorcery, along with disgusting foods and fluids, is classified as a violation of social boundaries. Third, the account is *too* contextual: wastes, corpses, and most bodily fluids are ubiquitously objects of disgust. Societies have great latitude to determine how ideas of contamination extend to other objects, but they seem not to have latitude to make these primary objects nondisgusting. Fourth, the idea of anomaly is too weak to explain why we find some things disgusting. Feces and corpses are disgusting but in no way anomalous. On the other hand, a creature like a dolphin is an anomaly in nature, being a sea-dwelling mammal, but nobody finds dolphins disgusting. There seems to be more going on in disgust than merely the idea of surprise or departure from social norms. That something is plausibly captured in Rozin's idea of anxiety about animality.[49]

Nussbaum's assessment of Douglas's work is not exactly persuasive. Firstly, Douglas did not set out to provide an account of disgust. Rather, she set out to explore purity and danger and, in doing so, laid the foundations for future accounts of disgust. Secondly, it is erroneous to say that Douglas runs together the idea of purity and the idea of disgust. Douglas barely mentions disgust. Instead, she is concerned with pollution. For Douglas, pollution is a type of danger that occurs only when strong lines of structure (cosmic or social) have been violated. By extension, it may be inferred that the emotion of disgust only arises when the values that an individual firmly subscribes to are violated. However, disgust is an emotion and, as such, it is relative to the individual. Certainly, it may be the case that an item may be impure without being disgusting, but this is due to the difference between socially endorsed values and individual values. Accordingly, what may be deemed as polluting at a social level may not be deemed revolting at an individual level. Thirdly, Douglas does not tend to assimilate disgust and danger. Sorcery may be classified as a violation of social boundaries but it may not disgust at an individual level. Again, because disgust is an emotion it is relative to the individual. Indeed, one's disgust at sorcery would be in direct proportion to how strongly one subscribed to societal injunctions concerning sorcery. Fourthly, if wastes, corpses, and most bodily fluids are ubiquitously objects of disgust then this is because they affect individuals at an emotional level, which is over and above societal determinations concerning what may be deemed contaminating. Fifthly, the idea of anomaly is not, in fact, too weak to explain why we find some things disgusting. Indeed, it is stronger than most of the other theories put forward in relation to disgust. Added to this, I would argue that excrement and corpses are in fact anomalous. As Julia Kristeva claims, "Dung signifies the other side of the border, the place where I am not and which permits me to be."[50] So, too, corpses, as Kristeva writes:

> *Show me* what I permanently thrust aside in order to live.... The corpse, the most sickening of wastes, is a border that has encroached upon everything. It is no longer I who expel, "I" is expelled.[51]

As to dolphins being anomalous but not disgusting, most people would not be overly concerned with their biological status. They would merely view them as sea-dwelling.

Just because Douglas does not *directly* address disgust in her account of purity and pollution does not mean that her work has little or no relevance to a theory of disgust. Disgust obviously plays a significant role in maintaining the structure of purity and pollution that Douglas outlines. Indeed, without the defining emotion of disgust there would be next to no pollution rituals for Douglas to explicate. If pollution is, as Douglas maintains, "a type of danger which is not likely to occur except where the lines of structure, cosmic or social, are clearly defined"[52] then it follows that there is a corresponding emotion which arises when one perceives a threat to the social/cosmic frameworks that one is committed to. This emotion, implicit in Douglas's thesis, is disgust. Accordingly, if disgust arises when one encounters death, it could be because one is committed to firm ideas concerning the sanctity of life; if disgust arises because one sees an infected wound, it could be because one is committed to strong ideas concerning the integrity of the body; and if disgust arises because one encounters a member of another race, creed, sex or sexual orientation, it could be because one holds firm ideas concerning the purity or superiority of one's own race, creed, sex or sexual orientation. Certainly, some might argue that there are limitations to this structural model of disgust.[53] However, it does undoubtedly highlight the fact that disgust frequently arises when one encounters matter that falls "outside of its culturally assigned place,"[54] and it also paves the way for deeper psychoanalytic analysis.

Turning now to psychoanalytic understandings of disgust, Freud described disgust as a psychological force operating to protect the integrity of the self.[55] However, Freud did not devote much attention to the emotion of disgust.[56] Indeed, as William Ian Miller puts it:

> He lumped disgust with shame and morality, treating them as "reaction formations," whose function it is to inhibit the consummation of unconscious desire; indeed reaction formations are part of the mechanism of repression that makes the desire unconscious.[57]

Susan B. Miller is in agreement:

> The Freudian view addresses instances of libidinal desire and the response of conscience against those, but misses the larger human conflict between isolation and openness to contact. The Freudian view is not apsychological, but it is limited in its psychological scope.[58]

For this reason, it is valuable to turn to Julia Kristeva's psychoanalytic and semiotic theory of abjection. This theory, while complex and at times problematic, nonetheless offers a much more comprehensive understanding of the role disgust plays in self-protection. Added to this, it significantly builds upon Mary Douglas's foundational model of disgust.

What is abjection? In a 1980 interview Kristeva was asked how she would translate the term *l'abjection* into English. Her response was as follows:

> L'abjection is something that disgusts you, for example, you see something rotting and you want to vomit — it is an extremely strong feeling that is at once somatic and symbolic, which is above all a revolt against an external menace from which one wants to distance oneself, but of which one has the impression that it may menace us from the inside. The relation to abjection is finally rooted in the combat that every human being carries on with the mother. For in order to become autonomous, it is necessary that one cut the instinctual dyad of the mother and the child and that one become something other.[59]

Kristeva thereby views abjection as "an extremely strong feeling" which is provoked by something that may be deemed revolting. Added to this, she believes that this feeling originates in the struggle for autonomy that every person wages with his or her mother. Kristeva thereby posits abjection as disgust, which is at base derived from the primordial universal imperative to separate from the mother. Certainly, Kristeva's seminal essay on abjection is called *Powers of Horror*, however throughout *Powers of Horror* "the logic of *exclusion* that causes the abject to exist"[60] is consistently made manifest through a lexis of disgust. Note, for instance, the high density of collocates relating to disgust in Kristeva's elaboration of abjection:

    Loathing an item of food, a piece of filth, waste, or dung. The spasms and vomiting that protect me. The repugnance, the retching that thrusts me to the side and turns me away from defilement, sewage, and muck. The shame of compromise, of being in the middle of treachery. The fascinated start that leads me toward and separates me from them.

    Food loathing is perhaps the most elementary and most archaic form of abjection. When the eyes see or the lips touch that skin on the surface of milk — harmless, thin as a sheet of cigarette paper, pitiful as a nail paring — I experience a gagging sensation and, still farther down, spasms in the stomach, the belly; and all the organs shrivel up the body, provoke tears and bile, increase heartbeat, cause forehead and hands to perspire. Along with sight-clouding dizziness, *nausea* makes me balk at that milk cream, separates me from the mother and father who proffer it. "I" want none of that element, sign of their desire; "I" do not want to listen, "I" do not assimilate it, "I" expel it. But since the food is not an "other" for "me," who am only in their desire, I expel *myself*, I spit *myself* out, I abject *myself* within the same motion through which "I" claim to establish *myself*.[61]

So while Kristeva focuses on "the horror of being"[62] both her depiction and understanding of abjection is bound up in the idiom of disgust. Commentators of Kristeva further underscore the semantic connection between abjection and disgust. According to Elizabeth Gross:

> Kristeva distinguishes three broad categories of abjects, against which various social and individual taboos are erected: food, waste, and the signs of sexual difference (roughly corresponding to oral, anal and genital erotogenic drives). The subject's reaction to these abjects is visceral: it is usually expressed in retching, vomiting, spasms, choking — in brief, in disgust.[63]

Correspondingly, Kelly Oliver asserts: "The abject is disgusting. It makes you want to vomit.... The abject is something repulsive that both attracts and repels. It holds you there in spite of your disgust."[64] While Anne-Marie Smith claims:

> Abjection can be experienced as disgust which is a bodily form of revolt or as a phobic reaction against the polarised experiences of fusion and separation. Total revolt is impossible and this impossibility is the very condition of abjection.[65]

By contrast, John Lechte (a former student of Kristeva) claims that abjection is "the psychoanalytical elaboration of universal horror."[66] This statement, however, is somewhat weakened by his general discussion of abjection:

> We recall, first of all, that in psychoanalytic theory of Lacanian inspiration, the acquisition of language during the mirror phase (6 to 18 months) marks the intervention of the symbolic (Name-of-the-Father) into the child's universe, and his/her separation from the idyllic state of harmony and continuity which, psychically, *is* the mother. A resultant experience of loss is constitutive of language and desire.... In my unarticulated fantasy, then, I desire the idyllic state which existed before my separation from my object.... Kristeva, on the other hand, suggests that the Lacanian position needs to be nuanced: its strokes are just a little too bold. Indeed, are there not things (let's not call them objects) outside of me which do not give

me the least satisfaction, and which I find repulsive. Whence, then, comes this repulsion, or, in its strongest form, this horror?[67]

Lechte here acknowledges that abjection is not always the feeling of horror. More often than not, it is the feeling of repulsion or disgust. Interestingly, Lechte, in delineating Kristeva's theory, appears to posit a continuum between disgust and horror. Accordingly, horror, within Kristevan terms, is the strongest form of disgust. This position may be understood with reference to William Ian Miller, who writes:

> Horror is horror because it is perceived as denying all strategy, all option. It seems that horror is a subset of disgust, being specifically that disgust for which no distancing or evasive strategies exist that are not in themselves utterly contaminating. Not all disgust evokes horror; there are routine petty loathings and gorge raisings which do not horrify. Disgust admits of ranges of intensity from relatively mild to major. But horror makes no sense except as an intense experience. Mild horror is no longer horror.[68]

It is clear, then, that abjection is primarily the reaction of disgust. However, in its most intense form it is the reaction of horror, and horror, as Miller notes, can be viewed as a subset of disgust.

It is important at this point to outline the forms that the abject can take. As Jon-Ove Steihaug writes: "It seems possible to trace two somewhat different versions of the abject, abjection understood in structural versus more substantial or material terms."[69] Abjection understood in structural terms relates to Kristeva's corroboration of Mary Douglas's structural analysis of defilement. For Kristeva (as for Douglas), "filth is not a quality in itself, but it applies only to what relates to a *boundary*,"[70] and more specifically it represents what has been cast out of that boundary. Accordingly, the abject is that which violates established boundaries, codes or categories:

> It is ... not lack of cleanliness or health that causes abjection but what disturbs identity, system, order. What does not respect borders, positions, rules. The in-between, the ambiguous, the composite.[71]

Indeed, the abject is exceedingly indeterminate. As Kelly Oliver says, "It is neither good nor evil, subject nor object, ego nor unconscious, but something that threatens the distinctions themselves."[72] Accordingly, the abject, as opposed to the object, does not anchor the subject within "the fragile texture of a desire for meaning."[73] Rather, as Kristeva states, it "is radically excluded and draws [one] toward the place where meaning collapses."[74] Despite its exclusion, however, the abject is alarmingly ever-present and potent:

> We may call it a border; abjection is above all ambiguity. Because, while releasing a hold, it does not radically cut off the subject from what treatens [sic] it — on the contrary, abjection acknowledges it to be in perpetual danger.[75]

In essence then, as Elizabeth Grosz writes, the abject "can never be fully obliterated but hovers at the borders of our existence, threatening the apparently settled unity of the subject with disruption and possible dissolution."[76]

Abjection understood in "substantial or material terms" primarily relates to Kristeva's assertion that filth is derived from the maternal and/or the feminine. Kristeva may clearly endorse Mary Douglas's structural view that filth or dirt is anomalous matter, and she may echo Douglas in maintaining that "the potency of pollution is therefore not an inherent one; it is proportional to the potency of the prohibition that founds it."[77] However, going beyond Douglas, Kristeva asks, "From where and from what does the threat [of filth] issue?"[78] Her answer is that "polluting objects fall, schematically, into two types: excremental and menstrual"[79] and these categories represent different dangers:

> Excrement and its equivalents (decay, infection, disease, corpse, etc.) stand for the danger to identity that comes from without: the ego threatened by the non-ego, society threatened by its outside, life by death. Menstrual blood, on the contrary, stands for the danger issuing from within the identity (social or sexual); it threatens the relationship between the sexes within a social aggregate and, through internalisation, the identity of each sex in the face of sexual difference.[80]

Further, Kristeva asks: "What can the two types of defilement have in common?" Her answer, as she is well aware, would not sit well with anthropologists:

> Without having recourse to anal eroticism or the fear of castration — one cannot help *hearing* the reticence of anthropologists when confronted with that explanation — it might be suggested, by means of another psychoanalytic approach, that those *two* defilements stem from the *maternal* and/or the feminine, of which the maternal is the real support.[81]

For Kristeva, then, there is a fundamental connection between impurity and women (especially the mother). In justification of her position, Kristeva claims it "goes without saying" that "menstrual blood signifies sexual difference."[82] As to linking "the *maternal* and/or the feminine" with the excremental, Kristeva's reasoning for this is grounded in her reading of psychoanalytic theory:

> It will be remembered that the anal penis is also the phallus with which infantile imagination provides the feminine sex and that, on the other hand, maternal authority is experienced first and above all, after the first essentially oral frustrations, as sphincteral training.... Through frustrations and prohibitions, this authority shapes the body into a *territory* having areas, orifices, points and lines, surfaces and hollows, where the archaic power of mastery and neglect, of the differentiation of proper-clean and improper-dirty, possible and impossible, is impressed and exerted. It is a "binary logic," a primal mapping of the body that I call semiotic to say that, while being the precondition of language, it is dependent upon meaning, but in a way that is not that of *linguistic* signs nor of the *symbolic* order they found. Maternal authority is the trustee of that mapping of the self's clean and proper body;

it is distinguished from paternal laws within which, with the phallic phase and acquisition of language, the destiny of man will take shape.[83]

According to Kristeva, maternal authority is "without guilt."[84] This kind of authority may be contrasted with "the order of the phallus" which, Kristeva claims, represents "a totally different universe of socially signifying performances where embarrassment, shame, guilt, desire, etc. come into play."[85] Interestingly, Kristeva deems that "the mapping of the self's clean and proper body" may be called semiotic. The semiotic represents Kristeva's challenge to Jacques Lacan's contention that linguistic signification is structured by paternal law or "the Symbolic." Under the Lacanian rubric, the Symbolic, as Judith Butler puts it,

> becomes a universal organizing principle of culture itself. This law creates the possibility of meaningful language, and hence, meaningful experience, through the repression of primary libidinal drives, including the radical dependency of the child on the maternal body.[86]

Kristeva, however, introduces the concept of the semiotic which, as Butler writes, "is a dimension of language occasioned by the primary maternal body." As such, it "not only refutes Lacan's primary premise, but serves as a perpetual source of subversion within the Symbolic."[87] The semiotic is manifest in language that conveys multiple meanings (i.e., poetic language) "which always recall the libidinal multiplicity which characterized the primary relation to the maternal body."[88] Kristeva's notion of the semiotic dimension of language has been the subject of much critical debate.[89] It is not my intention to enter into this debate. Whether or not the guilt free "primal mapping of the body" may be thought of as semiotic is immaterial to Kristeva's central contention that polluting objects can be divided into two categories, excremental and menstrual," and that these categories originate from the maternal and/or the feminine.

As one can see, unpacking Kristeva's notion of abjection means acknowledging both the structural and material dimensions of the abject, and while Steihaug claims that these versions are "somewhat different" I believe they are simply two sides of one coin. Why? Essentially, because within Kristeva's thesis, whether the abject takes a material or structural form, it is invariably linked to the maternal and/or the feminine.[90] Indeed, the structural version of the abject (i.e., that which violates or transgresses cultural categorization) is linked to the maternal and/or the feminine because it recalls the time (prior to identity, system and order) where the pre-subject existed in a state of fusion with the maternal body. So, too, the material version of the abject is linked to the maternal and/or the feminine because, from Kristeva's psychoanalytic perspective, the impure (i.e., the menstrual and the excremental) derives from the *maternal* and/or the feminine. Certainly, Kristeva may provide structural examples of what causes abjection that could be perceived as masculine: "the shameless rapist, the killer who claims he is a saviour."[91] However, such examples are, by implication, associated with "the maternal and/or the feminine" because they are "in opposition to a paternal rule-governed symbolic."[92]

Kristeva's theory of abjection or disgust is clearly indebted to Mary Douglas's structural work on pollution. Kristeva affirms Douglas's contention that filth is anomalous matter and she reinforces Douglas's view that the danger of pollution is not inherent but, rather, contingent upon the strength of the ideas that seek to define and contain it. However, Kristeva seeks to go beyond Douglas by determining (from a psychoanalytic perspective) the origins of the threat of filth. In such a way she is able to probe more deeply into the strong reaction (disgust) that subjects feel when they encounter anomaly, and she is able to suggest that there is a direct link between disgust and the universal primordial imperative to separate from the maternal body. The mother is thereby "*the 'object' of primal repression*"[93] and disgust, as it is derived from this fundamental need to expel the maternal, is arguably the primal emotion.

The problem with Kristeva's theory of abjection is similar to that of her theory of the semiotic, which, as Jacqueline Rose asserts, "finds itself face to face with, or even entrenched within, the most grotesque and fully cultural stereotypes of femininity itself."[94] Indeed, this is particularly apparent when Kristeva moves beyond plain descriptions of the processes of abjection. The following passage displays her tendency to reinforce stereotypical ideas concerning the feminine:

> The abject confronts us ... with our earliest attempts to release the hold of maternal entity even before ex-isting outside of her, thanks to the autonomy of language. It is a violent clumsy breaking away, with the constant risk of falling back under the sway of a power as securing as it is stifling. The difficulty a mother has in acknowledging (or being acknowledged by) the symbolic realm — in other words, the problem she has with the phallus that her father or her husband stands for — is not such as to help the future subject leave the natural mansion. The child can serve its mother as token of her own authentication; there is, however, hardly any reason for her to serve as go-between for it to become autonomous and authentic in its turn. In such close combat, the symbolic light that a third party, eventually the father, can contribute helps the future subject, the more so if it happens to be endowed with a robust supply of drive energy, in pursuing a reluctant struggle against what, having been the mother, will turn into an abject. Repelling, rejecting; repelling itsef, rejecting itself. Ab-jecting.[95]

This passage is quite offensive in its depiction of stifling maternal power. However, as Jacqueline Rose notes,

> unlike some of her most virulent detractors ... Kristeva at least knows that these images are not so easily dispatched. It is not by settling the question of their origins that we can necessarily dismantle their force.[96]

Kristeva is therefore prepared to tackle disgust head on even if the exercise, of necessity, trips her up in ghastly stereotypes of femininity. Added to this, she is also prepared to tackle one of the worst and most persistent forms that disgust can take: misogyny.[97] Indeed, in her work *Tales of Love* Kristeva contends that misogyny is essentially a misdirected or erroneous form of disgust. For Kristeva, misogyny arises because we do not have a cogent myth or discourse of maternity that can adequately absorb abjection. A myth is required which can allow us to abject the mother and come to terms with that abjection. Without such a myth, we effectively abject all women. Kristeva primarily attributes the degradation of women to a crisis in the religious myth of the Virgin. For Kristeva, the religious representation of maternity embodied in the Virgin once significantly served to absorb disgust concerning the mother. However, in a largely secular age, the currency of this myth has become eroded and women en masse have suffered the consequences:

> The image of the Virgin — the woman whose entire body is an emptiness through which the paternal word is conveyed — had remarkably subsumed the maternal "abject," which is so necessarily intrapsychic. Lacking that safety lock, feminine abjection imposed itself upon social representation, causing an actual denigration of women; this in turn gave rise to increased antifeminism.[98]

Kelly Oliver rightly questions Kristeva's thesis.[99] Oliver points out that women suffered oppression and denigration even at the height of the myth of the Virgin's popularity. Consequently, Kristeva's theory cannot serve to explain women's oppression before the nineteenth century. However, Oliver recognizes the importance of Kristeva's theory:

> I think that Kristeva's theory is useful for feminist consideration. It is not necessary to link a misdirected abjection to the crisis in the myth of the Virgin. After all, Kristeva does not endorse the myth of the Virgin. She merely points out that it is the only discourse of motherhood that is available to us; and that this discourse is inadequate.[100]

Oliver also acknowledges that Kristeva's account of the misdirected or misplaced reaction of disgust towards all women differs from other feminist theories:

> Her argument is different from other feminist positions that have considered women's oppression linked to reproduction or compulsory maternity for women. Kristeva maintains that it is not maternity or reproduction that are responsible for women's oppression but the representations of them. She suggests that we need to be able to consider the *maternal function* apart from women and individual mothers. If we can abject the maternal body as part of the maternal function and work through that abjection without abjecting the mother as a woman, then not only does the representation of woman change but also the representation of motherhood.[101]

As is evident, Oliver believes that Kristeva's theory provides a useful means to account for "women's oppression." Whilst this is indisputable, I believe that Oliver's position here is actually too mild. As I have sought to show, under the terms of Kristeva's theory, abjection is primarily the self-protective reaction of disgust, or in its worst form, horror. As such, the abjection of women is a reaction of sheer revulsion or horror towards women. When Kristeva speaks then of "feminine abjection," the "actual denigration of women," "increased antifeminism" and the lack of an adequate mythological "safety lock" to prevent the abjection of women through social representation, she offers up a useful means to account for misogyny.

As can be seen, while disgust may not have elicited enormous interest in various disciplines, it has nonetheless inspired a diverse range of responses amongst commentators who have not been concerned with the transference of "its unsociable stink." Of these responses, I believe that Mary Douglas's structural model and Julia Kristeva's psychoanalytic/semiotic model are the most compelling. Not only do they make the most sense (particularly when looked at together); they also "throw up" (so to speak) the most interesting possibilities for exegetic approaches to the discourse of disgust. In terms of the particular project that I am engaged in, they also afford the most fruitful terms of analysis. Mary Douglas's work, as I have shown, usefully serves to explicate Dickens's autobiographical fragment. Not simply does it shed light on Dickens's extreme aversion towards those, who for one reason or another, slip out of their expected place but it also gives us a platform to more readily identify the ways in which Dickens rhetorically constructs his mother as the foremost polluting and, by inference, disgusting person in his life. Furthermore, it helps us to see that Dickens displayed an all too similar rhetorical approach toward the characters who slip out of place in his major fictional autobiographies, and to uncover the fact that the key category slippage offenders/polluters and primary objects of narrative disgust in these works are the protagonists' mothers. These include the biological mothers of the protagonists (Clara Copperfield in *David Copperfield*, Lady Dedlock in *Bleak House* and Georgiana Pirrip in *Great Expectations*) and the women that come to stand in loco parentis to the protagonists (Betsey Trotwood in *David Copperfield*, Miss Barbary in *Bleak House* and Mrs. Joe Gargery in *Great Expectations*). This narrative disgust, in keeping with the way in which misogyny frequently operates, is, for the most part, insidiously conveyed, so while the central imperfect maternal characters may obviously "slip up" in terms of Dickens's "great expectations," his disgust at their actions is not always explicit. Instead, his narrative *implicitly* sets these characters up as objects of disgust. This is where Julia Kristeva's theory of abjection is particularly useful. Firstly, it helps, in a psychoanalytic sense, to pinpoint the disgust which underlies the depiction of these characters; secondly, it gives us the theoretical tools to explicate this veiled disgust; and thirdly, it serves to highlight the myriad ways in which misogynistic discourse produces its extremely damaging effects.

Clara Copperfield, Betsey Trotwood and the Construction of the Feminine Sublime in *David Copperfield*

> And now, as I close my task, subduing my desire to linger yet, these faces fade away. But one face, shining on me like a Heavenly light by which I see all other objects, is above them and beyond them all. And that remains.[1]

The character of Agnes Wickfield has, for some time, been viewed in an unfavorable light. For many critics, she is simply awful. George Orwell categorically writes: "Agnes is the most disagreeable of [Dickens's] heroines, the real legless angel of Victorian romance."[2] Harold Bloom opines, "Agnes is a disaster, and that dreadful 'pointing upward!' is not to be borne."[3] Barbara Hardy asserts: "I think the religious/feminine ideal presented in Agnes is repulsive."[4] Michael Slater declares: "It would be a bold critic indeed who would claim this character to be a success."[5] To put it mildly, then, critics are less than impressed with Agnes.[6] Nancy Klenk Hill perhaps best sums up the prevailing exegetic view of this character: "The very mention of Agnes Wickfield ... sends many critics into spasms of denunciation because Dickens is thought to have described [an] impossible paragon of virtue."[7] Certainly, it is difficult to argue with these views because the character of Agnes is so relentlessly virtuous. However, while I believe that Agnes is awful, it is for an entirely different reason. Agnes is awful, I submit, because Dickens was less interested in creating a believable woman character than in creating a pattern of feminine perfection that would enable his hero to completely transcend his less-than-perfect maternal origins and constitute himself as a "self-made man." Such a project is dubious, unrealistic and potentially disastrous, and this is, in all probability, why the character of Agnes stretches credulity. Dickens, however, goes to great lengths to present Agnes as the pinnacle of womanhood. Indeed, supplementing the hyperbolic praise that the protagonist, David Copperfield, heaps upon Agnes throughout the novel, Dickens, as I will seek to show, draws upon the discourse of the romantic sublime in order to construct Agnes as the natural object through which David can achieve authentic identity and originality.

Of course, in Edmund Burke's seminal treatise on the sublime and the beautiful, the sublime is figured as masculine and the beautiful is figured as feminine. Accordingly, it would be impossible under his treatise for a woman to be capable of raising ideas of the sublime (i.e., astonishment, terror, power, and infinity). However, the eighteenth-century tradition of the sublime, as commentators have noted, is a transformational discourse capable of transforming "both itself and its neighbouring discursive forms."[8] I would like to suggest that, in the nineteenth century, Charles Dickens tropologically transforms the romantic tradition of the sublime to include the possibility of an ideal woman producing an affect of sublimity and an illusion of self-creation. The character of Agnes Wickfield, then, should not be taken lightly. Not only is she a significant character in terms of mapping the transformation of the discourse of the sublime in the nineteenth century, but operating simultaneously as she does as the preeminent woman in Dickens's first major fictional autobiography — the creator of nothing less than his protagonist's soul,[9] and the antithesis of his protagonist's flawed biological and adoptive mothers — she "pointedly" reveals the depth of Dickens's disgust in relation to maternal ineptitude and arguably represents his most idealistic attempt to expunge maternal pollution.

There can be no doubt that Dickens strongly identified with *David Copperfield*. In terms of his literary output he regarded it as nothing less than his "favourite child"[10] and, nearing its completion, he wistfully wrote: "I seem to be sending some part of myself into the Shadowy World."[11] However, while Dickens knew that the novel was self-revelatory, he was also conscious that this was more than qualified by his artistry: "I really think I have done it ingeniously, and with a very complicated interweaving of truth and fiction."[12] Critics have not always appreciated the complex nature of this novel. Edmund Wilson, in particular, is quite dismissive:

> *Copperfield* is not one of Dickens's deepest books: it is something in the nature of a holiday. David is too candid and simple to represent Dickens himself; and though the blacking warehouse episode is utilized, all the other bitter circumstances of Dickens's youth were dropped when he abandoned the autobiography.[13]

Whether or not Copperfield represents Dickens himself, it is simply erroneous to claim that "all of the other bitter circumstances of Dickens's youth" were not utilized in this novel. Firstly, the most bitter circumstance of Dickens's youth was arguably the revulsion that he felt towards his less than ideal mother and this is most certainly woven into this novel through the barbed portrayal and symbolic repudiation of David Copperfield's biological mother Clara Copperfield, and his adoptive mother Aunt Betsey. Secondly, it is important to note that the inclusion of bitter autobiographical circumstances does not necessarily grant depth to a work of literature. Depth can just as readily be achieved without incorporating autobiographical material or, as I would like to explore here, through the inclusion and fictional transmutation of cherished autobiographical circumstances. As noted previously, perhaps Dickens's most favorable interaction with a woman in his childhood was his encounter, as fleeting as it was, with the sympathetic and admiring wife of the landlord in the public-house. Certainly, in David Copperfield's account of his time at Murdstone and Grinby's warehouse, there is a very similar encounter to what Dickens described in his autobiographical fragment. Indeed, much of it is simply lifted word for word from the fragment:

> I was such a child, and so little, that frequently when I went into the bar of a strange public-house for a glass of ale or porter, to moisten what I had had for dinner, they were afraid to give it to me. I remember one hot evening I went into the bar of a public-house, and said to the landlord:
>
> "What is your best — your *very best*— ale a glass?" For it was a special occasion. I don't know what. It may have been my birthday.
>
> "Twopence-halfpenny," says the landlord, "is the price of the Genuine Stunning ale."
>
> "Then," says I, producing the money, "just draw me a glass of the Genuine Stunning, if you please, with a good head to it."
>
> The landlord looked at me in return over the bar, from head to foot, with a strange smile on his face; and instead of drawing the beer, looked round the screen and said something to his wife. She came out from behind it, with her work in her hand, and joined him in surveying me. Here we stand, all three, before me now. The landlord in his shirt-sleeves, leaning against the bar window-frame; his wife looking over the little half-door; and I, in some confusion, looking up at them from outside the partition. They asked me a good many questions; as, what my name was, how old I was, where I lived, how I was employed, and how I came there. To all of which, that I might commit nobody, I invented, I am afraid, appropriate answers. They served me with the ale, though I suspect it was not the Genuine Stunning; and the landlord's wife, opening the little half-door of the bar, and bending down, gave me my money back, and gave me a kiss that was half admiring and half compassionate, but all womanly and good, I am sure [216].

The key difference between this passage and the passage in the autobiographical fragment is that, in addition to bending down and giving David an admiring and compassionate kiss, the landlord's wife gives David his money back. This is very significant because in the autobiographical fragment the extremely self-conscious and money-conscious Dickens wishes, in retrospect, that the suppliers of goods and services had not taken the coins that he had proffered as a child:

Once, I remember tucking my own bread (which I had brought from home in the morning) under my arm, wrapped up in a piece of paper like a book, and going into the best dining-room in Johnson's alamode beef-house in Clare Court, Drury Lane, and magnificently ordering a small plate of alamode beef to eat with it. What the waiter thought of such a strange little apparition, coming in all alone, I don't know; but I can see him now, staring at me as I ate my dinner, and bringing up the other waiter to look. I gave him a halfpenny, and I wish, now, that he hadn't taken it.[14]

The fictional landlord's wife, then, not only fulfills one of Dickens's most deeply held wishes but is even more kind and considerate than the flesh and blood "all womanly and good" landlord's wife that she was clearly based on. It would seem then that, on reflection, Dickens felt that the real landlord's wife could have gone just one step further in order to more fully deserve the appellation "all womanly and good." Indeed, it suggests that in Dickens's mind, a truly good woman must be above material considerations and not motivated by personal interest. In short, his ideal woman would be more than human. If there is one woman character in *David Copperfield* that meets these criteria it must surely be Agnes. Indeed, as Michael Slater puts it: "Agnes ... is sanctified for her creator as well as for David and so, by her very nature, will show no ... signs of human weakness."[15] Certainly, throughout the novel, Agnes is depicted as exceedingly kind and disinterested. Always, no matter what the cost, she puts others before herself. As Edwin Eiger writes:

> Readers have often complained that Agnes is an infuriatingly unreal character, that, especially in her disinterested attitude towards David's love for Dora, she goes beyond the pale even of saintly womanhood.[16]

This extraordinary selflessness is perhaps most tellingly conveyed when David provides a summary of the fervent letter that he receives from Agnes while he is in the Alps. In this letter, which is part of a packet of letters that reaches David on his travels when other packets have missed him, Agnes, like the fictional landlord's wife, is revealed as not simply self-denying but filled with compassion and admiration for David:

> The packet was in my hand. I opened it, and read the writing of Agnes.
> She was happy and useful, was prospering as she had hoped. That was all she told me of herself. The rest referred to me.
> She gave me no advice; she urged no duty on me; she only told me, in her own fervent manner, what her trust in me was. She knew (she said) how such a nature as mine would turn affliction to good. She knew how trial and emotion would exalt and strengthen it. She was sure that in my every purpose I should gain a firmer and a higher tendency, through the grief I had undergone. She, who so gloried in my fame, and so looked forward to its augmentation, well knew that I would labour on. She knew that in me, sorrow could not be weakness, but must be strength. As the endurance of my childish days had done its part to make me what I was, so greater calamities would nerve me on, to be yet better than I was;

and so, as they had taught me, would I teach others. She commended me to God, who had taken my innocent darling to His rest; and in her sisterly affection cherished me always, and was always at my side go where I would; proud of what I had done, but infinitely prouder yet of what I was reserved to do [888].

Interestingly too, along with being selfless, Agnes is from the outset associated with womanliness. Notably, when David first sees Agnes, she seems so like her mother's portrait that through a trick of imagination, David thinks that "the portrait had grown womanly" (279) while its subject has remained a child. As Philip M. Weinstein puts it:

> Agnes emerges, even as a child as a mature housekeeper.... Agnes is disciplined and harmonious from birth on. She seems to have emerged full-grown from her mother's portrait."[17]

In addition, it is worth considering that while the all-womanly and good Agnes may not be the wife of a landlord in a public-house, she is nonetheless, throughout most of the book, tied to a man, her father, who is an alcoholic and therefore constantly associated with alcohol. However, while Agnes can be likened to the landlord's wife, she is a much more full-blown version. Indeed, in his description of the landlord's wife, Dickens essentially adumbrates the qualities that will be magnified many times over in Agnes. So while the young David could, without any trouble, appreciate the qualities of the landlord's wife and view her in a very human light, the older David is so in awe of Agnes's superlative qualities that he actually constructs her as sublime.

Just as a packet of letters, against the odds, reaches David in the Alps, the novel itself does not get beyond the reach of Dickens's enduring preoccupations. Accordingly, far from representing something in the nature of a textual holiday away from Dickens's deepest concerns, *David Copperfield* is rather, just as Dickens deemed it to be, a highly ingenious work which engages in a very complicated interweaving of truth and fiction. Dickens may have abandoned his autobiography but in this, his most autobiographical novel, he does not (at least in relation to his formative experiences with women) abandon either his bitterest memory or his sweetest.

Bitter

If David Copperfield's fictional autobiography is examined carefully, it becomes evident that David is preoccupied with displacement. The famous opening lines of the novel display the protagonist's considerable uncertainty in terms of claiming his proper place: "Whether I shall turn out to be the hero of my own life, or whether that station will be held by anybody else, these pages must show" (49). John O. Jordan states: "In all the speculation about what

David means by the term 'hero,' no one has stopped to look at the evidence most closely at hand, the noun that he puts in apposition to 'hero' within his opening sentence."[18] This noun of course is "station" and while I agree with Jordan that it is important to give due consideration to this word, my reasons differ from his in terms of its meaning. For Jordan:

> the difficulty David has in knowing whether he is the hero of his own life has to do with his uncertainty about the relation between heroism and social station. David does not know whether heroes are born, like Steerforth, or whether they can make themselves through industry and earnestness, as he himself tries to do.[19]

While I can appreciate this interpretation, I am more concerned to place emphasis on "station" as "a neutral term meaning place, position, or location."[20] By underscoring this definition, I wish to show that David's difficulty in knowing whether he is the hero of his own life lies primarily in his uncertainty about the relationship between heroism and ontological placement. Indeed, David does not know whether he can be deemed the hero of his own life because he is all too aware that he fell from his original station as the hero of his *mother's* life.

David's first notable episode of displacement occurs when his caul is "advertised for sale, in the newspapers, at the low price of fifteen guineas" (49). A caul in the biological sense means the "membrane enclosing the foetus" which "is occasionally found on a baby's head at birth,"[21] but in a superstitious sense it means that a person born with it will be lucky in life and preserved from drowning. To have it put up for sale, then, is to experience loss on at least four fronts: personal good fortune, safety, heritage, and maternal connection. It is not altogether clear in the text who is responsible for putting the caul up for sale as it not directly stated. However, it is most probably David's mother Clara because David's father is not alive when he is born. Certainly, it appears that David's mother is not happy with the only bid for the caul, as David writes:

> All I know is, that there was but one solitary bidding, and that was from an attorney connected with the bill-broking business, who offered two pounds in cash, and the balance in sherry, but declined to be guaranteed from drowning on any higher bargain. Consequently the advertisement was withdrawn at a dead loss — for as to sherry, my poor dear mother's own sherry was in the market then — and ten years afterwards, the caul was put up in a raffle down in our part of the country, to fifty members at half-a-crown a head, the winner to spend five shillings. I was present myself, and I remember to have felt quite uncomfortable and confused, at a part of myself being disposed of in that way [50].

The way that this episode is related is very ambiguous. It appears that David's mother already has sherry up for sale, so the balance of the attorney's bid in sherry does not suit her needs. However, this is inferred rather than made explicit and the sentence in which this is conveyed is particularly elliptical. Dashes allow David to skip over the exact details of who is responsible for putting the caul up for sale on both occasions. Nevertheless, at the heart of the sentence lies David's "poor dear" mother, and whether or not she has been forced to put David's caul on the market on either occasion owing to straitened circumstances, the imputation is that she is prepared to sell off the aforementioned benefits conferred by the caul, which include David's tangible connection to her. Unsurprisingly, David remarks "I ... remember to have felt quite uncomfortable and confused at a part of myself being disposed of in that way" (50). Such a statement, of course, is all too reminiscent of Dickens's incredulous "autobiographical fragment" statement: "It is wonderful to me how I could have been so easily cast away at such an age."[22] To suffer, in any sense, a feeling of personal displacement or negation is one thing, but to suffer this as a result of the actions of one's mother (regardless of her motives) is extremely disquieting. Added to this, David's caul is eventually purchased by an old lady who "very reluctantly" produces "the stipulated five shillings, all in halfpence, and two pence half penny short" (50). Part of David is thereby sold at a discount to an ungracious woman who, as it turns out, need not have entered into the transaction in the first place because for the rest of her days she made it her business to never go anywhere near the water "except on a bridge" (50).

The digression about the sale of the caul is, to all intents and purposes, purely a means to add local color and to create humor. However, if considered at a deeper level, it offers a key to the broader novel. In this story we have two instances in David's formative years where his caul is put up for sale by an unspecified vendor. As indicated, while no one is held directly responsible for putting the caul up for sale, there is nonetheless a distinct reference to his mother at the heart of the story and there is clearly a penny-pinching woman who purchases the caul at a discount when she really had no business to do so (given her future avoidance of water). The sale of David's caul is thereby "tied up" with two women, and while there is ambiguity around expressing the full details of the sale, there is evidently repressed anger directed at money-conscious women who pursue personal agendas at the expense of masculine security.

It is also interesting to explore the significance of the caul in terms of Julia Kristeva's psychoanalytic elaboration of abjection. Under the terms of Kristeva's thesis, a caul could be viewed as a by-product of birth and a residual reminder of the enveloping symbiotic and undivided relation between mother and child. A person who enters the socio-symbolic signifying order engulfed in the inner membrane issuing from maternity could thereby be viewed as abject. For Kristeva:

Abjection preserves what existed in the archaism of pre-objectal relationship, in the immemorial violence with which the body becomes separated from another body in order to be — maintaining that night in which the outline of the signified thing vanishes and where only the imponderable affect is carried out.[23]

In a symbolic sense, one might expect that a person born with a caul would later experience a rather tenuous grasp on his or her own identity. One might also expect that a person who enters the world with the vestiges of his or her relation to maternity, will go on to be profoundly torn between a fascination and repulsion for the abject. However, the fact that David's mother seems to be keen to sell his caul on at least one occasion complicates David's relation with the abject, for not only is he born with the vestiges of the archaic maternal on display, but it appears that his mother is prepared to very publicly renounce this maternal association for the sake of monetary gain. Filthy lucre is also seemingly more important to her than the guarantor of her son's luck and immunity from drowning. David's fascination with the abject would thereby be offset by his awareness of maternal rejection. Accordingly, rather than alternating between absolute fascination and absolute repulsion for the abject, David can be said to alternate between a form of passive-aggressive fascination and outright repulsion. By the term "passive-aggressive fascination" I mean that David's fascination for the abject is always undercut by his need to expose its deficiencies. David's encounters with the abject are never simple. In David's world, there is no such thing as "pure" fascination for the abject. His fascination of necessity carries a stinging critique. For David, fascination and repulsion for the abject are very closely linked. There is no distinct disjunction between the two states.

If David wants to matter in anyone's life, it is in his mother's. Clara Copperfield is far and away the love of David's life. Initially, David feels "right at home" with her. In her eyes, he feels himself to be a king. David's future stepfather, Murdstone, is well aware of this:

As my mother stopped down on the threshold to take me in her arms and kiss me, the gentleman said I was a more highly privileged little fellow than a monarch [67].

David clearly loves to be the sole "fellow" in his mother's life. When Little Em'ly relates how she never knew her father owing to his death, David excitedly conveys his own fatherless but blissful and apparently indissoluble domestic arrangement:

I immediately went into an explanation how I had never seen my own father; and how my mother and I had always lived by ourselves in the happiest state imaginable, and lived so then, and always meant to live so; and how my father's grave was in the churchyard near our house, and shaded by a tree, beneath the boughs of which I had walked and heard the birds sing many a pleasant morning [84–85].

David is not at all upset about his father's nearby grave because he is so happy with his mother. The grave is simply a tranquil, pleasant fact of life. Indeed, David's sequestered existence with his mother appears idyllic:

> And now I see the outside of our house, with the latticed bed-room-windows standing open to let in the sweet-smelling air, and the ragged old rooks'-nests still dangling in the elm-trees at the bottom of the front garden. Now I am in the garden at the back, beyond the yard where the empty pigeon-house and dog-kennel are — a very preserve of butterflies, as I remember it, with a high fence, and a gate and padlock; where the fruit clusters on the trees, riper and richer than fruit has ever been since, in any other garden, and where my mother gathers some in a basket, while I stand by, bolting furtive gooseberries, and trying to look unmoved. A great wind rises, and the summer is gone in a moment. We are playing in the winter twilight, dancing about the parlour. When my mother is out of breath and rests herself in an elbow-chair, I watch her winding her bright curls round her fingers, and straitening her waist, and nobody knows better than I do that she likes to look so well, and is proud of being so pretty [64–65].

However, while the above sketch is quite glorious in its ambient evocation of childhood happiness, it nonetheless contains more than a hint of tension. The "sweet-smelling air" is offset by the decrepit rooks'-nests perilously hanging from the elm trees. The pigeon-house and dog-kennel are disused and neglected to the point where they have incongruously become a "very preserve of butterflies." The garden with its ripe, rich and abundant fruit appears to be a place of infinite plenitude, however the high fence, gate and padlock imply that it is a limited place that requires security. The image of David's mother benignly gathering fruit is juxtaposed with David giving in to temptation and engaging in an act of recalcitrance. "A great wind rises," ensuring that summer gives way in an instant to winter. David dances about the parlor with his mother, but her energy levels flag, the dancing stops and he is aware of her vanity. Indeed, in just one paragraph a series of conflicting images is presented highlighting David's conflicted views about his mother. Despite the pervading rosy glow, negative metaphors predominate. There are metaphors of insecurity and abandonment (the dangling, ragged old rooks'-nests, empty pigeon-house and kennel); temptation and transgression (David bolting down gooseberries); deception and pretense (David trying to look unmoved); transience (the great wind blowing summer away); cessation (the dancing drawing to a close); weakness (Clara out of breath and resting in an elbow chair); and vanity (Clara's obvious pride in her appearance). The presiding metaphor, however, is that of Eden, the garden where Adam and Eve lived. Of course, in the Adam and Eve paradigm, sin originated with Eve. Before her forbidden-fruit episode, man could live in Paradise for eternity, but owing to her sin, man is deprived of Paradise and condemned to suffering and mortality. In David's "Garden of Eden" however, sin originates with David, and while he consumes forbidden fruit he does not take ownership of the stealthy nature of his act. Instead of standing by *furtively* bolt-ing gooseberries, David bolts "furtive gooseberries." Hence, the gooseberries are made to carry the burden of his sin. They have been underhanded rather than him. So while an Edenic metaphor is invoked, it is not the woman who commits original sin but rather a boy, and this boy, while culpable, does not take any responsibility for his deception. Rather, he seeks to cast the forbidden fruit in a sly, compromised light. Why would David impute misconduct to the gooseberries rather than himself? The answer surely is that he views his mother as forbidden fruit and as such she is questionable within his estimation. In ana-lyzing this scene, Gail Turley Houston writes:

> Using Klein's explanation of child development, I suggest that Dickens depicts Clara Copperfield as the embodiment of all nature's treasure, which David desires to ingest. As he furtively bolts the gooseberries, he also seems to consume his mother's nutritive riches, for this image, so metonymically associated with his mother, represents the female as food. In this scene, David intuitively realizes his mother's sexual power and attraction, and he may also fantasize consuming her in a sexual sense.[24]

While I am largely in agreement with this interpretation, I feel that Houston's failure to see that the gooseberries are figured as furtive, rather than David, means that her analysis does not recognize how the text speciously works to place Clara Copperfield (David's forbidden fruit) in a morally suspect light, rather than David. Unpacking this Edenic allusion, I believe, is very important because it provides an essential clue to the circuitous way in which this novel works to set up guilt. Deficient mothers are never directly charged with origi-nating the ills of the Copperfield world, but David's narrative insidiously works to highlight the ways in which their actions invariably lead to most of its suf-fering and pain.

There is no doubt that Clara Copperfield is depicted as flawed and furtive in terms of her dealings with her son. While David is clearly fascinated with "her pretty hair and youthful shape" (61), his account of her actions is shot through with implicit disgust and condemnation. The first time that she is shown to be furtive is when she leaves David in the care of her servant Peggotty to spend "the evening at a neighbour's" (65) but returns home with a strange man. Whilst she is gone David reads to Peggotty about crocodiles, but when tiredness overwhelms him, he breaks off to ask her about her marital status: "Peggotty," says I, suddenly, "were you ever married?" (65) Peggotty, taken aback, cannot understand why marriage has entered David's mind. David responds:

> "I don't know!—You mustn't marry more than one person at a time, may you, Peggotty?"
> "Certainly not," says Peggotty, with the promptest decision.

> "But if you marry a person, and the person dies, why then you may marry another person, mayn't you, Peggotty?"
>
> "You MAY," says Peggotty, "if you choose, my dear. That's a matter of opinion" [66].

Peggotty's equivocal response suggests that she is skeptical about the propriety of marrying again after the death of a spouse. In such a way, the text not only implies that such an act is morally questionable but it presages the second marriage of Clara Copperfield. Ever observant, David notes that Peggotty has not stated her true feelings on the subject. Accordingly, he asks "But what is your opinion, Peggotty?" (66). Peggotty, unwilling to pursue the subject, appears to become annoyed with David. Again, David seeks to know how she is feeling:

> "You an't cross, I suppose, Peggotty, are you?" said I, after sitting quiet for a minute.
>
> I really thought she was, she had been so short with me; but I was quite mistaken: for she laid aside her work (which was a stocking of her own), and opening her arms wide, took my curly head within them, and gave it a good squeeze. I know it was a good squeeze, because, being very plump, whenever she made any little exertion after she was dressed, some of the buttons on the back of her gown flew off. And I recollect two bursting to the opposite side of the parlour, while she was hugging me [66].

Peggotty's "good squeeze" and concomitant button bursting symbolically underscores the fact that she feels extremely sorry for David. No doubt aware that Clara's night out may mark the beginning of a courtship, she is obviously worried about the implications for David. Eager to change the subject, she bids David to read to her again: "Now let me hear some more about the Crorkindills," said Peggotty, who was not quite right in the name yet, "for I an't heard half enough" (66). The mispronunciation of the word *crocodile* is interesting. The first part of the word brings to mind the word *crook*, which, of course, implies dishonest conduct, while the middle part of the word *kin* hints at a blood relation. Finally, the last part of the word *dill*, brings to mind the plant with bitter seeds but aromatic leaves. Hence, while the word itself appears innocent enough, several different negative notes are struck which, when considered together, point to a duplicitous blood relative.

Interestingly, too, much later in the novel another mother, the crafty "Old Soldier"[25] Mrs. Markleham, after receiving her comeuppance, is explicitly associated with crocodiles:

> "That's a settler for our military friend, at any rate," said my aunt, on the way home. "I should sleep the better for that, if there was nothing else to be glad of!"
>
> "She was quite overcome, I am afraid," said Mr. Dick, with great commiseration.
>
> "What! Did you ever see a crocodile overcome?" inquired my aunt.
>
> "I don't think I ever saw a crocodile," returned Mr. Dick, mildly.

"There never would have been anything the matter, if it hadn't been for that old Animal," said my aunt, with strong emphasis [732].

We cannot assume, then, that the earlier reference to crocodiles is devoid of extra-linguistic meaning. Indeed, great hostility underlies David's crocodile reading:

> We returned to those monsters, with fresh wakefulness on my part, and we left their eggs in the sand for the sun to hatch; and we ran away from them, and baffled them by constantly turning, which they were unable to do quickly, on account of their unwieldy make; and we went into the water after them, as natives, and put sharp pieces of timber down their throats; and in short ran the whole crocodile gauntlet [67].

Added to this, during this recital, Peggotty "thoughtfully [sticks] her needle into various parts of her face and arms, all the time" (67). The scene, then, quite graphically reveals the repressed anger and aggression that David and his sympathetic surrogate mother, Peggotty, feel towards Clara Copperfield. Quite obviously, they are not only anxious about her potential to remarry but also about her fecundity. Through the medium of his reading material, David casts himself and Peggotty in the role of violent natives pursuing and killing fertile, confused "monsters." However, at the same time, he is not so sure if Peggotty is as invested as he is, because she seems more engaged in self-mutilation. Peggotty's self-harm carries a clear message. It is "thoughtfully" undertaken as opposed to thoughtlessly undertaken. Peggotty is thereby all too aware of Clara's matrimonial potential and is palpably distressed by it. In addition, Clara's sexual currency is plainly a tremendous threat to David's domestic harmony, and at some level he would rather she be attacked with sharp instruments than to be let loose to find another mate.[26] He is also, at another level, averse to her having any more children. This is reflected by his identification with attacking the crocodiles while their eggs are left in the sand for the sun to hatch. The whole scene then quite disingenuously sets Clara up as a monster. Before she even gets home from her social appointment, she is figuratively attacked and killed. In addition, in a metaphoric sense, her offspring are abandoned. Moral disgust at Clara's sexual attractiveness along with her capacity to remarry and reproduce is thereby insidiously conveyed.

This premonitory judgment of Clara is confirmed when Clara returns home "looking unusually pretty" (67) with a vigorous-looking man at her side. David instinctively recoils from this man, who has "beautiful black hair and whiskers" and a "deep voice" (67). He even pushes the man's hand away when the man pats his head because he is "jealous that his hand should touch my mother's in touching me — which it did" (67). David also uses "the wrong hand" (68) to shake the man's hand because his mother holds his "right hand" (68). The gentleman laughs at this action and David's mother tries to draw his "right hand forward" (68) but David resolves not to give his right hand to the man. David is clearly threatened and cannot help but express his jealousy by clinging to his mother and physically eschewing the man that she has unexpectedly brought home.

The fact that Clara's actions have been imprudent is verified by Peggotty's sarcastic declaration when the man has left:

> "— Hope you have had a pleasant evening, ma'am," said Peggotty, standing as stiff as a barrel in the centre of the room, with a candlestick in her hand.
> "Much obliged to you, Peggotty," returned my mother, in a cheerful voice, "I have had a *very* pleasant evening."
> "A stranger or so makes an agreeable change," suggested Peggotty.
> "A very agreeable change, indeed," returned my mother [68].

In addition, Peggotty stresses how Clara's first husband would have disapproved of Clara's choice: "Not such a one as this, Mr. Copperfield wouldn't have liked," said Peggotty. "That I say, and that I swear!" (68). At this, Clara reproaches Peggotty for saying such a thing when she knows that Clara does not have "a single friend to turn to" (69). Peggotty counters emphatically: "The more's the reason ... for saying that it won't do. No! That it won't do. No! No price could make it do. No!" (69). Peggotty supplies the adult voice of outrage and censure that is not available to David. Her vehement response guides readers to view Clara as giddy and unwise. As Gail Turley Houston writes:

> if David's infantile memories, which register but cannot directly state his desire for and fear of the maternal, are so intense and dangerous, Dickens seems to displace his protagonist's anxiety and rage into the mouths of carnivalesque characters. For instance, through the voices of Peggotty and Betsey Trotwood, David gives a straightforward account of his mother's flaws, flaws that would be inappropriate for the protagonist to mention. Likewise, David's distinct memories of the arguments between Clara Peggotty and Clara Copperfield indirectly articulate the latter's narcissism and misjudgement, which result in her marriage to Murdstone.[27]

David's violent internal struggle with Clara's sexual allure is also reflected in Clara's own words:

> "How can you go on as if it was all settled and arranged, Peggotty, when I tell you over and over again, you cruel thing, that beyond the commonest civilities nothing has passed! You talk of admiration. What am I to do? If people are so silly as to indulge the sentiment, is it my fault? What am I to do, I ask you? Would you wish me to shave my head and black my face, or disfigure myself with a burn, or a scald, or something of that sort? I dare say you would Peggotty, I dare say you'd quite enjoy it" [69].

This extreme charge strikes a false, strained note. This is the lexicon of misogyny, not the words of a young, feckless woman reprimanding her out-of-line servant. The words reveal more about David's need to blot out his mother's sexual potency than about Clara's indignation. So, too, Clara's next completely unfounded and incongruous statement appears to be more about David's need to highlight Clara's foolish and willful neglect of her duty of care than about Clara's distress:

> "And my dear boy," cried my mother, coming to the elbow-chair in which I was, and caressing me, "my own little Davy! Is it to be hinted to me that I am wanting in affection for my precious treasure, the dearest little fellow that ever was!" [69].

Peggotty goes on to deny that this was her inference but Clara persists with this line of thought and defends herself by citing a trivial sacrifice that she has made on behalf of David:

> "You know as well as I do, that on his account only last quarter I wouldn't buy myself a new parasol, though that old green one is frayed the whole way up, and the fringe is perfectly mangy? You know it is, Peggotty. You can't deny it" [69].

Again, this statement is designed to highlight Clara's vain and misguided nature and this is underscored by her subsequent inflammatory questions:

> "Am I a naughty mama to you, Davy? Am I a nasty, cruel, selfish, bad mama? Say I am, my child; say 'yes,' dear boy, and Peggotty will love you; and Peggotty's love is a great deal better than mine, Davy. *I* don't love you at all, do I?" [69].

The textual inference is that yes, Clara is a bad mama; yes, she doesn't love David properly and yes, Peggotty's love is indeed superior. The words are put into Clara's mouth, however, because David and his surrogate mother cannot express them without forfeiting the sympathetic interest of the reader.

Clara, of course, continues to see the man with dark whiskers, whom David later comes to know as Mr. Murdstone, and the courtship continues to disturb Peggotty. The narrative also maintains its implicitly condemning strain:

> Sometimes I fancied that Peggotty perhaps objected to my mother's wearing all the pretty dresses she had in her drawers, or to her going so often to visit at that neighbour's; but I couldn't, to my satisfaction, make out how it was [70].

David, then, never speaks out of turn about his mother, but Peggotty serves as a convenient and consistent barometer for his repressed anger:

> ... Mr. Murdstone dismounted, and, with his horse's bridle drawn over his arm, walked slowly up and down on the outer side of the sweetbriar fence, while my mother walked slowly up and down on the inner to keep him company. I recollect Peggotty and I peeping out at them from my little window; I recollect how closely they seemed to be examining the sweetbriar between them, as they strolled along; and how, from being in a perfectly angelic temper, Peggotty turned cross in a moment, and brushed my hair the wrong way, excessively hard [71].

The act of brushing David's hair the wrong way mirrors David's refusal to give Murdstone his right hand. Murdstone clearly rubs David and Peggotty the wrong way. David, as a child, may not be able to adequately explain why:

I liked him no better than at first, and had the same uneasy jealousy of him; but if I had any reason for it beyond a child's instinctive dislike, and a general idea that Peggotty and I could make much of my mother without any help, it certainly was not *the* reason that I might have found if I had been older. No such thing came into my mind, or near it. I could observe, in little pieces, as it were; but as to making a net of a number of these pieces, and catching anybody in it, that was, as yet, beyond me [70].

Nevertheless, the narrative effectively nets Murdstone and shows him to be as "excessively hard" as Peggotty's distracted grooming. The very name Murdstone suggests that he is a "tough shit"[28] and by bringing home this "tough shit" Clara inadvertently works to contaminate the Copperfield household.

According to Michael Steig, "Turveydrop possesses what is the most scatological name in all of Dickens except perhaps for Merdle."[29] I would suggest that the name Murdstone seriously challenges Turveydrop and Merdle for this dubious honor. Indeed Murdstone stands out as one of the most odious characters in the Dickens canon. His only redeeming feature appears to be his prepossessing appearance. David is certainly aware of Murdstone's good looks. This is particularly evident when David travels on horseback with Murdstone to visit some of Murdstone's male friends in Lowestoft:

Several times when I glanced at him, I observed that appearance with a sort of awe, and wondered what he was thinking about so closely. His hair and whiskers were blacker and thicker, looked at so near, than even I had given them credit for being. A squareness about the lower part of his face, and the dotted indication of the strong black beard he shaved close every day, reminded me of the wax-work that had travelled into our neighbourhood some half-a-year before. This, his regular eyebrows, and the rich white, and black, and brown, of his complexion — confound his complexion, and his memory!–made me think him, in spite of my misgivings, a very handsome man. I have no doubt that my poor dear mother thought him so too [71].

Here the phrase "my poor dear mother" tellingly reappears. As may be recalled, David first referred to his "poor dear mother" in relation to the rejected bid for his caul. In that instance, Clara was ambiguously associated with offering for sale the tangible biological connection between herself and her son. In this instance, she is revealed as a woman who was, in her son's estimation, undoubtedly and lamentably attracted to the pleasing physical appearance of a highly unsuitable man. While the phrase can assuredly be viewed simply as David's sympathetic way of referring to his dearly departed mother, it can also be viewed more darkly as yet another means by which David casts his mother in a less than admirable light.[30]

The narrative certainly shows that Clara is attracted to Murdstone's good looks rather than his good character. She is also extremely flattered by his obvious appreciation of her looks. When David is dropped at home by Murdstone after his journey to Lowestoft, Clara wastes no time in inquiring about what the men said and did throughout the day, and she is shown to be well pleased when David tells her that the gentleman described her as bewitching. Indeed, she so relishes the compliment that later that day, before she bids David good-night, she asks him to repeat what was said about her:

"What was it they said, Davy? Tell me again. I can't believe it."
"'Bewitching —'" I began.
My mother put her hands upon my lips to stop me.
"It was never bewitching," she said, laughing. "It never could have been bewitching, Davy. Now I know it wasn't!"
"Yes, it was. 'Bewitching Mrs. Copperfield,'" I repeated stoutly. "And, '"pretty.'"
"No, no, it was never pretty. Not pretty," interposed my mother, laying her fingers on my lips again.
"Yes, it was. 'Pretty little widow.'"
"What foolish, impudent creatures!" cried my mother, laughing and covering her face. "What ridiculous men! An't they? Davy dear —"
"Well, Ma" [74].

Clara's attraction to Murdstone is also registered by her heightened physical state. As we recall, when she first brings Murdstone home, David notices that she looks "unusually pretty" (67). So, too, when Murdstone remarks that there is no need to wonder at David's devotion to his mother, David writes, "I never saw such a beautiful colour on my mother's face before" (67). This would suggest that Clara's appearance here even surpasses the radiance that she displayed when she danced about the parlor with David in the winter twilight. In addition, Clara also manifestly wishes to see Murdstone as much as possible and to draw him in by enhancing her natural beauty.[31] Finally, when Murdstone first takes his leave after walking Clara home, Clara is visibly distracted: "My mother, contrary to her usual habit, instead of coming to the elbow-chair, by the fire, remained at the other end of the room, and sat singing to herself" (68). Rather than taking up her "natural" maternal position at the hearth, Clara instead wishes to be alone with her thoughts about Murdstone. The fact that her reverie is pleasurable is made clear, when oblivious to Peggotty's distress, she confirms that she has indeed had a *very* pleasant evening" (68).

Clara's questionable attraction to Murdstone is also conveyed through her furtive actions. At no stage is she honest with her son about her feelings for Murdstone. David is completely kept in the dark while his world, by virtue of his mother's physical attraction to Murdstone, is progressively turned upside down. Indeed, Clara is so interested in Murdstone that she not only symbolically eschews her maternal role at the hearth and rejects "that honest creature" (70) Peggotty's good counsel, but she is also obliged to lie by omission to her son. This occurs, firstly, when she, innocuously enough, goes to spend the evening at a neighbor's (65) but is later escorted home by a comparative stranger. As

David writes, his mother appeared with a gentleman "who had walked home with us from church last Sunday" (67). Secondly, she lies by omission when, in a premeditated fashion, she arranges for Peggotty to take David to spend a fortnight with Peggotty's family at Yarmouth. The visit to Yarmouth, as is later made evident, is arranged to give Clara the freedom to marry Murdstone and to allow him to move in and take charge of the family home.

Certainly, Clara's lies may have been made with the intention of protecting David's feelings, but the fact remains that Clara deceives her son on more than one occasion in order to achieve her own agenda. There is even a suggestion in the text that Clara's blind attraction to Murdstone leads her to act in a nefarious way towards her son. This occurs when Clara (watched by a disapproving Murdstone) bids David a tearful farewell as he leaves with Peggotty for Yarmouth in the carrier's cart. David writes:

> I sat looking at Peggotty for some time, in a reverie on this supposititious case: whether, if she were employed to lose me like the boy in the fairy tale, I should be able to track my way home again by the buttons she would shed [76].

The sentence disingenuously and fancifully alludes to the fact that Peggotty's buttons burst off when she exerts herself. However, it should be remembered that the only preceding example of this event was when Peggotty gave David "a good squeeze" at a point where she was feeling particularly worried about David's welfare owing to Clara Copperfield's first formal social engagement with Murdstone. At that time, only two buttons burst off the back of her gown. In David's reverie above, however, he envisages Peggotty shedding so many buttons that it would be possible for him to find his way home again. This would suggest that David is aware that Peggotty now feels *extreme* concern for his welfare. There is also a chilling implication that someone wants to get rid of David and may have, to that end, enlisted Peggotty's services. This someone would appear to be Clara who, magnetized by Murdstone, is unable to prevent herself from this act of maternal perfidy. Here again, the text insidiously works to posit Clara as an object of moral disgust.

Peggotty's "full blown" concern for David is fully justified when they return home from Yarmouth. Arriving at Blunderstone Rookery "on a cold grey afternoon, with a dull sky, threatening rain," (91) David is met at the door by a servant rather than his mother. Extremely distressed, he turns to Peggotty for answers. After an awkward interval, Peggotty tries to present the situation to David in the best possible light: "What do you think? You have got a Pa!" (92). Unfortunately, this ambiguous news merely adds to David's distress:

> I trembled, and turned white. Something — I don't know what, or how — connected with the grave in the churchyard, and the raising of the dead, seemed to strike me like an unwholesome wind [92].

David naturally is deeply disturbed. How could his dead and buried father be alive again? Qualifying her statement, Peggotty says: "A new one" (92). Then gasping, "as if she were swallowing something that was very hard" (93), Peggotty takes David into the best parlor to see the new father and David's mother. There he finds the hard-hearted Mr. Murdstone who immediately sets about inhibiting the responses of David's mother: "Now, Clara, my dear," said Mr. Murdstone. "Recollect! control yourself, always control yourself!" (93). Forced into a stilted greeting with Mr. Murdstone and his mother, David states:

> I could not look at her, I could not look at him, I knew quite well that he was looking at us both; and I turned to the window and looked out there, at some shrubs that were drooping their heads in the cold [93].

The shrubs mimetically represent David's grief stricken and "out in the cold" psychological state. Clearly, David feels that his mother is lost to him, and the fact that he cannot look at her or Mr. Murdstone is not just a reaction to Murd-stone's gaze, it is an indication of his profound sense of betrayal. After all, Clara did not at any stage directly prepare David for such news. Rather she steadfastly hid her conjugal plans from him. This is later highlighted when Peggotty receives a marriage proposal from Barkis. Unlike Clara and the subterfuge that she engages in to hide her marital plans from David, Peggotty quite naturally asks David about his feelings in relation to the proposal:

> "Davy dear, what should you think if I was to think of being married?"
> "Why — I suppose you would like me as much then, Peggotty, as you do now?" I returned, after a little consideration [192].

Peggotty, sensitive to the trust that David places in her, not only emphatically confirms her "unalterable love" (192) but sincerely declares:

> "I wouldn't so much as give it another thought ... if my Davy was anyways against it — not if I had been asked in church thirty three times over, and was wearing out the ring in my pocket" [193].

This scene is highly significant because David, like Dickens in the autobiographical fragment, indirectly "shows up" his biological mother through juxtaposing the approach of a woman who considers David's needs over and above her own. Peggotty also notably arranges for David and Little Em'ly to be with her on the day of her wedding and even shares a "very comfortable" (201) celebratory meal with her new husband and the two children. Again, this is in stark contrast to the actions of David's mother, who marries only after she has ensured that David is completely off the scene. Interestingly, too, David reports that after the wedding of Peggotty and Barkis, Peggotty "could not hug me enough in token of her unimpaired affection" (201). Peggotty, like the landlord's wife in the autobiographical fragment, is quite naturally demonstrative. Furthermore, the newly married Peggotty reassures David that there will always be not simply a place in her home for David but an *unchanging* place:

> "Young or old, Davy dear, as long as I am alive and have this house over my head ... you shall find it as if I expected you here directly minute. I shall keep it every day, as I used to keep your little room, my darling; and if you was to go to China you might think of it as being kept just the same, all the time you were away" [203].

Here, the reader is prompted to recall the altered state of David's home when he returns from Yarmouth to find that his mother has married Murdstone. Unlike the ever-thoughtful Peggotty, Clara does not ensure that the family home is kept as before:

> My old dear bedroom was changed, and I was to lie a long way off. I rambled downstairs to find anything that was like itself, so altered it all seemed; and roamed into the yard. I very soon started back there, for the empty dog-kennel was filled up with a great dog — deep mouthed and black-haired like Him — and he was very angry at the sight of me, and sprang out to get at me [93].

Accordingly, David's affection for his home is shaken and his narrative takes on a deeply critical tenor. Speaking of his bedroom, he writes:

> I thought of the oddest things. Of the shape of the room, of the cracks in the ceiling, of the paper on the walls, of the flaws in the window-glass making ripples and dimples on the prospect, of the washing-stand being rickety on its three legs, and having a discontented something about it, which reminded me of Mrs. Gummidge under the influence of the old one [93–94].

The reference to Mrs. Gummidge is significant because Mrs. Gummidge throughout the novel is associated with discomfort. Owing to her self-pitying moods she consistently casts a pall over the Peggotty household in Yarmouth; and David finds her singularly objectionable to the point where he wishes that the household could be cleansed of her presence. Clara Copperfield, then, like Elizabeth Dickens in the autobiographical fragment, is linked to negatively altering the face of her son's home. Clara may not have arranged to sell off all of the possessions in the home like Elizabeth Dickens, but she might as well have because the changes that she has made to accommodate Murdstone mean that nothing in the home is as it was. Like the young Dickens's London home, it is an empty shell devoid of its former meaning and devoid of all comfort.

When David learns that the hateful Murdstone has married his mother and taken up residence in the Copperfield abode, he experiences a ghastly psychic rupture. Firstly, he loses what had appeared immutable — his mother's absolute and undivided love; secondly, he loses the trust that he had placed in her; thirdly, he loses his sense of home. Clara Copperfield is thereby depicted as a polluting person. Owing to the choices that she makes, she effectively taints everything that her son once held dear. It should not be forgotten, however, that David's biological father is also represented as Clara's hapless victim. This is again done in a disingenuous way. In the first chapter David writes:

> I was a posthumous child. My father's eyes had closed upon the light of this world six months, when mine opened on it. There is something strange to me, even now, in the reflection that he never saw me; and something stranger yet in the shadowy remembrance that I have of my first childish associations with his white gravestone in the churchyard, and of the indefinable compassion I used to feel for it lying out alone there in the dark night, when our little parlour was warm and bright with fire and candle, and the doors of our house were — almost cruelly, it seemed to me sometimes — bolted and locked against it [50–51].

David here is very conscious that his father has died not long after impregnating his mother. Indeed, he even defines himself by this fact — "I was a posthumous child." The sexual act, if not occasioning his father's death, has certainly preceded it. Accordingly, it is not unrealistic to maintain that at some level, David holds his mother responsible for his father's demise. Her sexuality has effectively "murdered" Copperfield Senior and all that remains is his pristine gravestone in the churchyard. Copperfield Senior is thereby the original Murdstone — the murdered man beneath the gravestone. Certainly, the text does not directly accuse Clara of her husband's death but it does accuse her, albeit obliquely, of cruelty. To the young David, his mother has piteously locked out his father and left him alone in the cold. It doesn't matter to David that his father is dead. All he can see is that his mother is oblivious to his father's condition. Her lack of feeling for his father is also underscored by the epithet that she uses to describe herself:

> My mother was, no doubt, unusually youthful in appearance even for her years; she hung her head, as if it were her fault, poor thing, and said, sobbing, that indeed she was afraid she was but a childish widow, and would be but a childish mother if she lived [53].

Critics routinely describe Clara Copperfield as a child-wife[32] (just like her son David's first wife, Dora). However, little is ever said about Clara's admission that she is a "childish widow," which of course implies that she is not as a widow should be or does not possess the maturity that a widow should have.

Clara, as a widow, has been well provided for. The first chapter explicitly shows that David's father not only "spoilt" (56) his much younger wife[33] but also unconditionally left his assets to her:

> "David had bought an annuity for himself with his money, I know," said [Miss Betsey], by and by. "What did he do for you?"
> "Mr. Copperfield," said my mother, answering with some difficulty, "was so considerate and good as to secure the reversion of a part of it to me."
> "How much?" asked Miss Betsey.
> "A hundred and five pounds a year," said my mother [57].

This annuity enables Clara to continue her lifestyle and to employ a servant. She is also left with the family home, Blunderstone Rookery. As Betsey Trotwood makes clear, this position of advantage is in stark contrast to her life before she met Mr. Copperfield:

> "You were an orphan, weren't you?
> "Yes."
> "And a governess?"
> "I was nursery-governess in a family where Mr. Copperfield came to visit. Mr. Copperfield was very kind to me, and took a great deal of notice of me, and paid me a good deal of attention, and at last proposed to me. And I accepted him. And so we were married," said my mother simply [56].

Clara's charms do not impress the nagging Betsey Trotwood[34]:

> "Ha! Poor Baby!" mused Miss Betsey, with her frown still bent upon the fire. "Do you know anything?"
> "I beg your pardon, ma'am," faltered my mother.
> "About keeping house, for instance," said Miss Betsey.
> "Not much I fear," returned my mother. "Not so much as I could wish. But Mr. Copperfield was teaching me —"
> ("Much he knew about it himself!") said Miss Betsey in a parenthesis [56].

However, while Betsey Trotwood may be critical of her nephew's ability to manage a house, she is mindful of his higher station: "You were not equally matched, child — if any two people *can* be equally matched" (56). Clara's failure to match Copperfield Senior in the matrimonial stakes is later justified when after his death she does not honor either the advantages that he bestowed on her or the trust that he placed in her. Instead, she succumbs to the flattery of a handsome man of dubious character and unwisely marries him. In doing so, she insults the memory of her husband. For Mary Poovey, Clara's "vanity betrayed both David's father's unworldly trust and the boy's unsuspecting love."[35] So while Copperfield Senior may have, as Poovey puts it, "placed no restrictions on his bequest to [Clara] and therefore made no independent provision for his son,"[36] this trust could have been more than repaid had Clara used more discrimination and foresight. Unfortunately, however, she places a higher premium on the fact that "foolish, impudent" men consider her to be a "pretty little widow" (74) and that one, in particular, wishes to court her.

If David, at some level, holds his mother responsible for murdering his father; he also, at some level, holds her responsible for murdering his father's memory. Here again, nothing to this effect is directly stated, but the symbolism that David uses makes this obvious. In the first chapter of the novel, we are told that each Sunday, in her widowhood, Clara reads to Peggotty and David in the best parlor of the house:

> There is something of a doleful air about the room to me, for Peggotty has told me — I don't know when, but apparently ages ago — about my father's funeral, and the company having their black cloaks put on [62].

It is not clear whether a wake for David's father was held in this room or whether the deceased Copperfield Senior was laid out for viewing in this room, but apparently the room is very much associated with his death. Such a memory, however, does not appear to disturb Clara. Rather than avoiding the room, Clara uses it on a weekly basis. One Sunday night, we are told, she even reads to Peggotty and David the story of how Lazarus was raised from the dead. David's narrative does not for a moment suggest that such reading matter is highly inappropriate or even distasteful (given the room's history) but it does reveal that it left him in a state of abject fear:

> I am so frightened that they are afterwards obliged to take me out of bed, and shew [sic] me the quiet churchyard out of the bedroom window, with the dead all lying in their graves at rest, below the solemn moon [62].

Manifestly, David is so disturbed that he cannot rest until he is convinced that there is no chance of his father coming back to life. Mirroring her insensitive use of this room, Clara sits in the best parlor when David returns from Yarmouth to find that he has a new father. Choosing such a place to convey such unexpected news is not only irresponsible (given David's memories of the room) but shockingly disrespectful to the memory of his father. Certainly, Clara, even at this early stage, appears to be very much under her new husband's control and it might have been *his* wish to use the best parlor to convey their news, but the fact remains that Clara is implicated in the negation of her husband's memory. One is prompted at this point to recall that after Dickens's father went to prison, all of his household possessions were sold off (including his library) and his young family was forced to camp in the two parlors of the emptied London house. Could parlors thereby be associated in Dickens's mind with disturbing endings and even death? As with the best parlor in *David Copperfield*, there would certainly have been a doleful air in the parlors that the Dickens family lived in after Dickens Senior went to prison. Further, could parlors be linked in Dickens's mind with the negation of paternal or symbolic meaning?

As I have sought to show, Clara Copperfield is depicted as a dangerous woman. For all her pretty curls and David's apparent adoration, there is a consistent undermining strain in his narrative that does not simply highlight her flaws but depicts her as pathologically insensitive, selfish and deflating. To be sure, David is brought down by Clara's choices in life. After her remarriage, David effectively "falls" and feels like dirt: the Copperfield kingdom is sacked, he is deposed and painful uncertainty becomes the hallmark of his life. In

Chapter 19, David claims his first 'fall' in life occurs when a dirty and disheveled man takes his place on the Canterbury coach:

> I have always considered this as the first fall I had in life. When I booked my place at the coach office I had had "Box Seat" written against the entry, and had given the book-keeper half-a-crown. I was got up in a special great-coat and shawl, expressly to do honour to that distinguished eminence; had glorified myself upon it a good deal; and had felt that I was a credit to the coach. And here, in the very first stage, I was supplanted by a shabby man with a squint, who had no other merit than smelling like a livery stables, and being able to walk across me, more like a fly than a human being, while the horses were at a canter!
>
> A distrust of myself, which has often beset me in life on small occasions, when it would have been better away, was assuredly not stopped in its growth by this little incident outside the Canterbury coach. It was in vain to take refuge in gruffness of speech. I spoke from the pit of my stomach for the rest of the journey, but I felt completely extinguished and dreadfully young [342–43].

Despite this contention, it is nonetheless obvious that his first real "fall" occurs when he is usurped in his mother's affections by the odious Murdstone. David's association with Murdstone is in fact characterized by repeated falls. The first night of David's homecoming, Murdstone makes it clear that David can expect to be knocked down if he steps out of place:

> "David," he said, making his lips thin, by pressing them together, "if I have an obstinate horse or dog to deal with, what do you think I do?"
>
> "I don't know."
>
> "I beat him."
>
> I had answered in a kind of breathless whisper, but I felt, in my silence, that my breath was shorter now.
>
> "I make him wince, and smart. I say to myself, 'I'll conquer that fellow'; and if it were to cost him all the blood he had, I should do it [95–96].

David may not lose all the blood in his body at Murdstone's hands, but Murdstone makes him feel much worse than did the shabby man with the squint on the Canterbury coach. The lessons, for instance, that Mr. Murdstone subjects him to, are associated with feelings of "disgust" (103); "reluctance" (103); forgetfulness[37]; "drowning" (103); tripping; embarrassment[38]; stupidity[39]; hopelessness[40]; degradation[41]; dirtiness[42]; and victimization.[43] David describes these lessons as "the death-blow of my peace, and a grievous daily drudgery and misery" (103). The terrible beating that Murdstone gives David after he has performed badly in one of his lessons provides another example:

> He had my head as in a vice, but I twined round him somehow, and stopped him for a moment, entreating him not to beat me. It was only a moment that I stopped him, for he cut me heavily an instant afterwards, and in the same instant I caught the hand with which he held me in my mouth, between my teeth, and bit it through. It sets my teeth on edge to think of it.
>
> He beat me then, as if he would have beaten me to death. Above all the noise

we made, I heard them running up the stairs, and crying out — I heard my mother crying out — and Peggotty. Then he was gone; and the door was locked outside; and I was lying, fevered and hot, and torn, and sore, and raging in my puny way, upon the floor [108].

In addition to his physical pain, David feels terrible guilt:

My stripes were sore and stiff, and made me cry afresh, when I moved; but they were nothing to the guilt I felt. It lay heavier on my breast than if I had been the most atrocious criminal, I dare say [108].

David feels like a criminal because he knows that he has literally gotten under the skin of the authority figure Murdstone and rendered him vulnerable. Later he reveals: "Mr. Murdstone's hand was bound up in a large linen wrapper" (109). As Kristeva puts it: "Any crime, because it draws attention to the fragility of the law, is abject."[44] Certainly, Murdstone treats David like a criminal. For five long days, he imprisons David in his room: "The length of those five days I can convey no idea of to any one. They occupy the place of years in my remembrance" (109).

Biting Murdstone marks a turning point for David and not just because Murdstone arranges to send him away to school. Prior to this he has seen his mother, under the influence of Murdstone, become more and more alienated from him. All of her actions are monitored by Murdstone to the point where she even feels ashamed to show any affection to her son.[45] Following the biting incident, however, Clara turns against her son completely. Not only does she not try to slip away from Murdstone to relay comfort to her son, as Peggotty does, but she actually comes to endorse Murdstone's negative view of her son:

"Oh, Davy!" she said. "That you could hurt anyone I love! Try to be better, pray to be better! I forgive you; but I am so grieved, Davy that you should have such bad passions in your heart."

They had persuaded her that I was a wicked fellow, and she was more sorry for that than for my going away. I felt it sorely. I tried to eat my parting breakfast, but my tears dropped upon my bread-and-butter, and trickled into my tea. I saw my mother look at me sometimes, and then glance at the watchful Miss Murdstone, and than [sic] look down, or look away [112].

While he does not say anything directly against his mother, one senses that this incident represents the ultimate betrayal for David. Here, we are reminded of the autobiographical fragment because Clara, like Dickens's mother, is *warm* for her son to be sent away. In addition David, again like Dickens in his auto-biographical fragment, employs juxtaposition to show up the deficiencies of his mother. Just as Dickens celebrated the virtues of the landlord's wife, David celebrates the virtues of the ever faithful Peggotty. After Peggotty has consoled the imprisoned David through fervently declaring her love and kissing the keyhole of his bedroom door, David states:

From that night there grew up in my breast a feeling for Peggotty which I cannot very well define. She did not replace my mother; no one could do that; but she came into a vacancy in my heart; which closed upon her, and I felt towards her something I have never felt for any other human being [111].

So, too, after David has been sent off to school and has traveled half a mile in a cart, he tells us how the devoted Peggotty bursts out from a hedge and climbs into the cart:

She took me in both her arms, and squeezed me to her stays until the pressure on my nose was extremely painful, though I never thought of that till afterwards when I found it very tender. Not a single word did Peggotty speak. Releasing one of her arms, she put it down in her pocket to the elbow, and brought out some paper bags of cakes which she crammed into my pockets, and a purse which she put into my hand, but not one word did she say. After another and a final squeeze with both arms, she got down from the cart and ran away; and, my belief is, and has always been, without a solitary button on her gown. I picked up one, of several that were rolling about, and treasured it as a keepsake for a long time [112–13].

Here again, the button-squeezing metaphor is employed to convey Peggotty's extreme concern for David. Unlike his mother, she knows that David requires a tangible expression of love. Certainly, if we consider the contents of the purse, it appears that Clara is behind Peggotty's cart-jumping attempt to see David or she at least condones it:

It was a stiff leather purse, with a snap, and had three bright shillings in it, which Peggotty had evidently polished up with whitening, for my greater delight. But its most precious contents were two half-crowns folded together in a bit of paper, on which was written, in my mother's hand, "For Davy. With my love" [113].

However, the fact remains that Peggotty *demonstrably* shows how much she cares rather than revealing this at a remove. Again, one cannot help but recall that the landlord's wife in the autobiographical fragment spontaneously stooped down and kissed Dickens. Peggotty's unexpected jump into the cart to be with David could be said to parallel this action.

There is no doubt that David psychologically cuts off from his mother after he is sent away to school. His thoughts as he travels to the new school on the coach are particularly revealing:

When we passed through a village, I pictured to myself what the insides of the houses were like, and what the inhabitants were about; and when boys came running after us, and got up behind and swung there for a little way, I wondered whether their fathers were alive, and whether they were happy at home. I had plenty to think of, therefore, besides my mind running continually on the kind of place I was going to — which was an awful speculation. Sometimes, I remember, I resigned myself to thoughts of home and Peggotty; and to endeavouring, in a confused blind way, to recall how I had felt, and what sort of boy I used to be, before I bit Mr. Murdstone [121].

In this passage, home is linked to Peggotty and there is no mention of David's mother. The words "I wondered whether their fathers were alive, and whether they were happy at home" also associate happiness at home with having a biological father. Although David apparently has "plenty to think of," he doesn't, apparently, think of his mother. The fact that David tries to recall how he was before he bit Mr. Murdstone is interesting. It is as if the Murdstone biting episode marks a disjunction in terms of David's identity. There is the good David and there is the bad David. For David, biting Murdstone means that he has overstepped the line and become corrupted. Of course, if his father were still alive there would be no Murdstone to bite and he would be as happy and carefree as one of the boys running after the coach. However, his father is dead and his mother has replaced him with another man. The general tenor of the passage then suggests that his mother is responsible for his corruption.

Arriving at an inn in the Whitechapel district, David faces an awkward interval before anyone comes to escort him to his new school. During this time, David wonders what will happen if no one ever comes to fetch him. Myriad thoughts enter his mind, including the possibility that he might starve to death and the owners of the inn will be put to the inconvenience of paying for his funeral expenses. He also wonders if he should try to get back home:

> If I started off at once, and tried to walk back home, how could I ever find my way, how could I ever hope to walk so far, how could I make sure of anyone but Peggotty, even if I got back? [124].

Clearly, David has no confidence in his mother. Peggotty is the only person whom he can feel sure about. When David (owing to Murdstone's instructions) is forced to wear a placard at school bearing the words: "*Take care of him. He bites*" (130) he dreams at night of his mother but, significantly, he sees her only "as she used to be" (131). His mother is, in fact, so little in his thoughts that when he feels "very sad and solitary" (132) at school, his longings for solace and comfort are only associated with Peggotty: "I picture myself going up to bed, among the unused rooms, and sitting on my bed-side crying for a comfortable word from Peggotty" (132).

When David has to go home for the holidays he is not happy about the prospect:

> Ah, what a strange feeling it was to be going home when it was not home, and to find that every object I looked at, reminded me of the happy old home, which was like a dream I could never dream again! The days when my mother and I and Peggotty were all in all to one another, and there was no one to come between us, rose up before me so sorrowfully on the road, that I am not sure I was glad to be there — not sure but that I would rather have remained away, and forgotten it in Steerforth's company [161–62].

Returning home, however, he finds to his delight that his mother does not have Mr. Murdstone and his sister Miss Murdstone at her side. Conveniently, they are out on a visit in the neighborhood. In her arms, however, she has a baby:

> I spoke to her, and she started, and cried out. But seeing me, she called me her dear Davy, her own boy! and coming half across the room to meet me, kneeled down upon the ground and kissed me, and laid my head down on her bosom near the little creature that was nestling there, and put its hand to my lips.
> I wish I had died. I wish I had died then, with that feeling in my heart! I should have been more fit for Heaven than I ever have been since [162].

This is an extraordinary admission. Essentially, David wishes that he could be struck dead at the point where he feels that he is once again his mother's own dear boy or the highly privileged monarch that Murdstone spoke of. In that moment, it doesn't matter to him that his mother has a new dear boy in her arms. The baby is secondary to the unadulterated and uninhibited love that she displays towards him. The fact that David associates being fit for Heaven with a return to his mother's breast is very interesting. Does this mean that David fundamentally believes that people are fit for Heaven only if they possess their mother's pure and absolute love? It would seem from his words that if one does not experience complete maternal love then one is fundamentally impure. Dying in this rapturous, purified state however, is not an option for David, as Harry Stone writes:

> David's alienation, as he will soon discover, cannot be assuaged by a momentary return to his mother's breast. His infant brother is an emblem of irreversible change, a sign that David has been permanently displaced; indeed, David has been doubly supplanted. For only his brother may rightfully remain at his mother's breast; and his brother is a child not of David's father, but of the usurper, the evil Mr. Murdstone.[46]

Although David's wish is not granted, he nonetheless goes on to spend a happy day with his mother, her new baby and Peggotty. However, even this day is tainted by a quarrel that Peggotty has with Clara. The quarrel starts because Peggotty indirectly accuses Clara of not providing adequately for her son and speculates if his Aunt Betsey might leave him something in her will:

> "—I wonder, if she was to die, whether she'd leave Davy anything?"
> "Good gracious me, Peggotty," returned my mother, "what a nonsensical woman you are! when you know that she took offence at the poor dear boy's ever being born at all."
> "I suppose she wouldn't be inclined to forgive him now," hinted Peggotty.
> "Why should she be inclined to forgive him now?" said my mother, rather sharply.
> "Now that he's got a brother, I mean," said Peggotty.
> My mother immediately began to cry, and wondered how Peggotty dared to say such a thing.

"As if this poor little innocent in its cradle had ever done any harm to you or anybody else, you jealous thing!" said she. "You had much better go and marry Mr. Barkis, the carrier. Why don't you?" [166].

Clara churlishly tries to get back at Peggotty by telling her to marry Mr. Barkis. This is totally illogical given the fact that Clara has only a little earlier selfishly begged Peggotty to stay with her and not to marry Barkis while she is alive. The interaction with Peggotty provides yet another chance for readers to see that Clara is a self-absorbed, difficult woman and that David has been hard done by. It also serves to highlight Clara's vanity. During the quarrel, Clara explains to Peggotty why Miss Murdstone has taken over the running of the house:

"Haven't you heard her say, over and over again, that she thinks I am too thoughtless and too — a — a —"
"Pretty," suggested Peggotty.
"Well," returned my mother, half laughing, "and if she is so silly as to say so, can I be blamed for it?" [167].

Clara is again flattered by the notion that people think she is pretty. Indeed, this matters more to her than the fact that she has actually become disenfranchised in her own home. Significantly, too, during the quarrel Clara takes ownership for her feckless ways: "I very well know that I am a weak, light, girlish creature" (167). There is no escaping the fact, then, that Clara Copperfield is depicted as a foolish woman and a bad mother. Indeed, at every possible opportunity in David's daedal narrative this is reinforced: Peggotty's insinuations, David's thoughts and dreams, Clara's admissions, Aunt Betsey's censorial assertions — all of these rhetorical strategies not only point to her inadequacy as a mother but they also effectively prime the text with a thick undercoat of disgust.

David's holiday at home is nothing short of dreadful. The Murdstones continue to treat him like dirt and his mother is afraid to speak to him or be kindly "lest she should give them some offence by her manner of doing so" (171). Indeed, things are so unremittingly bad that David comes to feel he has absolutely no place within the family:

What yawns and dozes I lapsed into, in spite of all my care; what starts I came out of concealed sleeps with; what answers I never got, to little observations that I rarely made; what a blank space I seemed, which everybody overlooked, and yet was in everybody's way; what a heavy relief it was to hear Miss Murdstone hail the first stroke of nine at night, and order me to bed! [174].

At last, when it is time to go, David is not sorry to leave his mother because he cannot help but feel that "the gulf between us was there, and the parting was there, every day" (174). However, the actual parting from her is etched in his memory:

> I was in the carrier's cart when I heard her calling to me. I looked out, and she
> stood at the garden-gate alone, holding her baby up in her arms for me to see. It
> was cold still weather; and not a hair of her head, nor a fold of her dress, was
> stirred, as she looked intently at me, holding up her child.
>
> So I lost her. So I saw her afterwards, in my sleep at school — a silent presence
> near my bed — looking at me with the same intent face — holding up her baby in
> her arms [174–75].

At this point Clara is effectively dead to David and it isn't much longer
before we read of her actual death. Two months later, back at school, David is
summoned:

> Mr. Sharp entered and said:
> "David Copperfield is to go into the parlour."
> I expected a hamper from Peggotty, and brightened at the order. Some of the
> boys about me put in their claim not to be forgotten in the distribution of the
> good things, as I got out of my seat with great alacrity.
> "Don't hurry, David," said Mr. Sharp. "There's time enough, my boy don't
> hurry" [175–76].

David's thoughts are again of Peggotty and she is associated with abundance.
His mother, however, is the reason why he is singled out. To David's shock, he
learns from the headmaster's wife, Mrs. Creakle, that his mother has died and
that her baby is also likely to die. David is very upset. However after his tears
are spent his thoughts all too quickly turn to subjects other than his mother:

> I stood upon a chair when I was left alone, and looked into the glass to see how
> red my eyes were, and how sorrowful my face. I considered, after some hours were
> gone, if my tears were really hard to flow now, as they seemed to be, what, in con-
> nexion with my loss, it would affect me most to think of when I drew near home —
> for I was going home to the funeral. I am sensible of having felt that a dignity
> attached to me among the rest of the boys, and that I was important in my afflic-
> tion.
> If ever child were stricken with sincere grief, I was. But I remember that this
> importance was a kind of satisfaction to me, when I walked in the playground that
> afternoon while the boys were in school. When I saw them glancing at me out of
> the windows, as they went up to their classes, I felt distinguished, and looked more
> melancholy, and walked slower. When school was over, and they came out and
> spoke to me, I felt it rather good in myself not to be proud to any of them, and
> to take exactly the same notice of them all, as before [177].

David's grief is mixed up with his thoughts concerning his appearance and
the impression that he conveys. The phrases that he uses are very interesting:
"a dignity attached to me"; "I was important"; "a kind of satisfaction to me";
"I felt distinguished"; "I felt it rather good in myself." How revealing, too, that
he self-consciously tries to look "more melancholy" and walks slower. Whilst
David's honesty here lends authenticity to his narrative,[47] it does nonetheless
strike a rather hollow note. The days preceding the funeral and the funeral itself

are also marked by David's detailed observations, but again hardly any of these observations center on his feelings towards his mother. Even as the clergyman speaks, David's thoughts turn to Peggotty rather than memories of his mother:

> Now there is a solemn hush, which we have brought from home with what is resting in the mould; and while we stand bareheaded, I hear the voice of the clergyman, sounding remote in the open air, and yet distinct and plain, saying: "I am the Resurrection and the Life, saith the Lord!" Then I hear sobs; and, standing apart among the lookers-on, I see that good and faithful servant, whom of all the people upon earth I love the best, and unto whom my childish heart is certain that the Lord will one day say: "Well done" [184].

This comment is rather distasteful given the nature of the occasion. Could David for instance say with the same certainty that his mother would receive such an endorsement from the Lord? Certainly, there is nothing within David's narrative that suggests that his mother deserves a celestial "pat on the back." She has categorically not done a good job and her son's grief is far from whole hearted. Indeed, David cannot bear to think of his mother as she was after she met Murdstone. He wishes to think of her only as she was before Murdstone entered her life. Tellingly, after Peggotty has conveyed to David the exact circumstances of his mother's death, he states:

> From the moment of my knowing of the death of my mother, the idea of her as she had been of late had vanished from me. I remembered her, from that instant, only as the young mother of my earliest impressions, who had been used to wind her bright curls round and round her finger, and to dance with me at twilight in the parlour. What Peggotty had told me now, was so far from bringing me back to the later period, that it rooted the earlier image in my mind. It may be curious, but it is true. In her death she winged her way back to her calm untroubled youth, and cancelled all the rest.
>
> The mother who lay in the grave, was the mother of my infancy; the little creature in her arms, was myself, as I had once been, hushed for ever on her bosom [186–87].

Like the sinister Duke in Browning's poem "My Last Duchess" who keeps his wife's wondrous portrait but orders her death, David treasures wonderful, controlled images of his mother but nonetheless sentences her to death in his mind. Interestingly, too, in his imagination, he places himself in the grave with "the young mother of [his] earliest impressions," but this fanciful act, while extreme, cannot be viewed as a deeply affecting sign of his grief. Indeed, it carries similar problematic and insidious connotations because, rather than being wracked with grief to the point where he wants to join his mother in death, he instead wishes to stop his life at the point before he lost his innocence and became aware of her fallibility as a human being and more importantly as his mother.[48]

Accordingly, in a passive-aggressive way, David's narrative systematically highlights the deficiencies of his mother and, following her death, repudiates the part of her life which he could not accept. A close reading of the text assuredly reveals this. Disgust is decidedly behind Clara Copperfield's portrait. It is also, as I will show, behind the portrait of his adoptive mother, Aunt Betsey.

Aunt Betsey has, by and large, been viewed in a positive light.[49] Critics consistently highlight her realistic character development and the way that she comes to provide a safe haven for her "wooly-witted protégé"[50] Mr. Dick and young David when he turns to her in desperation after his mother has died and he has escaped from Murdstone and Grinsby. Sylvère Monod is very impressed with the portrayal of Aunt Betsey. For Monod, Betsey Trotwood is nothing less than the novel's "most powerful creation"[51] and she is highly credible:

> The presence of Betsey Trotwood in *David Copperfield* is the supreme achievement of Dickens' art in his autobiographical novel. Betsey is an entirely imaginary creation, yet she is fully as convincing, as lively, and as real as the characters painted from identifiable originals.[52]

Similarly, Françoise Basch believes that Aunt Betsey is a very convincing character:

> She is revealed as an admirable adoptive mother, who is in fact a victim wife whose maternal gifts lie fallow. In the course of the novel, Betsy [sic] Trotwood undergoes a development as spectacular as Bella Wilfer in *Our Mutual Friend* and Caddy Jellyby in *Bleak House*. She is shown at first as an eccentric type, enclosed in behaviour patterns, manias that are not purely grotesque inventions but reveal a denial of certain traumatic aspects of life ... [She] for a time ... only accepts the male sex in the form of an innocent and an orphan both entirely dependent on her for their subsistence. Little by little there emerges from rigid behaviour patterns a personality at once strong, tender and generous, which overcomes the neurosis created by her disastrous marriage.[53]

Michael Slater holds much the same view. For Slater, Betsey "compels us to suspend our disbelief in the existence of real-life fairy godmothers." In addition, he states: "Betsey is, I believe, the finest flowering of Dickens's concentration on women in the novels of his mid-career."[54] Natalie E. Schroeder and Ronald A. Schroeder are also enthusiastic: "Though she is clearly a secondary character in the novel, she is one of Dickens's triumphs of characterization."[55] Finally, Natalie McKnight describes Betsey "as one of Dickens's most complete portraits of an ideal mother."[56] To be sure, Aunt Betsey is not a one-dimensional character and she is shown to be benevolent and capable of change; however, even Aunt Betsey does not escape the narrator's disgust at maternal ineptitude.

Aunt Betsey quite suddenly appears in the very first chapter of the novel: "She gave my mother such a turn, that I have always been convinced I am indebted to Miss Betsey for having been born on a Friday" (52). Thoroughly boisterous and critical, she virtually scares Clara Copperfield into labor. However, when Clara gives birth to a boy, she leaves just as suddenly as she came. Aunt Betsey, as she indicates before David's birth, is only prepared to accept the birth of a girl:

> "You were speaking about its being a girl," said Miss Betsey. "I have no doubt it will be a girl. I have a presentiment that it must be a girl. Now child, from the moment of the birth of this girl —"
>
> "Perhaps boy," my mother took the liberty of putting in.
>
> "I tell you I have a presentiment that it must be a girl," returned Miss Betsey. "Don't contradict. From the moment of this girl's birth, child, I intend to be her friend. I intend to be her godmother, and I beg you'll call her Betsey Trotwood Copperfield. There must be no mistakes in life with *this* Betsey Trotwood. There must be no trifling with *her* affections, poor dear. She must be well brought up, and well guarded from reposing any foolish confidences where they are not deserved. I must make that *my* care."
>
> There was a twitch of Miss Betsey's head, after each of these sentences, as if her own old wrongs were working within her, and she repressed any plainer reference to them by strong constraint [55].

Accordingly, Aunt Betsey's brand of love is highly conditional and selfish. The child must be a girl so that Aunt Betsey can atone for her own mistakes. When speaking to the doctor, Mr. Chillip, shortly after the birth, the possibility of the baby being a boy doesn't even enter her head:

> "The baby," said my aunt. "How is she?"
>
> "Ma'am," returned Mr. Chillip, "I apprehended you had known. It's a boy."
>
> My aunt said never a word, but took her bonnet by the strings, in the manner of a sling, aimed a blow at Mr. Chillip's head with it, put it on bent, walked out, and never came back. She vanished like a discontented fairy; or like one of those supernatural beings, whom it was popularly supposed I was entitled to see; and never came back any more [60].

As is clear from the text, David knows that his great-aunt wanted nothing to do with him when she discovered that he was a boy. There are mitigating circumstances, however. Before conveying the details of his birth, David gives us a potted history of Aunt Betsey's life. He explains that she had once been married to a younger man. This man, while handsome, had an ugly nature:

> he was strongly suspected of having beaten Miss Betsey, and even of having once, on a disputed question of supplies, made some hasty but determined arrangements to throw her out of a two pair of stairs' window. These evidences of an incompatibility of temper induced Miss Betsey to pay him off, and effect a separation by mutual consent. He went to India with his capital, and there, according to a wild legend in our family, he was once seen riding on an elephant, in company with a Baboon; but I think it must have been a Baboo — or a Begum. Anyhow, from India tidings of his death reached home, within ten years. How they affected my aunt, nobody knew; for immediately upon the separation, she took her maiden name again, bought a cottage in a hamlet on the sea-coast a long way off, established

herself there as a single woman with one servant, and was understood to live secluded, ever afterwards, in an inflexible retirement.

My father had once been a favourite of hers, I believe; but she was mortally affronted by his marriage, on the ground that my mother was "a wax doll." She had never seen my mother, but she knew her to be not yet twenty [51].

Aunt Betsey, it appears, had originally cared for two men. The first, her husband, had mistreated her and the second, her nephew, had disappointed her. There are reasons, thereby, for her violent repudiation of the male sex. However, while motives are provided for her behavior, it is clear from the plot that her anti-male position is far from acceptable. Accordingly, as if to show Aunt Betsey that her ideas of atonement are completely misguided, the narrative dubiously provides her with a more fitting atonement program. Indeed, rather than getting a great-niece who, at her behest, would have been egotistically called Betsey Trotwood, Aunt Betsey ends up taking care of and completely relying upon the advice of a mentally disturbed *man* who insists on being called Mr. Dick:

> "You are not to suppose that he hasn't got a longer name, if he chose to use it," said my aunt, with a loftier air. "Babley — Mr. Richard Babley — that's the gentleman's true name."
>
> I was going to suggest, with a modest sense of my youth and familiarity I had been already guilty of, that I had better give him the full benefit of that name, when my aunt went on to say:
>
> "But don't you call him by it, whatever you do. He can't bear his name. That's a peculiarity of his. Though I don't know that it's much of a peculiarity, either; for he has been ill-used enough, by some that bear it, to have a mortal antipathy for it, Heaven knows. Mr. Dick is his name here, and everywhere else, now — if he ever went anywhere else, which he don't. So take care child, you don't call him anything but Mr. Dick" [257].

"Dick," as Aunt Betsey stresses, is an abbreviation of Richard, but in coarse slang it means penis. Certainly, Mr. Dick may adopt an abridgement of his name because he wishes to psychically distance himself from the pain of his past. However, if we take into account the slang meaning of his name, then there is the decided implication that Aunt Betsey not only needs a "dick" in her life but more importantly, the advice of a "dick":

> "Is he — is Mr. Dick — I ask because I don't know, aunt — is he at all out of his mind, then?" I stammered; for I felt I was on dangerous ground.
>
> "Not a morsel," said my aunt.
>
> "Oh, indeed!" I observed faintly.
>
> "If there is anything in the world," said my aunt, with great decision and force of manner, "that Mr. Dick is not, it's that."
>
> I had nothing better to offer, than another timid, "Oh, indeed!"
>
> "He has been *called* mad," said my aunt. "I have a selfish pleasure in saying that he has been called mad, or I should not have had the benefit of his society and advice for these last ten years and upwards — in fact, ever since your sister, Betsey Trotwood, disappointed me" [259].

As William C. Spengemann notes, Mr. Dick "came under [Aunt Betsey's] protection at the very hour of David's birth."[57] Just at the point, then, where the very sane Aunt Betsey determines that a boy can have no meaning in her life, she ironically becomes wholly responsible for a mentally challenged man with a phallic name who miraculously happens to possess excellent moral judgment. Added to this, she becomes wholly reliant upon his wisdom. So while Aunt Betsey might have vanished like a discontented fairy straight after David's birth, the text just as magically ensures that a man immediately materializes to show her just how indispensable the male sex is. The narrative thereby implicitly suggests that a woman's reasoning is *off* unless it is backed up by the advice of a man. Indeed any man's advice is better than the independent reasoning of a woman. Even, it seems the advice of a man who happens to be "all out of his mind."

Some commentators suggest that the character of Mr. Dick is, to some degree, a conscious authorial self-portrait.[58] After all, his name is an abbreviation of Dickens's name[59]; he is "a prolific writer"[60] working on an allegorically expressed memorial which Aunt Betsey indicates is about "his own history" (261); he believes the troubled thoughts of a beheaded king (whose Christian name was the same as Dickens), Charles the First, have been put into his head[61]; he seeks to send his memorial out into the world (albeit not through publishing but through putting his words on a kite with plenty of string so that it may fly high); and his troubled mind is the result of a "domestic catastrophe."[62] If this is the case, then one cannot treat Mr. Dick's guardian, Aunt Betsey, in an uncritical light. One should not, for instance, ignore the fact that Aunt Betsey never seems to know what to do with David until the penetrating Mr. Dick sets her straight. Indeed, Aunt Betsey's role is less about guiding Mr. Dick than about *being guided by* Mr. Dick, and all too often the narrative reveals that Aunt Betsey is woolly, irrational and wrong-headed, as opposed to Mr. Dick who is "as sharp as a surgeon's lancet" (249).

When David, for instance, first turns up at Aunt Betsey's garden gate, her first inclination is to get rid of him:

> There came out of the house a lady with her handkerchief tied over her cap, and a pair of gardening gloves on her hands, wearing a gardening pocket like a toll-man's apron, and carrying a great knife. I knew her immediately to be Miss Betsey, for she came stalking out of the house exactly as my poor mother had so often described her stalking up our garden at Blunderstone Rookery.
> "Go away!" said Miss Betsey, shaking her head, and making a distant chop in the air with her knife. "Go along! No boys here!"
> I watched her, with my heart at my lips, as she marched to a corner of her garden, and stooped to dig up some little root there [246–47].

David is not so easily dispatched:

> "If you please, aunt, I am your nephew."

> "Oh, Lord!" said my aunt. And sat flat down in the garden-path.
>
> "I am David Copperfield, of Blunderstone, in Suffolk — where you came, on the night when I was born, and saw my dear mama. I have been very unhappy since she died. I have been slighted, and taught nothing, and thrown upon myself, and put to work not fit for me. It made me run away to you. I was robbed at first setting out, and have walked all the way, and have never slept in a bed since I began the journey." Here my self-support gave way all at once; and with a movement of my hands, intended to show her my ragged state, and call it to witness that I had suffered something, I broke into a passion of crying, which I suppose had been pent up within me all the week [247].

Aunt Betsey, in response, "collars" (247) her nephew and takes him inside to administer a series of questionable restoratives. As David notes, "I think they must have been taken out at random, for I am sure I tasted aniseed water, anchovy sauce, and salad dressing" (247). This strange, far from efficacious move is followed by more awkward maneuvers. Firstly, she gets David to lie down on the sofa with a "handkerchief from her own head under my feet, lest I should sully the cover" (248); and secondly, she sits behind a screen, and out of David's vision, repeatedly exclaims "Mercy on us!" (248)

Certainly, her inept reaction to David's unexpected arrival may well be viewed in a humorous light, but it can also be viewed as decidedly suspect because Aunt Betsey is clearly incapable of responding in an appropriately empathetic fashion. Indeed, she is so devoid of fellow-feeling that she must call upon Mr. Dick to offer guidance: "Now here you see young David Copperfield, and the question I put to you is, what shall I do with him?" (249) Mr. Dick thoughtfully proposes that David should be given a bath. This idea, while simplistic, is nevertheless far superior to Aunt Betsey's confused and rejecting treatment of her highly distressed great-nephew, and this is further underscored by Aunt Betsey's own words. Turning to her maid, she says, "Mr. Dick sets us all right. Heat the bath!" (249) Mr. Dick does indeed serve to set Aunt Betsey right, and most of her "right" moves are shown to be underlaid by his logic. David describes the bath that he receives as a "great comfort" (251), but this sense of comfort unravels when later, in the evening, Aunt Betsey does nothing to alleviate his fears:

> All this time I was deeply anxious to know what she was going to do with me; but she took her dinner in profound silence, except when she occasionally fixed her eyes on me sitting opposite, and said, "Mercy upon us!" which did not by any means relieve my anxiety [252].

After dinner, Aunt Betsey gets David to tell his story to Mr. Dick, and at its conclusion she intimates that Clara Copperfield was mad to have remarried: "Whatever possessed that poor unfortunate Baby, that she must go and be married again," said my aunt, when I had finished, "*I* can't conceive" (252). Mr. Dick, not illogically, suggests that she might have fallen in love. Incredulous,

Aunt Betsey asks him what he could possibly mean and furthermore what business did Clara Copperfield have to fall in love? Mr. Dick's answer is more than a little telling: "Perhaps," Mr. Dick simpered, after thinking a little, "she did it for pleasure" (252). This answer, while ostensibly guileless, is also highly revealing. In effect, it provides the text's last word or final judgment in relation to Clara Copperfield. If Mr. Dick is as sharp as Aunt Betsey gives him credit for and if Mr. Dick operates as Dickens's "coded self-identification" then what is really being said here is that Clara Copperfield sacrificed her son's wellbeing and future prospects to pursue nothing less than her own sexual pleasure. Aunt Betsey, of course, ever guided by Mr. Dick's piercing logic, goes on to point out that such pleasure seeking only led to Clara Copperfield's ill-usage. Indeed, Aunt Betsey says that Clara had to go and marry "a Murderer — or a man with a name like it" (253). This pronouncement, while designed to generate humor, nonetheless carries a stinging barb. There is the distinct suggestion here that Clara, owing to her sexual impulses, was incapable of preventing herself from marrying a pathologically dangerous man. However, if Clara was incapable of succumbing to a "Murderer," it should not be forgotten that Aunt Betsey was almost pathologically incapable of providing even the most basic ongoing support and advice, which might have prevented the impressionable Clara from falling prey to a "Murderer." As Schroeder and Schroeder put it:

> Clara's problem with Aunt Betsey was that Miss Trotwood did leave, and at a time when the frail young widow was most vulnerable. Aunt Betsey carelessly abandoned Clara during that critical hour when David was born. As she confesses later, even on the eve of the boy's birth, she knew that Clara would remarry, but she had hoped "it wouldn't have been as bad as it turned out." Her deserting the young mother and infant, then, was directly related to the Murdstones' subsequent abuse of Clara and David.... Because she left her niece prey to the Murdstones, Aunt Betsey must share the guilt for Clara's death.[63]

Unsurprisingly, if Aunt Betsey couldn't find it within herself to provide any level of support for the distressed widow of her nephew and the mother of her great-nephew, it stands to reason that she would be equally maladroit with her frightened and upset great-nephew. Later that evening, she again solicits Mr. Dick's advice:

> "What would you do with him, now?"
> "Do with David's son?" said Mr. Dick.
> "Ay," replied my aunt, "with David's son."
> "Oh!" said Mr. Dick. "Yes. Do with — I should put him to bed."
> "Janet!" cried my aunt, with the same complacent triumph that I had remarked before. "Mr. Dick sets us all right. If the bed is ready, we'll take him up to it" [254].

Mr. Dick's advice is all too obvious, but in its simple appreciation for the fundamental things that David needs, it gives David a sense of security. Again, this is in stark contrast to Aunt Betsey's bungling and lack of awareness. Indeed, aside from her willingness to follow Mr. Dick's advice, Aunt Betsey gives David very little to feel secure about. Sharing breakfast with his aunt, David notes:

> I never could look at her for a few moments together but I found her looking at me — in an odd thoughtful manner, as if I were an immense way off, instead of being on the other side of the small round table [256].

This kind of limited vision will be echoed in the portraits of Miss Barbary and Mrs. Jellyby in *Bleak House*. David, however, is not some distant speck on the horizon but a living, breathing child (and a relative no less) who needs her love and assistance in the here and now. Nevertheless, she provides him with no assurances:

> "I have written to him," said my aunt.
> "To —?"
> "To your father-in-law," said my aunt. "I have sent him a letter that I'll trouble him to attend to, or he and I will fall out, I can tell him!"
> "Does he know where I am, aunt?" I inquired, alarmed.
> "I have told him," said my aunt, with a nod.
> "Shall I — be — given up to him?" I faltered.
> "I don't know," said my aunt. "We shall see."
> "Oh! I can't think what I shall do," I exclaimed, "if I have to go back to Mr. Murdstone!"
> "I don't know anything about it," said my aunt, shaking her head. "I can't say, I am sure. We shall see."
> My spirits sank under these words, and I became very downcast and heavy of heart. My aunt, without appearing to take much heed of me, put on a coarse apron with a bib, which she took out of the press; washed up the teacups with her own hands; and, when everything was washed and set in the tray again, and the cloth folded and put on the top of the whole, rang for Janet to remove it [256].

Aunt Betsey's distant way of relating to her great-nephew is also emphasized when she conveys the particulars of Mr. Dick's existence to David. While she may address David, he knows that his presence has little to do with her discourse:

> If I could have supposed that my aunt had recounted these particulars for my espe-cial behoof, and as a piece of confidence in me, I should have felt very much dis-tinguished, and should have augured favourably from such a mark of her good opinion. But I could hardly help observing that she had launched into them, chiefly because the question was raised in her own mind, and with very little reference to me, though she had addressed herself to me in the absence of anybody else [261].

Aunt Betsey, like Dickens's mother in the autobiographical fragment, is quite unaware of her negating behavior. However, thanks to her association with Mr. Dick, David is given the chance to start a new life. When the horrible Murdstone arrives with his sister to take the very fearful David away and dispose of him as he sees fit, Aunt Betsey calls upon Mr. Dick to once again provide his advice:

> "Mr. Dick," said my aunt, "what shall I do with this child?"
> Mr. Dick considered, hesitated, brightened, and rejoined, "Have him measured for a suit of clothes directly" [269].

At this, Aunt Betsey swiftly banishes Mr. Murdstone and his sister from the house and determines that the best course of action is to bring up David (or Trotwood as she decides to call him) in conjunction with Mr. Dick. David is thereby enabled to drop a curtain on all of his past pain.

Aunt Betsey assuredly goes on to become David's loving, supportive and clear-sighted aunt but the fact remains that without Mr. Dick's sharp suggestions, Aunt Betsey would quite literally not have known what to do with David. According to Stanley Tick, the fact that Mr. Dick is at his most serene when his kite/manuscript is flying but disturbed when it descends "seems pointed in the direction of the novelist as self-therapist."[64] Similarly, Mr. Dick's role as Aunt Betsey's adviser in relation to her handling of David points in this direction. At some level, Dickens deemed that the character of Aunt Betsey was incapable of recognizing the needs of a sensitive little boy unless she received assistance from a benign masculine figure. Accordingly, he consciously created the "metaphor" of "coded self-identification" Mr. Dick to simultaneously set a bad mother figure straight and to help his brainchild or inner child David to achieve proper placement. In the opening chapter of the novel, Aunt Betsey is nothing short of outraged when Clara Copperfield gives birth to a boy rather than a girl. In fact, she is so outraged that she uses her bonnet as a weapon against the attending doctor and then puts it back on her head, bent out of shape. David's narrative, I believe, carries a similar but much more buried sense of outrage. He may not take aim at Aunt Betsey directly, but through a bent narrative design he ensures that Aunt Betsey is ironically paid back for her misandry. Indeed, she is put back in place by not just a man but a man with a resoundingly masculine name, who also happens to be insane. So while David may not express any anger or bitterness at his aunt's rejection of his sex or her particular brand of maternal ineptitude, his narrative indirectly works to get back at her for her "disgusting" behavior.

As I have worked to show, disgust is very much a feature (albeit implicit) of Dickens's portrayal of David Copperfield's biological and adoptive mothers. Both of these mothers repeatedly displace David in a variety of different ways. However, at the end of the novel David Copperfield emerges as an apparently integrated Victorian hero. Just how does he do this given the failings of his biological and adoptive mothers? David's trip to the Alps towards the end of the novel, I believe, provides the key to this question.

Sweet

The Alps in *Frankenstein* is a place where Dr. Frankenstein retreats in order to take a break from the horrors associated with creating a monster. Far from getting away from it all, however, Frankenstein gets confronted with it all. Despite the "terrifically desolate"[65] nature of the place, the hideous and reproachful creature assiduously manages to hunt Frankenstein down for the express purpose of recounting its exceedingly miserable life-story. Correspondingly, the Alps in Sigmund Freud's classic case history "Katharina" is a place where Freud goes in order to take a break from hysterical women patients. Amusingly enough, while partaking of its enveloping serenity, he is approached by yet another hysterical woman who quite suddenly needs high altitude counseling. As he remarks: "I was interested to find that neuroses could flourish in this way at a height of over 6,000 feet."[66] While these texts may seem light-years away from *David Copperfield*, their respective Alpine scenes, with their evasion followed by collision framework, do, to a significant degree, parallel the *David Copperfield* Alps scene. Throughout most of the novel, Agnes Wickfield weighs heavily on David's mind as *the* woman above all others, yet not the woman that David believes he is fit for. Admittedly, he doesn't go to the Alps to literally get away from her, and she, by the same token, doesn't unexpectedly show up to entreat him and disturb his peace of mind. Rather, he goes there as part of his tour of Europe following the deaths of Dora, Ham and Steerforth. Agnes has not been the catalyst for the trip nor has she physically interrupted it. Nevertheless, she does quite successfully punctuate his Alpine sojourn through her fervent and stirring letter. Indeed, this letter is so stirring that David experiences a profound awakening:

> I put the letter in my breast, and thought what had I been an hour ago! When I heard the voices die away, and saw the quiet evening cloud grow dim, and all the colours in the valley fade, and the golden snow upon the mountain-tops become a remote part of the pale night sky, yet felt that the night was passing from my mind, and all its shadows clearing, there was no name for the love I bore her, dearer to me, henceforward, than ever until then.
>
> I read her letter, many times. I wrote to her before I slept. I told her that I had been in sore need of her help; that without her I was not, and I never had been, what she thought me; but, that she inspired me to be that, and I would try [888].

As a consequence of Agnes's letter, then, David's vision clears. No longer in the dark, he simultaneously realizes his love for Agnes and he becomes aware of the fact that she sees something in him that he dearly wishes to become. Accordingly, he accepts her vision of him and single-mindedly sets about to become the man that he believes he has never been. Remaining in Switzerland, he sets to work:

> I worked early and late, patiently and hard. I wrote a Story, with a purpose growing, not remotely, out of my experience, and sent it to Traddles, and he arranged for

its publication very advantageously for me; and the tidings of my growing repu-tation began to reach me from travellers whom I encountered by chance. After some rest and change, I fell to work, in my old ardent way, on a new fancy, which took strong possession of me. As I advanced in the execution of this task, I felt it more and more, and roused my utmost energies to do it well. This was my third work of fiction [889].

Of course, all of this becomes possible because Agnes not only assures him of a place in her heart but she points the way for him to achieve his place in the world. Through Agnes, David gets beyond his original displacement and expe-riences a kind of terrified delight in his own possibilities. Indeed, her pure and unbounded perception of him enables him to discover nothing less than an image of his own greatness.

Significantly, David only realizes his love for Agnes in the Alps. Why? The Alps is of course an awe-inspiring place which represents for many the essence of purity. Indeed, it is probably *the* site within romantic discourse which is most associated with raising ideas of the sublime. What better place, then, for David to come to grips with his over the top feelings for Agnes. For Agnes is, in David's mind, "all womanly and good" and he is throughout the novel com-pletely in awe of her. Indeed, he is so overwhelmed that until his epiphany in the Alps, he doesn't just put her on a pedestal; he actually constructs her as awful and sublime.

The first thing that strikes one about the Alps scene is that Dickens directly invokes Edmund Burke's notion of the sublime:

> If those awful solitudes had spoken to my heart, I did not know it. I had found sublimity and wonder in the dread heights and precipices, in the roaring torrents, and the wastes of ice and snow; but as yet, they had taught me nothing else [887].

The allusion may be intentional or Dickens may have just absorbed it through the osmotic process of reading romantic texts like Wordsworth's *The Prelude*, which employ similar lexical arrangements. In this respect, it is particularly interesting to note that Dickens actually purchased a copy of *The Prelude* just before he wrote of Dora's death and David's sojourn in the Alps, as Leon Litvak explains:

> *The Prelude* [was] published in July 1850 and bought by Dickens soon thereafter (Account 1, 17 August 1850), at a time when he was working on the closing monthly numbers of *David Copperfield*. While the poem — which, like Dickens's novel uses imaginative memory to produce a spiritual and psychological experience of personal history — cannot be seen to have guided the overall conception of *David Copperfield*, it is interesting to speculate on how Dickens's reading of Wordsworth at this time might have affected those portions of the novel following on the death of Dora (written by Dickens in August 1850). In chapter 58 (which opened the final double number in November 1850) David goes to the Alps, and engages in a retrospec-tive — but assertive — self-examination and spiritual awakening, which recalls for several critics the pattern adopted in *The Prelude*.[67]

However, regardless of the reason for David's invocation, Burke's notion of the sublime is certainly alluded to in this passage and as such it should be explored.

If we turn to Edmund Burke's treatise on the sublime, we find that the sublime elicits very strong emotions, the chief amongst them being astonishment: "that state of the soul, in which all its motions are suspended with some degree of horror."[68] As Agnes is very much associated with the Alps, I would like to argue that astonishment is the prevailing emotion that David feels towards her. David makes many statements throughout the book that corroborate this assertion. David is at all times very much in awe of Agnes. He is daunted and even paralyzed by her superior qualities. A handful of David's assertions should serve to illustrate this point:

> "You are like no one else. You are so good, and so sweet-tempered. You have such a gentle nature, and you are always right" [333].
> "There is no one that I know of, who deserves to love *you*, Agnes" [333].
> Agnes was too superior to me in character and purpose. (430)
> I had accustomed myself to think of her, when we were both mere children, as one who was far removed from my wild fancies [890].
> "All my life long I shall look up to you, and be guided by you" [916].
> "Until I die, my dearest sister, I shall see you always before me, pointing upward!" [916].
> "You were so much better than I" [936].

The sublime is also powerful. According to Burke: "I know of nothing sublime which is not some modification of power."[69] This is a quality which Agnes is assuredly endowed with. Agnes is omnipotent, as David's words attest. She is totally good and always right. She is all-knowing, as her Alps letter confirms:

> *She knew* (she said) how such a nature of mine would turn affliction to good. *She knew* how trial and emotion would exalt and strengthen it. *She was sure* that in my every purpose I should gain a firmer and a higher tendency, through the grief I had undergone. *She*, who so gloried in my fame, and so looked forward to its augmentation, *well knew* that I would labour on. *She knew* that in me, sorrow could not be weakness, but must be strength [888; emphasis added].

She is also omnipresent, as David says: she "was always at my side go where I would" (888). She even apparently creates David:

> "What I am, you have made me, Agnes. You should know best."
> "*I* made you, Trotwood?"
> "Yes, Agnes, my dear girl!" [916].

As Nina Auerbach writes:

> With no more theological authority than the light that filters through the man-made church windows, Agnes is endowed with a virtually unlimited power of creation. From making tea she goes on to make order, to make abstractions (goodness,

peace, and truth), and finally, to make David himself. On returning to her after many trials, he recognizes not only his true wife but the source of his being. Agnes' role in the novel makes sense only if we accept his tribute literally.[70]

There is one quality of the sublime that Agnes does not possess — she is not associated with darkness. Burke claims: "darkness is more productive of sublime ideas than light."[71] As we know, Agnes is not exactly imbued with darkness, shining as she does "like a Heavenly light" (950) above and beyond all objects. Nevertheless, Agnes's brand of light may still be perceived as sublime because for Burke, some light "by its very excess is converted into a species of darkness."[72] This is certainly true of Agnes because by virtue of her purity she effectively overcomes David's organs of sight. As Aunt Betsey knows, David is "blind, blind blind" (565) to Agnes.

Another quality of the sublime, according to Burke, is that it is generally cloaked in obscurity:

> To make anything very terrible, obscurity seems in general to be necessary. When we know the full extent of any danger, when we can accustom our eyes to it, a great deal of the apprehension vanishes. Every one will be sensible of this, who considers how greatly night adds to our dread.[73]

Certainly, Agnes is obscure. The reader never really gets a strong sense of her physicality. In fact, she is so shrouded in abstractions that she just about floats off the page. Virginia Woolf claimed:

> As a creator of character [Dickens] creates wherever his eyes rest — he has the visualizing power in the extreme. His people are branded upon our eyeballs before we hear them speak.[74]

This is decidedly not the case with Agnes, as Philip Collins remarks:

> Unlike Dora, she is not visualized: Dora has that delightful "shape" and pretty hair, Agnes merely has sides against which her keys hang, and the adjectives about her all refer to her disposition and moral qualities.[75]

David is also very aware of Agnes's moral qualities. She is a fountain of strength. Despite all the odds, she never wavers in terms of her loyalty or her sense of duty. David states at one point: "I had always felt my weakness in comparison with her constancy and fortitude" (890). And to Agnes, he says: "I really believe ... that you could be faithfully affectionate against all discouragement, and never cease to be so, until you ceased to live" (917). According to Burke:

> Those virtues which cause admiration and are of the sublimer kind, produce terror rather than love. Such as fortitude, justice, wisdom and the like.... The great virtues turn principally on dangers, punishments, and troubles, and are exercised rather in preventing the worst mischiefs than in dispensing favours; and are therefore not lovely, though highly venerable ... we submit to what we admire, but we love what submits to us; in one case we are forced, in the other we are flattered into compliance.[76]

Certainly up until the Alps scene it is clear that David feels that Agnes is highly venerable rather than highly lovable. How is it then that in the Alps he effectively gets over his terror of Agnes and discovers his love for her? The answer, I believe, may be found if one considers Burke's conception of the sublime. According to Burke, the experience of the sublime is one of simultaneous terror and delight. However, Burke is mindful that terror and delight are generally viewed as mutually exclusive feelings:

> If the sublime is built on terror, or some passion like it, which has pain for its object; it is previously proper to enquire how any species of delight can be derived from a cause so apparently contrary to it.[77]

Accordingly, Burke suggests that it is the removal or modification of pain or danger which distinguishes the sublime experience from that of absolute terror:

> When danger or pain press too nearly, they are incapable of giving any delight, and are simply terrible; but at certain distances, and with certain modifications, they may be, and they are delightful, as we every day experience.[78]

Under the Burkean conception of the sublime, then, if pain or danger is experienced at a certain remove or distance, delight may also be experienced. Removal can, however, be construed in a number of different ways. According to Tom Furniss:

> The notion of "removal" can imply that the danger is "removed" (at a certain distance, or at one remove) and that delight may arise simultaneously with fear because the danger is not quite adjacent. "Removal" can also imply that the delight succeeds the terror after the removal of the threat — the sublime experience thereby being akin to the great relief felt at the cessation of pain or the escape from danger. Finally, "removal" can mean that the act of removal is itself the source of the delight which "accompanies" it — the sublime therefore being the experience of the threatened self seeming to overcome or master danger through effort. The sublime may be read, then, as a moment or synchronic structure, a sequence of different states, or as a concerted action or movement. It is the last of these possibilities which is of most importance to Burke, for whom the sublime experience is an escape from fatal stasis through strenuous action.[79]

Indeed, within Burke's theory of the sublime, pain or fear can not only induce "an unnatural tension of the nerves"[80] but also "extraordinary weakness"[81] or passivity. Such a condition is far from desirable because for Burke: "Melancholy, dejection, despair, and often self-murder, is the consequence of the gloomy view we take of things in this relaxed state of body."[82] Accordingly, it is crucial for the subject to overcome this state through effort. For Burke:

> The best remedy for all these evils is exercise or *labour*; and labour is a surmounting of *difficulties*, an exertion of the contracting power of the muscles; and as such resembles pain, which consists in tension or contraction, in every thing but degree.

Labour is not only requisite to preserve the coarser organs in a state fit for their functions, but it is equally necessary to these finer and more delicate organs, on which, and by which, the imagination, and perhaps the other mental powers act.[83]

Unless the subject engages in labor, he or she does not have the requisite mental strength to transcend his or her subjection to that which had aroused pain or fear. As Furniss puts it:

The crucial thing in Burke's account is the way the subject *responds* to pain or fear — whether he or she remains immobilized in face of them or acts to overcome them and so experience delight and achieve sublimity."[84]

Some may therefore become trapped in the passive, overawed phase of the sublime, these being, as Burke asserts, "weaker subjects, which are the most liable to the severest impressions of pain and fear."[85] By contrast, others may through labor reverse their subjection and accordingly experience the delightful or elevated stage of the sublime. Furniss translates this in contemporary terms:

Today, we might call it a rush of adrenalin which energizes an extraordinary defensive response. The delight is that of the self, saved from pain or danger, but it also arises from the activity which accomplishes self-preservation (it is both an energy which empowers exertion, and an exertion which releases energy). As such, it is at once a sense of relief and a sense of mastery, of mastering danger through effort.[86]

Rather prosaically then, Burke's notion of the sublime helps to reinforce middle-class ideology. Indeed, as Frances Ferguson notes: "All [the sublime's] strainings follow the dictate of the work ethic."[87]

In light of the above, if we consider David's relationship to Agnes, there is no doubt that he becomes trapped in the transfixed or paralyzed phase of the sublime for an extended period. However, in the Alps, at a sufficient remove from her, he reads her stirring letter and decides to remain in Switzerland to work hard, writing, as he says, "early and late, patiently and hard" (889). In doing so, he stays true to the common but nonetheless singular labor practices that Agnes had apparently earlier helped to awaken in him:

My meaning simply is, that whatever I have tried to do in life, I have tried with all my heart to do well; that whatever I have devoted myself to, I have devoted myself to completely; that in great aims and in small, I have always been thoroughly in earnest. I have never believed it possible that any natural or improved ability can claim immunity from the companionship of the steady, plain, hard-working qualities, and hope to gain its end. There is no such thing as such fulfillment on this earth. Some happy talent, and some fortunate opportunity, may form the two sides of the ladder on which some men mount, but the rounds of that ladder must be made of stuff to stand wear and tear; and there is no substitute for thorough-going, ardent, and sincere earnestness. Never to put one hand to anything, on which I could throw my whole self; and never to affect depreciation of my work, whatever it was; I find, now to have been my golden rules.

> How much of the practice I have just reduced to precept, I owe to Agnes, I will not repeat here [672].

Ordinarily, one would expect that the above ethos would have been instilled by a parent but as David was a posthumous child and like Dickens in the autobiographical fragment, had little or no respect for his mother's ability to impart knowledge, he ingeniously suggests that it was Agnes who inspired him to adopt these golden, highly successful rules. This is made even more obvious in the Alps when David comes to read Agnes's highly inspirational letter:

> I read her letter, many times. I wrote to her before I slept. I told her that I had been in sore need of her help; that without her I was not, and I never had been, what she thought me; but, that she inspired me to be that, and I would try [888].

David then is so affected by Agnes's elevated view of him that he discovers a vision of his own greatness and then actively sets about to achieve it. This is very much in keeping with Burke's assertion that the sublime produces a kind of self-deception:

> Now whatever either on good or bad grounds tends to raise a man in his own opinion, produces a sort of swelling and triumph that is extremely grateful to the human mind; and this swelling is never more perceived, nor operates with more force, than when without danger we are conversant with terrible objects, the mind always claiming to itself some part of the dignity and importance of the things which it contemplates. Hence proceeds what Longinus has observed of that glorying and sense of inward greatness, that always fills the reader of such passages in poets and orators as are sublime....[88]

David, through hard work and isolation in the Alps, claims to himself some of the dignity and importance that he had originally attributed to Agnes. In such a way he transcends his original subjection to her finer qualities and achieves an experience of sublimity or delightful horror. For much of the book Agnes was in David's mind, simply grand and terrible. Her superior qualities were indelibly impressed on his mind. She was *the* woman above all others and, perhaps more importantly, above his all-too-human biological mother and adoptive mother. Accordingly, she was awesome but not delight producing. However, when David travels far away from her and labors in the manner that she would expect of him, she becomes an object of terror and delight that raises David in his own opinion to the point where he is able to reinvent himself as a self-made man. As Tom Furniss states:

> The sublime occasions, and is occasioned by, an illusion of original creativity: the self's "creation," and mastery of what it has heard or seen, raises it in its own opinion and produces "a sort of swelling and triumph." The self responds to the perhaps already fictional threat with the creative labour of metaphor-making, a gesture which defends and reaffirms a sense of self, or perhaps constitutes a new understanding of the self as an originating subject. A new model of the self is "born,"

then, through its own sublime labour or the labour of the sublime.... The sublime thus operates as an indispensable trope through which the "self-made man" (in philosophical and/or economic terms) is constituted. Although the sublime seems a mere dumb show, its denouement — the emergence of the individual ("Self begot, self raised / By our own quickening power" (*Paradise Lost*, v 860–1)) — bears an important ideological load.[89]

In *David Copperfield*, Agnes, is, whether readers like it or not, the natural object or aesthetic vehicle through which David achieves authentic identity and originality. As such she is "made" by David (and his sympathetic, hardworking creator Dickens) to bear the novel's "important ideological load." However, as Furniss notes:

> If the sublime's role is to reaffirm the sense of self as a kind of heroic labourer, purging itself of weakness through individual effort, the sublimity of the victorious subject is perhaps more an efficacious fiction than a genuine transcendence.[90]

Agnes's role therefore is not completely successful. While David assiduously records both his protracted weakness in relation to Agnes and his eventual transcendence, fittingly experienced in the Alps, a location typically associated with sublimity, his victory nonetheless strikes one as hollow. Dickens may have "ingeniously" ensured that David got beyond his original displacement at the hands of his biological and adoptive mothers and largely hid his disgust for their misguided behavior. He may have also ensured that David was able to get over his unmitigated terror for the pure woman who effectively displaced his mothers, but he cannot ensure that readers will get beyond the fact that Agnes is simply too "womanly and good" to be credible.

Miss Barbary, Lady Dedlock and the Disfigurement of Esther Summerson in *Bleak House*

I had never been a beauty, and had never thought myself one; but I had been very different from this. It was all gone now. Heaven was so good to me, that I could let it go with a few not bitter tears, and could stand there arranging my hair for the night quite thankfully.[1]

The preceding chapter on *David Copperfield* sought to show that the hero was largely able to conceal the disgust that he felt towards his biological and adoptive mothers, and even achieved a measure of transcendence by displacing them with the sublime pinnacle of feminine purity that was Agnes; but the protagonist of the next major fictional autobiography that Dickens would come to write is arguably not nearly so fortunate. The protagonist is Esther Summerson and the autobiography that she writes constitutes approximately half of the novel that is *Bleak House*.[2] Esther is much like David Copperfield in that she conveys the disgust that she feels towards her adoptive and biological mothers in a covert way, but unlike David whose maternal disgust goes hand in hand with self-pity. Esther's disgust towards her adoptive and biological mothers (Miss Barbary and Lady Dedlock) goes hand in hand with internalized guilt and shame. Such a toxic combination is bound to produce an unhealthy outcome. Accordingly, this chapter will suggest that the disfiguring disease that Esther accidentally contracts is actually something that she seeks out at a subconscious level in order to punish her mothers and herself. Furthermore, Esther's feverish disease may be paralleled to the spontaneous combustion of the rag-and-bone merchant Krook, because just as Krook's death provides Dickens with the means to burn the novel's "black Nemesis" (the iniquitous Court of Chancery) in effigy,[3] Esther's ravaging disease provides her with the means (albeit subconscious and self-destructive) to burn in effigy the disgraceful and abandoning mothers who jointly constitute her "black Nemesis." According to Geoffrey Thurley, "There is throughout [*Bleak House*] a disgust which transcends its origination and a sense of waste which by far exceeds the inadequacies of the legal system."[4] However, while there might be a pervasive thread of disgust that runs throughout this large novel, it is rarely, if ever, thought to extend to the protagonist, Esther Summerson. Disgust is not even a word that would feature prominently in Esther's vocabulary. Mild and consistently self-denying, Esther would appear to be beyond such extremes of emotion. Nevertheless, if one closely scrutinizes the language in which Esther presents her mothers and considers the less-than-accidental way in which she catches her disfiguring disease, there is compelling evidence to suggest that Esther actually feels revulsion toward her mothers and even wishes (at her own expense) to blast them out of her life.

In terms of the novel's exegesis, no critic or commentator has suggested that Esther's face-ravaging disease is the means by which she subconsciously seeks to punish her cruel surrogate mother, Miss Barbary, and her fallen biological mother, Lady Dedlock. In addition, no one has suggested that Esther's disease may be paralleled to the symbolic "Spontaneous Combustion" destruction of the Court of Chancery. Certainly if we take the novel at "face value" one could hardly arrive at such conclusions, but if we get beyond the novel's epidermal layer and analyze the consistently disdainful lexicon that Esther employs to describe her mothers and some of her questionable actions there is much to support this line of thought.

The third chapter of *Bleak House*, called "A Progress," introduces Esther Summerson, who writes in the first person:

> I have a great deal of difficulty in beginning to write my portion of these pages, for I know I am not clever. I always knew that. I can remember, when I was a very little girl indeed, I used to say to my doll, when we were alone together, "Now Dolly, I am not clever, you know very well, and you must be patient with me, like a dear!" And so she used to sit propped up in a great arm-chair, with her beautiful complexion and rosy lips, staring at me — or not so much at me, I think, as at nothing — while I busily stitched away, and told her every one of my secrets [62].

The first paragraph that Esther writes, then, records her memory of confiding to her beautiful doll that she is not clever. Following this, Esther recalls the intense feelings that she had for the doll:

> My dear old doll! I was such a shy little thing that I seldom dared to open my lips, and never dared to open my heart, to anybody else. It almost makes me cry to think what a relief it used to be to me, when I came home from school of a day, to run upstairs to my room, and say, "O you dear faithful Dolly, I knew you would be expecting me!" and then to sit down on the floor, leaning on the elbow of her great chair, and tell her all I had noticed since we parted. I had always rather a

noticing way — not a quick way, O no! — a silent way of noticing what passed
before me, and thinking I should like to understand it better. I have not by any
means a quick understanding. When I love a person very tenderly indeed, it seems
to brighten. But even that may be my vanity [62].

Esther's deep love for the doll is conveyed here. Clearly, the doll afforded Esther
a safe space to convey her observations, but a shadow hangs over this touching
tableau and very soon we find out just why Esther was so painfully shy:

I was brought up, from my earliest remembrance — like some of the princesses in
the fairy stories, only I was not charming — by my godmother. At least I only knew
her as such. She was a good, good woman! She went to church three times every
Sunday, and to morning prayers on Wednesdays and Fridays, and to lectures whenever there were lectures; and never missed. She was handsome; and if she had ever
smiled, would have been (I used to think) like an angel — but she never smiled.
She was always grave, and strict. She was so very good herself, I thought, that the
badness of other people made her frown all her life. I felt so different from her,
even making every allowance for the differences between a child and a woman; I
felt so poor, so trifling, and so far off; that I never could be unrestrained with
her — no, could never even love her as I wished [63].

The rhetoric that Esther employs here is particularly interesting. In the first
sentence, she alludes to a traditional fairytale upbringing with a godmother but
she undercuts this by unequivocally declaring that she was a child devoid of
charm. Immediately then, Esther links her godmother with what can only be
described as self-disdain. In the next sentence, she swiftly moves to cast doubt
on the legitimacy of her godmother's role — "At least I only knew her as such."
This is followed by the exclamatory assertion that her godmother was exceedingly or emphatically good. However this is again undercut by Esther's next
sentence because Esther ingenuously suggests that her godmother's goodness is
more about obsessive churchgoing than demonstrating consistent kindness or
compassion. Esther then claims that her godmother is good-looking and even
potentially angelic in appearance but this potentiality is not realized because
she "never" smiled. To add to this, Esther teams her godmother's dour coun-
tenance with a rigid and severe outlook: "She was always grave and strict." In
a fanciful bid to reconcile her godmother's severity, Esther suggests that her
godmother was so good that she could not help but frown at the badness of
other people. This pronouncement, as innocent as it sounds, is really just another
way for Esther to preemptively undermine her godmother because, in essence,
it implies that her godmother was so self-righteous that she spent every waking
moment judging the actions of "lesser" individuals. To complete this extremely
negative portrait, Esther records the way that she feels in her godmother's presence. Not simply does she feel of little or no significance but all of her natural
impulses are blocked. Indeed, she cannot even love her godmother according
to her want. In just one paragraph, then, Esther lays before the reader a damning

indictment of her primary care giver. While this woman may have brought her up, she is dubiously connected to Esther; fanatically religious; dour; severe; judgmental; distant; unbending and plain unlovable. Moreover, the lexicon that Esther employs to describe her godmother is nothing short of extreme. For Esther, there are no shades of grey in relation to her godmother. Indeed, her godmother *never* misses a religious activity; *never* smiles; is *always* grave and strict; and frowns at the badness of others *all her life*. So, too, Esther's response to her godmother is far from tempered: she could *never* be unrestrained with her and she could *never* even love her as she wished.

To reinforce the sense of alienation that she feels, Esther goes on to directly attribute her timidity and introspection to her impoverished relationship with her godmother: "This made me, I dare say, more timid and retiring than I naturally was, and cast me upon Dolly as the only friend with whom I felt at ease" (63). Tragically, Esther suggests that she feels more at ease with an inanimate object than with her flesh and blood primary caregiver. Craving meaning, comfort and worth outside of the artificial sanctuary that she has with her doll, Esther seeks to know something of her mother but despite her efforts she finds no validation:

> I had never heard my mama spoken of. I had never heard of my papa either, but I felt more interested about my mama. I had never worn a black frock, that I could recollect. I had never been shown my mama's grave. I had never been told where it was. Yet I had never been taught to pray for any relation but my godmother. I had more than once approached this subject of my thoughts with Mrs. Rachael, our only servant, who took my light away when I was in bed (another very good woman, but austere to me), and she had only said, "Esther, good night!" and gone away and left me [63].

Again, this paragraph is notable for its extreme rhetoric. Characterized by a series of negative assertions, the words "I had never" appear no less than six times. Such vehemence directly implicates her godmother in a plot to blot out all traces of her ancestry. Owing to her godmother's apparently relentless and selfish cover-up, Esther knows nothing of her parents and has not even been permitted to mourn their loss. Attempts to find answers from the servant Mrs. Rachael correspondingly yield nothing. Complicit in the denial of Esther's origins, she treats Esther with the dismissive obduracy modeled by Esther's godmother.

As to opportunities for social interaction, Esther is a day pupil at a school where there are seven girls but her godmother ensures from the outset that Esther's chances for friendship are quashed:

> One of [the girls], in the first week of my going to the school (I remember it very well), invited me home to a little party, to my great joy. But my godmother wrote a stiff letter declining for me, and I never went. I never went out at all [64].

Here again the word "never" is foregrounded. Esther *never* went to the party or for that matter anywhere at all. Indeed, as Judith Wilt puts it, "Her godmother imposed a soul-eating quarantining of her, as if she had been a disease."[5] She also *never* experienced the joy of celebrating her own birthday because her godmother effectively expunged it from the household calendar and claimed that she should *never* have been born: "It would have been far better, little Esther, that you had had no birthday; that you had never been born!" (64) This horrifically cruel pronouncement is justified by a set of punitive beliefs:

> "Your mother, Esther is your disgrace, and you were hers. The time will come — and soon enough — when you will understand this better, and will feel it too, as no one save a woman can. I have forgiven her" — but her face did not relent — "the wrong she did to me, and I say no more of it, though it was greater than you will ever know — than any one will ever know, but I, the sufferer. For yourself, unfortunate girl, orphaned and degraded from the first of these evil anniversaries, pray daily that the sins of others be not visited upon your head, according to what is written. Forget your mother and leave all other people to forget her who will do her unhappy child that great kindness.... Submission, self-denial, diligent work, are the preparations for a life begun with such a shadow on it. You are different from other children, Esther, because you were not born, like them, in common sinfulness and wrath. You are set apart" [65].

So while Esther is permitted to live under Miss Barbary's roof, Miss Barbary displaces Esther in a number of different ways: she denies Esther knowledge of her parents; she makes it clear (through the negation of Esther's birthday) that Esther is a waste of space; she refuses to allow Esther to associate with other children; and by telling Esther that she is "set apart" she not only eliminates Esther from the worldview that she subscribes to but also denies Esther a legitimate place in the human race.

Traumatized, Esther turns to her doll for solace and cries herself to sleep. In the days that follow, she compulsively conveys to the doll the account she has been given of her birth and makes resolutions to atone for her congenital fault:

> Dear, dear, to think how much time we passed alone together afterwards, and how often I repeated to the doll the story of my birthday, and confided to her that I would try, as hard as ever I could, to repair the fault I had been born with (of which I confessedly felt guilty and yet innocent), and would strive as I grew up to be industrious, contented, and kind-hearted, and to do some good to some one, and win some love to myself if I could [65].

This passage is particularly significant. If one stops for a moment to think about it, the image that comes before us is that of an enormously distressed (if not to say disturbed) little girl who spends much of her time repeating a litany to a doll. The litany may not be conveyed word for word, but if we take into account the history that Esther has put before us, it would in all probability go along the following lines: "My mother is my disgrace. I am my mother's disgrace. I will come to understand and feel this better when I am a woman. My mother did something so awful to my godmother that she has barely forgiven her. My birthday is evil and I am degraded. I must pray daily that the sins of my mother are not visited on my head. I must forget my mother and let all other people forget her too. I am different from others and set apart. My life has a shadow on it. I cannot hope to be loved as I am, but if I am submissive, self-denying and hard-working I might be able to win some love for myself." The story that Esther's godmother has conveyed to her may be evil and erroneous, but the fact that Esther compulsively repeats it, commits to a program of reparation, and pledges to try and win some love means that she has completely internalized the extreme views of her godmother and even believes, as William Axton claims that she is inherently "tainted" and "repulsive."[6] This is particularly significant because, as I will show, her godmother's warnings and directives (as harmful and wicked as they are) actually come to pass within the idiosyncratic terms of Esther's narrative. Indeed, Esther does go on to set herself apart from others by contracting a disfiguring disease which is quite literally visited upon her head; and she forgets her "disgraceful" biological mother and seeks to ensure that all others forget her by firstly, "accidentally" divesting herself (through disease) of her mother's good looks; secondly, painting a consistently negative (if not to say repellent) portrait of her; and thirdly, omitting to speak of her following her death.

Esther's vow to win some love is also significant for another reason. According to Marcia Renee Goodman:

> The belief that if she does "some good to someone" she will be loved, and the notion that love can be "won," that it is an achievement for which one works, rather than a feeling that two people come to share and to nurture between them, mark Esther's masculine gender affiliation, her aspirations in the symbolic, abstract, hierarchical world of the father in which achievement promises acceptance. Love here is something one earns or competes for, a mark of success rather than a reciprocal, shared process.[7]

Goodman's argument here stems from her conviction that "the characterization of Esther portrays many of Dickens' own psychological conflicts,"[8] so while Esther may portray "many of the characteristics which our culture still recognizes and reproduces as important constituents of feminine identity," she also "enacts the conflicts, tensions, angers, fears, and hurt of the masculine constructed psyche."[9] For Goodman, the masculine side of Esther's character becomes manifest primarily in relation to her mother. Esther's godmother is not, of course, Esther's biological mother, but she is effectively her surrogate mother and she is also, as Lawrence Frank puts it, "the woman who has perhaps done more to define her being than even the mother whose 'disgrace' she is."[10] Accordingly, it is telling that the first real glimpse of Esther's masculine dimension appears just after she has described the profound trauma that she has suffered at the hands of her primary caregiver. However, while I would agree that Esther goes on to display a masculine gender affiliation in seeking to maximize all of her chances to *win* love, I believe she can equally be said to display this affiliation because she maximizes all of her chances to *defeat* those who do not allow her to win their love. Certainly, Esther successfully wins the hearts of many throughout the book (including all of the staff and boarders at Greenleaf; John Jarndyce, Ada, Richard, Caddy Jellyby, Charley and Mr. Woodcourt), but there are two people who, while close to Esther in a familial sense, nevertheless resolutely refuse to be "won over" by Esther. Regrettably for Esther, these people are her "mothers," Miss Barbary and Lady Dedlock; and Esther uses all the powers at her disposal (as limited as they are) to diminish, negate, and expel them from her life.

How does Esther defeat Miss Barbary? There are a number of ways in which Esther attempts to get back at the woman who takes it upon herself to become her primary caretaker but nonetheless treats her with coldness and cruelty. Primarily, she does this in a retrospective or delayed sense. As indicated earlier, as an adult she employs from the outset emotive rhetoric in her first-person narrative to implicitly condemn her godmother. Added to this, she sets up a binary opposition in her narrative between her "dear old doll" and Miss Barbary. The beautiful doll, although inanimate, nevertheless "listens" to Esther's secrets and is "patient" with her shortcomings. She is also "faithful" and receptive towards Esther. Indeed, she "expects" or even looks forward to seeing Esther, and within her presence Esther is immediately put at ease. By contrast, Miss Barbary may be angelic in appearance but her temperament is ugly. Severe and cruel, she could never be called "dear" or "faithful." Displaying no interest in Esther (let alone her secrets or observations) she is appallingly blunt and condemning about Esther's ostensible faults and inherited guilt. In addition, she displays no allegiance to Esther, is singularly unapproachable and does everything within her power to put up barriers to intimacy. With her doll Esther feels "at home" and unrestrained, but with Miss Barbary she feels "so poor, so trifling and so far off" (63). The stark juxtaposition between the two even extends to their respective endings. As Keith Easley states:

> The affectionate burial of the doll "under the tree that shaded my old window" contrasts with the aunt's funeral, limited to a passing reference that it happened the day after. When the "dear old doll" later comes to [Esther's] mind, we are told once more where it, not the aunt, was buried.[11]

Certainly, the doll is not a person and Esther projects positive qualities on to it but the doll still possesses all of the qualities that Esther's godmother does not. Accordingly, the same rhetorical strategy that Dickens uses in the autobiographical fragment (and *David Copperfield*) appears here: a deficient "mother" is pointedly set against an "all good" person; the only difference is that in *this* case the person[12] is inanimate. Interestingly, too, of the little intelligence that Esther is prepared to credit herself with, none of it can be said to have been passed on by her primary caretaker. Esther, as we know, states from the outset that her powers of comprehension are enhanced when she loves a person "very tenderly" (63) but because this assertion comes directly after the eulogistic treatment of her faithful doll and there is no mention at this stage of her primary caretaker, there is the strong suggestion that the much loved doll is the one who has inspired or awakened Esther's capacity for understanding. This is highly significant if one recalls Dickens's autobiographical fragment. In that document, Dickens, as noted, was not prepared to give his mother any credit for his powers of observation even though she was openly admired for her intensely observant nature and extraordinary gifts of narration, mimicry and acting.

Dickens indeed effectively denied the influence of his mother and structured his autobiographical piece to imply that he alone was responsible for his considerable powers of perception. If we compare this to Esther's explanation for her "silent way of noticing" (63) we can see that a similar dynamic is at work. Esther's mental apprehension becomes brighter when *she* favorably concentrates *her feelings* upon another person. She *alone* is responsible for her mental powers. It is also important to note that Esther links comprehension to love. As a result, she effectively asserts, as Keith Easley puts it, that "love is the key to better understanding,"[13] and again, as she has devoted the first two paragraphs of her "portion of these pages" (62) to a panegyric of her doll rather than her primary caretaker, there is the distinct intimation that her primary caretaker is either unloving or unlovable and therefore devoid of perspicacity. Casting about for support, Esther turns to her faithful doll and obsessively relates the story of her birthday. She also chatters to the doll about her deep wish to mend the "fault" that she was born with. However, this "fault" is something for which she feels guilty and yet innocent. This paradoxical state of guilty innocence is again all too reminiscent of Dickens's autobiographical fragment. As we know, after he began his servitude at the blacking warehouse and was forced to live away from his family, Dickens wrote: "I (small Cain that I was, except that I had never done harm to anyone) was handed over as a lodger to a reduced old lady."[14] As his mother, owing to financial circumstances, was forced to take the rest of the family to live with Dickens's father in the Marshalsea Prison, we can safely assume that it was his mother who handed him over as a lodger to the reduced old lady. This is not stated in Dickens's narrative, but there is definitely a muted accusation that his mother has unfairly found him guilty or unworthy and has accordingly "sentenced" him to this awful fate away from his family.[15] The "story," then, is not all that different from Esther's "story."

Esther at heart believes herself to be innocent, yet she has been made to feel guilty, displaced, unworthy and shameful by her godmother and while, like Dickens, she doesn't confront her primary caregiver about this or *directly* condemn her within her retrospective narrative, there is nonetheless a very similar veiled accusation in her narrative that her godmother has unjustly "sentenced" her to an awful fate of damnation.

Perhaps the most direct way that Esther seeks to hit out at her godmother is through an "all too apt" Bible reading. "One dreadful night" Esther reads aloud to her godmother a passage from the Bible which deals with Christ's mercy towards the woman who has been condemned for adultery:

> "So when they continued asking him, he lifted up himself and said unto them, He that is without sin among you, let him first cast a stone at her!"
> I was stopped by my godmother's rising, putting her hand to her head, and crying out, in an awful voice, from quite another part of the book:
> "Watch ye therefore! Lest coming suddenly he find you sleeping. And what I say unto you, I say unto all, Watch!"
> In an instant, while she stood before me repeating these words, she fell down on the floor. I had no need to cry out; her voice had sounded through the house, and been heard in the street.
> She was laid upon her bed. For more than a week she lay there, little altered outwardly; with her old handsome resolute frown that I so well knew, carved upon her face. Many and many a time, in the day and in the night, with my head upon the pillow by her that my whispers might be plainer to her, I kissed her, thanked her, prayed for her, asked her for her blessing and forgiveness, entreated her to give me the least sign that she knew or heard me. No, no, no. Her face was immovable. To the very last, and even afterwards, her frown remained unsoftened [66–67].

As is obvious, the cause of Miss Barbary's death is nothing less than her extreme reaction to a key passage in the Bible. This passage concerns the importance of not entering into judgment because no one is without sin. In addition, it stresses the importance of extending compassion and mercy to those who may have sinned. Apparently outraged by this passage, Miss Barbary quotes from an entirely different section of the Bible which concerns the Second Coming of Christ and "St. Mark's call for vigilance against sin."[16] Following this, she conveniently enough drops to the floor and shortly thereafter dies. Certainly, one can view Esther's reading in an entirely innocent light. Jasmine Yong Hall, for instance, writes: "That she is narrating God's words to her godmother removes any sense of Esther's own motivation in reading this particular story."[17]

Nevertheless, because the moral of this parable is so pertinent and obvious, it is not unreasonable to speculate that she may have specifically chosen this passage to highlight the grievously false and deluded nature of her godmother's thinking. After all, it is clear that Esther has a good working knowledge of the Bible because she is immediately aware that her godmother has cried out a quote from "quite another part of the book." At least one critic is of this opinion. According to Lawrence Frank, "Esther implicitly challenges and condemns her aunt by reading from St. John [and] Miss Barbary's response is her desperate attempt to justify herself, and to warn Esther."[18] Frank, however, is bemused by Miss Barbary's choice of quotation: "The lines from St. Mark remain forever ambiguous."[19] A number of critics have sought to explain Miss Barbary's warning. Raymond Conlon, for instance, believes that Miss Barbary's incongruous response reveals "the depth of her fear and dread of sexuality." For Conlon, Miss Barbary senses "that 'he' (personified sexuality, and perhaps 'he' the generic male) attacks when she and others are sleeping."[20] Other critics, however, have viewed this scene as an example of Dickens's antipathy toward religious zealots. Gordon D. Hirsch states:

> Aunt Barbary and her "distorted religion" (xvi) are ridiculed mercilessly by the author — for example, the immediate cause of the aunt's demise is her horrified response to a reference to Christ's mercy toward the woman taken in adultery.[21]

David A. Ward goes a step further and claims that Miss Barbary's extreme reaction may specifically display Dickens's distaste for religious Dissenters:

> In this scene Dickens may have ... intended to use the apocalyptic warning of Miss Barbary and her dramatic physical collapse to align her with the teachings of one of the most well-known and controversial of early nineteenth-century preachers, Edward Irving, who was noted for his millenarianism (i.e., the belief that Christ would soon return to set up a thousand-year reign on earth) as well as for the wild, emotional services at his London chapel, in which worshipers, in the words of one historian, "became 'infected'" with the gift of speaking in tongues.[22]

Explanations aside, there are two important points that should be made about this scene. Firstly, Esther does not reveal just how she came to read this particular passage from the Bible. All Esther tells us is that at the age of fourteen she read the Bible to her godmother at the regular appointed hour and that the particular passage on that evening was taken from St. John and concerned Christ's encounter with "the sinful woman." Esther would appear to be devoid of calculation, but is it wise or even profitable in a critical sense to assume that Esther is artless? Refreshingly, Lawrence Frank is not afraid to question Esther's apparent purity: "Sinned against as she may be, Esther is not fully the innocent, the victim. Her attempts to cope with herself may involve her, like David [Copperfield], in the violation of others."[23] I am sympathetic to this assessment but I am more of the belief that it is Esther's attempts to cope with *others* that involve her in a violation of *her own* integrity. Esther's interaction with Miss Barbary in this scene affords a key example of this. Certainly, Esther may have proceeded to read the passage from St. John because it was simply where she was up to in terms of her nightly readings to Miss Barbary, or she may by chance have opened the Bible to this page; but because we are not told how she alighted on this page, we are left in the dark as to her motivation for reading this "sinful woman" passage. Accordingly, there is a room to posit a third option and that is that Esther is not altogether the victim and is not above wanting to hoist Miss Barbary by her own petard. Indeed, at the age of fourteen the justifiably hurt Esther is very capable of choosing a particularly apposite passage from the Bible and using it as the means by which she can cast the first "stone" that she is able to at her godmother. From this perspective, Miss Barbary's extreme "watch yourself" reaction makes much more sense. Certainly, Esther may wish to present herself as an innocent, nonjudgmental victim, but her lack of contextualization in this instance leaves room to question her intentions and her integrity.

The second point to be made about this memorable scene is the fact that the chapter in which it occurs is called "A Progress." According to Carolyn Dever, the chapter title "refers to its own internal events, to its commencement *in medias res* in the life of Esther Summerson, and also to its position as the third chapter, not the first, of *Bleak House*."[24] David A. Ward holds a different view:

> That [Miss Barbary] dies in a chapter entitled "A Progress" suggests something about the author's attitude toward her religious values. (The chapter perhaps also alludes to John Bunyan's famous allegory of the Christian life, indicating to readers that Esther's story will likewise be a spiritual autobiography.)[25]

Certainly, these conjectures are valid, but here again, perhaps more to the point is the question, Who wrote the chapter title? Has Esther written the title herself or has she left that honor to the omniscient narrator? At no point in *Bleak House* is it clear whether Esther chose her own chapter titles. Nevertheless, the question begs to be asked: If Esther is capable of writing a sizeable "portion" (62) of the tome that is *Bleak House*, why wouldn't she be capable of writing her own chapter titles as well? Some of these titles, as we know, are quite arch. Indeed, two in particular spring to mind — "Telescopic Philanthropy" and "Covering a Multitude of Sins" — and both of these chapters significantly highlight the deficiencies of particular mothers, Mrs. Jellyby and Mrs. Pardiggle respectively. The title "A Progress" is in a similar vein, and there is no disputing the fact that a significant part of the "progress" involves the death of a mother (albeit surrogate) who has been depicted as exceedingly deficient. If we consider the "choice" Bible reading and the "pointed" chapter title, and then take into account the very few avenues for resistance that would have been available to Esther (both as a child and as an adult), it is not too farfetched to suggest that Esther was so hurt and horrified by her godmother's damning condemnation of herself and her biological mother that she subversively employed the Bible to challenge her godmother and this action quite unintentionally precipitated her death. So, too, it is not beyond the realm of possibility that Esther's enduring disgust for her godmother could not only lead her to view her godmother's inglorious demise as little more than a necessary step in her journey towards advancement but also to suggest this through the means of a chapter title within her first-person narrative.

Finally, Esther's wish to defeat Miss Barbary (and, for that matter, her biological mother) is made manifest through what I believe are her self-destructive actions. Critics have focused in various ways on Esther's character. She has by turns been described as selfless; self-deceiving; self-abnegating; self-sacrificing; self-denying; self-depreciating; self-congratulating; self-affirming; self-deprecating; self-restrained and so on,[26] but the idea of her being self-destructive does not appear to have been considered. Most people, however, would consider that a person who recklessly puts herself in harm's way is somewhat self-destructive — and Esther, as I will show, does just that. Indeed, she becomes disfigured and nearly dies as a consequence of her rash actions, but for some reason critics have elided the possibility that she might not be entirely life-affirming. Let us, however, consider Esther's less than ideal background. As we know, Esther as a child suffered horrific, degrading, nullifying verbal abuse — the kind that made her feel responsible for her mother's sexual "sin" and ashamed to be alive. Directly engaging in self-harm may not have been the way that she dealt with this disgusting abuse, but there is room to suggest that when Miss Barbary told Esther to pray daily that the sins of others would not be visited upon her head and to forget her mother and leave all other people to forget her, she left Esther with an internalized revulsion for both herself and her biological mother; and this in turn resulted in Esther developing subconscious destructive desires. These desires, as I will maintain, involved the wish to be consumed by a disease in order to, firstly, relieve or expiate the guilt that she felt at being her mother's disgrace; secondly, rid herself of any genetic resemblance to her apparently disgraceful mother; and, thirdly, punish in effigy both her godmother for her cruelty and her biological mother for her shameful, transgressive behavior.

Certainly, given her sheltered sphere, the opportunities for self-harm would have been minimal, but the means did eventually arise through Esther's ostensibly altruistic determination to put aside considerations for her own safety in order to help others. As we know, Miss Barbary told Esther that it would have been far better if she had never been born. According to John Harrison, a medical practitioner and the author of the provocatively titled book *Love Your Disease: It's Keeping You Healthy*, if a parent tells a child that she was not wanted the child will grow up with a "'don't exist' injunction"[27] and the strength or influence of this injunction will depend upon the force with which it was given. Children of such parents may, as a consequence, go on not to take care of themselves, as Harrison writes:

If someone believes "I shouldn't exist," then certain events are made more likely. He neglects to protect himself against dangerous or life-threatening situations. These people may engage in dangerous sports (motorcycle racing, daredevil stunts). They may join the armed forces and apply for active duty, or become mercenaries. They may become involved in dangerous occupations like illegal drug-trafficking or, in some parts of the world, become policemen. Not all people in the above categories are trying to fulfil their parent's messages to not exist, but dangerous occupations do attract people who are ambivalent about living. So does cancer.

Most people who decide that their parents didn't want them and who subsequently don't take all available measures to stay alive, do not become mercenaries. Instead they may drive under the influence of drugs or alcohol. In these ways they put their lives at risk, getting a thrill from flirting with death, often with tacit parental approval. When these people eventually seriously hurt themselves or kill themselves, we all cry, "What bad luck, to have a fatal accident at such a young age!" But often that was no accident. Why did the young woman, apparently enjoying life and with a successful career, fail to notice the bald tyre on her car? Or if she noticed it, why didn't she take the time and effort to have it changed? Why did the handsome young lawyer fail to notice the oncoming bus as he stepped from the kerb? These people weren't trying hard enough to stay alive. In other words, they had manifested their early childhood decision to "not exist" and exploited available hazards to effect that decision.[28]

While the above argument may consist of modern examples, the general import of Harrison's assertions is, I believe, particularly relevant to the protagonist of *Bleak House*. Esther, I propose, not only neglects to protect herself against dangerous or life-threatening situations, she actually goes out of her way to put herself in these situations. This is not something that critics have generally considered. Geoffrey Thurley, for instance, views the disease that Esther contracts as well outside Esther's control:

> The smallpox that attacks Esther Summerson has the force of a punitive visitation: it is as though she is being punished for the sins of her parents.... There is, in ... Dickens's novel, evidence of that deep ineradicable association of sex and disease, of carnal pleasure and guilt, which occurs in so much great tragedy, and which is perhaps its *raison d'être*.[29]

On the surface it may appear that the disease that attacks Esther has the force of a punishment sent by God, but if we turn to the chapter in the book where Esther contracts the disease — "Nurse and Patient" — we will see that Esther, of her own volition, puts herself in harm's way not just once but twice. In the first instance, Esther is told by her little maid, Charley, that while Esther was away from Bleak House, the brickmaker's wife, Jenny, had come to the property three or four days running hoping to see Esther. Unsuccessful in this quest, Jenny was later seen by Charley at the doctor's shop where she was apparently trying to get medicine for a poor, sick orphan boy who had come tramping from London and didn't know his destination. Charley, as Esther notes, is very affected by the boy's plight and keen to take Esther to see him at Jenny's house:

> My little maid's face was so eager, and her quiet hands were folded so closely in one another as she stood looking at me, that I had no great difficulty in reading her thoughts. "Well, Charley," said I, "it appears to me that you and I can do no better than go round to Jenny's and see what's the matter."
>
> The alacrity with which Charley brought my bonnet and veil, and, having dressed me, quaintly pinned herself into her warm shawl and made herself look like a little old woman, sufficiently expressed her readiness. So Charley and I, without saying anything to any one, went out [484].

With no consideration for the consequences, Esther immediately sets out to see someone who is obviously sick and highly disoriented. Recklessly, she does not tell her guardian that she is going out and strangely, given her wish to help, she takes nothing with her in the way of medicine, blankets or food. Arriving at Jenny's place, Esther sees the "wretched boy" (485) cowering and shaking uncontrollably and she watches as Charley sits him down and draws his rags around him to keep him warm. Shortly thereafter, Esther ineffectually explains to the boy why she has come: "I came to see if I could do you any good," said I. "What is the matter with you?" (486) The boy then describes his symptoms:

> "I'm a-being froze," returned the boy, hoarsely, with his haggard gaze wandering about me, "and then burnt up, and then froze, and then burnt up, ever so many times in an hour. And my head's all sleepy, and all a-going mad-like — and I'm so dry — and my bones isn't half so much bones as pain" [486].

Certainly, as we know, Esther has declared that she is not clever and has "always" known it (62) but under the circumstances even the most foolish or unworldly person would realize that the boy is probably highly contagious. This is, in fact, confirmed when, after Esther has taken the boy home with her, "the dear old infant" (577) Skimpole immediately cautions Mr. Jarndyce against having him at Bleak House:

> "You had better turn him out," said Mr. Skimpole.
>
> "What do you mean?" inquired my guardian, almost sternly.
>
> "My dear Jarndyce," said Mr. Skimpole, "you know what I am: I am a child. Be cross to me, if I deserve it. But I have a constitutional objection to this sort of thing. I always had, when I was a medical man. He's not safe, you know. There's a very bad sort of fever about him" [489].

While Skimpole's suggestion is no doubt intended to reflect badly upon him, there is no mistaking the fact that Esther's actions have been highly irresponsible. Not only has she put herself at risk but she has endangered her maid Charley, Mr. Jarndyce, Mr. Skimpole and all of the servants at Bleak House. At no stage, however, does such a consideration even cross her mind. Indeed, she is so oblivious that she actually takes pleasure (quite condescendingly) in the kindness that the Bleak House servants display towards the sick boy:

> The servants compassionating his miserable state, and being very anxious to help, we soon got the loft-room ready; and some of the men about the house carried

him across the wet yard, well wrapped up. It was pleasant to observe how kind they were to him, and how there appeared to be a general impression among them that frequently calling him "Old Chap" was likely to revive his spirits. Charley directed the operations, and went to and fro between the loft-room and the house with such little stimulants and comforts as we thought it safe to give him [491].

Esther's irresponsibility here is particularly ironic in light of the fact that she later takes Skimpole to task for his irresponsibility:

I delicately said, that there was a responsibility in encouraging Richard.

"Responsibility, my dear Miss Summerson? He repeated, catching at the word with the pleasantest smile. "I am the last man in the world for such a thing. I never was responsible in my life — I can't be."

"I am afraid everybody is obliged to be," said I, timidly enough: he being so much older and more clever than I [586].

Esther might fundamentally believe that everybody is obliged to be responsible but her own highly questionable earlier actions most certainly belie this. Added to this, Esther may say that she had no idea when she took it upon herself to go and see the sick boy what might befall her, but there is clear evidence that at a subconscious level she was very aware of the serious ramifications of her decision. Indeed, on the cold, wild and gloomy night when she rushes off to assist Jenny with the sick boy she is ominously aware that the experience will fundamentally change her:

I had no thought, that night — none, I am quite sure — of what was soon to happen to me. But I have always remembered since, that when we had stopped at the garden-gate to look up at the sky, and when we went upon our way, I had for a moment an undefinable impression of myself as being something different from what I then was. I know it was then, and there, that I had it. I have ever since connected the feeling with that spot and time, and with everything associated with that spot and time, to the distant voices in the town, the barking of a dog, and the sound of wheels coming down the miry hill [484–85].

Despite her presentiment, Esther does not immediately contract the disease. Rather, the boy, Jo (perhaps, unlike Esther, considering the risk of infecting others) runs away from Bleak House. A search is mounted for five days but no trace of him is found. Following this, Esther's attention is "diverted" (493) by the fact that her maid has contracted the disease:

As Charley was at her writing again in my room in the evening, and as I sat opposite to her at work, I felt the table tremble. Looking up, I saw my little maid shivering from head to foot.

"Charley," said I, "are you so cold?"

"I think I am miss," she replied. "I don't know what it is. I can't hold myself still. I felt so, yesterday; at about this same time, miss. Don't be uneasy. I think I'm ill" [493–94].

Here then is the second instance where Esther decides to put herself in harm's way. Immediately, Esther determines that she will take care of Charley during her illness. In addition, rather than moving Charley to another part of the house, Esther decides to put Charley in her own bedroom. Esther's resolve is so strong that her guardian, Jarndyce, appears to have little or no say in the matter:

> Charley fell ill. In twelve hours she was very ill. I moved her to my room, and laid her in my bed, and sat down quietly to nurse her. I told my guardian all about it, and why I felt it was necessary that I should seclude myself [494].

During the protracted illness, Charley falls "into heavy danger of death" (494) but Esther sits by her all the while and holds her head in her arms. Again, at no point does Esther consider her own safety but, significantly, she is very worried about her darling Ada's welfare and takes every precaution to ensure that Ada will not get the disease:

> Ada called to me to let her in; but I said, "Not now, my dearest. Go away. There's nothing the matter; I will come to you presently." Ah! it was a long time, before my darling girl and I were companions again" [494].

Esther is so frightened in fact of Ada coming in contact with the disease that whenever Ada comes beneath the window to talk to Esther, she stands "behind the window-curtain listening and replying, but not so much as looking out!" (494). Unsurprisingly, given her readiness to put herself in risky situations, Esther catches the disease, but her chief concern during her illness is to protect Ada:

> "Now Charley, when she knows I am ill, she will try to make her way into the room. Keep her out, Charley, if you love me truly, to the last! Charley, if you let her in but once, only to look upon me for one moment as I lie here, I shall die!" [497].

Not simply courting death, Esther threatens death. However, while one can identify a willingness to flirt with death, it is questionable whether Esther actually wants to die. Dying, one suspects, would be too easy for the guilt-plagued Esther. Instead, she wants at a subconscious level to physically harm herself to atone for the guilt that she feels at being her mother's disgrace and, secondly, to punish her punitive godmother and disgraceful mother in absentia for their sins against her and against themselves. There are two ways that these motives become manifest. The first motive, atonement, may be found in the hallucinations that Esther experiences at the height of her feverish disease, and the second motive, revenge, may be found in the various ways that Esther describes her appearance after she has "recovered" from the disease.

In the first recorded hallucination that Esther experiences, she labors up enormous staircases "piled up to the sky" (544), but all the way, like "a worm in a garden path" (544), she encounters obstacles and is forced to turn back only to labor again. According to David Ward:

> The worm that she likens herself to implies, of course, the lowliness of her own self-image, but ... a religious frame of reference might apply, whether it be "worm" as a term of self-revilement common to religious discourse (it appears, for example, in a famous hymn by the Nonconformist theologian Isaac Watts) or as a symbol of the terrors of hell awaiting the damned, "Where their worm dieth not, and the fire is not quenched" [Mark 10:9].[30]

As we recall, Miss Barbary told Esther that she was set apart from others because she and her mother had sinned. So, too, the last words that she uttered exhorted Esther to be ever vigilant against sin. A deep sense that she has been condemned to hell and a corresponding need to atone for this is thereby displayed in this graphic image. Esther's guilt is in fact so profound that she believes that no matter what she does, she will never get beyond it. Endless, daunting, hard labor is her sentence, and this, of course, is perfectly in keeping with Miss Barbary's prescription for her benighted state: "Submission, self-denial, diligent work, are the preparations for a life begun with such a shadow on it" (65).

In the second hallucination, Esther experiences even greater distress:

> Dare I hint at that worse time when, strung together somewhere in great black space, there was a flaming necklace, or ring, or starry circle of some kind, of which *I* was one of the beads! And when my only prayer was to be taken off from the rest, and when it was such inexplicable agony and misery to be a part of the dreadful thing? [544].

Critics have tended to single out this passage because of its extreme angst. For Lawrence Frank:

> The passage is unique in Dickens's novels. There is no other place in which Dickens so completely expresses what we would call both religious and existential despair. Esther's prayer "to be taken off from the rest" is her denial of herself and the chain of interconnectedness which comprises the human condition.[31]

Helena Michie, while sympathetic to this reading, goes a step further and claims that in this passage, Esther effectively prefigures her separation from her ornamental mother:

> While this moment in Esther's illness has been seen as indicating her desire to separate herself from the community and from her attendant responsibilities, it can also be seen as a prophetic separation from her mother whose association with jewelry begins with her introduction into the text as living in a world wrapped up in "jeweller's cotton." "Necklace" and "ring" suggest a feminized image of teleology and the marriage toward which novelistic teleology moves. Esther seems to be resisting the novel's apparent insistence that she, like Rosa, become one of her mother's "beads," that she be joined and reunited with her mother.[32]

For Timothy Peltason, however, the passage signifies the point in Esther's life where she indulges (albeit briefly) in a "death wish."[33] Certainly, at this stage of her narrative Esther evinces an exceedingly strong desire to remove herself from something, but whether it is from the community, her mother, or her life is a moot point. Perhaps the most plausible explanation for Esther's second hallucination is provided by David Ward:

> It is Biblical images of damnation that, more than anything else, seem to lie behind Esther's most bizarre and horrifying apparition, in which she is part of a "flaming necklace, or ring, or starry circle" that is "strung together somewhere in great black space." The terror here is of a loss of control — an understandable fear for someone in the throes of a life-threatening illness — but it seems also, given our knowledge of Esther's childhood trauma, a terror of divine retribution, of the ominous Scriptural edicts that the Godless would be "cast out into outer darkness" (Matthew 8:12), that they would be "wandering stars to whom is reserved the blackness of darkness forever" (Jude 13). It was Miss Barbary, of course, who had implanted such horrors in Esther's mind, telling her that she had been "set apart" as a special object of God's displeasure, and it is scenes like this one on Esther's troubled sickbed that reveal how difficult it is for her to completely disown that imputed image.[34]

This is a very persuasive reading. By this token, if Esther wants to get beyond anything it is her belief (erroneous as it may be) that she is godless and set apart. Praying to be taken off the awful starry circle is thereby yet another indication that Esther feels incredibly guilty about the shame of her birth and, one suspects, she will go to *any* length to atone for this, even if it means jeopardizing her life.

Turning now to the ways in which Esther describes her appearance after she has recovered from her disease, it is particularly interesting that the ravages of the disease appear to be confined to Esther's head. As we recall, Miss Barbary's injunction to Esther was to "pray daily that the sins of others be not visited upon your head, according to what is written" (65). Ironically enough, through the medium of the disease, this quite literally comes to pass. There is no sense that the rest of Esther's body is scarred at all. Certainly, Dickens may have shied away from describing bodily scars owing to concerns about modesty and propriety but even so, it is very strange that there is nothing in the text to suggest that anything other than Esther's face was subject to the devastation of the disease. At the very least, one would expect that Esther's hands or arms would have been scarred but this is not even remotely intimated:

> I put my hair aside, and looked at the reflection in the mirror, encouraged by seeing how placidly it looked at me. I was very much changed — O very, very much. At first, my face was so strange to me, that I think I should have put my hands before it and started back, but for the encouragement I have mentioned. Very soon it became more familiar, and then I knew the extent of the alteration in it better than I had done at first. It was not like what I had expected; but I had expected nothing definite, and I dare say anything definite would have surprised me.
> I had never been a beauty, and had never thought myself one; but I had been very different from this. It was all gone now. Heaven was so good to me, that I could let it go with a few not bitter tears, and could stand there arranging my hair for the night quite thankfully [559].

Notably, too, Esther is able to "let [her face] go" quite easily. Indeed, earlier when Charley can't help but give in to grief over the loss of Esther's good looks, Esther consoles her with the words: "It matters very little, Charley. I hope I can do without my old face very well" (546). So while the disease has "gone" to Esther's head she refuses to let it get to her at a deeper level. Assuredly, Dickens may have wished to stress that the virtuous Esther was devoid of vanity, but the fact remains that Esther sheds but "a few" tears and only fleetingly feels the loss of her "old face," as she says:

> I knew the worst now, and was composed to it. I shall not conceal, as I go on, the weaknesses I could not quite conquer; but they always passed from me soon, and the happier frame of mind stayed by me faithfully [560].

Furthermore, as Esther seeks to reestablish her strength, she comes to view the loss of her former face as a minor event which can be easily be forgotten:

> I had scarcely any time to think about that little loss of mine, and was almost always cheerful. If I did think of it at odd moments now and then, I had only to be busy and forget it. I felt it more than I had hoped I should, once, when a child said "Mother, why is the lady not a pretty lady now, like she used to be?" But when I found the child was not less fond of me, and drew its soft hand over my face with a kind of pitying protection in its touch, that soon set me up again [561–62].

As is evident, Esther's "masculine" childhood resolve to *win* warmth and affection takes precedence over the pain of losing her good looks. That Esther was considered to be attractive[35] is made clear by the child's innocent question. So while Esther may be able to dismiss her previous looks with the words "I had never been a beauty, and had never thought myself one," she nevertheless records an encounter with an artless child to stress the enormity of her loss. In addition, the "fond" child draws its "soft hand" over Esther's face "with a kind of pitying protection in its touch." This suggests that the child seeks to protect the poor, defenseless Esther by covering her face. This is particularly significant because this action is actually analogous to what Esther can be said to have done to herself through contracting a feverish, scar-inducing disease. Indeed, while in one sense the disease damages or ravages Esther's appearance, in another it affords her the opportunity to protectively cover herself so that she no longer needs to directly face her "disgraceful" self or her tainted maternal inheritance. According to Helena Michie, Esther's illness provides her with the means to preemptively reject her mother: "Before Lady Dedlock can reject Esther, Esther has inscribed the difference between them on her own face. The bodily cost of difference is, for Esther, worth the possession, no matter how tenuous, of a self."[36] Certainly, this is a very valid point, but I would instead argue that Esther's illness provides her with the means to abject both her biological mother and her adoptive mother[37] and to "re-cover" from them.[38]

Aside from the near-fatal disease that Esther contracts (which conveniently overwrites any resemblance that she may have to her biological mother) how else does Esther subconsciously express the disgust that she feels towards the woman who brought her into the world? The first thing, as we know, that Esther learns about her mother is that her mother is her disgrace just as she is her mother's disgrace. Owing to this, she is directed by Miss Barbary to forget her mother and to allow "all other people" to forget her (65). Miss Barbary is, of course, depicted in a far from favorable light, but her warped answer to Esther's plight is nonetheless completely borne out by the novel. Esther, whether she knows it or not, makes it her mission to judge her mother as disgraceful and to ultimately erase her from her consciousness and the consciousness of others. Indeed, even before Esther knows that Lady Dedlock is her mother, she instinctively views her in a highly judgmental way. Added to this, as soon as she becomes aware that Lady Dedlock is her mother, she rejoices over the loss of her physical resemblance to her mother; obliterates all traces of her through burning her confessional letter; unfavorably juxtaposes her mother's actions against those of her much more loving friend Ada; and at the last, consigns her mother to oblivion (in her mind and in her narrative) after her mother has all too obligingly died of "terror and [her] conscience" (864).

The first time that Esther sees her biological mother (although she doesn't know her as such) is in a church and, significantly, her mother's entrance is presaged by the words of the service: "Enter not into judgement with thy servant, O Lord, for in thy sight —" (304). While speaking of not entering into judgment, the words are those of imputation and they are immediately linked to the commanding presence of a beautiful woman who "throws" Esther into a state of extreme perturbation:

> But why her face should be, in a confused way, like a broken glass to me, in which I saw scraps of old remembrances; and why I should be so fluttered and troubled (for I was still), by having casually met her eyes; I could not think [304].

Esther also unaccountably recalls the lingering pain of her childhood:

> And, very strangely, there was something quickened within me, associated with the lonely days at my godmother's; yes, away even to the days when I had stood on tiptoe to dress myself at my little glass, after dressing my doll. And this, although I had never seen this lady's face before in all my life — I was quite sure of it — absolutely certain [304].

A state of being lonely, small, entirely unsupported and not quite "in the picture" is therefore associated with this handsome woman. So, too, a state of quasi-mothering (Esther dressing her doll), rather than being mothered, is linked to this woman's face. Interestingly, the words of the service are taken over in Esther's mind by the voice of her godmother: "Very strangely, I seemed to hear them, not in the reader's voice, but in the well-remembered voice of my godmother" (305). This leads Esther to consider the physical resemblance between her godmother and Lady Dedlock:

> This made me think, did Lady Dedlock's face accidentally resemble my god-mother's? It might be that it did, a little; but the expression was so different and the stern decision which had worn into my godmother's face, like weather into rocks, was so completely wanting in the face before me, that it could not be that resemblance which had struck me. Neither did I know the loftiness and haughtiness of Lady Dedlock's face, at all, in any one [305].

While the sermon may ostensibly prompt Esther to become aware of the physical similarity between Lady Dedlock and Miss Barbary, the fact that it concerns judgment and is spoken in Esther's mind by the highly judgmental Miss Barbary, would suggest that Lady Dedlock is a woman who evokes judgment or has done something that would immediately elicit censure. This is confirmed when Esther cannot refrain from judging Lady Dedlock herself. Indeed, even though Lady Dedlock has not spoken a word, Esther definitively tells us that she has never before come across such arrogance in a person. Lady Dedlock is thereby cast in an extremely negative light, and this is reinforced by the incongruous connection that Esther seeks to forge between Lady Dedlock and her miserable childhood:

> And yet I—I, little Esther Summerson, the child who lived a life apart, and on whose birthday there was no rejoicing — seemed to arise before my own eyes, evoked out of the past by some power in this fashionable lady, whom I not only entertained no fancy that I had ever seen, but whom I perfectly well knew I had never seen until that hour [305].

While this sentence seeks to draw an inexplicable association between the lowly Esther and the powerful, fashionable Lady Dedlock, there is nonetheless an unmistakable hint of reproach. Indeed, Esther's jumbled words and apparent confusion cannot mask the fact that she believes that Lady Dedlock is directly responsible for drawing forth an image of herself as a neglected, damned and isolated child. In such a way, she implicitly implicates Lady Dedlock in the agony of her childhood.

Esther gradually overcomes her "strange emotion" (305), but the lasting sense is that the beautiful and self-possessed Lady Dedlock has not awoken any positive emotions in Esther. Indeed, she has served only to elicit feelings of abandonment, desolation and powerlessness. Such an extreme reaction is strange, to say the least. Even if we credit Esther with a sixth sense, it must be said that her negative response is decidedly illogical and premature. Given Lady Dedlock's evident stature within the community and handsome appearance one would expect that Esther would feel nervous excitement, admiration or even awe. So, too, one would expect that the humble Esther would wax lyrical about seeing such a fine lady. Certainly, she would not have written about her in the kind of terms that Skimpole reserves for Sir Leicester: "Mighty potentate, here *is* my homage!"(306) Nonetheless a modicum of admiration from the young woman who had, as a child, resolved to grow up to be "industrious, contented, and kind-hearted" would have been a decidedly more appropriate and credible reaction.

If the first impression that Esther forms of Lady Dedlock is not affirmative, then the second impression that she forms is hardly more favorable. Close to a week later, while rambling in the woods, Esther and her companions Jarndyce and Ada are forced to take shelter in a keeper's lodge when a storm breaks. There, they encounter Lady Dedlock, who has also sought shelter. Hearing her speak for the first time, Esther once again inexplicably sees visions of herself, and when Lady Dedlock happens to stand close to her, she responds with something akin to fear:

> She stood behind my chair, with her hand upon it. I saw her with her hand close to my shoulder when I turned my head.
> "I have frightened you?" she said.
> No. It was not fright. Why should I be frightened? [309].

Esther may deny that she feels frightened and ask why she should feel fright but she has nonetheless had a visceral reaction that would easily sit within the continuum of mild trepidation to outright horror, and here again, given the context, her negative reaction makes little sense. Even if Esther were aware at some level that this grand lady bore some relation to her life, a more natural and comprehensible reaction would have been one of nervous surprise. This, however, is out of the question. Esther, it seems, is far from impressed with Lady Dedlock. Describing Lady Dedlock's interaction with Mr. Jarndyce, Esther writes:

> She had given him her hand, in an indifferent way that seemed habitual to her, and spoke in a correspondingly indifferent manner, though in a very pleasant voice. She was as graceful as she was beautiful; perfectly self-possessed; and had the air, I thought, of being able to attract and interest any one, if she thought it worth her while [309].

Certainly, while Esther details some of Lady Dedlock's pleasing features, this is nonetheless a damning portrait which implicitly asserts that Lady Dedlock is indifferent, false, feckless and self-interested. Warming to her theme, Esther continues in this highly critical and arch manner: "There was something very winning in her haughty manner..." (310), and this is reinforced by the way that Esther speaks of her formal presentation to Lady Dedlock:

> "Miss Summerson really is my ward," said Mr. Jarndyce. "I am responsible to no Lord Chancellor in her case."
> "Has Miss Summerson lost both her parents?" said my Lady.
> "Yes."
> "She is very fortunate in her guardian."
> Lady Dedlock looked at me, and I looked at her, and said I was indeed. All

at once she turned from me with a hasty air, almost expressive of displeasure or dislike [310].

Here Esther unequivocally depicts Lady Dedlock as rejecting her just after she has spoken to her for the very first time. Lady Dedlock even turns away from Esther as though she is repulsed, and in such a way Esther suggests that Lady Dedlock eliminates her from her consciousness before she has even got to know her. So, too, Esther suggests that Lady Dedlock is so self-centered that she is barely conscious of anyone else:

> With her air of superiority, and power, and fascination, and I know not what, she seemed to regard Ada and me as little more than children. So, as she slightly laughed, and afterwards sat looking at the rain, she was as self-possessed, and as free to occupy herself with her own thoughts, as if she had been alone [310].

Finally, when Lady Dedlock's carriage arrives to collect her, Esther pointedly remarks that Lady Dedlock specifically ignores her in her leavetaking: "She took a graceful leave of Ada — none of me" (311). The kind of favoritism that is displayed here is also apparent in Lady Dedlock's treatment of her servants. When Lady Dedlock's maid Hortense arrives in a carriage with a pretty girl attendant, Lady Dedlock humiliates Hortense for presuming that she was called upon to attend her:

> "What now?" said Lady Dedlock. "Two!"
> "I am your maid, my Lady, at the present," said the French-woman. "The message was for the attendant."
> "I was afraid you might mean me, my Lady," said the pretty girl.
> "I did mean you, child," replied her mistress, calmly. "Put that shawl on me."
> She slightly stooped her shoulders to receive it, and the pretty girl lightly dropped it in its place. The Frenchwoman stood unnoticed, looking on with her lips very tightly set [311].

To add insult to injury, Lady Dedlock then drives off in the carriage with the pretty girl in attendance, leaving Hortense behind to make her own way back. Deeply incensed, Hortense slips off her shoes and walks back barefooted "through the wettest of the wet grass" (312). A thoroughly discreditable portrait of Lady Dedlock is thereby drawn. Indeed, Esther leaves no doubt that Lady Dedlock is interested in acknowledging only those that she deems to be of value. All others are cast aside as so much waste.

Turning now to Esther's final encounter with her mother, it is very interesting that this encounter is directly preceded by an event that displays Esther's condoning attitude towards those who are prepared to cover up the truth in the interests of protecting those who suffer from a deficiency. This event, ostensibly connected with Esther's sense of inferiority owing to the scars that she has been left with following her illness, has Esther championing deception and elevating its adherents to the ranks of the noble:

There were many little occurrences which suggested to me, with great consolation, how natural it is to gentle hearts to be considerate and delicate towards any inferiority. One of these particularly touched me. I happened to stroll into the little church when a marriage was just concluded, and the young couple had to sign the register.

The bridegroom, to whom the pen was handed first, made a rude cross for his mark; the bride, who came next, did the same. Now I had known the bride, when I was last there, not only as the prettiest girl in the place, but as having quite distinguished herself in the school; and I could not help looking at her with some surprise. She came aside and whispered to me, while tears of honest love and admiration stood in her bright eyes, "He's a dear good fellow, miss; but he can't write, yet — he's going to learn of me — and I wouldn't shame him for the world!" Why, what had I to fear, I thought, when there was this nobility in the soul of a labouring man's daughter! [562].

For Esther it is noble, then, to engage in an illusion or a fraud if one is to protect the feelings of an "inferior" person, and this is just what she does when she comes to understand that Lady Dedlock — the woman whom she has formerly depicted as inferior despite her elevated rank — is in actual fact her "disgraceful" mother.

Coming with Charley to rest at "a favourite spot of mine in the park-woods of Chesney Wold" (562) Esther nonetheless describes her strong aversion towards the house at Chesney Wold:

The indefinable feeling with which Lady Dedlock had impressed me, may have had some influence in keeping me from the house even when she was absent. I am not sure. Her face and figure were associated with it, naturally; but I cannot say that they repelled me from it, though something did. For whatever reason or no reason, I had never once gone near it, down to the day at which my story now arrives [563].

Just as the house in which Lady Dedlock resides is strangely repellent to Esther, so, too, is Lady Dedlock when she rushes towards Esther with an expression of maternal love and solicitude:

I was fluttered by her being unexpectedly so near (she was almost within speaking distance before I knew her), and would have risen to continue my walk. But I could not. I was rendered motionless. Not so much by her hurried gesture of entreaty, not so much by her quick advance and outstretched hands, not so much by the great change in her manner, and in the absence of her haughty self-restraint, as by a something in her face that I had pined for and dreamed of when I was a little child; something I had never seen in any face; something I had never seen in hers before.

A dread and faintness fell upon me, and I called to Charley [563].

Lady Dedlock's look may have been something that Esther had always pined for but it clearly brings her no joy. Instead, Esther instinctively wishes to flee, feels horror and seeks to protect herself by calling over her attendant. Moderating her behavior, Lady Dedlock tries to calm Esther, but Esther feels powerless, disoriented and sick:

I could no more have removed my eyes from her pale face, than I could have stirred from the bench on which I sat. She gave me her hand; and its deadly coldness, so at variance with the enforced composure of her features, deepened the fascination that overpowered me. I cannot say what was in my whirling thoughts.

"You are recovering again?" she asked kindly.

"I was quite well but a moment ago, Lady Dedlock" [563–64].

Here Esther is beset by abjection. As Julia Kristeva writes:

A massive and sudden emergence of uncanniness, which, familiar as it might have been in an opaque and forgotten life, now harries me as radically separate, loathsome. Not me. Not that. But not nothing, either. A "something" that I do not recognize as a thing. A weight of meaninglessness, about which there is nothing insignificant, and which crushes me. On the edge of non-existence and hallucination, of a reality that, if I acknowledge it, annihilates me.[39]

Esther may acquiesce to Lady Dedlock's request to send her attendant Charley home but she is terrified of this woman who reminds her of death:

Lady Dedlock sat down on the seat beside me.

I cannot tell in any words what the state of my mind was, when I saw in her hand my handkerchief, with which I had covered the dead baby.

I looked at her; but I could not see her, I could not hear her, I could not draw my breath. The beating of my heart was so violent and wild, that I felt as if my life were breaking from me [565].

Not simply are Lady Dedlock's hands as cold as death but she carries the very article that Esther had used to cover up death. Like a corpse, then, Lady Dedlock is "death infecting life"[40] and Esther is stricken with horror. Compounding matters, Lady Dedlock reveals that Esther is intimately and inextricably tied to her. Indeed, she is nothing less than Esther's mother:

But when she caught me to her breast, kissed me, wept over me, compassionated me, and called me back to myself; when she fell on her knees and cried to me, "O my child, my child, I am your wicked and unhappy mother! O try to forgive me!"—when I saw her at my feet on the bare earth in her great agony of mind, I felt, through all my tumult of emotion, a burst of gratitude to the providence of God that I was so changed as that I never could disgrace her by any trace of likeness; as that nobody could ever now look at me, and look at her, and remotely think of any near tie between us [565].

Shockingly, Esther feels no elation at finding her mother at long last but only gratitude that her scars have covered up her likeness to her mother so that she cannot disgrace her. Like the young woman who "nobly" sought to cover up her literacy so that she would not bring shame upon her illiterate husband, Esther "nobly" feels relief that her scar-covered face means that she cannot bring shame upon her self-confessed "wicked" mother. Immediately then, Esther's only joy at meeting her mother stems from the fact that she has been able through God's help to cover up her inherited beauty in the interests of denying her connection with her mother. According to Lawrence Frank:

> Esther's gratitude is double-edged to say the least. The tie binding the two, and seemingly sundered by Esther's illness, reaches beyond that between mother and daughter. The relinquished likeness is a relinquished potentiality. Esther will never encounter the situation which led to her mother's love for Captain Hawdon and her own birth. *She* will never be humbled, as Lady Dedlock so gratifyingly is, before the living embodiment of a past indiscretion.[41]

This is a very valid point. Esther is only too aware that Lady Dedlock feels ashamed and guilty about her questionable past, and along with this knowledge would be the feeling that "there but for the grace of God go I." So while Esther may feel inferior to others owing to her disfigurement she will never feel anywhere near as inferior as her erring mother plainly does. Losing her mother's looks, then, is something to rejoice in rather than to grieve over.

Raising her mother up, Esther tries to tell her mother that she has forgiven her:

> I told her — or I tried to tell her — that if it were for me, her child, under any circumstances to take upon me to forgive her, I did it, and had done it, many, many years. I told her that my heart overflowed with love for her; that it was natural love, which nothing in the past had changed, or could change. That it was not for me, then resting for the first time on my mother's bosom, to take her to account for having given me life; but that my duty was to bless her and receive her, though the whole world turned from her, and that I only asked her leave to do it. I held my mother in my embrace, and she held me in hers; and among the still woods in the silence of the summer day, there seemed to be nothing but our two troubled minds that was not at peace [565].

Significantly, Esther indicates that the reconciliation with her mother brings her no peace. Could this mean that she prefers to remain upset and disturbed by her mother in much the same way that Dickens was by his mother? Interestingly, too, Esther may speak the words of forgiveness but there is something distasteful about the way she puts this. As Lawrence Frank writes: "Her forgiveness of her mother is a terrible rebuke.... How deftly the knife is turned in the wound!"[42] In saying that it is her duty to accept her mother even if the rest of the world turns away from her, Esther underscores the enormity of her mother's transgression and the depth of her guilt. In addition, she implicitly denies her mother a place within society in much the same way as she was denied a place in society due to the extremely unwarranted condemnation of her "godmother," Miss Barbary. However, just as Esther denies Lady Dedlock a place within the world, Lady Dedlock denies Esther a continuing place within her life:

> She had followed me down here, to speak to me but once in all her life. We never could associate, never could communicate, never probably from that time forth

could interchange another word, on earth. She put into my hands a letter she had written for my reading only; and said, when I had read it, and destroyed it — but not so much for her sake, since she asked nothing, as for her husband's and my own — I must evermore consider her as dead [566].

In a premeditated way, then, Lady Dedlock has determined that she will speak with her daughter, but only once, and she will give her daughter a letter, but after her daughter has read it she must destroy it and consider her mother as dead. In such a way, Lady Dedlock ensures that she will be free to pursue her miserable, self-imposed course of action: "The dark road I have trodden for so many years will end where it will. I follow it alone to the end, whatever the end be. It may be near, it may be distant; while the road lasts, nothing turns me" (567). Such a rigid stance, of course, brings to mind Miss Barbary. As we know, Miss Barbary *never* diverged from her chosen path. She never missed church; never smiled; never spoke to Esther about her parents; never allowed Esther to wear mourning clothes; never taught her to pray for any relation other than herself; never allowed Esther to go out; never celebrated Esther's birthday; never stopped frowning and never gave Esther her final blessing. So, too, Lady Dedlock resolves to *never* associate in any way with Esther again and to *never* diverge from the dark road that she has trodden for so many years. Interestingly, this road is not a road to atonement but rather a road to obdurate and wretched triumph:

> "Dear mother, are you so resolved?"
> "I *am* resolved. I have long outbidden folly with folly, pride with pride, scorn with scorn, insolence with insolence, and have outlived many vanities with many more. I will outlive this danger, and outdie it, if I can" [567].

Such an intransigent agenda is dubious at best, but it is nonetheless the agenda that has motivated her above all others, even if it means that everything else (including her child) "falls" by the wayside. As nothing and no one can stop her, least of all her daughter, Lady Dedlock then melodramatically exits Esther's life with the intention of never meeting with her again and never receiving forgiveness in the afterlife:

> "My child, my child!" she said. "For the last time! These kisses for the last time! These arms upon my neck for the last time! We shall meet no more. To hope to do what I seek to do, I must be what I have been so long. Such is my reward and doom. If you hear of Lady Dedlock, brilliant, prosperous, and flattered; think of your wretched mother, conscience-stricken, underneath that mask! That the reality is in her suffering, in her useless remorse, in her murdering within her breast the only love and truth of which it is capable! And then forgive her, if you can; and cry to Heaven to forgive her, which it never can!" [568].

Traumatized, Esther eventually composes herself and returns to the sanctuary of her room wherein she reads her mother's letter and learns that she was not abandoned at birth:

I had not been abandoned by my mother. Her elder and only sister, the godmother of my childhood, discovering signs of life in me when I had been laid aside as dead, had in her stern sense of duty, with no desire or willingness that I should live, reared me in rigid secrecy, and had never again beheld my mother's face from within a few hours of my birth. So strangely did I hold my place in this world, that, until within a short time back, I had never, to my own mother's knowledge, breathed — had been buried — had never been endowed with life — had never borne a name [569].

However, while she learns that she was not consciously disowned by her mother, Esther, through the letter, is made to feel negated. Indeed, as Chiara Briganti puts it: "The letter, by conjuring up a time during which for her mother she did not exist and was nameless, poses for her the threat of non-existence."[43] In addition, Esther has clearly shown that her mother has consistently rejected her: Upon giving birth, she literally leaves Esther for dead; upon being introduced and hearing Esther speak for the first time, she summarily turns away from her with a look of distaste; upon taking leave, she specifically ignores Esther; and upon meeting with Esther after she has learned that Esther is her child, she cruelly resolves that she must murder within her breast the love that she feels for her. Indeed, as Brian Cheadle puts it: "For all her avowal of motherly love, she abandons Esther after finding her."[44] Esther, then, is radically expelled by her mother in every sense of the word. Completely powerless and jettisoned, her only recourse is to abject a part of herself, and it would appear that this part is the love that she feels, despite everything, for her mother. Certainly Esther does not make the ferocious resolution that she must murder within her breast the residual love that she feels towards her mother, but through her actions she as good as murders it. How does she do this? Essentially, it is a three-step process which involves burning, implicit condemnation through the means of structural antithesis, and negation.

Esther may have received advice from her mother to burn her letter, but when she comes to do this, her execution of this act is severe, to say the least: "My first care was to burn what my mother had written, and to consume even its ashes" (569). Certainly, Esther was told by her mother that the letter should be read and then destroyed, but the extent of the burning ironically mirrors the extreme combustion of Krook and the drastically altering nature of the feverish disease that Esther contracts. So just as the Lord Chancellor of the Court of Chancery, through Krook's spontaneous combustion, symbolically dies "the death of all Lord Chancellors in all Courts, and of all authorities in all places under all names soever, where false pretenses are made, and where injustice is done" (511), Lady Dedlock, through Esther's *extremely* dutiful combustion of her letter, dies the death of all mothers who have pursued falseness over substance and injustice over "love and truth" (568).

It should be noted that while the action of burning her mother's letter allows Esther to symbolically get back at her mother, she is still beset with absolute self-revilement:

> I hope it may not appear very unnatural or bad in me, that I then became heavily sorrowful to think I had ever been reared. That I felt as if I knew it would have been better and happier for many people, if indeed I had never breathed. That I had a terror of myself, as the danger and the possible disgrace of my own mother, and of a proud family name. That I was so confused and shaken, as to be possessed by a belief that it was right, and had been intended, that I should die in my birth; and that it was wrong, and not intended, that I should be then alive.
>
> These are the real feelings that I had. I fell asleep, worn out; and when I awoke, I cried afresh to think that I was back in the world, with my load of trouble for others. I was more than ever frightened of myself, thinking anew of her, against whom I was a witness; of the owner of Chesney Wold; of the new and terrible meaning of the old words, now moaning in my ear like a surge upon the shore, "Your mother, Esther, was your disgrace, and you are hers. The time will come — and soon enough — when you will understand this better, and will feel it too, as no one save a woman can." With them, those words returned, "Pray daily that the sins of others be not visited upon your head." I could not disentangle all that was about me; and I felt as if the blame and the shame were all in me and the visitation had come down [569].

Here Esther views herself as nothing short of monstrous. Fundamentally, she feels that in being born, she crossed the boundary between good and evil and became polluting. Accordingly, her life does not simply endanger her mother but also the proud family name that she married into. In addition, her god-mother's dire words take on new meaning to the point where she, in essence, comes to believe that her body[45] and her disfigured face are signs of her difference and impurity. These thoughts are intensified when Esther goes for a walk alone and ends up at the Ghost's Walk wherein she scares herself into thinking that she is the horrific agent of defilement who will bring down the patrilineal edifice that is Chesney Wold:

> My echoing footsteps brought it suddenly into my mind that there was a dreadful truth in the legend of the Ghost's Walk; that it was I, who was to bring calamity upon the stately house; and that my warning feet were haunting it even then. Seized with an augmented terror of myself which turned me cold, I ran from myself and everything, retraced the way by which I had come, and never paused until I had gained the lodge-gate, and the park lay sullen and black behind me [571].

Interestingly, though, these terrifying thoughts dissipate when Esther goes back to her room and finds two letters from Ada and Jarndyce that, unlike her mother's negating letter, serve to affirm her place in the world. Esther then becomes reconciled to her life and to her innocence:

> For, I saw very well that I could not have been intended to die, or I should never have lived; not to say should never have been reserved for such a happy life. I saw very well how many things had worked together, for my welfare; and that if the

sins of the fathers were sometimes visited upon the children, the phrase did not mean what I had in the morning feared it meant. I knew I was as innocent of my birth as a queen of hers; and that before my Heavenly Father I should not be punished for birth, nor a queen rewarded for it [571].

Following this, Esther prays for herself and for her "unhappy mother" (571) and begins to feel "the darkness of the morning" (571) pass away. By the next day it is completely gone. The phrase "the darkness of the morning" is an interesting one. Euphemistic in tone, it refers to the morning meeting with her mother, and there is a strong sense that Esther wishes to place it behind her and wipe it from her memory. Certainly, within a day Esther finds something that replaces any lingering thoughts concerning her mother. That something is the prospect of meeting her dear friend Ada again following her illness. All the next day after seeing her mother, Esther worries about revealing her scarred face to Ada, but to her relief, when Ada finally sees her, she is completely accepting:

She ran in, and was running out again when she saw me. Ah, my angel girl! the old dear look, all love, all fondness, all affection. Nothing else in it — no, nothing, nothing!
O how happy I was, down upon the floor, with my sweet beautiful girl down upon the floor too, holding my scarred face to her lovely cheek, bathing it with tears and kisses, rocking me to and fro like a child, calling me by every tender name that she could think of, and pressing me to her faithful heart [573].

This is an extremely telling passage. As Christine Van Boheemen-Saaf remarks:

It is highly significant that the chapter that has as its central event the relatively restrained recognition of the kinship between Esther and her mother should end in a climax of much greater emotional intensity with the reunion of Esther and Ada. Here we see Ada play the mother role, accepting Esther's face, "bathing it with tears and kisses, rocking [her] to and fro like a child, calling [her] by every tender name that she could think of."[46]

Indeed, the contrast between the two scenes is quite startling. Not simply is Ada far more joyous at the prospect of seeing Esther but she is far more maternal that Esther's biological mother. Unlike Esther's fear-oppressed and far from devoted mother, nothing, quite simply, can stand in the way of her love and devotion for Esther. Interestingly too, Van Boheemen-Saaf views Ada with her beautiful skin and rosy lips as the "reincarnation of [Esther's] long buried doll."[47] This is a fascinating point because it helps us to trace a direct link between Esther's portrait of Miss Barbary and her portrait of Lady Dedlock. Indeed, just as Miss Barbary was unfavorably set against Esther's "all good" beautiful doll with its "imagined loving gaze,"[48] Lady Dedlock is in this chapter unfavorably set against Esther's "all good," beautiful and ever-loving friend Ada; and even the reunion that she has with Esther is, in the final analysis, structurally eclipsed by the climactic reunion that Esther has with Ada.

Finally, Esther engages in a systematic process of negation in relation to the thoughts that she has of her mother. Indeed, while Esther's dark "morning" of the soul is succeeded over time by thoughts of her mother, these are always qualified, minimized or denied. When Esther is reunited with Ada she resolves to keep the meeting with her mother a secret. Thoughts of her mother still creep into her consciousness, but the disciplined Esther restricts these to the nocturnal hours: "Though often when [Ada] was asleep, and all was quiet, the remembrance of my mother kept me waking, and made the night sorrowful, I did not yield to it at another time" (573). Later Esther prefaces her thoughts about her mother with a deprecating phrase: "It matters little now, how much I thought of my living mother who had told me evermore to consider her dead" (647); "It matters little now how often I recalled the tones of my mother's voice" (647); "It matters little that I watched for every public mention of my mother's name" (647). Speaking of her emotions as if they are long gone and of little consequence, Esther completely distances herself from her mother: "It is all, all over. My lot has been so blest that I can relate little of myself which is not a story of goodness and generosity in others. I may well pass that little, and go on" (647). This contention is particularly ambiguous. It is as if Esther wishes to dismissively consign her mother to the past so that she can relate the much more palatable aspects of her life. The goodness and generosity of others has been her lot, she seems to say, so what is the point in dwelling on a connection that can go nowhere?

Not long after, the goodness and generosity of others is demonstrated when Esther decides to confide in her guardian, Jarndyce. Rising to the occasion, Jarndyce helps Esther to integrate her thoughts around her mother:

> I would have told him all my mother's letter, but he would not hear it then. He spoke so tenderly and wisely to me, and he put so plainly before me all I had myself imperfectly thought and hoped in my better state of mind, that, penetrated as I had been with fervent gratitude towards him through so many years, I believed I had never loved him so dearly, never thanked him in my heart so fully, as I did that night [662].

So, too, the next day, he agrees to keep her secret and pledges to help her mother in the future if he can:

> And if the time should come when I can stretch out a hand to render the least service to one whom it is better not to name even here, I will not fail to do it for her dear daughter's sake [664].

Esther thanks him wholeheartedly, and from that moment on her burden is lightened. It is so lightened, in fact, that Esther's thoughts scarcely turn to her mother until the point where she is roped in by Inspector Bucket to find Lady Dedlock after she has disappeared following the murder of Tulkinghorn. This pursuit, or "death chase,"[49] as Virginia Blain describes it, leads Esther to find a letter written by her mother which essentially states that she has no purpose but to die and that it is right that she should die of terror and her conscience (864). Not much later, Esther and Mr. Bucket find her mother "cold and dead" (869) at the gate of the pestiferous burial ground "where the man was buried that took the sleeping-stuff" (866). According to Chiara Briganti, the nature of Esther and Inspector Bucket's pursuit is somewhat suspect:

> After a night-long pursuit, Esther and Inspector Bucket finally succeed in catching up with Honoria Barbary at the burial ground where she has joined her dead lover. The relentless character of Esther and Inspector Bucket's pursuit, even though steeped in loving concern, is reminiscent of Esther's thoroughness in destroying Lady Dedlock's letter and suggests that [Thomas] Hanzo may very well be right in indicating that "structurally ... Esther is guilty of wishing the mother's death (with Bucket, does she hound her mother to her doom?)"[50]

Whilst I concur with Briganti and Hanzo, I am of the opinion that Esther's reaction after finding her mother is even more suspect. As soon as Esther finds her mother cold and dead the chapter ends, and the next chapter, called "Perspective," officiously opens with the words:

> I proceed to other passages of my narrative. From the goodness of all about me, I derived such consolation as I can never think of unmoved. I have already said so much of myself, and so much still remains, that I will not dwell upon my sorrow. I had an illness, but it was not a long one; and I would avoid even this mention of it, if I could quite keep down the recollection of their sympathy.
> I proceed to other passages of my narrative [869].

Here again the goodness and generosity of others takes precedence over the thoughts that Esther has for her mother. Esther in fact barely mentions her grief at the death of her mother. The sorrow that she ostensibly feels does not even refer to her mother, and the illness or relapse that Esther undergoes is so brief that it is only mentioned to affirm the sympathy extended to her by everyone in her orbit. That Esther recovers very quickly from her illness and from her sorrow is in no doubt. Also in no doubt is Esther's wish to move on to other matters. Indeed, the repeated sentence "I proceed to other passages of my narrative," while clearly conforming to literary tradition, is nonetheless rather offensive owing to its purgative tone[51] and the dismissive and all too obvious sense of haste that it conveys. If, structurally, Esther is indeed guilty of wishing her mother's death, then she is guilty here of working to obliterate all traces of her mother. Interestingly too, as Deborah Epstein Nord points out, this startling erasure is replicated at the end of the novel:

> Even in Esther's final chapter, in which she sums up the fate of the major players in her story, no further mention of the dead mother is made. Esther's own maternity takes its place.[52]

Paralleling the way that she sought, through combustion, to consume even the ashes of her mother's letter, Esther then seeks through narrative negation to completely destroy her mother. However, while she may successfully dispatch her mother by such means, she can never bury the fact that her mother chose to eject her from her life.

If Geoffrey Thurley is right and there is "a disgust [in *Bleak House*] which transcends its origination and a sense of waste which far exceeds the inadequacies of the legal system,"[53] the disgust and sense of waste, I propose, originates with the protagonist Esther Summerson who, not unlike Dickens,[54] never gets over the way that both of her mothers "eliminate" her from their world views. Esther, as I have shown, through the medium of her narrative implicitly demonizes and attacks her mothers in various ways, and eventually seeks to abject them by burning them in effigy, just as the omniscient narrator burns the Court of Chancery in effigy. However, while the text appears to successfully destroy these execrable faces of maternal dereliction, the essential thing about the Abject is that "it is something rejected from which one does not part."[55] Accordingly, the novel ends with the disfigured heroine unconvinced by her success. Sitting on the porch of the new Bleak House and married to the man that she loves, the respected doctor Allan Woodcourt, she tells him of her thoughts:

> "I have been thinking about my old looks — such as they were."
> "And what have you been thinking about *them*, my busy bee?" said Allan.
> "I have been thinking, that I thought it was impossible that you *could* have loved me any better, even if I had retained them."
> "'Such as they were'?" said Allan, laughing.
> "Such as they were, of course."
> "My dear Dame Durden," said Allan, drawing my arm through his, "do you ever look in the glass?"
> "You know I do; you see me do it."
> "And don't you know that you are prettier than you ever were?"
> I did not know that; I am not certain that I know it now. But I know that my dearest little pets are very pretty, and that my darling is very beautiful, and that my husband is very handsome, and that my guardian has the brightest and most benevolent face that ever was seen; and that they can very well do without much beauty in me — even supposing [935].

The last sentence is marked by its lack of closure. Were Esther to have finished it, it would have probably been to the effect "they can very well do without much beauty in me — even supposing that what my husband says is true." The fact that she doesn't finish the sentence might be because she knows that she is nowhere near as pretty as she was before. It is worthwhile, after all, to remember that Esther contracted a very serious disease, as Maura Spiegel writes: "Esther is disfigured by a disease which neither she nor the omniscient narrator chooses to call by name. There is no question that the disease is smallpox, or that Dickens's contemporaries would have any doubt about that."[56] Smallpox was nothing short of horrendous. As Thomas Babington Macaulay claimed, smallpox left "on those whose lives it spared the hideous traces of its power, turning the babe into a changeling at which the mother shuddered, and making the eyes and cheeks of the betrothed maiden objects of horror to the lover."[57] Further, Spiegel maintains: "The extent of the scarring, which often permanently denuded eyelashes, eyebrows and large patches of the scalp, left the face ridged and deeply pitted."[58] Esther might, therefore, know that her husband, like the bride of the illiterate, is lying to make her feel better, or she might half believe him because she did after all victoriously "win" his love. Indeed, at Woodcourt's declaration of love, Esther writes:

> He had called me the beloved of his life, and had said I would be evermore as dear to him as I was then; and I felt as if my heart would not hold the triumph of having heard those words [891].

"Triumph"—what an extraordinary and discordant word to use in this context. The relentlessly retiring and apparently unselfish Esther feels *triumphant* rather than simply happy or joyous when the man she adores tells her of his love! Still, if we recall that Esther's masculine gender affiliation to earn or compete for love emerged after she had vowed to repair the congenital fault that Miss Barbary had traumatically saddled her with, it makes much more sense and this brings us to the crux of the matter. Esther's husband may or may not be telling the truth, but it hardly matters. Esther knows that she has won him over and many others despite all the odds during the course of her life, but she can't forget the fact that she did not win over her mothers. She may have psychically "defeated" them by erasing her genetic resemblance to them and acquiring an altogether "new" look, but she knows that she never gained their enduring love and was never beautiful in their eyes.

Georgiana Pirrip, Mrs. Joe and the Case for the Hero's Disgust in *Great Expectations*

As I have sought to show, the first-person narrators David Copperfield and Esther Summerson both seek to cleanse themselves of the repellent taint they rightly or wrongly associate with their respective biological and adoptive mothers. In David's case, this leads him to construct the "all good" Agnes Wickfield as the natural object through which he can achieve an illusion of self-creation; and in Esther's case, this leads her to contract a disfiguring and near fatal disease which results in what she describes as an "altered self."[1] Turning now to the final autobiographical novel that Dickens wrote, *Great Expectations*, a close reading of the text assuredly reveals a similar underlying anti-maternal drive, but in Pip's case, we can detect the beginnings of a shift in the paradigm because there is evidence that Pip is, at least at *some* level, aware that "bad" mothers are not, of themselves, always totally to blame.

For many critics the dominant theme in *Great Expectations* is guilt. Indeed, in seeking to explicate the novel in terms of shame, Robert Newsom writes: "There would be no question about discussing shame in this novel at length were it not for all the critics who have emphasized guilt at the expense of shame."[2] Certainly, since the second half of the twentieth century, the theme of guilt in this novel has repeatedly captured the attention of critics.[3] The most cited work in this area must surely be Julian Moynahan's seminal article, "The Hero's Guilt: The Case of *Great Expectations*." In addition, shame is a central theme in the novel and the exploration of its importance has yielded significant exegetic gains.[4] In this chapter, however, I would like to emphasize the importance of disgust in *Great Expectations* over and above guilt or shame. Indeed, I would like to argue that disgust is actually the dominant (albeit veiled) theme of the novel and the chief emotion that propels the putative hero Pip throughout his expectant journey. Further, the disgust that drives Pip is, I suggest, first and foremost directed at two of the most significant people in his life: the woman who bore him and the woman who raised him.

Pip is not normally associated with disgust. If critics do consider disgust in relation to Pip, they generally point to the revulsion that Pip feels in relation to the criminal men that cross his path or to the loathing that Pip has for masculinity. Of the former consideration, David Trotter, for instance, directs us to the part of the novel where Pip travels by coach to Kent to see Miss Havisham and finds, to his disgust, that two of his fellow passengers are prisoners. Sickened by their "coarse mangy ungainly" appearance, Pip likens them to "lower animals."[5] Further, when one of the men sits directly behind him, Pip registers his extreme discomfort:

> It is impossible to express with what acuteness I felt the convict's breathing, not only on the back of my head, but all along my spine. The sensation was like being touched in the marrow with some pungent and searching acid, and it set my very teeth on edge. He seemed to have more breathing business to do than another man, and to make more noise in doing it; and I was conscious of growing high-shouldered on one side, in my shrinking endeavours to fend him off [250].

Of this passage, Trotter writes:

> The feeling [the convicts] provoke is not horror, or anger, or pity, but disgust. Disgust enabled Dickens to understand mess as contingency's signature. That the heavy breather had once brought Pip some money from Magwitch, and thus recalls to him a misplaced charitable impulse he would now rather forget, is of less significance than the pungent and searching acid of the breath, and the disgust it provokes.[6]

Further, Trotter points to the part of the novel where Pip goes to the Cheapside coach office to meet Estella several hours before she is due to arrive. Here, Pip unexpectedly comes across Wemmick, and in order to kill some time he agrees to accompany him on a tour of Newgate Prison. On the tour, Wemmick directs Pip to notice one of the prisoners in particular:

> Almost as soon as he had spoken, a portly upright man (whom I can see now, as I write) in a well-worn olive-coloured frock-coat, with a peculiar pallor overspreading the red in his complexion, and eyes that went wandering about when he tried to fix them, came up to a corner of the bars, and put his hand to his hat — which had a greasy and fatty surface like cold broth — with a half serious and half-jocose military salute [281].

Trotter writes:

> The fact that Pip can still "see" this man as he writes has less to do with his criminal accomplishments than with his peculiar pallor, and above all his hat, which occupies a very striking parenthesis. There is only one term for the feeling the hat arouses: disgust. It is not so much that Pip can "see" in his mind's eye a portly

upright reprobate, as that he knows what it would be like to touch the greasy and fatty surface of the man's hat.[7]

This meeting, for Trotter, contributes towards Pip's memorable "meditation"[8] on his sense of being encompassed by "all this taint of prison and crime" (284) and regret at having allowed himself to accompany Wemmick:

> I thought of the beautiful young Estella, proud and refined, coming towards me, and I thought with absolute abhorrence of the contrast between the jail and her. I wished that Wemmick had not met me, or that I had not yielded to him and gone with him, so that, of all days in the year on this day, I might not have had Newgate in my breath and on my clothes. I beat the prison dust off my feet as I sauntered to and fro, and I shook it out of my dress, and I exhaled its air from my lungs. So contaminated did I feel [284].

The other primary scene that critics refer to in relation to Pip's disgust for criminal men is when Pip learns, to his disgust, that it is the "dunghill dog" (337) Magwitch rather than Miss Havisham who is his benefactor[9]: "The abhorrence in which I held the man, the dread I had of him, the repugnance with which I shrank from him, could not have been exceeded if he had been some terrible beast" (337). Of this scene, John Lucas writes: "Of what service is the notion of a gentleman to Magwitch? Its final achievement is to make him seem abhorrent to the gentleman his money has created."[10]

As to the disgust that Pip feels in relation to masculinity, the key exponent of this position is Sharon Marcus. In her thought provoking examination of *Great Expectations*, Marcus proposes that Pip identifies so strongly with "the homoerotic female dyad"[11] of Miss Havisham and her adopted daughter Estella that he actively seeks to "annihilate his masculinity"[12] and tries to "transform himself into a female accessory."[13] Added to this, Marcus believes that "Pip dislikes masculinity in others as well as in himself"[14] and cites Pip's loathing for Pumblechook; repugnance for Magwitch; aversion towards Trabb's boy; and love for Joe, whom he "persistently associates ... with femininity"[15] as evidence of this. Marcus's argument is definitely an advance on previous treatments of Pip's disgust, but because Marcus is more interested in focusing on desire within the novel, in particular the "desire between women"[16] she hinges Pip's disgust for his own sex on somewhat questionable[17] erotic imperatives and fails to see the disgust that Pip has for the opposite sex. Of course, the "very sensitive" (92) aspiring gentleman Pip is not generally associated with disgust towards women. Here, however I will argue that there are strong grounds to suggest that Pip is not simply associated with disgust towards women but actually consumed by it. Indeed, his self-described "blind and thankless" life (410) may quite plausibly be understood as a reflection of the unacknowledged disgust that he feels towards his deceased mother, Georgiana Pirrip, and his sister and foster mother "by necessity."[18] Mrs. Joe Gargery.

In order to chart the disgust that underlies the depiction of Pip's mothers, one must firstly explore the manifest ambivalence that Pip displays towards his deceased biological father. *Great Expectations* opens with the first-person narrator declaring that he named himself:

> My father's family name being Pirrip, and my christian name Philip, my infant tongue could make of both names nothing longer or more explicit than Pip. So, I called myself Pip, and came to be called Pip [35].

A number of critics have remarked on these two key sentences, and the views expressed are manifold,[19] but for the purposes of this study there are two areas of commentary that are particularly relevant. The first concerns the way that Pip appears to subvert authority. According to Peter Brooks: "This originating moment of Pip's narration and his narrative is a self-naming that already subverts whatever authority could be found in the text of the tombstones."[20] So, too, Anny Sadrin traces a subversive strain in Pip's opening paragraph:

> The circuitous phrase, "my father's family name," shows lasting impertinence on the part of the narrator — no longer the blundering, inarticulate infant whose tongue slipped inadvertently, but an elderly, polite gentleman — and expresses an ambivalent claim to kinship and alienation. No legitimate son in his right mind would ever choose, unless in jest, to introduce himself so deviously when a plain statement, "my family name," would do just as nicely. The incongruous interpolation of the genitive creates a grammatical and sentimental disruption in the sentence and distorts the relationship between possessor and possessed: the name belongs to the father, the father belongs to the son, and the son belongs nowhere. And if, undeniably, the formulation gives pride of place to the child's sire as life-giver, it also most cheekily dismisses him as name-transmitter.[21]

This seemingly subversive strain might also help to account for the interesting fact that Pip's father's name, "Philip Pirrip, is truncated twice over in Pip's."[22] As to the second area of commentary, this concerns Pip's inability to speak his father's name and the autonomy that this implies. Carolyn Brown, for instance, stresses the way in which Pip makes himself unlike his father through his incapacity to master his father's name: "He is 'Pip'; he has acquired this name through his inability to speak his father's name which he has been given. He shares his father's name, even as he differentiates himself from it."[23] Echoing this line of thought, Nicola Bradbury highlights the transformative nature of Pip's self-naming. For Bradbury, Pip's name "both is and is not that of his father. His 'infant tongue' has transformed it ('infant' means, etymologically, non-speaking) into his own."[24] So, too, Catherine Waters focuses on the independence that is implied through Pip's act of self-naming but stresses (by reference to Pip's subsequent contemplation of the family tombstones) that this is qualified by the fact that his identity is already inscribed by historically determined notions of sexual difference:

Despite the assertion of autonomy implied in Pip's self-naming on the novel's opening page, the determination of his identity by a familial context and the difference made by gender in these arrangements are made apparent in his contemplation of the family tombstones.... The tombstone text inscribes divisions of power within the family which are registered in Pip's reading, and indicate that the process of identity-formation expressed here is not conducted in some neutral linguistic medium. The language Pip works with is already gendered.[25]

Christopher D. Morris also challenges Pip's apparent autonomy. According to Morris, Pip's belief in his own freedom to self-name displays bad faith. For Morris, it is essentially erroneous to "presume the existence of some self apart from language."[26] Whether or not Pip is actually autonomous, his inability to speak his father's name, his act of self-naming and his apparent refusal even years later to take ownership of his family name certainly gives pause for thought. Might there be, one wonders, a subconscious reason behind Pip's evident distaste in relation to his father's name? Could it be that Pip wants to disassociate himself from his father? Could Pip even be ashamed of his father? And if so, why?

At the beginning of the second paragraph, Pip tells us that he was aware that his surname was Pirrip owing to the authority of his father's tombstone and his sister, "Mrs. Joe Gargery, who married the blacksmith" (35). However, while his sister (who is formally referred to in terms of her marital status and her husband's occupation rather than in terms of endearment) may have told Pip that his surname was Pirrip, it would appear that she did not convey to him what their mother and father looked like:

> As I never saw my father or my mother, and never saw any likeness of either of them (for their days were long before the days of photographs), my first fancies regarding what they were like, were unreasonably derived from their tombstones. The shape of the letters on my father's, gave me an odd idea that he was a square, stout, dark man, with curly black hair. From the character and turn of the inscription, "*Also Georgiana Wife of the Above*," I drew a childish conclusion that my mother was freckled and sickly. To five little stone lozenges, each about a foot and a half long, which were arranged in a neat row beside their grave, and were sacred to the memory of five little brothers of mine — who gave up trying to get a living, exceedingly early in that universal struggle — I am indebted for a belief I religiously entertained that they had all been born on their backs with their hands in their trousers-pockets, and had never taken them out in this state of existence. (35)

Pip's fancies about his parents' looks were, as he reveals, "unreasonably derived from their tombstones." This statement, of course, refers to the unreasonable assumption that one can infer anything about what a person looks like from a tombstone, but it also calls attention (by virtue of the fact that his sister has already been mentioned) to the unreasonable nature of Pip's circumstances in that he should be reduced to seeking this fundamental knowledge from such a bizarre and morbid source. Indeed, it implies that even a tombstone is more giving and informative than an immediate surviving relative.

Turning to Pip's actual fancies about his deceased relatives, it is very interesting that Pip imagines that his father was swarthy and vigorous looking but his mother was marked and ill and his five brothers quickly gave up on life and were all born in a supine state "with their hands in their trousers-pockets."[27] Certainly, a lively imagination is at work here and the vision is endearing in its whimsy. Of this fanciful description, Max Byrd, for instance, writes:

> Pip's illiterate, "unreasonable" readings of these tombstones are both childish and charming, and the reader is expected to see along with him, now speaking in his adult voice, that the child's fantasizing is not to be taken seriously.[28]

However, on a purely structural or spatial level, it is impossible to ignore the fact that Georgiana lies at the heart of Pip's imaginative construction as the sick and blemished member of the family and all about her lie the corpses (no less than *six*) of Pip's immediate male relatives. Accordingly, she is figured as a dangerously anomalous member of the Pirrip family, and it is as if Pip fancifully holds her responsible for the deaths of his father and five brothers. Mary Douglas's thesis on concepts of pollution and taboo is pertinent here because, as Douglas puts it: "Ideas about contagion can certainly be traced to reaction to anomaly."[29] So while Georgiana Pirrip may, on the tombstone, be defined only in relation to her husband, she nevertheless looms very large in Pip's mind. In fact, by his infant reckoning she is an awful agent of contagion who has laid waste to six male members of his family. This would explain why the words on the tombstone "*Also Georgiana Wife of the Above,*" are, as Carolyn Brown puts it, "more central within that first paragraph as a name, than the father's."[30] For Brown, this can be attributed to "Pip's infancy" but it might be profitable to go a step further and suggest that the centrality of her name within this key paragraph reveals the threatening prominence that she holds in Pip's infant mind. A woman who apparently has the power to bring down a virile husband and five male children is not to be dismissed, and this is arguably why Pip gives her the pivotal position at the opening of his narrative. Indeed, as her only surviving male child he cannot help but be horrified by her gender-specific lethal touch, and here it should be recalled that horror as William Ian Miller explains is the strongest form of disgust: "Horror is a subset of disgust, being specifically that disgust for which no distancing or evasive strategies exist that are not in themselves utterly contaminating."[31]

Perhaps this helps to explain why Pip (as a child) can't or won't master the pronunciation of his father's name and why (as an adult) he doesn't take direct ownership of the family name. If his infant tongue *could* make his father's name clear (Philip Pirrip) and his adult tongue could unequivocally lay claim to his family name ("my" family name)—then he would be effectively telling the world that he was just like his father and thereby equally capable of succumbing to the contagion of his mother. Conflating the name Philip Pirrip as a child and incongruously speaking of his *father's* family name as an adult thereby provides Pip with the means to distance himself from his father's fate. His father may have been drawn to "the place where meaning collapses"[32] and reduced to the state of a corpse, "the most sickening of wastes,"[33] but his only surviving son will (through denominative repudiation) convulsively extricate himself from this fallen state. The identity of the narrating Pip is then founded on the horror that he feels towards his mother and the fear of being viewed like his apparently weak and susceptible father — Philip Pirrip. "Not me. Not that."[34] Accordingly, the opening paragraph of the novel with its key statements "My father's family name" and "I called myself Pip" all at once stands as an emphatic act of subversion, differentiation, transformation, autonomy *and self-protection*. Pip may share his father's name and it may be a part of him, but he must reject it in order to protect his "condition as a living being."[35] As Kristeva puts it: "I expel *myself*, I spit *myself* out, I abject *myself* within the same motion through which 'I' claim to establish *myself*."[36]

Interestingly, later in Chapter Seven when Pip describes his education he alludes to the family tombstones again:

> At the time when I stood in the churchyard, reading the family tombstones, I had just enough learning to be able to spell them out. My construction even of their simple meaning was not very correct, for I read "wife of the Above" as a complimentary reference to my father's exaltation to a better world; and if any one of my deceased relations had been referred to as "Below," I have no doubt I should have formed the worst opinions of that member of the family [73].

Here Pip claims that he assumed that the words on the epitaph that refer to his mother respectfully signaled that his father had gone on to a higher place. Notably, the words, for Pip, do not pay the same "complimentary reference" to his mother. Instead, Pip claims that if any one of his other deceased relations had been referred to as "Below" he would have "no doubt" thought very badly towards "that member of the family." These words are highly ambiguous. Just which member of the family is Pip referring to? He has only one extant relative — his sister, Mrs. Joe — and as to his deceased relatives, why would he single out only *one* member of the family to speculatively view in the "worst" possible light? Moreover, why does he speculate in this way at all? It would appear that he only speculates in this way because he has subconsciously formed "the worst opinions" of one member of his family and that member could logically only be his mother "Below" or his sister, Mrs. Joe. Interestingly, too, while Pip may assume that the epitaph pays a compliment to his father, he does not pay the same compliment to his father by reaching the conclusion that his father has actually gone on to a higher place; so while Philip Pirrip may be favorably designated as "Above" on the epitaph, it would appear that his son views him in a less than exalted light. One might even say that his son has judged him as being tainted by his association with the "worst" wife "Below" him.

Another distinct feature of the second paragraph of Pip's narrative is the fact that Pip displays a strong propensity for creating or more accurately re-creating things according to his want. Indeed, he effectively conjures up his family from his subjective interpretation of the inscriptions on their tombstones, as Jolene Zigarovich writes: "It is as if the graphic symbols — the manner in which the engraved letters are painted and shaped — have become directly mimetic."[37] His father, mother and five brothers are thereby the products of his own imagination. Nowhere in this paragraph do we get a sense that Pip actually *wanted* to know what his deceased relatives were really like, actively sought further more accurate information, or even worried that his mental pictures might be incorrect.[38] He may have "unreasonably" derived his sketchy assumptions about them from their tombstones, but he seems all too satisfied with these reductive fancies.

The third paragraph of the first chapter moves to situate the young Pip alone at late afternoon in a churchyard, looking at the tombstones of his father, mother and five siblings:

> Ours was the marsh country, down by the river, within, as the river wound, twenty miles of the sea. My first most vivid and broad impression of the identity of things, seems to have been gained on a memorable raw afternoon towards evening. At such a time I found out for certain, that this bleak place overgrown with nettles was the churchyard; and that Philip Pirrip, late of this parish, and also Georgiana wife of the above, were dead and buried; and that Alexander, Bartholomew, Abraham, Tobias, and Roger, infant children of the aforesaid, were also dead and buried; and that the dark flat wilderness beyond the churchyard, intersected with dykes and mounds and gates, with scattered cattle feeding on it, was the marshes; and that the low leaden line beyond, was the river; and that the distant savage lair from which the wind was rushing, was the sea; and that the small bundle of shivers growing afraid of it all and beginning to cry, was Pip [35–6].

Of this passage, Moshe Ron writes: "His first authentic experience was that of his utter and radical separation from the world around him and by the same token, from himself."[39] In a similar vein, Colin N. Manlove asserts: "His first true impression of life is of death."[40] Iain Crawford also recognizes "the narrator's preoccupation with death, a preoccupation, which is also to become the underlying motive for much of Pip's life."[41]

Certainly Pip makes a clear linkage here between identity and death. The condition of being a specific thing or person is thereby inextricably bound up in Pip's mind with non-being. This is underscored by the fact that Pip divests *himself* of identity by speaking of himself in the third person: "the small bundle of shivers growing afraid of it all and beginning to cry, was Pip." In such a way, he "dies" at the very point where he claims to have become conscious of life.[42]

Further, all of the things that he identifies on this memorable afternoon are far from life affirming: the churchyard is "bleak"; his father, mother and five brothers are all "dead and buried"; the marshes beyond the churchyard are "dark" and "flat"; the river is "low" and "leaden"; and the sea is a "distant savage lair" from which the wind rushes. The description of the sea, in particular, is noteworthy. A lair is, of course, the resting place of a wild animal — not something one would normally associate with the sea — but the fact that the sea (something traditionally figured as feminine) is presented in such hostile terms and that it constitutes the limit of Pip's experience, interest or knowledge is of some import. Here again, along with displaying his aforementioned propensity to re-create things according to his own imagination, Pip displays, at this very early stage of his narrative, a pronounced fear and deep distrust of the feminine and even a wish to run, like the wind, away from it. How ironic then that just at this very moment, "a fearful man" leaps out at Pip "from among the graves" (36). The man, as we soon learn, is not his father escaped from the tomb and the contaminating grip of his wife but he is nonetheless a fugitive ("frantically trying to avoid the nemesis of being 'laid hands on'"[43]) who has appeared "in the immediate vicinity"[44] of Pip's father's grave. All too tellingly, he immediately demands to know Pip's name:

> "Tell us your name!" said the man. "Quick!"
> "Pip, sir."
> "Once more," said the man, staring at me. "Give it mouth!"
> "Pip, Pip, sir" [36].

Of this exchange, Anny Sadrin writes:

> That an escaped convict should prove so eager to know the name of a child whom he has just met by chance and whom in all likelihood he will never meet again (there is at this stage no reason why he should) seems quite inexplicable, even goes against common sense. This behaviour cannot be ascribed to vain curiosity or be taken for convict "manners." Yet the question is asked twice, as if the man wanted to make sure that he gets the answer right. The obvious explanation that comes to mind is that this verbal exchange meets dramatic requirements: Dickens wants to secure the future of his story and how could a sheep-farmer from the depths of Australia ever find the track of the boy unless he knew him by name?[45]

Sadrin's explanation makes perfect sense but if we divorce the exchange from the imperatives of the plot, there is a beautiful irony in the convict's eagerness to know Pip's name and his apparent frustration at Pip's timid and monosyllabic response. It is as if Pip, in retrospect, needs to record an exchange at the site of his father's grave where he repeatedly asserts the name he has given himself rather than his father's name. So, too, it is a beautiful irony that the next part of the exchange concerns Pip's living arrangements: "Show us where you live," said the man. "Pint out the place!" (36) Pip's response situates him at quite a distance — "a mile or more" (36) — from the graveyard, and this again affirms his singular identity as he is not by any stretch aligned to his father either by name or location. At this, the fugitive convict or "spectral anti-father"[46] (almost vengefully) turns Pip upside down, takes bread from his emptied pockets and threatens to eat his "fat cheeks" (36). Extremely frightened and distressed, Pip is rendered powerless, that is, until the convict demands to know the whereabouts of his mother: "Now lookee here!" said the man. "Where's your mother?" (37). Pip's literal response ironically serves (albeit momentarily) to turn the tables on the man, and he even breaks out into a run:

> "There, sir!" said I.
> He started, made a short run, and stopped and looked over his shoulder.
> "There, sir!" I timidly explained. "Also Georgiana. That's my mother."
> "Oh!" said he, coming back. "And is that your father alonger your mother?"
> "Yes, sir," said I; "him too; late of this parish."

Finding that Pip's mother is nothing other than an inscription on a tombstone, the relieved man presses to know who his primary caregiver is:

> "Ha!" he muttered then, considering. "Who d'ye live with — supposin' you're kindly let to live, which I han't made up my mind about?"
> "My sister, sir — Mrs. Joe Gargery — wife of Joe Gargery, the blacksmith, sir."
> "Blacksmith, eh?" said he. And looked down at his leg [37].

Interestingly, the man's question elicits a detailed response from Pip which readily identifies the familial relation that the person holds to him; her marital name; and her position as the wife of the region's blacksmith, but, mirroring the second paragraph of his narrative, it glaringly conveys little or no affection for her. Pip does not, for instance, preface his detailed response with "my dear sister." While his response is, of course, mitigated by fear, it nonetheless foregrounds her domestic and social position as opposed to the position that she holds within his heart.

Seizing on the fact that Pip lives with a blacksmith, the man tells Pip to get him a file and "wittles" or "I'll have your heart and liver out" (37). In addition, he tells Pip that if he keeps his encounter with him a secret he will be permitted to live but if he fails to do this, a younger fellow fugitive will make sure that Pip's heart and liver are torn out. At this, the fearful Pip immediately confirms that he will obtain the required items and will return with them the next morning. However, rather than running from the scene with all the celerity that one would expect from a boy who has just had his life threatened in the most awful terms, Pip strangely finds the time to watch the man as he limps away and he even engages in fanciful imaginings that the dead people in the cemetery wish to drag him down to be with them:

> He hugged his shuddering body in both his arms — clasping himself, as if to hold himself together — and limped towards the low church wall. As I saw him go, pick-

ing his way among the nettles, and among the brambles that bound the green mounds, he looked in my young eyes as if he were eluding the hands of the dead people, stretching up cautiously out of their graves, to get a twist upon his ankle and pull him in [38].

In Pip's vision of Magwitch attempting to elude the arms of the dead people we have a prime example of abjection as understood in substantial or material terms. As discussed in Chapter Two of this book, for Kristeva, pollution in the form of excrement and its equivalents (i.e., decay, infection, disease, the corpse) is derived from the maternal and/or the feminine, "of which the maternal is the real support,"[47] and this pollution represents the danger to identity that emerges from without: "the ego threatened by the non-ego, society threatened by its outside, life by death."[48] It matters not, then, whether the grasping corpses in the churchyard were male or female because if we take into account Kristeva's thesis, there is a direct connection between impurity (in this case, corpses) and women (especially the mother). However, while Pip may have an underlying fear of a mother's capacity to bring the male sex down (even to the point of death) it is notable that he takes the time (despite being under the threat of death himself) to imagine that it is the convict rather than himself who is actually being hunted down by the infecting hands of death. This is particularly interesting in light of Kristeva's thesis because what is essentially happening here is a convulsive attempt by Pip to project his fears of maternal pollution onto someone else. Certainly, Pip may have taken himself to the churchyard to look at the graves of his relatives and projected his fears about his mother onto a man who was loitering about the graveyard, but *on no account* does he want to be drawn beyond "the border of [his] condition as a living being."[49] Rather, he psychically extricates himself from this border by imagining that another male (aptly one who has appeared near his father's grave) is instead wanted by the defiling clutches of death.

Just after Pip has this ghoulish grasping vision, the man turns back to look at him and Pip tells us that he set his sights on home and "made the best use of my legs" (39). However while Pip may break out into a sprint he is not so frightened that he can't look over his shoulder to track, in detail, the man's movements. Once again, he finds the time to stop and engage in high-flown imaginings about the man:

> The marshes were just a long black horizontal line then, as I stopped to look after him; and the river was just another horizontal line, not nearly so broad nor yet so black; and the sky was just a row of long angry red lines and dense black lines intermixed. On the edge of the river I could faintly make out the only two black things in all the prospect that seemed to be standing upright; one of these was the beacon by which the sailors steered — like an unhooped cask upon a pole — an ugly thing when you were near it; the other a gibbet, with some chains hanging to it which had once held a pirate. The man was limping on towards this latter, as if

he were the pirate come to life, and come down, and going back to hook himself up again. It gave me a terrible turn when I thought so; and as I saw the cattle lifting their heads to gaze after him, I wondered whether they thought so too. I looked all round for the horrible young man, and could see no signs of him. But, now I was frightened again, and ran home without stopping [39].

While the vision is atmospheric and memorable, it is nonetheless quite bizarre that Pip can suspend his fear long enough to actually stop and indulge in fantastical imaginings about the escaped man which amount to the man's transmutation into an executed criminal who comes back to life only to voluntarily return to the state of being hanged and exposed to public scorn. Just why Pip has literally taken the time to reconfigure the man in this way may also be attributed to his fears concerning maternal defilement. Firstly, it would seem that Pip gives himself this "terrible turn" because he fears that he might have actually encountered a dead person (significantly, a pirate, and thereby linked or wedded to the "savage" sea) who has briefly returned to life. Such a thought would horrify Pip because he is fundamentally driven by his need to eschew direct contact with the pollution derived from the maternal (being, in this case, the danger to identity that emerges from death). Indeed, Pip is so driven by this impulse that it actually "stops him dead" in his tracks at a time when he should be running for his life.

This is particularly interesting in light of the direct association that distraction has with abjection, as Iris Marion Young writes:

> Abjection is the feeling of loathing and disgust the subject has in encountering certain matter, images, and fantasies — the horrible, to which it can only respond with aversion, with nausea and distraction.[50]

Secondly, the fact that Pip associates the man who has emerged in the vicinity of his father's grave with a pirate who has been executed and exposed to public scorn would suggest that Pip feels a profound degree of shame for his father. The depth of Pip's shame is illustrated by the fact that, in his imagination, the pirate willingly returns to his degraded state at the gibbet. Such a weak and resigned action could be viewed in a disgraceful light, and for this reason one can surmise that Pip subconsciously feels that his father has disgraced the family name by giving in to his wife's contaminating touch. Little wonder, then, that he refers in his opening paragraph to "my father's family name" (35) rather than "my family name." This might also explain why he seeks to project his "terrible" thought onto the nearby grazing cattle. It is as if he wants some form of public endorsement (if only bovine) that his father can be perceived in a guilty (even criminal) and shameful light. As Robert A. Stein writes: "Shame depends upon being exposed to others' eyes; it is an immensely public emotion."[51]

Very few critics, if any, focus at any length on Pip's biological mother.

Michal Peled Ginsburg is typical. In a footnote Ginsburg claims that "the father's tombstone is given a special status as the site of the authority for the family's identity" and Georgiana is "clearly inscribed as dependent on [Philip Pirrip] (hence secondary), in life as in death."[52] Such an assessment does not take into account the ways in which *Pip's identity* is actively shaped by his creative thoughts concerning his mother. Whilst he may say little about her in his narrative (just as Dickens says little about his own mother in his autobiographical fragment), there is, I submit, a profound degree of fear and disgust that is registered by Pip towards her. In a structural sense, he makes her responsible for the deaths of his father and five brothers and in a rhetorical sense he situates her at the limit of his troubled mind. Just as the negatively presented marshes and river lead to a hostile sea, everything bad that Pip can identify can be attributed to his mother who is implicitly presented as flawed, toxic, distant, savage, and anti-male. Added to this, Pip's identity is also actively shaped by his creative thoughts concerning his father. As I have sought to show, there is evidence that Pip subconsciously wishes to disassociate himself from his father because he believes that his father has shamefully fallen under his mother's contaminating hands. Further, Pip projects his fears concerning maternal contagion and paternal weakness onto a "fearful" escaped criminal and this is why, while under the threat of death, he distractedly captures the man in his mind —firstly as someone who is running from the hands of dead people and secondly as an executed pirate who has quite literally been held up for public scorn.

Turning to Pip's foster mother and sister, Mrs. Joe, it is highly significant that the first description of her that Pip provides refers in a damning sense to her "hands on" approach:

> My sister, Mrs. Joe Gargery, was more than twenty years older than I, and had established a great reputation with herself and the neighbours because she had brought me up "by hand." Having at that time to find out for myself what the expression meant, and knowing her to have a hard and heavy hand, and to be much in the habit of laying it upon her husband as well as upon me, I supposed that Joe Gargery and I were both brought up by hand [39].

Moreover, Pip uncharitably speculates that she must have applied physical abuse to get Joe to marry her: "She was not a good-looking woman, my sister; and I had a general impression that she must have made Joe Gargery marry her by hand" (39). Clearly, time has not softened Pip's perception of his sister, and from the outset he is intent on ridiculing what would appear to be her two chief achievements in life: bringing him up "by hand" and marrying the local blacksmith Joe Gargery. Mrs. Joe's pride in rearing him, presumably from birth, is scornfully referred to. She has merely let everyone know about what she has done and has convinced herself and others that she is a person to be held in high esteem. Further, her achievement is negligible because it is outweighed by the physical abuse which she is alleged to have meted out to her husband and brother. Certainly, Pip's words are intended to be humorous, but they do not conceal his fundamental belief that his foster mother has dealt his foster father if not a death blow then something very nearly akin to it — a marital blow. Immediately, then, we have a concrete reason for the implicit disgust that weighs down the portrait of Pip's biological mother and the subconscious shame that Pip displays in relation to his biological father. Like the sickly Georgiana, Mrs. Joe is a woman who, in Pip's mind, possesses the power to nullify the male sex. While her "manual conduct"[53] may not be as lethal as her mother's, it is nonetheless heavy, savage and sweeping in scope. So while Mrs. Joe may (like her mother, "*Georgiana Wife of the Above*") be dependent on her husband and secondary (in a societal sense) to him, she nevertheless, in Pip's mind at least, possesses the power to bring him down through forcing him into marriage and then undercutting him as the site of the authority within the family.

Pip very naturally would associate his mother with his sister. After all, his sister stands in proxy to his mother and is her only daughter. In addition and significantly, Mrs. Joe's name, as Pumblechook later confirms "was Georgiana M'ria from her own mother" (484). True, Pip draws no direct physical link between them. Mrs. Joe is hardly sickly and pale (as Georgiana's freckles would connote). In fact, quite the opposite:

> My sister, Mrs. Joe, with black hair and eyes, had such a prevailing redness of skin that I sometimes used to wonder whether it was possible she washed herself with a nutmeg-grater instead of soap. She was tall and bony, and almost always wore a coarse apron, fastened over her figure behind with two loops, and having a square impregnable bib in front, that was stuck full of pins and needles. She made it a powerful merit in herself, and a strong reproach against Joe, that she wore this apron so much. Though I really see no reason why she should have worn it at all: or why, if she did wear it at all, she should not have taken it off, every day of her life [40].

Nevertheless, a link can be made in terms of Mrs. Joe's threatening presence. Gail Turley Houston writes: "With her arsenal of needles and pins sticking to the bodice of her apron, this "all-powerful sister" is literally the bad breast."[54] Houston's terms "arsenal" and "bad breast" aptly highlight the dangerous and polluting side of Mrs. Joe. Like her mother before her, Mrs. Joe has the capacity (or ammunition) to bring down the unfortunate male who enters her orbit. Indeed, her "arsenal" is exceedingly dangerous:

> My sister had a trenchant way of cutting our bread-and-butter for us, that never varied. First, with her left hand she jammed the loaf hard and fast against her bib — where it sometimes got a pin into it, and sometimes a needle, which we afterwards got into our mouths [42].

The dangerously culpable depiction of Mrs. Joe is all too reminiscent of the depiction of Elizabeth Dickens in the autobiographical fragment because, as we recall, Dickens illogically linked the failure of her rescue plan ("MRS. DICKENS'S ESTABLISHMENT"[55]) to the fall (imprisonment) of his father. It should also be recalled that in the autobiographical fragment Dickens could not bring himself to acknowledge his mother's good qualities: her enterprising nature, resourcefulness, and teaching skills. So, too, in the portrait of Mrs. Joe, Pip cannot acknowledge any of Mrs. Joe's good qualities. As discussed, her primary achievements in life are dismissed and her work within the household is negated. Indeed, Pip displays no understanding at all that his sister must have worn herself ragged every day cleaning, scrubbing, cooking and sewing. To him, even in retrospect, there was no sense in her having reddened, raw skin, nor was there any explicable reason for having frequently worn an apron festooned with pins and needles.[56] All of her efforts and hard work were of no importance. In his estimation, she was simply a weapon of male destruction — unattractive, dangerous, repellent and callous.

At this point, it is important to note that Pip's refusal to acknowledge any of his sister's good qualities can actually be said to be derived from his foster father's tutelage. After all, the reasons that Joe gives Pip for marrying Mrs. Joe are scant to say the least. Indeed, it would appear that aside from loneliness, he only married her because he was physically attracted to her:

> "It were but lonesome then," said Joe, "living here alone, and I got acquainted with your sister. Now, Pip;" Joe looked firmly at me, as if he knew I was not going to agree with him; "your sister is a fine figure of a woman."
> I could not help looking at the fire, in an obvious state of doubt.
> "Whatever family opinions, or whatever the world's opinions, on that subject may be, Pip, your sister is," Joe tapped the top bar with the poker after every word following, "a —fine —figure — of — a — woman!" [77–78].

Certainly, Joe does mention the fact that Mrs. Joe was generally admired for bringing Pip up by hand: "When I got acquainted with your sister, it were the talk how she was bringing you up by hand. Very kind of her too, all the folks said, and I said, along with all the folks" (78). However, it must be said that the vigorous and rhythmic way in which he uses his poker to tap out his strongly held vision of Mrs. Joe's attractive figure would suggest that his proposal was primarily based on sexual attraction.[57] Indeed, even after Mrs. Joe has died and Pip enquires into his feelings on the day of the funeral, Joe refers to *nothing* about Mrs. Joe other than the fact that she was once attractive:

> Poor dear Joe, entangled in a little black cloak tied in a large bow under his chin, was seated apart at the upper end of the room; where, as chief mourner, he had evidently been stationed by Trabb. When I bent down and said to him, "Dear Joe, how are you?" he said, "Pip, old chap, you knowed her when she were a fine figure of a–" and clasped my hand and said no more [298–99].

It would appear, then, that to Joe a woman is valuable only in so far as she is physically desirable. Little wonder that Pip, who at the beginning of his narrative can confidently declare that his sister was "not a good-looking woman" (39), will credit her with no redeeming features and will find nothing good to say about her after her life is over. This is precisely what Joe has taught him to do.

Notably, Mrs. Joe possesses the considerable clout of her husband's Christian name, which she has for some unknown reason adopted under all circumstances. Even within the privacy of her own home, she is consistently referred to as Mrs. Joe. This strangely formal and butch epithet brings up a series of questions. Did Mrs. Joe insist that Pip call her "Mrs. Joe"? Or did she not give him a name to use when he addressed her and so he named her Mrs. Joe in the same childish way that he named himself? Or did he call her Mrs. Joe because Joe and the other villagers customarily referred to her as Mrs. Joe? Whatever the reason, there is no doubt that the name has the effect of distancing, ridiculing and masculinizing her. Of the latter point, it is interesting to note Brenda Ayres's comment on the subject:

> When a Victorian woman marries, she loses her name and is to assume the signification of her husband. So why not call her Mrs. Joe? Actually, this is not what the text is overtly attempting with her epithet. Instead, it facetiously calls her Mrs. Joe to convey that the woman has stolen masculine power.[58]

Ayres's point is valid, but Donald Hall's assessment of the situation is perhaps more to the point: "The threat to male equanimity which she poses as the novel unfolds comes not from her attempts to acquire power — which is a *fait accompli* — but from her continuing misuse of it; after all, she fills a power void that is not of her own making."[59] Indeed, the fact that the name Mrs. Joe is used as a matter of course within the Gargery household means that her husband has effectively conferred his power on her. It would seem that he has complacently given away or weakly allowed her to appropriate the very name that distinguishes him as a man. Moreover, by doing so he has legitimized whatever way that she deems fit to use that power. Of course, as the text makes clear, Mrs. Joe uses her power in the "worst" possible way — to physically and emotionally abuse those closest to her, her husband and her younger brother.

As we know, according to Mary Douglas's thesis, an out-of-place person is an active form of dirt: "Bringing pollution ... is a capacity which men share with animals."[60] Pollution arises when a human does not fit in with or conform to commonly held notions, and it doesn't matter whether the person intentionally transgressed these notions because "displacement unleashes danger for someone."[61]

The pollution within the Gargery household has arisen, then, because Joe has not conformed to (or has eschewed) commonly held notions concerning masculinity and thus has created a power vacuum in his household which has been filled by his wife. However, rather than using her power judiciously, Mrs. Joe has chosen to treat her husband and brother with nothing less than contempt. As such, she has inverted traditional sexual power relations and placed herself in the ignominious and polluting realm of a "gender offender."[62] The original "gender offender," however, was Joe.

Pip's first description of Joe Gargery is tender and nostalgic:

> Joe was a fair man, with curls of flaxen hair on each side of his smooth face, and with eyes of such a very undecided blue that they seemed to have somehow got mixed with their own whites. He was a mild, good-natured, sweet-tempered, easygoing, foolish dear fellow — a sort of Hercules in strength, and also in weakness [39–40].

Joe is pleasing in appearance and temperament, and his foolish, weak side is humored. Notably, his prodigious physical strength is outweighed by his mild nature. Here, we start to encounter the rhetorical device of structural antithesis that is so much a feature of the autobiographical fragment and the preceding autobiographical novels. Clearly, Joe will be the good person that Pip will juxtapose and contrast with his less than good sister and foster mother, Mrs. Joe. However, even at this very early stage of his depiction, we can see that Joe differs somewhat from the "all good" counterpoint figures of the earlier autobiographical works. To be sure, the words that Pip uses are warm and affectionate but the portrait contains the seeds of discontent. Joe's eyes are disturbingly "mixed up" and "in-between." Instead of being definitively blue, they are a "very undecided blue," and while he may be attractive, mild, good-natured, sweet-tempered, easy-going, and extremely strong, he is nevertheless foolish and weak. Here, one recalls Julia Kristeva's contention:

> It is thus not lack of cleanliness or health that causes abjection but what disturbs identity, system, order. What does not respect borders, positions, rules. The in-between, the ambiguous, the composite.[63]

In *Great Expectations*, significantly Dickens's last autobiographical novel, we have then the beginnings of Dickens's awareness that it is not always possible to radically separate oneself from what Kristeva would call "the shame of compromise."[64] Indeed, the binary opposition — bad mother/"all good" person — is like most binary oppositions indefinite and tenuous for, as Kristeva asserts, "the ambiguous opposition I/Other, Inside/Outside [is] an opposition that is vigorous but pervious, violent but uncertain."[65] So while Pip may be driven to draw a boundary between what he wishes to separate (i.e., his dangerous foster mother from his good foster father) he cannot help but display just how porous this boundary is. Pip's narrative may (like Dickens's other autobiographical narratives) seek to juxtapose an all-good person against a deficient mother, but in this final autobiographical novel it would appear that this rhetorical strategy has begun to lose its potency. The fact remains that even though he can't admit it to himself, Pip fundamentally views his foster father as dangerously weak and "mixed up." Pip's portrait of Joe therefore recalls the earlier portrait of his biological father. As previously explored, a close reading of Pip's statements concerning his father reveals that Pip viewed him as troublingly strong and weak.[66] He is initially described as rugged, yet his strength is nonetheless put into question by his association with his "sickly" blemished wife, the tragic loss of his five sons and his premature death. Accordingly, there would appear to be a strong connection between Pip's feelings for his foster father and his biological father.

While Pip may at some level be aware that his foster father is far from ideal, this is not something that he wishes to explore at any length and there are only two other points in the text where we get any inkling that Pip subconsciously views him as an agent of pollution. The first is when Pip as a child writes a letter to Joe on his slate which touchingly conveys his wish to teach him, be apprenticed to him and be close to him (75). According to John O. Jordan:

> Its naive phonetic spelling accurately transcribes Pip's working-class rural dialect, and its intended message is clearly one of loyalty and devotion to Joe. The written form of the message, however, distorts its content and produces an ironically prophetic subtext. Pip closes the letter by writing, "BLEVE ME INF XN PIP" (7. 75). He means to say "in affection," but he writes "infection." This inadvertent pun, made possible only by writing, discloses the shame that Pip has already begun to feel at Joe's lack of education. Literacy, it appears, is a social disease that divides one class from another and can infect even the best of friends.[67]

This is an excellent point, but I would like to suggest that the written form of the message can also be taken to reveal Pip's subconscious knowledge that his alliance with his foster father is contaminating. Indeed, Pip at base knows that the behavior that his foster father has modeled (particularly in relation to women) has been grossly deficient and has damaged him in ways that he cannot (at this tender age) even begin to imagine. In this respect, it is interesting to cite Christopher D. Morris's comment on one of the possible meanings of Pip's name:

A pip is also a disease or the symptom of a disease, so the semantic values of the word begin to cancel or contradict each other: a seed that is a disease, a growth that is dying.[68]

The second point is when Pip slips into a delirium towards the end of the book and confuses ostensible murderers with Joe:

> That I sometimes struggled with real people, in the belief that they were murderers, and that I would all at once comprehend that they meant to do me good, and would then sink exhausted in their arms, and suffer them to lay me down, I also knew at the time. But, above all, I knew that there was a constant tendency in all these people — who, when I was very ill, would present all kinds of extraordinary transformations of the human face, and would be much dilated in size — above all, I say, I knew that there was an extraordinary tendency in all these people, sooner or later to settle down into the likeness of Joe [472].

However, while Pip is aware in the very dim recesses of his mind that his foster father is to some degree responsible for the injustice and pain that he suffers in his life,[69] he never comes to grips with this on a conscious level and instead implicitly renders his sister and his biological mother as objects of disgust.

Shortly after the introduction of his sister and Joe, Pip returns from the graveyard to find from his "fellow-sufferer" Joe that his sister has been looking for him:

> "Mrs. Joe has been out a dozen times, looking for you, Pip. And she's out now, making it a baker's dozen."
> "Is she?"
> "Yes, Pip," said Joe; "and what's worse, she's got Tickler with her."
> At this dismal intelligence, I twisted the only button on my waistcoat round and round, and looked in great depression at the fire. Tickler was a wax-ended piece of cane, worn smooth by collision with my tickled frame [40].

Ruefully, Joe alerts Pip that Mrs. Joe plans to whip him for having left the house without her permission, yet there is no sense that Joe is against such corporal punishment. So, too, by euphemistically referring to the cane as "Tickler" Joe minimizes the damage that it will do to Pip. Seeking further intelligence, Pip asks Joe how long Mrs. Joe has been gone and in the narrative explains: "I always treated him as a larger species of child, as no more than my equal" (40). Clearly, Pip does not respect Joe as an authority figure but he nevertheless views him as benign. When Mrs. Joe comes to the door, Joe tells Pip to get behind the door. Pip does this, but Mrs. Joe quickly finds him and she quite literally throws him at Joe. A stronger man would rebuke his wife, but Joe merely fences Pip up in the chimney with "his great leg" (41). At this, Mrs. Joe lets loose:

> "Where have you been, you young monkey?" said Mrs. Joe, stamping her foot. "Tell me directly what you've been doing to wear me away with fret and fright and worrit, or I'd have you out of that corner if you was fifty Pips, and he was five hundred Gargerys."
> "I have only been to the churchyard," said I, from my stool, crying and rubbing myself.
> "Churchyard!" repeated my sister. "If it warn't for me you'd have been to the churchyard long ago, and stayed there. Who brought you up by hand?"
> "You did," said I.
> "And why did I do it, I should like to know?" exclaimed my sister.
> I whimpered, "I don't know."
> "*I* don't!" said my sister. "I'd never do it again! I know that. I may truly say I've never had this apron of mine off, since born you were. It's bad enough to be a blacksmith's wife (and him a Gargery) without being your mother."
> My thoughts strayed from that question as I looked disconsolately at the fire. For, the fugitive out on the marshes with the ironed leg, the mysterious young man, the file, the food, and the dreadful pledge I was under to commit a larceny on those sheltering premises, rose before me in the avenging coals. "Hah!" said Mrs. Joe, restoring Tickler to his station. "Churchyard, indeed! You may well say

churchyard, you two." One of us, by-the-bye, had not said it all. "You'll drive *me* to the churchyard betwixt you, one of these days, and oh, a pr-r-recious pair you'd be without me!" [41].

The implication of Mrs. Joe's words is serious to say the least. In her eyes, her brother and her husband are out of place within the scheme of her life. By her estimation, they have caused her nothing but suffering and a loss of freedom. Furthermore, she believes that they possess the power to put her in an early grave. Such a view is entirely in keeping with the anthropologist Mary Douglas's theory of out of place matter being contaminating because not simply does Mrs. Joe regard her husband and brother as offensive but she also believes that they are potentially lethal.

Significantly, too, Pip's thoughts stray to his meeting with the escaped convict and the "dreadful pledge" that he has undertaken to steal a file and food from his sister's house. Of particular note, these errant thoughts emanate from "the avenging coals." Certainly, Pip might fancifully imagine that the coals will take vengeance on behalf of the house for the crime that he is about to commit. However, the fact that the thoughts of the pending crime actually arise from "the avenging coals" just after his sister has questioned why she brought him up would suggest that Pip wants to get revenge against his sister but cannot admit this to himself and thereby projects such thoughts on to the nearby inanimate coals.[70] It is particularly interesting, too, that straying, in Pip's mind, is linked to revenge, because it should be remembered that Pip's encounter with the escaped convict (which led to his pledge to commit larceny on his sister's "sheltering premises") occurred only because he quite literally *strayed* from home. One should note, at this point, that Pip never explains why he went to the graveyard. Accordingly, his motives are open for interpretation. Did he, for instance, go to the graveyard to seek some sort of connection with his deceased relatives (if only that of fancifully drawing conclusions about them from their tombstones)? Could he have gone there in the hopes of enlisting some kind of support? As Weissman and Cohan write:

> In discovering that his parents and brothers are dead, Pip must face the shocking realization that he has no strong allies — strong either in age or in number — who could help him resist his cruel and unloving adopted mother.[71]

Did he go to the graveyard to get away from Mrs. Joe and her abuse? Or did he go because he wanted to make her worry about him? Indeed, was it his vengeful way of saying to her "I know you hate me and wish me dead. Now you can see what it's like to not have me around." The last motive is not as farfetched as it would seem. Pip clearly does not hold his sister in high regard, and as we later discover, he has (rather implausibly) borne a grudge towards her since the time that he was a baby:

> Within myself, I had sustained, from my babyhood, a perpetual conflict with injustice. I had known, from the time when I could speak, that my sister, in her capricious and violent coercion, was unjust to me. I had cherished a profound conviction that her bringing me up by hand, gave her no right to bring me up by jerks. Through all my punishments, disgraces, fasts and vigils, and other penitential performances, I had nursed this assurance; and to my communing so much with it, in a solitary and unprotected way, I in great part refer the fact that I was morally timid and very sensitive [92].

The extreme rhetoric of this passage recalls Dickens's autobiographical fragment. Just like the self-described "solitary and self-dependent"[72] Dickens who "might easily have been for any care that was taken of me, a little robber or a little vagabond,"[73] Pip is "solitary and unprotected." So, too, the depiction of Mrs. Joe as "capricious" and violently coercive may be likened to the defiance and force that Elizabeth Dickens displayed in flagrantly going against her husband's wishes and getting her son reinstated in the blacking warehouse. Finally, the "perpetual" and "cherished" sense of injustice that Pip harbors towards his sister is all too reminiscent of the undying sense of injustice that Dickens clings to: "I never afterwards forgot, I never shall forget, I never can forget, that my mother was warm for my being sent back."[74]

If all of these things are taken into consideration, then it is quite possible that Pip subconsciously went to the graveyard to get back at his sister. Interestingly, going against a tide of critics, Tyson Stolte suggests that Pip's ownership of "a perpetual conflict with injustice" serves as nothing less than "a motivation for revenge."[75] However, although he cites the passage where Pip directly connects his "conflict with injustice" with his sister's actions, he claims that Pip's desire for vengeance is generalized: "Pip very much does wish to hurt others in order to gain vengeance."[76] I would agree that Pip wishes to get revenge, but I am of the opinion that his wish is subconscious because it springs from the unacknowledged disgust that he feels towards his sister. Furthermore, I believe that it is his sister *above all* whom he wants to get back at.

In seeking to provide an "in-depth examination of how Pip exacts his vengeance,"[77] Tyson Stolte argues that "the meeting with Magwitch that opens the text first reveals to Pip the possibility of free expression of the aggression that his abused childhood has fostered in him, although the model of violence that Magwitch offers is one that Pip cannot fully employ."[78] Whilst I can appreciate this contention, I believe that far from offering a model of vengeance, Magwitch instead offers Pip the first opportunity to subconsciously get back at Mrs. Joe. As we know, Pip never connects the larceny that he commits on his home with his foster father, Joe: "The guilty knowledge that I was going to rob Mrs. Joe — I never thought I was going to rob Joe, for I never thought of any of the housekeeping property as his ... almost drove me out of my mind" (44).

Mrs. Joe is thereby, in Pip's mind, the outright victim of his impending law-lessness. In addition, as I have shown, the threatening Magwitch, firstly, appears just at the point in the text where Pip has figuratively aligned his mother to pollution; secondly, is fancifully enlisted by Pip to evade the defiling touch of corpses which are, in Kristevan terms, associated with the feminine; and, thirdly, possesses the potential (at least in Pip's vivid imagination) to shamefully and perhaps irrevocably "hook himself up" with the pollution of death (which, of course, within Kristevan terms is derived from the maternal). In such a way, Magwitch is intimately connected, in Pip's mind, with the dangers of coming in contact with feminine or maternal pollution. However, the fact that Mag-witch wants food and an implement to liberate himself from his shackles also aligns him in Pip's mind with a fundamental drive to escape death/pollution. Clearly, Magwitch wants to extricate himself from the border of his "condition as a living being,"[79] and as such, he gives the equally driven Pip a viable oppor-tunity to get back at some level at the actual woman who threatens to nullify his existence, his sister and adoptive mother, Mrs. Joe.

The opportunity that Magwitch presents, however, is not without its dan-gers, and Pip is beside himself with fear at going through with the robbery:

> Since that time, which is far enough away now, I have often thought that few people know what secrecy there is in the young, under terror. No matter how unreasonable the terror, so that it be terror. I was in mortal terror of the young man who wanted my heart and liver; I was in mortal terror of my interlocutor with the ironed leg; I was in mortal terror of myself, from whom an awful promise had been extracted; I had no hope of deliverance through my all-powerful sister, who repulsed me at every turn; I am afraid to think of what I might have done, on requirement, in the secrecy of my terror [46–47].

Pip's admission that he is afraid to think of what he might have done if pushed is noteworthy, and it is particularly significant that this admission immediately follows his contention that his sister (though "all-powerful") would not have used her ample resources to set him free from his awful quest. The inference that may be drawn from this is that Pip might have been induced "on require-ment" to have killed somebody and that somebody would logically have been his cold and unsupportive sister because, just as he never thought he was going rob Joe, he would never have thought of killing him either. Accepting this as a possibility paves the way for us to understand exactly why the highly disturbed Pip goes on to dream that the executed pirate is accusing him of a crime that demands the punishment of execution:

> If I slept at all that night, it was only to imagine myself drifting down the river on a strong spring-tide, to the Hulks; a ghostly pirate calling out to me through a speaking-trumpet, as I passed the gibbet-station, that I had better come ashore and be hanged there at once, and not put it off. I was afraid to sleep, even if I had

been inclined, for I knew that at the first faint dawn of morning I must rob the pantry. There was no doing it in the night, for there was no getting a light by easy friction then; to have got one, I must have struck it out of flint and steel, and have made a noise like the very pirate himself rattling his chains [47].

Here Pip is haunted by abjection. Not only has he just realized that under certain conditions he is capable of murder, but he is also about to commit a premeditated crime in broad daylight. As Kristeva writes: "Any crime, because it draws attention to the fragility of the law, is abject, but premeditated crime, cunning murder, hypocritical revenge are even more so because they heighten the display of such fragility."[80] Pip's need to commit the crime in daylight may even be said to underscore the tenuous nature of the law, and this might account for his hyperbolic claim that the noise of striking a light would have sounded like "the very pirate himself rattling his chains." However, his identification with the pirate at this point seems overdetermined. There would appear to be other, stronger reasons for comparing himself to the executed pirate, and the awful thought of killing his sister could well be one of them.

The vast majority of critics have claimed that Pip's sense of guilt is disproportionate to the crimes that he actually commits,[81] but I would respectfully submit that this is because the critics have not sufficiently addressed Pip's subconscious desire for revenge against his sister and his terrifying secret — just what he might have done to her if he'd been forced. Pip, of course, does not go on to murder his sister. His crime is only that of robbery, but in his heart he knows that he could very well have gone further. If we accept this, it can help us to understand not simply his over-identification with the executed pirate but also his immediate "ownership" of the horrific crime that is later committed against Mrs. Joe:

> I was at first disposed to believe that *I* must have had some hand in the attack upon my sister, or at all events that as her near relation, popularly known to be under obligations to her, I was a more legitimate object of suspicion than any one else [147].

This sense of ownership is compounded by the fact that the weapon that was used in the attack upon his sister was a filed-off leg iron, most probably the one that was filed off by the convict that Pip helped: "It was horrible to think that I had provided the weapon, however undesignedly, but I could hardly think otherwise" (148). Pip's terrifying secret may also help to explain his enduring sense of being surrounded by the odium of crime and incarceration:

> Mr. Wemmick and I parted at the office in Little Britain, where suppliants for Mr. Jagger's notice were lingering about as usual, and I returned to my watch in the street of the coach-office, with some three hours on hand. I consumed the whole time in thinking how strange it was that I should be encompassed by all this taint of prison and crime; that, in my childhood out on our lonely marshes on a winter

evening I should have first encountered it; that, it should have reappeared on two occasions, starting out like a stain that was faded but not gone; that, it should in this new way pervade my fortune and advancement [284].

His secret matricidal thoughts may also help us to understand why those around him regard him in a deficient and suspicious light. On Christmas Day, for instance, just after he has committed his theft against Mrs. Joe, Pip describes how the adult guests goad him and contemplate him with foreboding:

> It began the moment we sat down to dinner. Mr. Wopsle said grace with theatrical declamation — as it now appears to me, something like a religious cross of the Ghost in Hamlet with Richard the Third — and ended with the very proper aspiration that we might be truly grateful. Upon which my sister fixed me with her eye, and said, in a low reproachful voice, "Do you hear that? Be grateful."
>
> "Especially," said Mr. Pumblechook, "be grateful, boy, to them which brought you up by hand."
>
> Mrs. Hubble shook her head, and contemplating me with a mournful presentiment that I should come to no good, asked, "Why is it that the young are never grateful?" This moral mystery seemed too much for the company until Mr. Hubble tersely solved it by saying, "Naterally wicious." Everybody then murmured "True!" and looked at me in a particularly unpleasant and personal manner [57].

In the same scene, Pumblechook speculates on what Pip's life might have been like if he had been born as a pig:

> "You would have been disposed of for so many shillings according to the market price of the article, and Dunstable the butcher would have come up to you as you lay in your straw, and he would have whipped you under his left arm, and with his right he would have tucked up his frock to get a penknife from out of his waistcoat-pocket, and he would have shed your blood and had your life. No bringing up by hand then. Not a bit of it!" [58].

Later, in the scene where Mr. Pumblechook comes to get Pip to take him to visit Miss Havisham, Pumblechook pointedly reminds Pip to be especially grateful to Mrs. Joe who has, incidentally, gone to enormous efforts to clean him up for his visit:

> When my ablutions were completed, I was put into clean linen of the stiffest character, like a young penitent into sackcloth, and was trussed up in my tightest and fearfullest suit. I was then delivered over to Mr. Pumblechook, who formally received me as if he were the Sheriff, and who let off upon me the speech that I knew he had been dying to make all along: "Boy, be for ever grateful to all friends, but especially unto them which brought you up by hand!"
>
> "Good-bye, Joe!"
>
> "God bless you, Pip, old chap!"
>
> I had never parted from him before, and what with my feelings and what with soap-suds, I could at first see no stars from the chaise cart [83].

While all of these passages appear to reflect badly upon the adults around Pip, one should not ignore the fact that these adults indirectly charge him with displaying little or no gratitude towards his sister. Furthermore, they imply that he is vicious and potentially capable of wicked acts. Certainly, these comments can be put down to "a rule-governed Protestantism in which children are 'naterally wicious'"[82] but can't we perhaps accept that there might actually be something in the claims that these adults make? To be sure, these adults are presented as ignorant, insensitive oppressors but, notwithstanding their character flaws, they might just be capable of picking up on something that the seemingly sensitive Pip refuses to acknowledge within himself— his absolute repugnance for his foster mother. It is not, after all, outside the realm of possibility that Pip's disgust towards his sister might in fact be quite obvious to those around him. Pip could very well have not displayed any observable gratitude towards his sister and may have appeared vicious.[83] Certainly, there is nothing in the text to suggest that Pip ever thanked his sister for anything, and here again, Pip's behavior in this respect could very well be put down to the behavior that Joe has modeled for him. Indeed, if we engage in a close reading of the text it can be seen that Joe never actually thanks Mrs. Joe for any of her ministrations (performed even as they are with ill grace). Accordingly, he models exceedingly poor behavior towards a woman. Added to this, Joe never teaches Pip to apologize to Mrs. Joe for any of his misdemeanors. Perhaps the best example of this is the scene where Pip returns from his unsanctioned visit to the cemetery. Here, rather than telling Pip that his behavior has been unacceptable and asking him to apologize to his clearly distressed wife, Joe merely alerts Pip to Mrs. Joe's frenzied behavior: "Mrs. Joe has been out a dozen times, looking for you, Pip. And she's out now, making it a baker's dozen" (40). By doing so, he shows Pip that it is entirely acceptable to be uncaring and disrespectful towards Mrs. Joe. So, too, in the previously mentioned scene where Pip leaves to visit Miss Havisham, Joe does not take Pip to task when Pip (despite Pumblechook's flatulent "speech") disrespectfully ignores his wife and says good-bye only to him. Finally, Joe routinely doesn't answer his wife when she addresses him. The scene when Joe thinks Pip has bolted his food affords an example of this:

> The wonder and consternation with which Joe stopped on the threshold of his bite and stared at me, were too evident to escape my sister's observation.
> "What's the matter now?" said she, smartly, as she put down her cup.
> "I say, you know!" muttered Joe, shaking his head at me in very serious remonstrance. "Pip, old chap! You'll do yourself a mischief. It'll stick somewhere. You can't have chawed it, Pip."
> "What's the matter *now?*" repeated my sister, more sharply than before.
> "If you can cough any trifle on it up, Pip, I'd recommend you to do it," said Joe, all aghast. "Manners is manners, but still your elth's your elth."
> By this time, my sister was quite desperate, so she pounced on Joe, and, taking him by the two whiskers, knocked his head for a little while against the wall behind him: while I sat in the corner looking guiltily on.

"Now, perhaps you'll mention what's the matter," said my sister, out of breath, "you staring great stuck pig."

Joe looked at her in a helpless way; then took a helpless bite, and looked at me again.

"You know, Pip," said Joe, solemnly, with his last bite in his cheek, and speaking in a confidential voice, as if we two were quite alone, "you and me is always friends, and I'd be the last to tell upon you, any time. But such a–" he moved his chair and looked about the floor between us, and then again at me — "such a most oncommon Bolt as that!"

"Been bolting his food, has he? cried my sister.

"You know, old chap," said Joe, looking at me, and not at Mrs. Joe, with his bite still in his cheek, "I Bolted, myself, when I was your age — frequent — and as a boy I've been among a many Bolters; but I never see your Bolting equal yet, Pip, and it's a mercy you ain't Bolted dead."

My sister made a dive at me, and fished me up by the hair: saying nothing more than the awful words, "You come along and be dosed" [43–44].

This scene is probably intended to be darkly funny, but Joe's consistent negation of his wife is questionable to say the least. Certainly, Mrs. Joe's behavior is highly offensive, but there is nothing admirable about a husband treating his wife like she doesn't exist and especially in front of his impressionable adopted son.[84] Accordingly, a vicious cycle is set up whereby a lack of respect (modeled by Joe and emulated by Pip) is met with the anger, resentment, ill grace and abuse of Mrs. Joe (and the repeated censure of relatives and family friends). Certainly, in opposition to this, one might point to the key scene where Joe justifies his ineffectual stance towards his wife and appears to hold her in high regard:

"Your sister's a master-mind. A master-mind."

"What's that?" I asked, in some hope of bringing him to a stand. But, Joe was readier with his definition than I had expected, and completely stopped me by arguing circularly, and answering with a fixed look, "Her."

"And I an't a master-mind," Joe resumed, when he had unfixed his look, and got back to his whisker. "And last of all, Pip — and this I want to say very serous to you, old chap — I see so much in my poor mother, of a woman drudging and slaving and breaking her honest hart and never getting no peace in her mortal days, that I'm dead afeerd of going wrong in the way of not doing what's right by a woman, and I'd fur rather of the two go wrong the t'other way, and be a little ill-conwenienced myself. I wish it was only me that got put out, Pip; I wish there warn't no Tickler for you, old chap; I wish I could take it all on myself; but this is the up-and-down-and-straight on it, Pip, and I hope you'll overlook shortcomings."

Young as I was, I believe that I dated a new admiration of Joe from that night [79–80].

However, if we read this justification carefully we can see that in Joe's mind doing the right thing by a woman simply means ceding all of his power and authority to her (in order to meet his questionable psychological needs) and never so much as remonstrating with her if she chooses to abuse it. Fundamental respect towards a woman is thereby not on his agenda, and this is regrettably the stance that Pip comes to admire. According to Jeffrey Berman,

> On the basis of his admissions and family dynamics, Joe is implicated in his wife's sadistic treatment of Pip. An abused child, he seems to have chosen a spouse who resembles his abusive father. Unable to defend himself from a battering father, Joe prefers not to defend Pip from a battering stepmother. From the viewpoint of ego psychology, Joe identifies with the aggressor, suggesting his unconscious collusion with his wife's violence. Joe chooses to be helpless against his wife's onslaught, chooses to allow Pip to be abused. Bartleby's maddening refrain, "I would prefer not to," seems relevant to Joe's passive-aggressive behaviour. Ironically, his passivity infuriates his wife, further endangering Pip.
>
> Admittedly, the interpretation of Joe as a passive-aggressive sharply disagrees with the prevailing critical view.[85]

I am in agreement with Berman's critically divergent assessment of Joe as passive-aggressive but for entirely different reasons. Joe does indeed seem to have chosen a spouse who resembles his abusive father, but I believe he has done this not because he identifies with the aggressor but because he subconsciously blames his mother for failing to protect him from his father's abuse and seeks to indirectly deal with his hostility towards her through casting another woman — his wife — in the role of the aggressor. Joe, then is quite simply a man who has (through the means of passive aggression) made his wife assume the role of an aggressor so that he can get back (in a psychic and retrospective way) at his mother for her inability to, firstly, protect him from his abusive, alcoholic father and, secondly, to ensure that he received an adequate education. In terms of the latter point, this could account for Joe's firm but unsubstantiated belief that his wife wasn't in favor of having educated people within the family home:

> "And she an't over partial to having scholars on the premises," Joe continued, "and in partickler would not be over partial to my being a scholar, for fear as I might rise. Like a sort of rebel, don't you see?" [79].

According to Barickman, MacDonald and Stark, "Mrs. Joe is as desperate and harried in her own way as Magwitch, though the causes of her desperation are hidden while the forces that menace him are obvious."[86] This is to a large extent true and this is primarily because the forces that menace Mrs. Joe amount to nothing less than her husband's subconscious woman-hating, which perfectly serves to demonstrate what R. Howard Bloch would call "the elusiveness of misogyny."[87] Little wonder, then, that Pip is viewed by those around him as a vicious ingrate when he constantly has before him the example of his passively vicious foster father.

Interestingly, too, when Pip is older these family friends continue to view Pip in a highly suspicious light. Significantly, this becomes manifest on the very night that Mrs. Joe is viciously attacked. As Pip explains, he was loitering along the main street when he was accosted by Wopsle for the purposes of giving a reading to Pumblechook of "the affecting tragedy of George Barnwell" (144). Interestingly, what gets to Pip most about this protracted and tiresome reading is the way that Wopsle and Pumblechook appear to liken him to the murderous Barnwell:

> What stung me, was the identification of the whole affair with my unoffending self. When Barnwell began to go wrong, I declare that I felt positively apologetic, Pumblechook's indignant stare so taxed me with it. Wopsle, too, took pains to present me in the worst light. At once ferocious and maudlin, I was made to murder my uncle with no extenuating circumstances whatever; Millwood put me down in argument, on every occasion; it became sheer monomania in my master's daughter to care a button for me; and all I can say for my gasping and procrastinating conduct on the fatal morning, is, that it was worthy of the general feebleness of my character. Even after I was happily hanged and Wopsle had closed the book, Pumblechook sat staring at me, and shaking his head, and saying, "Take warning, boy, take warning!" as if it were a well-known fact that I contemplated murdering a near relation, provided I could only induce one to have the weakness to become my benefactor [145].

Pip's incredulous words "as if it were a well-known fact that I contemplated murdering a near relation" again should not blind us to the consideration that owing to the palpable and consistent repugnance that Pip has displayed towards his sister, it could well be a commonly held thought amongst those closest to the family that Pip would be capable of contemplating the murder of a near relation. So, too, it is more than a little telling that Orlick, the person who was directly responsible for attacking (and very nearly murdering) Pip's sister, can confidently maintain that Pip was the actual assailant:

> "I tell you it was your doing — I tell you it was done through you," he retorted, catching up the gun, and making a blow with the stock at the vacant air between us. "I come upon her from behind, as I come upon you to-night. *I* giv' it her! I left her for dead, and if there had been a limekiln as nigh her as there is now nigh you, she shouldn't have come to life again. But it warn't Old Orlick as did it, it was you" [437].

Orlick is of course an odious character, but here again, is this a good enough reason to deny him any insight into Pip's character? Working closely at the forge as a fellow apprentice with Pip, Orlick has after all been in a perfect position to observe the way in which Pip interacts with his sister and clearly he has detected within Pip an emotion towards Mrs. Joe that does not in any way resemble love.

It is all too easy to go along with Pip's narrative and assume that he is nothing less than "unoffending," but there is strong evidence to suggest that the people who have regularly interacted with Pip are not of the opinion that his attitude towards his sister is innocent or free from malice. Further, his "unof-

fending self" claim is somewhat undermined by his apparently innocent childhood wish that Joe would jettison Mrs. Joe from his life:

> "Your sister is given to government."
> "Given to government, Joe?" I was startled, for I had some shadowy idea (and
> I am afraid I must add, hope) that Joe had divorced her in favour of the Lords of
> the Admiralty, or Treasury.
> "Given to government," said Joe. "Which I meantersay the government of you
> and myself" [79].

This fairy tale solution to the problem of Mrs. Joe doesn't, of course, happen,
but it is interesting that the model that Pip imagines (one of separation from
Mrs. Joe through embracing a higher order) is exactly the course of action that
Pip follows. As we know, owing to the opportunistic motives of Mrs. Joe, Pip
is taken "up town" (81) to go and play at Miss Havisham's house. Mrs. Joe is
excited about the prospect because Pumblechook has all but convinced her that
"this boy's fortune may be made by his going to Miss Havisham's" (82). Pip
therefore leaves for Miss Havisham's with the full knowledge that his foster
mother is "warm" for him to go. Obvious parallels can be drawn here with the
autobiographical fragment. As Natalie McKnight writes:

> Mrs. Joe, another surrogate mother for Pip, also can be seen as a reworking of
> Dickens's hostilities toward his mother, since, like Elizabeth Dickens, she also
> seems willing to sell a young boy to the highest bidder in her eagerness to usher
> Pip off to Miss Havisham's.[88]

And certainly Mrs. Joe's eagerness to send Pip off could be viewed in a mercenary
light, as Gail Turley Houston writes: "Mrs. Joe also expects remuneration for
having raised Pip by hand, for obviously she hopes to advance her own fortunes
by placing him at Miss Havisham's."[89] So, too, Curt Hartog claims:

> [Pip] is seen as a burden until he can be exploited for his labor. When Miss Hav-
> isham employs him to play for her, Mrs. Joe's attitude is purely proprietary; like
> the Brobdingnagian farmer who exhibits little Gulliver for profit, she cares nothing
> for the performer's well-being.[90]

It is important to stress that along with knowing that his foster mother is
keen for him to go, Pip knows that if he plays his proverbial cards right the
reputedly "immensely rich" (81) Miss Havisham may see fit to bestow wealth
upon *him*. Accordingly, Miss Havisham represents for Pip another opportunity
to get back at Mrs. Joe, because if he were rich he would be able to thoroughly
distance himself from her (just as he originally sought to do through the means
of his trip to the cemetery) and thereby escape once and for all from her contaminating grip. If we view Miss Havisham in this light it goes a considerable
way to explain why Pip is not disgusted or horrified by Miss Havisham or her
house. As we know, when Pip first sees Miss Havisham he describes a night-
marish figure:

I saw that the bride within the bridal dress had withered like the dress, and like the flowers, and had no brightness left but the brightness of her sunken eyes. I saw that the dress had been put upon the rounded figure of a young woman, and that the figure upon which it now hung loose, had shrunk to skin and bone. Once, I had been taken to see some ghastly waxwork at the Fair, representing I know not what impossible personage lying in state. Once, I had been taken to one of our old marsh churches to see a skeleton in the ashes of a rich dress, that had been dug out of a vault under the church pavement. Now, waxwork and skeleton seemed to have dark eyes that moved and looked at me. I should have cried out, if I could [87].

However, Pip's first impulse to scream is one of the few natural responses that he has in relation to Miss Havisham. Following this, he successfully quells or even kills most of his natural impulses in the interests of gaining her favor. When she, for instance, directly asks him what his reaction is to her he immediately responds with a lie:

"Look at me," said Miss Havisham. "You are not afraid of a woman who has never seen the sun since you were born?"
I regret to state that I was not afraid of telling the enormous lie comprehended in the answer "No" [88].

So, too, when he later sees the vermin-infested room which houses Miss Havisham's rotten "bride-cake" (113) he displays no immediate dislike or aversion. Another child, one suspects, would immediately be repelled by such a sight and might even wish to run from the scene, but Pip does not express any disgust within his narrative or to Miss Havisham when she later enters the room. Indeed, the narrative almost naturalizes the scene because Pip chooses to render the vermin in quaint, anthropomorphic terms:

The most prominent object was a long table with a table-cloth spread on it, as if a feast had been in preparation when the house and the clocks all stopped together. An epergne or centre-piece of some kind was in the middle of this cloth; it was so heavily overhung with cobwebs that its form was quite indistinguishable; and, as I looked along the yellow expanse out of which I remember its seeming to grow, like a black fungus, I saw speckled-legged spiders with blotchy bodies running home to it, and running out from it, as if some circumstance of the greatest public importance had just transpired in the spider community.
I heard the mice too, rattling behind the panels, as if the same occurrence were important to their interests. But, the blackbeetles took no notice of the agitation, and groped about the hearth in a ponderous elderly way, as if they were short-sighted and hard of hearing, and not on terms with one another [113].

As a consequence, the insects and mice appear innocuous and even endearing and the scene is emptied of its horror. There is only one point in this scene where Pip registers any sense of repulsion: when Miss Havisham lays her hand on his shoulder and indicates that she intends to be laid out on the vermin-infested table when she is dead:

"This," said she, pointing to the long table with her stick, "is where I will be laid when I am dead. They shall come and look at me here."

With some vague misgiving that she might get upon the table then and there and die at once, the complete realization of the ghastly waxwork at the Fair, I shrank under her touch [113].

While Pip might momentarily shrink from Miss Havisham, it is interesting that he does not shrink from her because of her ghoulish wishes or disgusting domestic habits but, rather, because of his own fanciful thoughts. Even these do not sufficiently disturb him, because within moments he is dutifully walking her around and around the room in an effort to meet her sick commands. It is as if Pip feels quite at home amid this airless, dank, filthy, festering, noxious, verminous and insanitary environment. This is significant in light of Pip's earlier pejorative comment about his sister's housekeeping skills:

Mrs. Joe was a very clean housekeeper, but had an exquisite art of making her cleanliness more uncomfortable and unacceptable than dirt itself. Cleanliness is next to Godliness, and some people do the same by their religion [54].

Miss Havisham is everything that Mrs. Joe isn't. Dirty, unkempt (she wears only one shoe and a half-arranged veil when Pip first sees her) and thoroughly unhygienic, she is nonetheless, owing to her riches, a refreshing and pleasant prospect for Pip, and this is reflected in Pip's thoughts about her and her ward when he is away from them:

Whenever I watched the vessels standing out to sea with their white sails spread, I somehow thought of Miss Havisham and Estella; and whenever the light struck aslant, afar off, upon a cloud or sail or green hill-side or water-line, it was just the same.—Miss Havisham and Estella and the strange house and the strange life appeared to have something to do with everything that was picturesque [137].

This passage is particularly interesting because in the first chapter (where Pip's mother, Georgiana, featured so prominently) the sea was presented as dangerous and threatening. Here, Pip links the sea to Miss Havisham and Estella and speaks of it in light, fresh, free, pure and benign terms. The inability or refusal to see Miss Havisham or Estella in terms of pollution or danger is also conveyed by the fact that Pip believes that if he describes Miss Havisham and Estella to Mrs. Joe she will somehow sully them:

I felt convinced that if I described Miss Havisham's as my eyes had seen it, I should not be understood. Not only that, but I felt convinced that Miss Havisham too would not be understood; and although she was perfectly incomprehensible to me, I entertained an impression that there would be something coarse and treacherous in my dragging her as she really was (to say nothing of Miss Estella) before the contemplation of Mrs. Joe. Consequently, I said as little as I could, and had my face shoved against the kitchen wall [95].

The lie that Pip chooses to tell his sister and Pumblechook instead about Miss Havisham and Satis House (involving a velvet coach, a cake and wine, gold plates and four immense dogs fighting for veal cutlets out of a silver basket) is thereby his way of protecting the occupants of Satis House from the defiling apprehension of his sister and her ally while indirectly getting back at them through pulling the wool over their eyes and placing himself in a realm beyond their wildest imagination. However, as Peter Brooks remarks:

> The dream of Satis House is properly a daydream, in which "His Majesty, the Ego" pleasures himself with the phantasy of social ascension and gentility. Miss Havisham is made to play the role of the Fairy Godmother, her crutch become a magic wand, explicitly evoked twice near the close of part 1. This plot has adult sanction; its first expression comes from Pumblechook and Mrs. Joe when they surmise that Miss Havisham intends to "do something" for Pip, and Pip comes to believe in it, so that when the "Expectations" arrive he accepts them as the logical fulfilment of the daydream, of his "longings." Yet to identify Satis House with the daydream is to perform a repression of all else that Satis House suggests and represents — all that clusters around the central emblem of the rotting bride cake and its crawling things.[91]

Miss Havisham, her house and all that is in it would appear to be rotten to the core but, driven by his overwhelming desire to get beyond his foster mother and all that she represents, Pip turns a blind eye to this and instead pursues a foolish and misguided fantasy:

> She reserved it for me to restore the desolate house, admit the sunshine into the dark rooms, set the clocks a going and the cold hearths a blazing, tear down the cobwebs, destroy the vermin — in short, do all the shining deeds of the young Knight of romance, and marry the Princess [253].

Of this sad delusion, Robert Barnard claims:

> to him the insects and rot signify little more than wealth unused, and future glory promised him.... In fact the insects are symbolic of the repulsive desires and ambitions nurtured by the psychopathic woman who has laid waste the house.[92]

Eventually, Pip learns to his horror that Miss Havisham has not set him up as the hero of her life, but this is not before his love for her ward, Estella, has become so much a part of him that he cannot dislodge her from his imagination. This is perhaps the deepest irony in this novel of "great expectations" because Estella is fundamentally not that different from Mrs. Joe. Indeed, she resembles Mrs. Joe in so many ways that one could declare that Pip's expectations never really got much further than wanting to find a substitute for Mrs. Joe.

According to Brenda Ayers:

> Estella is the exact opposite of an angel-in-the-house. Instead of submissive, she is willful and domineering. Instead of gentle, kind, and tender, she is calculating, malicious, and hard. Instead of reserved, she is acrimonious. Instead of internalising her suffering, as was expected of a good Victorian woman, she inflicts suffering on men.[93]

Ayers could just as easily be speaking here of Mrs. Joe. At base, the two are almost interchangeable. We could add to this list of attributes: snobbish, resentful, capricious, unjust, heartless, hostile and physically abusive (Estella forcefully slaps Pip, for instance) and we could still be just as easily referring to Mrs. Joe. Like Mrs. Joe with her arsenal of pins and needles, Estella could even be said to be weapon-wielding, for as Robert R. Garnett states: "Estella wields her beauty like a weapon, a jeweled sword that dazzles and destroys."[94] Even Estella's sexuality may be likened to Mrs. Joe's sexuality because, like Mrs. Joe, the only time she appears to become aroused is when she has just witnessed two males fighting over her:

> There was a bright flush upon her face, as though something had happened to delight her. Instead of going straight to the gate, too, she stepped back into the passage, and beckoned me.
> "Come here! You may kiss me, if you like" [121].

This, of course, may be paralleled to Mrs. Joe's response after she has witnessed the fight between her husband and Orlick. As Robert Garnett recognizes, there is something distinctly sexual in Mrs. Joe's reaction:

> The only (reported) conjugal embrace between Joe and Mrs. Joe, just after she has witnessed him drubbing Orlick in the forge, shows her unmistakeably aroused. Swooning, she "was carried into the house and laid down ... and would do nothing but struggle and clench her hands in Joe's hair...."[95]

Even Estella's heritage can be likened to Mrs. Joe's. Estella turns out to be the daughter of a murderess and a convict who is ultimately given a death sentence; and Mrs. Joe, as Pip depicts her, is the daughter of a woman who is implicitly charged with the deaths of all of his male relatives and a man who is linked, in a figurative sense, to a pirate who has been executed.

Pip's responses to Estella are also very similar to Joe's responses to Mrs. Joe. Joe, as previously discussed, found Mrs. Joe physically attractive, but it would seem that there was nothing else that he particularly liked about her. So, too, Pip's attraction to Estella is primarily based on her physical desirability, and in his narrative he quite openly declares that there is nothing else about her that he finds remotely attractive:

> But, though she had taken such strong possession of me, though my fancy and my hope were so set upon her, though her influence on my boyish life and character had been all-powerful, I did not, even that romantic morning, invest her with any attributes save those she possessed. I mention this in this place, of a fixed purpose, because it is the clue by which I am to be followed into my poor labyrinth. According to my experience, the conventional notion of a lover cannot be always true. The unqualified truth is, that when I loved Estella with the love of a man, I loved her simply because I found her irresistible. Once for all; I knew to my sorrow, often and often, if not always, that I loved her against reason, against promise,

against peace, against hope, against happiness, against all discouragement that could be. Once for all; I loved her none the less because I knew it, and it had no more influence in restraining me, than if I had devoutly believed her to be human perfection [253–54].

Pip, then, is just as one-eyed as his foster father. Significantly, too, Pip speaks of Estella as having taken "such strong possession of me" and he regards her influence as "all-powerful." As we know, Pip believed that his foster father had been taken forcibly into marriage by Mrs. Joe (39), which is tantamount to saying that she had taken strong possession of him. Furthermore, Pip actually describes Mrs. Joe as "all-powerful" (46) and depicts his foster father as being completely under the influence of Mrs. Joe to the point where he views her as nothing less than a "master-mind" (79). Interestingly, too, just as Joe habitually chose to ignore what his wife had to say, Pip constantly chooses to ignore what Estella has to say. As we know, throughout the novel, Estella repeatedly warns Pip not to pursue her romantically:

"Pip, Pip ... will you never take warning?"
"Of what?"
"Of me."
"Warning not to be attracted by you, do you mean Estella?"
"Do I mean! If you don't know what I mean, you are blind" [319].

She also at every chance tells him that she is not interested in him but Pip consistently refuses to listen.

"When you say you love me, I know what you mean, as a form of words; but nothing more. You address nothing in my breast, you touch nothing there. I don't care for what you say at all. I have tried to warn you of this; now, have I not?
I said in a miserable manner, "Yes."
"Yes. But you would not be warned, for you thought I did not mean it. Now, did you not think so?
"I thought and hoped you could not mean it. You, so young, untried, and beautiful, Estella! Surely it is not in Nature."
"It is in *my* nature," she returned [376].

Estella's nature, however, is not what Pip is interested in. As his words reveal, he is interested only in the way that she looks, and her feelings are of little consequence to him. Indeed, nothing that she says has any meaning for him, as Hilary Schor notes: "To the very end, Estella says one thing and Pip hears another; while he insists he sees "no shadow of another parting," she says they "will continue friends apart."[96] Pip, then, is just as misogynistic towards Estella as Joe is to Mrs. Joe; and he is just as deluded about his actions toward her as his foster father is in relation to his treatment of Mrs. Joe. As we know, Joe likes to think of himself as a man who has consistently sought to do the right thing by a woman, but the fact is that he has pushed his wife into taking on the role of an aggressor so that he can, at a remove, work through the anger that he could not express towards his battered and beleaguered mother. So, too, Pip, as Ross Dabney puts it, "thinks of himself as a disinterested and selfless lover. But the fact is that he intends to take Estella as a gift from Miss Havisham, part of his expectations, a being who has no choice but to follow her guardian's money."[97]

The question of whether or not Pip and Estella actually "get together" is perhaps not worth asking because even if they did get together their union would in all likelihood come to resemble the only union that Pip has ever really known — the highly dysfunctional marriage of his angry and aggressive sister and her equally angry but passive-aggressive husband Joe. So while Pip's narrative may have convinced himself (on a conscious level) and most readers that Mrs. Joe is largely responsible for his sensitivity, moral timidity (92) and concomitant suffering, it is timely to consider that the implicit disgust towards women that his foster father modeled may have actually *forged* the "poor labyrinth" (253) that Pip got caught up in.

CHAPTER SIX

Postscript

> I believe that it is better to try to understand that someone who is a writer is not simply doing his work in his books, in what he publishes, but that his major work is, in the end, himself in the process of writing his books. The private life of an individual, his sexual preference, and his work are interrelated, not because his work translates his sexual life, but because the work includes the whole life as well as the text. The work is more than the work: the subject who is writing is part of the work.[1]

It would be a natural step to conclude this study by examining the "strange, haunting little story"[2] and fictional autobiography that Dickens wrote towards the end of his life, "George Silverman's Explanation." This bleak work of fiction which as Philip Hobsbaum claims, is "full of a pervading self-disgust,"[3] features a hero, George Silverman, who has a biological mother and a mother-surrogate. These women interestingly enough contribute to George's overwhelming sense of unworthiness and contamination, and while he assiduously tries throughout his life to pursue a pure and self-denying course, he cannot get beyond his feelings of guilt and taint, and finds himself at the last, as Q.D. Leavis puts it, "back where he started, repulsive to himself."[4] Whilst the story has obvious parallels to the autobiographical novels and is even thought by some to be the key to understanding Dickens,[5] I am of the opinion that another quite different area of Dickens's art provides this key.

Patricia Ingham in *Dickens, Women and Language* concludes her study with a postscript.[6] This postscript, titled "Rewriting Experience," examines extracts from Dickens's correspondence to show that his accounts of real women are as much literary constructs as the fictional women in his texts. Ingham, for instance, analyzes the sequence of letters that Dickens wrote after the death of his sister-in-law Mary Hogarth and shows how his descriptions of her evolved over time to the point where one can discern the evolution of a literary figure, "Mary." Indeed, Ingham suggests that in 1839 Dickens adapted the "firmly established literary exemplar"[7] of the Mary figure in order to write a *consolatium* for the publisher Bradbury when his young daughter died. So, too, Ingham considers the way that Dickens described his wife, Catherine, in the letters he wrote during and after their separation, and concludes that like the highly adaptable "Mary" figure, Dickens turned Catherine into a literary creation which could be shaped to suit different circumstances.[8] Finally, Ingham examines the ways in which Dickens described his mistress Ellen Ternan, and she contends that by representing her as simultaneously unfallen and fallen, Dickens created "his most sophisticated literary representation of a woman: one who enacts the ambiguity of his mapping of overtly contrasting groups of women."[9] Ingham, thereby, is concerned to show that life can imitate art rather than art imitating life. By contrast, I would like to conclude this study with a postscript that privileges the exegetic value of art rather than the mimetic value of life. Indeed, I will work to show that art can, if taken to the limit, actually provide the key to a writer's life.

Dickens's public readings of *Sikes and Nancy*[10] were, in their time, quite horrifying. Indeed, after Dickens had produced the *Sikes and Nancy* reading he was of two minds as to whether or not he should actually read it in public. According to Raymund Fitzsimons: "He adapted and cut the text with great care, but the result was so horrifying that he had been afraid to try it in public."[11] To try and resolve this question, Dickens decided to perform the reading to a select audience. His audience, however, agreed with him. After the reading, a member of the audience who happened to be a doctor told Dickens: "My dear Dickens, you may rely upon it that if only one woman cries out when you murder the girl, there will be a contagion of hysteria all over this place."[12] So, too, an invited critic was moved to such a degree that he candidly revealed to Dickens: "I am bound to tell you that I had an almost irresistible impulse to scream, and that, if anyone had cried out, I am certain I should have followed."[13] As for the public readings, while mass hysteria did not occur, audiences were nonetheless so convinced by "the Murder" that they actually lost track of where they were. During the first public reading, held at St. James's Hall in London on January 5, 1869, members of the audience "sat frozen in their seats," and it wasn't until Dickens had actually left the stage that they came back to life.[14] Certainly, the following extract, while set loose from its original dramatic moorings, is nonetheless sufficiently gruesome and graphic to disturb even the most desensitized modern reader:

> The housebreaker freed one arm, and grasped his pistol. The certainty of immediate detection if he fired, flashed across his mind; and he beat it *twice* upon the upturned face *that almost touched his own.*
> She staggered and fell, but raising herself on her knees, *she drew from her bosom a white handkerchief— Rose Maylie's — and holding it up towards Heaven, breathed one prayer, for mercy to her Maker.*

It was a ghastly figure to look upon. The murderer staggering backward to the wall, and shutting out the sight with his hand, seized a heavy club, and struck her down!!

The bright sun burst upon the crowded city in clear and radiant glory. *Through costly-coloured glass and paper-mended window, through cathedral dome and rotten crevice*, it shed *its equal ray*. It lighted up *the room* where *the murdered woman* lay. It did. He tried to shut it out, but *it would stream in*. If the sight had been a *ghastly* one in the *dull morning*, what was it, *now*, in all that *brilliant light!!!*

He had not moved; he had been afraid to stir. There had been a moan and motion of the hand; and, with terror added to rage, he had struck and struck again. Once he threw a rug over it; but it was worse to *fancy* the *eyes*, and imagine them moving towards him, than to see them glaring upward, as if *watching the reflection of the pool of gore that quivered and danced in the sunlight on the ceiling.* He had plucked it off again. And there was the body — mere flesh and blood, no more — but *such* flesh, *and so much blood!!!*

He struck a light, kindled a fire, and thrust the club into it. There was hair upon the end, which shrunk into a light cinder, and whirled up the chimney. Even that frightened him; but he held the weapon till it broke, and then piled it on the coals to burn away, and smoulder into ashes. He washed himself, and rubbed his clothes; there were spots upon them that would not be removed, but he cut the pieces out, and burnt them. *How those stains were dispersed about the room! The very feet of his dog were bloody!!!!*[15]

By all accounts, Dickens put everything into these readings and his performance was extraordinarily powerful and convincing. For one critic, "Never, probably, through the force of mere reading was a vast concourse held so completely in the grasp of one man."[16] For another:

> It was a masterpiece of reading, quite unparalleled in its way; and it is with no small pride one feels it can honestly be said that Mr. Dickens is the greatest reader of the greatest writer of the age.[17]

One reviewer even extravagantly declared that it was a performance which "our greatest histrionic artists might deem it the height of their ambition to produce."[18] Indeed, the great histrionic artist William Macready admitted as much when, after Dickens performed *Sikes and Nancy* in Cheltenham, he excitedly told Dickens: "In my — er — best times — er — you remember them, my dear boy — er — gone, gone!— no … it comes to this — er —Two Macbeths!"[19] The journalist Edmund Yates, in describing just one of the readings, was also in awe of Dickens's theatrical skills:

> Gradually warming with excitement he flung aside his book and acted the scene of the murder, shrieked the terrified pleadings of the girl, growled the brutal savagery of the murderer, brought looks, tones, gestures simultaneously into play to illustrate his meaning, and there was not one of those who had known him best or who believed in him most, but was astonished at the power and versatility of his genius.[20]

Technical virtuosity aside, however, it is my belief that Dickens's *Sikes and Nancy* readings were unparalleled for quite another reason and that reason is that they provide one of the clearest examples in the history of English literature of an author's direct engagement with and/or plunge into the realm of philosophical extremity that the philosopher Michel Foucault called "limit experience."

What is limit experience? There is no concise textbook definition of limit experience. The existential philosopher, Karl Jaspers used to speak of a "limit-situation," which is, basically, a situation occurring at the limit of one's existence where one can be sure of nothing. As Jaspers put it:

> there is nothing firm or stable, no indubitable absolute, no enduring support for experience or thought. Everything is in flux, in restless movement of question and answer; everything is relative, finite, split into opposites — nothing is whole, absolute, essential.[21]

But while Jaspers believed that in a limit-situation there is no firm ground and that everything is stripped from the subject, he nonetheless maintained that the subject would still retain its essential being. Writers after Jaspers came to dispute this notion. Maurice Blanchot, in particular, claimed that a limit-situation contained no existential consolation, as he states:

> The self has never been the subject of this experience. The "I" will never arrive at it, nor will the individual, this particle of dust that I am, nor even the self of us all that is supposed to represent absolute self-consciousness.... We speak as though this were an experience, and yet we can never say we have undergone it.[22]

For Blanchot, in a true limit-situation the subject is essentially without relation to itself. Accordingly, Blanchot maintains that limit experience is "the affirmation of a self that accepts being entirely outside itself, delivered over and boldly entrusted to the strangeness of the outside."[23]

One of the most influential writers in terms of limit experience was Georges Bataille. Indeed, Michel Foucault is said to have formulated his notion of limit experience through reading Georges Bataille's work,[24] in particular his 1943 text *Inner Experience.*[25] This work is essentially a fragmentary series of highly introspective, gnomic reflections on the nature of experience. Couched in quasi-mystical terms it attempts to question traditional Judeo-Christian notions of experience whereby subjects stand in relation to a transcendent God. For the atheist Bataille, such notions are unacceptable, as he writes: "Dogmatic presuppositions have provided experience with undue limits: he who already knows cannot go beyond a known horizon."[26] Accordingly, Bataille seeks to define a space where a subject can experience "ecstasy" or "rapture"[27] through a transgression of the subject's own limits, as opposed to the limits defined by morality, religion, or discourse. The governing principle of this state of rapture is what Bataille calls "non-knowledge"[28] because, as he puts it: "Experience is, in fever and anguish, the putting into question (to the test) of that which a man knows of being."[29] Bataille's thought parallels Jasper's thought as both see the limit experience as a space beyond absolutes. Bataille writes that it is "an experience laid bare, free of ties, even of an origin."[30] However, Bataille, like Blanchot, believes that the self is not the subject of this experience because at base it is about getting beyond all notions of identity.[31]

Taking his lead from Bataille, Foucault has defined limit experience as a state of concomitant self-destruction and self-fulfillment; a turbulent experience of "untamed exteriority" and "suffering-pleasure" which heralds truth; an experience that revels in exploring the depths of irrational aspects of human existence; a transformative mystical experience which produces a "changed" subject.[32] Foucault also believes, like Bataille, that a transgression of the subject's own limits is the only means to achieve ecstasy:

> Transgression carries the limit right to the limit of its being; transgression forces the limit to face the fact of its imminent disappearance, to find itself in what it excludes (perhaps, to be more exact, to recognize itself for the first time), to experience its positive truth in its downward fall?[33]

However, transgression should not be regarded as negative or positive:

> Transgression contains nothing negative, but affirms limited being — affirms the limitlessness into which it leaps as it opens this zone to existence for the first time. But correspondingly, this affirmation contains nothing positive: no content can bind it, since by definition, no limit can possibly restrict it.[34]

One of the most interesting things about Foucault is that in his own life he "deliberately"[35] sought out limit experience. He was fascinated by life episodes which could potentially invoke "a sacrifice, an actual sacrifice of life."[36] Such episodes were intrinsically tied up with notions of personal metamorphosis as they signified "a voluntary obliteration that does not have to be represented in books because it takes place in the very existence of the writer."[37] In Foucault's case, these kind of life episodes could best be achieved through consensual homosexual sado-masochistic sex. According to Foucault, sado-masochistic eroticism amounted to "the real creation of new possibilities of pleasure."[38] However, Foucault's notion of pleasure was extreme: "Complete total pleasure ... for me, it's related to death."[39] In his account of Foucault's life,[40] entitled, appropriately enough, *The Passion of Michel Foucault*, James Miller reveals the lethal nature of Foucault's pleasure-seeking, which took the form of sado-masochistic sexual encounters in San Francisco gay bathhouses during the early years of the AIDS epidemic:

> That fall [of 1983], he later told friends, he returned to the bathhouses of San Francisco. Accepting the new level of risk, he joined in the orgies of torture, trembling with "the most exquisite agonies," voluntarily effacing himself, exploding the

limits of consciousness, letting real, corporeal pain insensibly melt into pleasure through an alchemy of eroticism.[41]

According to Miller, in repeatedly seeking out these forms of limit experience, Foucault essentially gambled with his life:

> *Given the circumstances in San Francisco in the fall of 1983, as best I could reconstruct them, to have taken AIDS as a "limit experience," it seemed to me, would have involved engaging in potentially suicidal acts of passion with consenting partners, most of them likely to be infected already; deliberately throwing caution to the wind, Foucault and these men were wagering their lives together; that, at least, is how I came to understand what may have happened.*[42]

Admittedly, Miller's study of Foucault is not the last word on Foucault and there are other more conservative views concerning his death, but Miller provides detailed and plausible evidence to back up his suggestions. Indeed, in a 1990 interview, Foucault's long-time lover Daniel Defert[43] more or less stated that Foucault had consciously chosen to take AIDS as a limit experience: "He took AIDS very seriously.... When he went to San Francisco for the last time, he took it as *limit experience*."[44] As going to San Francisco involved not just academic engagements but a series of arguably unprotected sado-masochistic sexual experiences in homosexual bathhouses, one can readily surmise, then, that Foucault was courting death.

So what do gay bathhouses and AIDS have to do with Dickens? Infinitely little, but the potential relation between limit experience and death has considerable relevance to Dickens. There is a general consensus that Dickens's insistence on performing the *Sikes and Nancy* readings played a major role in contributing to his death. Dickens's son, Charley; Dickens's manager, George Dolby; Dickens's doctor, Frank Beard; and Dickens's friend and fellow novelist Wilkie Collins all believed that the final readings of *Sikes and Nancy* killed Dickens. Charley recalls how Dickens's doctor unequivocally said:

> I have had some steps put up against the side of the platform, Charley. You must be there every night, and if you see your father falter in the least, you must run up and catch him and bring him off with me, or, by Heaven, he'll die before them all.[45]

George Dolby claimed: "That the frequency with which he persisted in giving this Reading was affecting him seriously, nobody could judge better than myself, living and travelling with him as I was, day after day and week after week."[46] Wilkie Collins maintained that this reading "did more to kill Dickens than all his work put together."[47] Finally, Dickens's best friend and later biographer John Forster noted that Dickens's pulse rate rose to its highest levels whenever he did the *Sikes and Nancy* readings,[48] and while not directly linking this particular reading to Dickens's death, Forster nevertheless was in no doubt that Dickens's public readings contributed to his early death:

No supposed force in reserve, no dominant strength of will, can turn aside the penalties sternly exacted for disregard of such laws of life as were here plainly overlooked; and though no one may say that it was not already too late for any but the fatal issue; there will be no presumption in believing that life might yet have been for some time prolonged if these readings could have been stopped."[49]

As most commentators have remarked, the *Sikes and Nancy* reading quite literally obsessed Dickens. Edmund Wilson states: "Certainly the murder of Nancy had taken on something of the nature of an obsessive hallucination."[50] Philip Collins writes:

> Clearly his attachment to this piece went far beyond the understandable satisfaction of a professional performer in being able to create such an impression and win such acclaim for his talents.[51]

Robert Newsom bluntly claims that "he simply could not leave it alone."[52] Not only did it become the "most often-performed item of his readings repertoire in 1870" but it became "quite literally and fatally entrancing or captivating."[53] So, too, Peter Ackroyd asserts:

> He read it approximately four times a week and nothing on earth seemed to be able to prevent him from doing so, even at the cost of life and health. It took on, for him, an hallucinatory reality. It became almost a monomania.[54]

Certainly, contemporary testimonials relating to Dickens's actions at the time of these readings make the epithet "obsessive" seem mild. By all accounts, no matter what legitimate concerns were expressed by those closest to him, Dickens "would listen to no remonstrance in respect of it,"[55] and no matter what the cost to his health, Dickens's would not give up the horrific "Murder" from his repertoire. Dickens's son Charley, for instance, was, from the start, very much against the "Murder" readings. In November 1868 Dickens began to rehearse the readings at home. According to Raymund Fitzsimons:

> As with all his Readings, he rehearsed it over and over again, sometimes three or four times a day, striving for the effects that would arouse passion and horror in his audience. One afternoon his son, Charley, was working in the library at Gad's Hill with the windows open. He was startled to hear in the garden a voice raised violently followed by screams. He rushed outside and saw his father murdering an imaginary Nancy with ferocious blows. At dinner he mentioned to his father what he had seen and Dickens acted it for him again. At the end he asked his son what he thought of it. "The finest thing I have ever heard," said Charley, "but don't do it."[56]

Charley clearly had concerns about the effect of this strenuous reading on his father's health, but Dickens was determined to go ahead with it and shortly thereafter gave the aforementioned private reading of the "Murder" before a select audience. At the conclusion of the reading he again solicited his son's opinion: "'Well, Charley, and what do you think of it now?'" Charley replied:

'It is finer even then I expected, but I still say, don't do it.'[57] Apparently, just at that moment Edmund Yates came over to join Dickens and his son.

> "What do you think of this, Edmund?" Dickens asked. "Here is Charley saying it is the finest thing he has ever heard, but persists in telling me, without any reason, not to do it." Yates gave Charley a quick look and, to Dickens's amazement, said gravely: "I agree with Charley, sir."[58]

Dickens, however, was by then too caught up with his performance of the "Murder" to let it go, as his manager George Dolby wrote: "The horrible perfection to which he brought it acted as a charm to him and made him the more determined to go on with it come what might."[59] He so identified with it, in fact, that after the "Murder" had become a central part of his repertoire he admitted to having "a vague sensation of being 'wanted'"[60] as he walked about the streets, and at one stage claimed the morning after a reading that "the crime being completely off my mind, and the blood spilled, I am (like many of my fellow-criminals) in a highly edifying state today."[61] His letters at the time were also peppered with phrases like: "I am murdering Nancy"; "My preparations for a certain murder"; "I commit the murder again"; I have a great deal of murdering before me."[62] After readings, he was also known to jokingly refer to his "murderous instincts,"[63] which apparently so disturbed a group of friends who came to see him in his dressing room after one reading that they actually turned down Dickens's invitation to have supper with him and could not find the words to congratulate him.[64] Such reactions did not faze Dickens, because he genuinely believed that audiences had a "horror of me after seeing the murder."[65]

At the end of a typical *Sikes and Nancy* reading, Dickens's pulse rate, which was normally seventy-two, would shoot as high as one hundred and twenty-four[66] and "he would often have to lie on a sofa, quite unable to speak a word, for an interval of ten minutes before gathering his strength and staggering back to the platform to read another item."[67] On one particular occasion, in Edinburgh, Dickens became so vehement during a reading that he "drove all the breath out of his body" and upon leaving the platform "fell into the arms" of his manager Dolby and his valet, who had to support him into his dressing room.[68] Added to this, that same night, during supper, when Dolby suggested that Dickens ease up on the readings of *Sikes and Nancy* as the success of the tour was assured regardless of what Dickens chose to read, Dickens apparently

> jumped up from his chair in a paroxysm of rage. He threw his knife and fork down on his plate with such force that he shattered it, and shouted: "Dolby, your infernal caution will be your ruin one of these days."[69]

Of this episode, Raymund Fitzsimons writes:

> Perhaps he was angry at the implication that he was not up to the work. He always resented any reference to his failing health. But this does not explain the extent of

his anger. He was beside himself with rage. Dolby had never before seen him in such a temper. It is most probable that Dickens was angry because Dolby had taken from him any financial excuse for reading the "Murder" so frequently.[70]

Just what was Dickens's motivation for committing the "Murder" as many as four times a week when, firstly, his doctors had advised him against it owing to his fragile state of health, and, secondly, his farewell season of 1868–1869 readings was not only half completed but a clear financial success when he introduced the reading to his repertoire? There are two recorded reasons that Dickens gave. In the first place, he felt that he needed a powerful novelty to ensure that the agents of the farewell tour, the Chappells, would not lose any of their investment in the tour. As Forster stated:

> He was beset by a misgiving, that, for a success large enough to repay Messrs Chappell's liberality, the enterprise would require a new excitement to carry him over the old ground.[71]

The second reason that Dickens gave for performing these readings was that he wanted to leave behind him "the recollection of something very passionate and dramatic, done with simple means, if the art would justify the theme."[72] Certainly, these reasons appear quite plausible, but Dickens's own actions suggest that he had a much larger vested interest in the readings than his impresarios did, and that his concerns about creating passion and drama were not simply focused on the need to achieve lasting literary glory as this was already well assured.

Unsurprisingly, a number of biographers and critics have speculated on the real reasons as to why Dickens needed to keep committing the "Murder." Fred Kaplan in his biography of Dickens writes: "In repeatedly murdering her, he expressed himself with displaced violence against the horrible women of his life, his mother and his wife."[73] Raymund Fitzsimons says:

> The "Murder" Reading had become for him a means of expressing all the things he raged against in his mind, and as the ferocious blows rained down on the imaginary upturned face of Nancy, he was perhaps symbolically enacting his bitterness for his wife and his guilt over Ellen Ternan.[74]

Peter Ackroyd in his biography of Dickens conjectures:

> Can we not see [the condition of Dickens's childhood] revived here? But, on this occasion, only the horror and hatred which he had once felt. Killing his mother. Killing his sister.[75]

Sylvia Manning writes:

> The compulsion and the high stimulation both came as Dickens acted out the criminal violence he could not acknowledge in himself. It must have been a great relief. Dickens, was, and at bottom knew himself to be, a violent man.[76]

According to Robert Newsom:

> Dickens was drawn to the Murder not simply because of the added sense of power
> over his public that it gave him, but because it drew upon deeper emotions that
> even the frequent and obsessive repetitions of the performance did nothing to
> lessen, as is evident in Dolby's report that a "craving" to do it all again and indulge
> what Dickens "used jokingly to call his 'murderous instincts'" would return within
> hours after a performance.[77]

For Malcolm Andrews, Dickens simply wanted to bring people together:

> Night after night, luxuriating in polymorphousness and monopolylogue, the Old
> Enchanter tore himself to pieces, in order to fuse thousands of strangers into one
> community.[78]

Finally, Claire Tomalin simply states: "He wanted the excitement and the public
wanted to be horrified."[79] A variety of motives are thereby put forward, but significantly, all of these commentators suggest that Dickens used the medium of
popular entertainment to express the violent aspect of his nature. Popular entertainment therefore gave Dickens a space in which he could give vent to the
emotions that he suppressed in his own life.

The same could be said in a vicarious sense for the Victorian public. One
has only to consider what was perhaps the era's most powerful novelty, *Punch
and Judy*. This extremely violent puppet show was universally popular. During
this show, the eponymous Punch kills his wife, Judy, his child and his doctor.
Added to this, he strikes a dog called Toby; kills Toby's master; bashes a servant;
batters a blind man; kills his hangman; and kills the Devil. None of these
exploits deterred the Victorian public. Again and again, people from every
sphere of life flocked to see the show. As Bernard Blackmantle noted in 1826,
Punch's opening tune always served to

> act with talismanic power upon the locomotive faculties of all the peripatetics
> within hearing, attracting everybody to the travelling stage, young and old, gentle
> and simple; all the crowd seem as if magic chained them to the spot.[80]

Blackmantle also noted that when Punch appears, "Nothing is heard but one
deafening shout of clamorous approbation."[81] Certainly, the medium of pup-
petry dehumanized and distanced the show's violent material to the point where
it became a laughing matter. However, the fact remains that the Victorian
public repeatedly and enthusiastically converged to see this brutal show. As
Robert Leach writes:

> On the surface, *Punch and Judy* presents fairly childish knockabout, yet adults
> watch it compulsively. At least part of the reason for this lies in the ability of the
> adult subconscious to accept it as an imagistic and exploratory fantasy. This was
> probably particularly true for middle class Victorians, so much of whose sexual
> experience was either guilt-haunted or subliminal. During the fantasy the spectator
> suspends the moralising function of his brain so that he can indulge himself freely
> in a carnival of the imagination.[82]

Could it also be the case that the relentlessly violent nature of the show gave the Victorian public nothing less than an outlet to vicariously dip into the perilous waters of limit experience? Might it also be said that Dickens, as a devotee of this form of popular entertainment, relished the show's uninhibited celebration of crossing limits and even drew upon *Punch and Judy* in his *Sikes and Nancy* readings? After all Sikes bludgeons Nancy just as Judy is bludgeoned, and there is a dog at Sikes's side which is all too reminiscent of Toby. The puppet show *Punch and Judy* is also mentioned in just about every one of Dickens's books, and many of Dickens's characters remind readers of *Punch and Judy*, as Robert Morse, when considering the extraordinary scope of Dickens's concealed myths and archetypes, writes: "Who could Mr. and Mrs. Smallweed be, by the way, other than Punch and Judy?"[83] There is, of course, nothing funny about the *Sikes and Nancy* story or the readings that Dickens gave, but this does not mean that Dickens was not influenced at least to some degree by *Punch and Judy*. According to Grahame Smith, Dickens's lifelong enjoyment of popular entertainment not simply fed into but actually strengthened his writing at its most serious. Indeed, for Smith, this is "a key aspect of that confluence of forces we call Dickens."[84]

In working to understand what drove Dickens to obsessively perform this reading, there is yet another point which deserves to be considered. Dickens was not simply the perpetrator of the horrifying "Murder" he was also in every respect the victim for, as he put it at the time of the readings, he was currently being "nightly murdered by Mr. W. Sikes."[85] Indeed, according to Peter Ackroyd, Dickens had "a tendency towards self-punishment" that was "reflected by the fact that all the time he was delivering himself up to be "murdered" by Bill Sikes, just as he in turn became the foul murderer of a woman."[86] Dickens, then, in his *Sikes and Nancy* readings is a conflation of man and woman, murderer and victim. As a result, he cannot simply be regarded as a man who gets a perverse thrill out of simulating the murder of a young prostitute onstage. Rather, he is a man who is driven by sado-masochistic impulses and a man who, in the truest sense of the word, can be labeled a "Switch."

What's a "switch"? A switch, according to a popular late-twentieth-century text on sado-masochism, *Screw the Roses, Send Me the Thorns*, is "a person who enjoys taking either side in SM role or physical play; i.e., top or bottom, dom or sub."[87] Owing to this variable orientation, a switch is said to have "the best of both worlds."[88] But while Dickens, in performing his *Sikes and Nancy* readings may be viewed in S&M parlance as a switch, he is an interesting variation because he doesn't act out his shifting inclinations with a partner; rather, he takes on the roles of "top" and "bottom" in his own person. Accordingly, Dickens, through the vehicle of his *Sikes and Nancy* readings, may be said to seek the ultimate in terms of auto-erotic power.

At this point, some might say yes, Dickens is seeking power by acting as the perpetrator of his murder, but how could he be seeking power as the victim of his murder? He is seeking erotic power and achieving it because power is essentially a very fluid term in the world of S&M. The thing about "subs"' in S&M culture is that they generally get what they want. Because pure sado-masochism is consensual, submissives are always in charge as they have the capacity to say no to any act that displeases them. So while the submissive may appear to be in a position of helplessness and vulnerability, in reality this isn't the case. As Philip Miller and Molly Devon put it in *Screw the Roses, Send Me the Thorns*:

> The submissive obeys only because she chooses to. There is nothing compelling her obedience except her resolve. The submissive is, therefore, empowering the dominant by her decision. We call a consensual empowerment of the dominant by the submissive a power exchange. Just as she gave her consent, she can take it away at any time. Power in S&M flows from the bottom up.[89]

If we apply this to Dickens, we can see that by enthusiastically embracing both roles in *Sikes and Nancy*, Dickens clearly chooses at *a performance level* to murder and be murdered and at *an individual level* to enact a murder and run the risk of dying.[90] Further, these choices, when viewed in the light of sado-masochism, are nothing less than empowering, self-affirming acts. Of course, if one chooses to run the risk of dying there is the possibility that death will be the outcome, but this is a risk that Dickens is very willing to take, as Malcolm Andrews asserts:

> Dickens's willingness as an actor or Reader to indulge his "wayward" and "wild" impulses amounted to a public experiment in a kind of self-annihilation. This is the Dionysian part of him, the voluntary fissility of the self.[91]

Nowhere, perhaps is this better illustrated than by the fact that just before he gave his final performance of *Sikes and Nancy*, he whispered to a friend on his way to the platform: "I shall tear myself to pieces."[92] As Malcolm Andrews remarks, "This is a revealing phrase. Like the redeeming Ghost of Christmas Past Dickens in performance became an exhilarating medley of floating dis-memberment."[93] Further, Andrews definitively describes the readings as "acts of self-morcellation."[94] Dickens, accordingly, takes his particular auto-erotic brand of S&M to its very limits — the kind of limits that Foucault and others such as the Marquis de Sade explored in entirely different personal ways.

Dickens, of course, had been warned by many people that if he kept reading his murder story he might, at the very least, seriously impair his health, but Dickens vehemently *chose* to keep reading it. Incredibly, even when he had finished his farewell reading tour he could not give up the "Murder" perform-ance. As Philip Collins writes: "It is reported ... that a day or two before his death he was discovered in the grounds [of his house] at Gad's Hill re-enacting the murder of Nancy."[95] This is quite bizarre. If the tour was over and had been a clear financial success, why would the exhausted and unwell Dickens want to perform this reading *by himself* in his garden? Surprisingly, very few commentators have analyzed this extraordinary and highly disturbing episode in Dickens's life. The fact that this occurred at all gives rise to a series of questions. Had the performance become a ritualistic act to the point where it didn't really matter whether or not Dickens had an audience? Did the "Murder" even need to be performed in front of an audience? Indeed, was the performance less about Dickens's stated ideals (providing a powerful novelty to ensure the success of the reading tour or leaving behind the memory of "something very passionate") than about Dickens's obsessive need to tear himself to pieces? Did Dickens value performing the "Murder" over and above his life? Was Dickens less interested in horrifying audiences than in horrifying himself to death? Did Dickens want to get completely beyond *the* horror of his life — the fact that his mother was keen to return him to a place of degradation that amounted to the death of all of his hopes and dreams? Robert Newsom is useful here. Noting that the murder of Nancy essentially represented a return to one of Dickens's earlier novels, *Oliver Twist*, Newsom associates this with the pain of Dickens's childhood:

> The return to *Oliver Twist* no doubt signals a return to, or rather the survival of, the childhood fears associated with Warren's and his father's imprisonment, although Nancy's relationship to that material is indirect and complex — her plot effectively takes over the novel at a point when Oliver himself seems to drop out except as a mere counter in other people's games.[96]

While Nancy's relationship to the circumstances of Dickens's youth may appear indirect and complex it becomes clearer if one considers her essential role in *Oliver's* youth. Nancy, a prostitute leading a self-confessed "bad life"[97] among a gang of thieves, nevertheless risks her life to ensure that Oliver is kept safe from harm. Indeed, after overhearing a highly disturbing piece of intelligence concerning Oliver, she drugs her cruel partner, Sikes, with laudanum and rushes across London in a desperate bid to speak to Oliver's protectress Rose Maylie (later revealed to be Oliver's aunt) who is staying in "a family hotel in a quiet but handsome street near Hyde Park" (358). Arriving at her destination, Nancy is treated as a pariah by the servants in the establishment, but to Nancy's surprise, Rose treats her kindly:

> "It's a hard matter to get to see you, lady. If I had taken offence, and gone away, as many would have done, you'd have been sorry for it one day, and not without reason either."
> "I am very sorry if any one has behaved harshly to you," replied Rose. "Do not think of that. Tell me why you wished to see me. I am the person you inquired for."

The kind tone of this answer, the sweet voice, the gentle manner, the absence of any accent of haughtiness or displeasure, took the girl completely by surprise, and she burst into tears.

"Oh, lady, lady!" she said, clasping her hands passionately before her face, "if there was more like you, there would be fewer like me, — there would — there would!" [361].

Rose, as the text has previously shown, is quite perfect:

[She] was in the lovely bloom and spring-time of womanhood; at that age, when, if ever angels be for God's good purposes enthroned in mortal forms, they may be, without impiety, supposed to abide in such as hers.

She was not past seventeen. Cast in so slight and exquisite a mould; so mild and gentle; so pure and beautiful; that earth seemed not her element, nor its rough creatures her fit companions. The very intelligence that shone in her deep blue eyes, and was stamped upon her noble head, seemed scarcely of her age, or of the world; and yet the changing expression of sweetness and good humour, the thousand lights that played about the face, and left no shadow there; above all, the smile, the cheerful, happy smile, were made for Home, and fireside peace and happiness [264].

Completely taken by Rose's goodness and compassion, Nancy tells her of the terrible danger that she has placed herself in: "I have stolen away from those who would surely murder me, if they knew I had been here, to tell you what I had overheard" (362). What Nancy has overheard is a threat by Oliver's wicked half-brother Monks that he will relentlessly seek to wreck Oliver's life:

He said, with oaths common enough in my ears, but strange to yours, that if he could gratify his hatred by taking the boy's life without bringing his own neck in danger, he would; but, as he couldn't, he'd be upon the watch to meet him at every turn in life; and if he took advantage of his birth and history, he might harm him yet [363].

Determined to investigate the matter further, Rose persuades Nancy to meet with her and Oliver's guardian, Mr. Brownlow, at a later date. Nancy assents and tells Rose where she can be found: "Every Sunday night, from eleven until the clock strikes twelve ... I will walk on London Bridge if I am alive" (365). While Nancy is not able to get away to meet on the first Sunday, she manages, at great risk to herself, to keep the appointment on the following Sunday. At this meeting, Mr. Brownlow asks Nancy to deliver up Fagin but Nancy refuses to do this owing to her loyalty to Fagin and other gang members:

... bad life as he has led, I have led a bad life too; there are many of us who have kept the same courses together, and I'll not turn upon them, who might — any of them — have turned upon me, but didn't, bad as they are [412].

Nancy is, however, prepared to deliver up Monks if she can be given assurances that he will not be told of her actions:

"Monks would never learn how you knew what you do?" said the girl, after a short pause.

"Never," replied the gentleman. "The intelligence should be so brought to bear upon him, that he could never even guess" [413].

Satisfied with this pledge, Nancy provides a thorough description of the place where Monks can be located, "the best position from which to watch it without exciting observation, and the night and hour on which Monks was most in the habit of frequenting it" (413). She also provides a detailed description of Monks's physical appearance. Extremely grateful for her assistance, Brownlow offers Nancy the chance to start her life afresh:

> I do not say that it is in our power to offer you peace of heart and mind, for that must come as you seek it; but a quiet asylum, either in England, or, if you fear to remain here, in some foreign country, it is not only within the compass of our ability but our most anxious wish to secure you. Before the dawn of morning, before this river wakes to the first glimpse of daylight, you shall be placed as entirely beyond the reach of your former associates, and leave as utter an absence of all trace behind you, as if you were to disappear from the earth this moment. Come! I would not have you go back to exchange one word with any old companion, or take one look at any old haunt, or breathe the very air which is pestilence and death to you. Quit them all, while there is time and opportunity! [414].

Tragically, Nancy claims that she is absolutely beyond all help: "I am chained to my old life. I loathe and hate it now, but I cannot leave it" (415). Shocked and saddened by Nancy's determination to return to the streets, Rose Maylie cries: "What ... can be the end of this poor creature's life!" (415) Nancy's response is swift:

> Look before you, lady. Look at that dark water. How many times do you read of such as I who spring into the tide, and leave no living thing to care for or bewail them. It may be years hence, or it may be only months, but I shall come to that at last [415].

Desperately, Rose tries to at least give Nancy some money, but she refuses to take it:

> I have not done this for money. Let me have that to think of. And yet — give me something that you have worn: I should like to have something — no, no, not a ring — your gloves or handkerchief— anything I can keep, as having belonged to you, sweet lady. There. Bless you! God bless you! Good night, good night [415].

Money has not been Nancy's object. It is quite enough for her to accept a small keepsake from a woman who has treated her with kindness.

Nancy, it would seem, is a woman of extremes: she feels fundamentally and inescapably tainted; she is prepared to risk everything — even her life — for the welfare of an innocent child; she believes that she will in time be driven to take her own life; she is prepared to deliver up the person who would actively seek to ruin a child's life, but only if she is completely satisfied that the person will never even guess that she has done this; and perhaps, more than anything else, she values the kindness that a good person once extended to her. Indeed, she believes that good, kind people effectively serve to engender moral purity because, as her words make clear, if there were more good, kind people, there would be fewer corrupt and degraded individuals.

Turning, then, to consider Nancy's relationship to the traumatic circumstances of Dickens's youth, there are very interesting parallels. Dickens, as we know, felt absolutely soiled by his experience in the blacking warehouse and he never got over his mother's wish to reinstate him. In such a way, he was as chained to his memories as Nancy was chained to the life that she loathed. Dickens would also arguably have risked everything not to have suffered the blow that his mother dealt him (a blow that could have very nearly wrecked his life just as Oliver's life was very nearly wrecked). Indeed, perhaps at some deep level he was driven to take his own life as a means to get beyond his enduring sense of degradation.

Dickens is also willing to expose the person that he believed was most responsible for very nearly wrecking his life — his mother — but only if he can do this without her becoming aware. As I have worked to show, the rhetorical techniques he uses in his autobiographical fragment and the implicit disgust which underscores his depiction of the mothers of the protagonists in his first-person novels more than allows him to do this. Finally, as Dickens's autobiographical fragment shows, while Dickens may have felt irretrievably contaminated by his experiences, he nonetheless, through the kindness of a good person (the landlord's wife), experienced a glimpse of the humanity that he could not find in his mother, and later in his "autobiographical" writing he repeatedly transmuted this experience to structurally highlight the deficiencies of less-than-good mothers.

Accordingly, if viewed in this light, we can see that Dickens is prepared to go to the absolute limit (even the limit of his existence) in order to free himself from the contaminating effects of his mother's wish to reinstate him in the blacking warehouse. Was Dickens's life, for the most part then, about seeking to transcend in *every* possible way the horror of what he perceived as his mother's betrayal and the death of his childhood? Could his fame; prodigious work ethic; restlessness; prolific output as a writer; autobiographical novels; horrific *Sikes and Nancy* readings; and premature death all just be manifestations of his compulsive need to rise above the profound disgust that he felt towards his mother and his associated belief that in the moment of her "betrayal," the best part of himself—his innocence—had been thrown away? I believe so. According to Julia Kristeva:

> If it be true that the abject simultaneously beseeches and pulverizes the subject, one can understand that it is experienced at the peak of its strength when that sub-

ject, weary of fruitless attempts to identify with something on the outside, finds the impossible within; when it finds that the impossible constitutes its very *being*, that it *is* none other than abject. The abjection of self would be the culminating form of that experience of the subject to which is revealed that all its objects are based merely on the inaugural *loss* that laid the foundations of its own being.[98]

Dickens, I propose, was exceedingly "weary of fruitless attempts to identify with something on the outside." The fact that he obsessively sought to "tear himself to pieces" both on and offstage attests to this. Within the terms of Kristeva's theory of the abject, all subjects wish "to release the hold of *maternal entity*."[99] Dickens, like most subjects, may have broken away from his mother through "the autonomy of language,"[100] but again like most subjects, he was always at "risk of falling back under the sway of a power as securing as it is stifling."[101] However, while he was naturally attracted to his mother, he was also profoundly repulsed by her because, at base, he believed that she possessed the power to dispose of him. His strategies to deal with the pain of this belief are, I submit, made manifest through a careful examination of the rhetoric that he uses in his major autobiographical works — the autobiographical fragment and the novels which contain extended first-person narratives (*David Copperfield*, *Bleak House* and *Great Expectations*). All of these works, owing to their skilful deployment of implicit anti-maternal rhetoric, effectively enabled Dickens to hold at bay the sense that he was abject, but in the end they weren't enough and it would appear that the only way for him to overcome his self-disgust was to abject himself. The horrific but arguably autoerotic *Sikes and Nancy* readings apparently provided him with just the right means to do this.

Limit experience is not unique to French writers. Certainly it has been practiced throughout history. From time immemorial, people have sought out metamorphic experiences of "voluntary obliteration," but not everyone has taken such experiences to their absolute limit. However, popular entertainers (or celebrities as they are known in our own era) do appear to be more prone to engage in fatal or near-fatal limit experience. It would seem in fact that popularity is a natural precursor to taking on a limit attitude. Maybe when one has experienced everything life has to offer by way of approbation and power over others there is only one place left to go, and that place is to the limits of one's own identity.[102] Perhaps this is why limit experience is not just pleasurable but painful, as it essentially involves a rupture or tearing of individual integrity, and only through this anguished sacrifice may one open out to the power of the unknown.

According to James Miller, one of Foucault's most extravagant convictions was that a man's manner of dying may reveal, all at once, the "lyrical core" of his life,[103] "his invisible truth, his visible secret."[104] As the facts relating to Foucault's death amount to the bald solidity of the acronym AIDS, Miller naturally enough has the well-founded temerity to suggest that AIDS may have been Foucault's "deliberately chosen apotheosis."[105] Miller asks: "Does his conceivable embrace of a death-dealing 'disease of love' reveal, as he implied that it would, the 'lyrical core' of his life — *the* key to his 'personal poetic attitude'?"[106] In much the same spirit, I would like to suggest that Dickens's passionate embrace of an ultimately fatal reading of sado-masochistic, auto-erotic horror reveals, all at once, the truth and the secret of his life[107] as well as the essence of his "personal poetic attitude."

Chapter Notes

Preface

1. John Bowen, "A Garland for *The Old Curiosity Shop*," *Dickens Studies Annual* 37 (2006): 5.

2. Edmund Wilson, "Dickens: The Two Scrooges," *The Wound and the Bow: Seven Studies in Literature* (1941; London: Methuen, 1961) 1–93.

3. Lawrence J. Clipper, "The Blacking Warehouse Again: Another View," *Dickens Studies Newsletter* 12 (1981): 77.

4. Patricia Ingham, *Dickens, Women and Language* (New York: Harvester Wheatsheaf, 1992) 115.

5. See John Bowen's excellent article "Dickens and the Force of Writing," *Palgrave Advances in Charles Dickens Studies*, ed. John Bowen and Robert L. Patten (Basingstoke: Palgrave Macmillan, 2006) 255–72.

Chapter One

1. Goldie Morgentaler in *Dickens and Heredity: When Like Begets Like* (London: Macmillan Press, 2000) described *David Copperfield* and *Great Expectations* as "autobiographical" novels since they were "narrated in the first person by the central character" 72. I believe that *Bleak House* also fits this category as it contains a major fictional autobiography that constitutes approximately half of the book.

2. Charles Dickens, *David Copperfield*, ed. Trevor Blount (1849–50; Harmondsworth: Penguin Books, 1985) 259.

3. *David Copperfield* 52.

4. Nina Auerbach, "Performing Suffering: From Dickens to David," *Browning Institute Studies* 18 (1990): 15.

5. The autobiographical fragment is quoted in John Forster's biography of Dickens. See *The Life of Charles Dickens*, ed. A.J. Hoppe, Everyman's Library, 2 vols. (1872–74; London: Dent, 1969), I: 19–33.

6. It is very difficult to ascertain the exact date that the autobiographical fragment was written. See Nina Burgis, Introduction, *David Copperfield*, by Charles Dickens (Oxford: Clarendon, 1981) xv–xxii; and Philip Collins, "Dickens's Autobiographical Fragment and *David Copperfield*," *Cahiers Victoriens et Edouardiens* 20 (1984): 87–96.

7. Wilson 7.

8. Clipper 77.

9. Auerbach 16.

10. Alexander Welsh, *From Copyright to Copperfield: The Identity of Dickens* (Cambridge, MA: Harvard University Press, 1987) 156.

11. Charles Dickens, *Great Expectations*. Ed. Angus Calder (1965; Harmondsworth: Penguin, 1986) 142.

12. Welsh vii.

13. Welsh 10.

14. Welsh 9–11.

15. Robert Newsom, *Charles Dickens Revisited* (New York: Twayne Publishers, 2000) 101.

16. Linda M. Shires, "Literary Careers, Death and the Body Politics of David Copperfield," *Dickens Refigured: Bodies, Desires and*

Other Histories, ed. John Schad (Manchester & New York: Manchester University Press, 1996) 119–120.

17. Rosemary Bodenheimer, *Knowing Dickens* (Ithaca and London: Cornell University Press, 2007) 18.

18. Bodenheimer 18.

19. John Drew, "A Twist in the Tale," *Guardian Unlimited* November 1, 2003, January 22, 2008 http://books.guardian.co.uk/departments/classics/story/0,,1075112,00.html.

20. Drew par. 6.

21. Drew par. 7.

22. See John M.L. Drew, *Dickens the Journalist* (Basingstoke: Palgrave Macmillan, 2003) 17.

23. Drew, "A Twist in the Tale" par. 17.

24. Drew par. 20.

25. Drew, *Dickens the Journalist* 19.

26. Rosemarie Bodenheimer, "Dickens and the Writing of a Life," *Palgrave Advances in Charles Dickens Studies* ed. John Bowen and Robert L. Patten (New York: Palgrave Macmillan, 2006) 66.

27. Bodenheimer, *Knowing Dickens* 69.

28. Wilson 13.

29. See especially Edgar Johnson, *Charles Dickens: His Tragedy and Triumph*, 2 vols. (New York: Simon and Schuster, 1952) 2: 684; Walter Allen, *The English Novel* (1954; Harmondsworth: Penguin, 1965) 166; Clipper 9; Harry Stone, "*Oliver Twist* and Fairy Tales," *Dickens Studies Newsletter* 10 (1979): 34–39; Welsh 4.

30. Albert D. Hutter, "Reconstructive Autobiography: The Experience at Warren's Blacking," *Dickens Studies Annual* 6 (1977): 4.

31. Welsh 4.

32. See Robert Newsom, "The Hero's Shame," *Dickens Studies Annual*, 11 (1983): 18.

33. See Albert D. Hutter, "Nation and Generation in *A Tale of Two Cities*," *PMLA* 93 (1978): 448–462; Dianne F. Sadoff, *Monsters of Affection: Dickens, Eliot, and Bronte on Fatherhood* (Baltimore: John Hopkins University Press, 1982) 22–38; and Welsh 4–5.

34. Michael Slater, *Dickens and Women* (Stanford: Stanford University Press, 1983) 362.

35. Steven O'Connor, Rev. of Harry Stone's *The Night Side of Dickens: Cannibalism, Passion, Necessity, The Dickensian* 91.2 (1995): 127.

36. Patricia Ingham, *Dickens, Women and Language* (New York: Harvester Wheatsheaf, 1992) 11.

37. See John Carey, *The Violent Effigy: A Study of Dickens' Imagination* (1973; London & Boston: Faber and Faber, 1979) and Michael Slater, *Dickens and Women* (Stanford: Stanford University Press, 1983) .

38. Ingham 3.

39. Ingham 3.

40. Annette R. Federico, "Dickens and Disgust," *Dickens Studies Annual* 29 (2000): 146.

41. Federico 146.

42. Federico 146.

43. Federico 156.

44. Jack Lindsay, *Charles Dickens* (1950; London: Andrew Dakers, 1970) 380.

45. Earl Davis, *The Flint and the Flame: The Artistry of Charles Dickens* (Columbia: University of Missouri Press, 1963) 265.

46. Davis 264.

47. Michael Steig, "Dickens' Excremental Vision," *Victorian Studies* 13.3 (1970): 339.

48. Steig 343.

49. Steig 354.

50. Jeremy Tambling, *Dickens, Violence and the Modern State* (New York: St. Martin's Press, 1995) 198.

51. Tambling 198–99.

52. Tambling 199.

53. Tambling 199.

54. Forster I: 19.

55. Forster I: 19.

56. Qtd. Forster I: 19.

57. Forster I: 19.

58. Forster I: 19.

59. Forster I: 19.

60. Forster I: 20.

61. Qtd. Forster I: 13.

62. Forster I: 17.

63. Forster I: 16.

64. Forster I: 16.

65. Forster I: 17.

66. Forster I: 17.

67. Forster I: 17.

68. Forster I: 11.

69. Forster I: 18.

70. Charles Dickens, *Great Expectations*. Ed. Angus Calder (1965; Harmondsworth: Penguin, 1986) 54.

71. According to Forster, James Lamert was "a stepson to [Elizabeth Dickens's] sister, and therefore a sort of cousin" (1: 9).

72. Forster I: 21.

73. Johnson 1: 32.

74. Qtd. Forster 1: 21.

75. Qtd. Forster I: 21.

76. Qtd. Forster I: 32.

77. Una Pope-Hennessy, *Charles Dickens* (1945; London: The Reprint Society, 1947) 296.

78. Clipper 78.

79. Johnson 1: 45.

80. Christopher Hibbert, *The Making of Charles Dickens* (1967; Harmondsworth: Penguin Books, 1983) 72.

81. Wilson 5.

82. Hesketh Pearson, *Dickens: His Character, Comedy and Career* (1949; London: Cassell, 1988) 9.

83. Fred Kaplan, *Dickens: A Biography* (1988; London: Sceptre, 1989) 45.

84. Michael Allen, *Charles Dickens's Childhood* (New York: St. Martin's Press, 1988) 104.

85. Claire Tomalin, *Charles Dickens: A Life* (London: Penguin, 2011) 28.

86. Michael Allen, *Charles Dickens and the Blacking Factory* (St. Leonards: Oxford-Stockley, 2011) 95.

87. Peter Ackroyd, *Dickens* (London: Sinclair-Stevenson, 1990) 95.

88. Johnson 1: 45.

89. Qtd. Forster I: 21

90. Qtd. Forster I: 25.

91. Forster I: 13.

92. Gwen Watkins, *Dickens in Search of Himself: Recurrent Themes and Characters in the Work of Charles Dickens* (Basingstoke: Macmillan, 1987) 23.

93. Charles Dickens, *Dombey and Son*, ed. Peter Fairclough (1846–8; Harmondsworth: Penguin Books, 1986), 51.

94. *Dombey and Son* 79.

95. *David Copperfield* 174.

96. *David Copperfield* 174.

97. Charles Dickens, *Bleak House*, ed. Norman Page (1852–53: Harmondsworth: Penguin Books, 1985) 64.

98. Charles Dickens, *Hard Times*, ed. David Craig (1854; Harmondsworth: Penguin Books, 1986) 91.

99. *Hard Times* 60.

100. Charles Dickens, *Little Dorrit*, ed. John Holloway (1855–57; Harmondsworth: Penguin Books, 1985) 73.

101. *Little Dorrit* 80.

102. *Great Expectations* 39.

103. Qtd. Forster I: 25–26.

104. Forster I: 25.

105. Forster I: 9.

106. Forster I: 9.

107. Qtd. Forster I: 31–32.

108. Forster I: 33.

109. Watkins 22.

110. Forster I: 29.

111. Watkins 19.

112. Qtd. Forster I: 32.

113. Qtd. Forster I: 32.

114. Qtd. Forster I: 32.

115. Jeffrey Berman, *Narcissism and the Novel* (New York: New York University Press, 1990) 121.

116. Slater 5.

117. Slater 5.

118. Qtd. Michael Allen, 58.

119. Forster I: 30.

120. Qtd. Forster I: 30.

121. *Hard Times* 281–82.

122. Qtd. Forster I: 30–31.

123. Qtd. Forster I: 21.

124. Forster I: 15–16.

125. Slater 8.

126. Watkins 22.

127. Qtd. Forster I: 29.

128. Qtd. Forster I: 29.

129. Natalie J. McKnight, *Suffering Mothers in Mid-Victorian Novels* (New York: St. Martin's Press, 1997) 54–55.

130. Qtd. Forster I: 13.

131. Qtd. Forster I: 13.

132. Watkins 21.

133. Qtd. Forster I: 22.

134. Qtd. Forster I: 22.

135. Qtd. Forster I: 22.

136. Ackroyd 77–78.

137. Qtd. Forster I: 26.

138. Qtd. Forster I: 27.

139. Steven Marcus, *Dickens: From Pickwick to Dombey* (1965; London: Chatto and Windus, 1971) 367.

140. See June Foley, "Elizabeth Dickens: Model for Fagin," *Women's Studies* 30.2 (2001): 225–35. Foley cogently suggests that Elizabeth Dickens is actually "the primary prototype for Fagin" in *Oliver Twist* (229).

141. Slater 9. See also Peter Ackroyd's comments concerning Fagin, 77–78.

142. Newsom, "The Hero's Shame" 10.

143. See Hutter "Reconstructive Autobiography" 6.

144. Wilson 5.

145. Trevor Blount, "Introduction," *David Copperfield*, by Charles Dickens, ed. Trevor Blount (London: Penguin Books, 1971) 18.

146. Jack Lindsay, *Charles Dickens: A Biographical and Critical Study* (1950; London: Andrew Dakers, 1970), 60.

147. Newsom, "The Hero's Shame" 10.

148. Newsom, "The Hero's Shame" 11.

149. Forster I: 34.

150. Wilson 5–6.

151. Hibbert 72.

152. Hutter "Reconstructive Autobiography" 3.

153. Qtd. Forster I: 23.

154. Berman 118–19.

155. Hutter "Reconstructive Autobiography" 11.

156. Hutter "Reconstructive Autobiography" 9.

157. Berman 119.

158. Mary Douglas, *Purity and Danger: An Analysis of Concepts of Pollution and Taboo* (1966; London: Routledge, 1978) 35.

159. Douglas 35–36.

160. Douglas 113.

161. Douglas 113.

162. Douglas 113.

163. Douglas 113.

164. Charles Dickens, *David Copperfield* 208.

165. Ackroyd 95–96.

166. Qtd. Forster I: 32.

167. Slater 11.

168. Pearson 6.

169. Kaplan 43.

170. Lindsay 59.

171. Lindsay 49.

172. Claire Tomalin, *The Invisible Woman: The Story of Nelly Ternan and Charles Dickens* (1990; London: Penguin, 1991) 4.

173. Qtd. Forster I: 32–3.

174. Slater 12.

175. Slater 13.

Chapter Two

1. David Trotter, *Cooking with Mud: The Idea of Mess in Nineteenth-Century Art and Fiction* (Oxford: Oxford University Press, 2000) 8–9.

2. Trotter 9.

3. Trotter 2.

4. Trotter 172.

5. Trotter 160.

6. M.L. Phillips et al., "Disgust: the Forgotten Emotion of Psychiatry," *The British Journal of Psychiatry* 172 (1998): 373.

7. William Ian Miller, *The Anatomy of Disgust* (Cambridge, MA: Harvard University Press, 1997) 5.

8. Paul Rozin and April E. Fallon, "A Perspective on Disgust," *Psychological Review* 94.1 (1987): 23. For a useful summary of the study of the characteristic facial expression of disgust see Susan B. Miller, *Disgust: The Gatekeeper Emotion* (Hillsdale, NJ, and London: Analytic Press, 2004) 10.

9. Miller *Disgust* 2.

10. See Chapter One of Miller's *Disgust* 1–22.

11. Miller *Disgust* 2.

12. Valerie Curtis and Adam Biran, "Dirt, Disgust, and Disease: Is Hygiene in Our Genes?" *Perspectives in Biology and Medicine* 44.1 (2001): 18.

13. Andras Angyal, "Disgust and Related Aversions," *The Journal of Abnormal and Social Psychology* 36 (1941): 397.

14. Angyal 394.

15. Angyal 394.

16. Miller *Anatomy* 6.

17. Angyal 394.

18. Miller *Anatomy* 5.

19. Miller *Anatomy* 5.

20. Charles Darwin, *The Expression of the Emotions in Man and Animals* (1872; Oxford: Oxford University Press, 1998) 255.

21. Silvan Tomkins, *Affect, Imagery, Consciousness*, vol. 2 (New York: Springer, 1963) 232–33.

22. Rozin and Fallon 23.

23. Paul Rozin, Jonathan Haidt, and Clark R. McCauley, "Disgust," *Handbook of Emotions*, ed. M. Lewis & J.M. Haviland-Jones, 2nd ed. (New York: Guilford Press, 2000) 637.

24. Rozin, Haidt, and McCauley 639.

25. Rozin, Haidt, and McCauley 650.

26. Miller *Anatomy* 1.

27. Miller *Disgust* 10–11.

28. Miller *Disgust* 4.

29. There are other models of disgust, for instance the transgressive model, which is manifest in the work of the Marquis de Sade and Georges Bataille. See Robert Rawdon Wilson's discussion in *The Hydra's Tale: Imagining Disgust* (Edmonton: University of Alberta Press, 2002) 70–77. See also Chapter 8

of Winfried Menninghaus, *Disgust: The Theory and History of a Strong Sensation*, trans. Howard Eiland and Joel Golb (Albany: State University of New York Press, 2003). However, this model does not emphasize the self-protective role of disgust. Wilson also canvasses the social-constructionist model. This model explains disgust as a learned response "that takes place during a process of socialization within a particular socio-cultural context" (54). However, it is not clear from Wilson's account whether this theory places emphasis on self-protection or bodily protection.

30. See in particular Rozin, Haidt, and McCauley 642.

31. Miller *Anatomy* 49–50.

32. Miller *Anatomy* 1–2.

33. Miller *Anatomy* 194.

34. Wilson *Hydra's Tale* 52.

35. Martha Nussbaum, *Hiding from Humanity* (Princeton: Princeton University Press, 2004) 74.

36. Wilson *Hydra's Tale* 64.

37. Jean Paul Sartre, *Being and Nothingness*, trans. Hazel E. Barnes (1943; London: Methuen, 1972) 607.

38. Sartre 604.

39. Sartre 608.

40. Sartre 609.

41. Sartre 609.

42. See Toril Moi, *Simone de Beauvoir: The Making of an Intellectual Woman* (Oxford: Blackwell, 1994) 102.

43. Douglas 125.

44. Douglas 125.

45. Douglas 102.

46. Douglas 124.

47. Douglas 124.

48. Miller *Anatomy* 271.

49. Nussbaum 91–92.

50. Julia Kristeva, *The Powers of Horror: An Essay on Abjection* (New York: Columbia University Press, 1982) 3.

51. Kristeva 5–6.

52. Douglas 113.

53. See, for instance, Wilson *Hydra's Tale* 68.

54. Wilson *Hydra's Tale* 68.

55. See the examples cited by Miller *Disgust* 4–5.

56. Nor, for that matter, did he devote much attention to any of the emotions. According to Kathleen Woodward: "In his work as a whole Freud placed much more emphasis on a theory of drives than he did on the emotions. In fact he devoted remarkably little attention to the emotions in comparison, say, with Melanie Klein, whose work is a veritable theoretical atlas of the strong emotions of psychoanalysis" ("Anger ... and Anger: From Freud to Feminism," *Freud and the Passions*, ed. John O'Neill [Pennsylvania: Pennsylvania State University Press, 1996] 75).

57. Miller *Disgust* 5.

58. Miller *Disgust* 21.

59. Kristeva, Julia, interview with Elaine Hoffman Baruch, "Feminism and Psychoanalysis," *Julia Kristeva, Interviews*, ed. Ross Mitchell Guberman (New York: Columbia University Press, 1996) 118.

60. Kristeva *Powers of Horror* 65.

61. Kristeva 2–3.

62. Kristeva 208.

63. Elizabeth Gross, "The Body of Signification," *Abjection, Melancholia, and Love: The Work of Julia Kristeva*, ed. John Fletcher and Andrew Benjamin (London & New York: Routledge, 1990) 89.

64. Kelly Oliver, *Reading Kristeva: Unraveling the Double-bind* (Bloomington and Indianapolis: Indiana University Press, 1993) 55.

65. Anne-Marie Smith, *Julia Kristeva: Speaking the Unspeakable* (London & Sterling, VA: Pluto Press, 1998) 29.

66. John Lechte, *Julia Kristeva* (London & New York: Routledge, 1990) 158.

67. Lechte 159.

68. Miller *Anatomy* 26–7.

69. Jon-Ove Steihaug, "Abject/*Informe*/Trauma: Discourses on the Body in American Art of the Nineties," *ForArt* (1995): 4, January 24, 2005 http://www.forart.no/steihaug/toc.html.

70. Kristeva 69.

71. Kristeva 4.

72. Oliver 56.

73. Kristeva 1–2.

74. Kristeva 2.

75. Kristeva 9–10.

76. Elizabeth Grosz, *Sexual Subversions: Three French Feminists* (Sydney: Allen & Unwin, 1989) 71–72.

77. Kristeva 69.

78. Kristeva 69.

79. Kristeva 71.

80. Kristeva 71.

81. Kristeva 71.

82. Kristeva 71.

83. Kristeva 71–72.

84. Kristeva 74.

85. Kristeva 74.

86. Judith Butler, *Gender Trouble: Feminism and the Subversion of Identity* (New York & London: Routledge, 1990) 79.

87. Butler 79.

88. Butler 79.

89. See, for example, Butler, 79–93; Tina Chanter, "Kristeva's Politics of Change: Tracking Essentialism with the Help of a Sex/Gender Map," *Ethics, Politics, and Difference in Julia Kristeva's Writing*, ed. Kelly Oliver (New York and London: Routledge, 1993) 179–195; Nancy Fraser, "The Uses and Abuses of French Discourse Theories for Feminist Politics," *Revaluing French Feminism: Critical Essays on Difference, Agency, and Culture*, ed. Nancy Fraser and Sandra Lee Bartky (Bloomington and Indianapolis: Indiana University Press, 1992) 177–194; Diana T. Meyers, "The Subversion of Women's Agency in Psychoanalytic Feminism: Chodorow, Flax, Kristeva," *Revaluing French Feminism: Critical Essays on Difference, Agency, and Culture*, ed. Nancy Fraser and Sandra Lee Bartky (Bloomington and Indianapolis: Indiana University Press, 1992) 136–161; Jacqueline Rose, "Julia Kristeva — Take Two," *Sexuality in the Field of Vision* (London: Verso, 1986) 141–164; and Jennifer Stone, "The Horrors of Power: A Critique of Julia Kristeva," *The Politics of Theory*, Proc. of the Essex Conference in the Sociology of Literature, July 1982 (Colchester: University of Essex, 1983) 38–48.

90. Grosz is in no doubt that the abject is "placed on the side of the feminine and the maternal" 78.

91. Kristeva 4.

92. Grosz 78.

93. Kristeva 12.

94. Rose 157.

95. Kristeva 13.

96. Rose 157.

97. As R. Howard Bloch observes, the uniform terms of misogynistic discourse "still govern (consciously or not) the ways in which the question of woman is conceived by women as well as by men" ("Medieval Misogyny," *Misogyny, Misandry and Misanthropy*, ed. R. Howard Bloch and Frances Ferguson [Berkeley: University of California Press, 1989] 1).

98. Julia Kristeva, *Tales of Love*, Trans. Leon Roudiez (New York: Columbia University Press, 1987) 374.

99. Oliver 161.

100. Oliver 161.

101. Oliver 162.

Chapter Three

1. Charles Dickens, *David Copperfield*, ed. Trevor Blount (1966; reprint London: Penguin, 1985) 950. Further citations will be noted parenthetically in the text.

2. George Orwell, "Charles Dickens," *Collected Essays* (London: Mercury Books, 1961) 85.

3. Harold Bloom, "Introduction," *Charles Dickens's David Copperfield*, ed. Harold Bloom (New York: Chelsea House, 1987) 7.

4. Barbara Hardy, *The Moral Art of Dickens* (London: Athlone Press, 1970) 127–28.

5. Slater 250.

6. See also Robert R. Garnett, "Why Not Sophy? Desire and Agnes in *David Copperfield*," *Dickens Quarterly* 14 (1997): 213–31.

7. Nancy Klenk Hill, "Woman as Saviour," *Denver Quarterly* 18.4 (1984): 101.

8. Andrew Ashfield and Peter de Bolla, "Introduction," *The Sublime: A Reader in British Eighteenth-century Aesthetic Theory*, eds. Andrew Ashfield and Peter de Bolla (Cambridge: Cambridge University Press, 1996) 6.

9. See Nina Auerbach, *Woman and the Demon: The Life of a Victorian Myth* (Cambridge: Harvard University Press, 1982) 84–5.

10. Dickens, "Preface to Charles Dickens Edition," *David Copperfield* 47.

11. Qtd. Forster 2: 98.

12. Qtd. Forster 2: 48.

13. Wilson 39.

14. Qtd. Forster 1: 23.

15. Slater 251.

16. Edwin Eiger, *The Metaphysical Novel in England and America: Dickens, Bulwer, Melville, and Hawthorne* (Berkeley: University of California Press, 1978) 131.

17. Philip M. Weinstein, *The Semantics of Desire: Changing Models of Identity from Dickens to Joyce* (Princeton, NJ: Princeton University Press, 1984) 30.

18. John O. Jordan, "The Social Sub-Text of *David Copperfield*," *Dickens Studies Annual* 14 (1985): 64.

19. Jordan 65.

20. Jordan 64.

21. Note in *David Copperfield* 951.

22. Charles Dickens, qtd. Forster 1: 21.

23. Kristeva, *Powers of Horror* 9–10.

24. Gail Turley Houston, *Consuming Fictions: Gender, Class and Hunger in Dickens's Novels* (Carbondale and Edwardsville: Southern Illinois University Press, 1994) 103.

25. "Mrs. Strong's mama was a lady I took great delight in. Her name was Mrs. Markleham; but our boys used to call her the Old Soldier, on account of her generalship, and the skill with which she marshalled great forces of relations against the Doctor. She was a little, sharp-eyed woman, who used to wear, when she was dressed, one unchangeable cap, ornamented with some artificial flowers, and two artificial butterflies supposed to be hovering about the flowers. There was a superstition among us that this cap had come from France, and could only originate in the workmanship of that ingenious nation" (296).

26. Houston reads this scene quite differently. For Houston, the attack on the crocodiles may be viewed in the light of a family romance: "Perhaps frightened of his own Oedipal desires for his nourishing mother, David may project those desires onto Murdstone through the crocodile fantasy that conflates with Murdstone's toothy entry" (105).

27. Houston 104.

28. I take this idea from Simon Edwards's analysis of *David Copperfield*. Edwards writes of the "tyrannic sadism personified in Mr. Creakle and the 'tough shit' of Mr. Murdstone" ("*David Copperfield*: The Decomposing Self," in *David Copperfield and Hard Times*, ed. John Peck [Basingstoke and London: Macmillan, 1995] 75). He also speaks of "the discipline of the constipated Murdstone" (76).

29. Steig 347.

30. It is interesting to compare this phrase with the way that Thackeray referred to his mother. In a diary entry Thackeray wrote: "All sorts of recollections of my youth came back to me: dark and sad and painful with my dear good mother as a gentle angle interposing between me and misery" (*The Letters and Private Papers of William Makepeace Thackeray*, ed. Gordon N. Ray, vol. 2 [Cambridge, MA: Harvard University Press, 1946] 361). "My poor dear mother" does not compare nearly as favorably as "my dear good mother." Rather,

it has a condescending, even disparaging ring to it.

31. Indeed, as noted, she wears *all* of the pretty dresses that she had in her drawers (70).

32. In relation to the child-wife category in Dickens's oeuvre, see, for instance, Jane W. Stedman, "Child-Wives of Dickens," *The Dickensian* LIX (1963): 112–118.

33. David indicates that his father was "double my mother's age when he married" (51).

34. For Houston, "Betsey's nagging serves the rhetorical purpose of allowing the reader to recognize that David has experienced benign neglect without implicating his own bitterness" (104).

35. Mary Poovey, "The Man-of-Letters Hero: *David Copperfield* and the Professional Writer," *Uneven Developments: The Ideological Work of Gender in Mid-Victorian England* (London: Virago Press, 1989) 94.

36. Poovey 94.

37. "I begin to feel the words I have been at infinite pains to get into my head, all sliding away, and going I don't know where" (103).

38. "I trip over a word. Mr. Murdstone looks up. I trip over another word. Miss Murdstone looks up. I redden, tumble over half-a-dozen words, and stop" (103).

39. "I am very stupid" (104).

40. "The case is so hopeless, and I feel that I am wallowing in such a bog of nonsense, that I give up all idea of getting out, and abandon myself to my fate. The despairing way in which my mother and I look at each other, as I blunder on, is truly melancholy" (104).

41. "Mr. Murdstone comes out of his chair, takes the book, throws it at me or boxes my ears with it, and turns me out of the room by the shoulders" (104).

42. "[I make] a Mulatto of myself by getting the dirt of the slate into the pores of my skin" (105).

43. "I could have done very well if I had been without the Murdstones; but the influence of the Murdstones upon me was like the fascination of two snakes on a wretched young bird" (105).

44. Kristeva, *Powers of Horror* 4.

45. "I was timidly following her, when she turned round at the parlour door, in the dusk, and taking me in her embrace as she had been used to do, whispered me to love my new father and be obedient to him. She did this hur-

riedly and secretly, as if it were wrong, but tenderly; and, putting out her hand behind her, held mine in it, until we came near to where he was standing in the garden, where she let mine go, and drew hers through his arm" (97).

46. Harry Stone, "The Love Pattern in Dickens' Novels," in *Dickens the Craftsmen: Strategies of Presentation*, ed. Robert B. Partlow, Jr. (Carbondale and Edwardsville: Southern Illinois University Press, 1970) 7.

47. Gordon D. Hirsch ("A Psychoanalytic Rereading of *David Copperfield*," *The Victorian Newsletter* 58 [1980]: 3), for instance, says: "This may sound a bit selfish, but it is also touching and rings oddly true; surely one of the consolations in mourning is the attention, concern, and sympathy of others."

48. This passage has sparked a variety of critical responses. Bert G. Hornback maintains that in burying himself with his mother, David finds a way back to the past happiness that he had shared with her. See "*The Hero of My Life*": *Essays on Dickens* (Athens: Ohio University Press, 1981) 65. Dianne F. Sadoff believes that the passage heralds David's self-renewal: "This narrative moment banishes fathers, enshrines dead mothers, and kills that old young David, leaving him free to create himself" (*Monsters of Affection: Dickens, Eliot & Bronte on Fatherhood* 40). Gordon D. Hirsch claims that this "wish for reunion with the mother of his infancy" is "a grisly fantasy" (2).

49. See Edwin M. Eiger's "David Copperfield and the Benevolent Spirit," *Dickens Studies Annual* 14 (1985) 1–15 for a good summation of the critical responses to the character of Betsey Trotwood.

50. Johnson 2: 686.

51. Sylvère Monod, *Dickens the Novelist* (Norman: University of Oklahoma Press, 1968) 333.

52. Monod 335.

53. Françoise Basch, *Relative Creatures: Victorian Women in Society and the Novel* (New York: Schocken Books, 1974) 147.

54. Slater 275.

55. Natalie E. Schroeder and Ronald A. Schroeder, "Betsey Trotwood and Jane Murdstone: Dickensian Doubles," *Studies in the Novel* 21.3 (1989): 268.

56. McKnight 48. McKnight's view is, however, somewhat qualified by her justification for this assessment: "She is the kind of

maternal authority Dickens can stomach — a loving, intelligent woman who still bows to the advice of the man of the house, even though he's an idiot" (48).

57. William C. Spengemann, *The Forms of Autobiography: Episodes in the History of a Literary Genre* (New Haven and London: Yale University Press, 1980) 129.

58. See in particular, Stanley Tick, "The Memorializing of Mr. Dick," *Nineteenth-Century Fiction* 24.2 (1969): 142–53; and William C. Spengemann, *The Forms of Autobiography* 126–29.

59. Stanley Tick writes: "'Dick' was a signature which Dickens himself used when corresponding with Clarkson Stanfield — the man described by J.W.T. Ley as 'the best-loved friend that Dickens ever had.' Ley suggests that 'Dick' was a private nickname given by Stanfield to the author. Could it be that 'Mr. Dick' was a coded self-identification put in by Dickens only for his closest friends?" (149).

60. Spengemann 127.

61. According to Stanley Tick: "Fortunately, novelist Charles Dickens had nothing quite like Mr. Dick's intrusive figure of King Charles' head to prevent him from achieving his recollections. Nevertheless, like Mr. Dick, he could not bring himself to express directly certain of the circumstances of his disturbing experiences. Exactly like Mr. Dick, Dickens required adequate similes in order to confront the outrage of his past" (145).

62. Tick 144.

63. Schroeder and Schroeder 275.

64. Tick 150.

65. Mary Shelley, *Frankenstein or The Modern Prometheus*, The World's Classics, ed. James Kinsley and M.K. Joseph (Oxford: Oxford University Press, 1980) 97.

66. Sigmund Freud, "Katharina," *Studies on Hysteria*, trans. James and Alix Strachey, ed. Angela Richards, vol. 3. (Harmondsworth: Penguin, 1986) 190.

67. Leon Litvak, "What Books did Dickens Buy and Read? Evidence from the Book Accounts with His Publishers," *The Dickensian* 94.2 (1998): 94.

68. Edmund Burke, *A Philosophical Enquiry into Our Ideas of the Sublime and Beautiful*, ed. James T. Boulton (London: University of Notre Dame Press, 1968) 57.

69. Burke 64.

70. Auerbach 84.

71. Burke 80.

72. Burke 80.

73. Burke 58–59.

74. Virginia Woolf, "*David Copperfield*," *Nation*, August 22, 1925.

75. Philip Collins, *Charles Dickens: David Copperfield* (London: Edward Arnold, 1977) 48.

76. Burke 110–13.

77. Burke 134.

78. Burke 40.

79. Tom Furniss, *Edmund Burke's Aesthetic Ideology: Language, Gender, and Political Economy in Revolution* (Cambridge: Cambridge University Press, 1993) 25.

80. Burke 132.

81. Burke 132.

82. Burke 135.

83. Burke 135.

84. Furniss 26.

85. Burke 132.

86. Furniss 29.

87. Frances Ferguson, "Sublime of Edmund Burke, or the Bathos of Experience," *Glyph: John Hopkins Textual Studies* 8 (1981): 76.

88. Burke 50–51.

89. Furniss 30–31.

90. Furniss 29.

Chapter Four

1. Charles Dickens, *Bleak House*. Ed. Norman Page (1971; reprint London: Penguin, 1985) 559. Further citations will be noted parenthetically in the text.

2. As Richard J. Dunn writes: "The thirty-three chapters that Esther presents in the first person, past tense, balanced the thirty-four chapters that the omniscient author presents in the third person, present tense." "Esther's Role in *Bleak House*," *The Dickensian* 62 (1966): 163.

3. Michael Goldberg, *Carlyle and Dickens* (Athens: University of Georgia Press, 1972) 71.

4. Geoffrey Thurley, *The Dickens Myth: Its Genesis and Structure* (St. Lucia: University of Queensland Press, 1976) 179.

5. Judith Wilt, "Confusion and Consciousness in Dickens's Esther," *Nineteenth-Century Fiction* 32.3 (1977) 289.

6. William Axton, "Esther's Nicknames: A Study in Relevance," *The Dickensian* 62 (1966): 160.

7. Marcia Renee Goodman, "'I'll Follow the Other': Tracing the (M)other in *Bleak House*," *Dickens Studies Annual* 19 (1990): 161.

8. Goodman 147.

9. Goodman 150.

10. Lawrence Frank, "'Through a Glass Darkly': Esther Summerson and *Bleak House*," *Dickens Studies Annual* 4 (1975): 92.

11. Keith Easley, "Dickens and Bakhtin: Authoring in *Bleak House*," *Dickens Studies Annual* 34 (2004): 194.

12. It is worth noting that in all likelihood, Esther's doll was an adult woman, as Sharon Marcus states: "Dolls representing mature girls or adult women dominated the market throughout the nineteenth century, and baby dolls sold in large numbers only after 1914" [*Between Women: Friendship, Desire, and Marriage in Victorian England* (Princeton and Oxford: Princeton University Press, 2007)] 155.

13. Easley 193.

14. Qtd. Forster, I: 24.

15. Interestingly, it seems never to have occurred to Dickens that his mother might have paid for his board and lodging away from the family precisely because she knew how sensitive he was and how mortifying it would be for him to live in a debtors' prison.

16. Jacob Korg, Introduction, *Twentieth-Century Interpretations of Bleak House* (New Jersey: Prentice-Hall, 1968) 14.

17. Jasmine Yong Hall, "What's Troubling About Esther? Narrating, Policing, and Resisting Arrest in *Bleak House*," *Dickens Studies Annual* 22 (1993) 176.

18. Frank 93.

19. Frank 93.

20. Raymond Conlon, "*Bleak House*'s Miss Barbary: A Psychological Miniature," *Dickens Studies Newsletter* 14.3 (1983): 91.

21. Gordon D. Hirsch, "The Mysteries in Bleak House: A Psychoanalytic Study," *Dickens Studies Annual* 4 (1975): 137.

22. David A. Ward, "Distorted Religion: Dickens, Dissent, and *Bleak House*," *Dickens Studies Annual* 29 (2000): 213.

23. Frank 94.

24. Carolyn Dever, *Death and the Mother from Dickens to Freud: Victorian Fiction and the Anxiety of Origins* (Cambridge: Cambridge University Press, 1998) 87.

25. Ward 213.

26. See, for instance: Paul Eggert, "The Real Esther Summerson," *Dickens Studies*

Newsletter 11.3 (1980): 74–81; William Axton, "Esther's Nicknames: A Study in Relevance," *The Dickensian* LXII (1966): 158–63; William Axton, "The Trouble with Esther," *Modern Language Quarterly* 26 (1965): 545–57; and Robert Newsom, "*Villette* and *Bleak House*: Authorizing Women," *Nineteenth-Century Literature* 46.1 (1991): 54–81.

27. John Harrison, *Love Your Disease* (London: Angus & Robertson, 1984) 28.

28. Harrison 28–9.

29. Thurley 178.

30. Ward 219.

31. Frank 100.

32. Helena Michie, "'Who Is This in Pain?': Scarring, Disfigurement, and Female Identity in *Bleak House* and *Our Mutual Friend*," *Novel* 22.1 (1989): 206.

33. Timothy Peltason, "Esther's Will," *ELH* 59.3 (1992): 673.

34. Ward 219.

35. On the question of Esther's beauty, see Diane L. Jolly, "The Nature of Esther," *The Dickensian* 86.1 (1990): 29–40.

36. Michie 207.

37. See Dever 100. Dever claims that Esther's disease-ravaged face "enacts a symbolic rejection of the mother who rejected, and all that that mother represents." I believe that Esther's face also enacts a symbolic rejection of her adoptive mother.

38. See Dever's suggestive claim that "Esther Summerson effectively literalizes the argument Paul de Man makes in 'Autobiography as Defacement': that the signifier precedes, and indeed shapes, changes, and even creates its referent" (100).

39. Kristeva, *Powers of Horror* 2.

40. Kristeva 4.

41. Frank 103.

42. Frank 103.

43. Chiara Briganti, "The Monstrous Actress: Esther Summerson's Spectral Name," *Dickens Studies Annual* 19 (1990): 216.

44. Brian Cheadle, "Mystification and the Mystery of Origins," *Dickens Studies Annual* 25 (1996): 32.

45. As Barbara Creed writes: "The fully symbolic body must bear no indication of its debt to nature. In Kristeva's view the image of woman's body, because of its maternal functions, acknowledges its 'debt to nature' and consequently is more likely to signify the abject" [*The Monstrous-Feminine: Film, Fem-*

inism, Psychoanalysis, (1993; London and New York: Routledge, 1994) 11].

46. Christine Van Boheemen-Saaf, "'The Universe Makes an Indifferent Parent': *Bleak House* and the Victorian Family Romance," *Interpreting Lacan*, eds. Joseph H. Smith and William Kerrigan (New Haven and London: Yale University Press, 1983) 247.

47. Van Boheemen-Saaf 246.

48. Wilt 290.

49. Virginia Blain, "Double Vision and the Double Standard in *Bleak House*: A Feminist Perspective," in *New Casebooks: Bleak House*, ed. Jeremy Tambling (London: Macmillan, 1998) 79. For Blain, "Esther, in a sense, has to 'kill' her mother within herself, in order to escape her contagion. The chase by Bucket, with the passive collusion of Esther, ostensibly to 'save' Lady Dedlock, has in fact resulted in her death — since the more relentless their pursuit, the more desperate her flight, and the more inevitable her end" (81).

50. Briganti 221. See also Thomas A. Hanzo, "Paternity and the Subject in *Bleak House*," in *The Fictional Father: Lacanian Readings of the Text*, ed. Robert Con Davis (Amherst: University of Massachusetts Press, 1981): 27–47.

51. Robert E. Lougy is particularly sensitive to Esther's purificatory purpose here. See "Filth, Liminality, and Abjection in Charles Dickens's *Bleak House*," *ELH* 69 (2002): 492.

52. Deborah Epstein Nord, *Walking the Victorian Streets: Women, Representation and the City* (Ithaca and London: Cornell University Press, 1995) 107.

53. Thurley 179.

54. "I never afterwards forgot, I never shall forget, I never can forget, that my mother was warm for my being sent back." Qtd. Forster I: 32.

55. Kristeva, *Powers of Horror* 4.

56. Maura Spiegel, "Managing Pain: Suffering and Reader Sympathy in *Bleak House*," *Dickens Quarterly* 12 (1995): 8.

57. Qtd. Spiegel 8.

58. Spiegel 8–9.

Chapter Five

1. Charles Dickens, *Bleak House*. Ed. Norman Page (1971; reprint London: Penguin, 1985) 549.

2. Newsom, "The Hero's Shame," 18.

3. See, for example, Dorothy Van Ghent, "On *Great Expectations*," *The English Novel: Form and Function* (New York: Holt, Rinehart and Winston, 1953) 125–38; G. Robert Stange, "Expectations Well Lost; Dickens' Fable for His Time," *College English* 16.1 (1954): 9–17; J. Hillis Miller, *Charles Dickens: The World of His Novels* (Cambridge, MA: Harvard University Press, 1958) 251; Julian Moynahan, "The Hero's Guilt: The Case of *Great Expectations*," *Essays in Criticism* 10 (1960): 60–79; Q.D. Leavis, "How We Must Read *Great Expectations*," in F.R. Leavis and Q.D. Leavis, *Dickens the Novelist* (1970; Harmondsworth: Penguin, 1980) 360–428; Robert Barnard, "Imagery and Theme in *Great Expectations*," *Dickens Studies Annual* 1 (1970): 238–51; Lawrence Jay Dessner, "*Great Expectations*: 'The Ghost of a Man's Own Father,'" *PMLA* 91.3 (1976): 436–49; Colin N. Manlove, "Neither Here nor There: Uneasiness in *Great Expectations*," *Dickens Studies Annual* 8 (1980): 61–71; Peter Brooks, "Repetition, Repression, and Return: The Plotting of *Great Expectations*," in *Reading for the Plot: Design and Intention in Narrative* (Oxford: Clarendon Press, 1984) 113–42; Michal Peled Ginsburg, "Dickens and the Uncanny: Repression and Displacement in *Great Expectations*," *Dickens Studies Annual* 13 (1984): 115–24; Shuli Barzilai, "Dickens's *Great Expectations*: The Motive for Moral Masochism," *American Imago* 42.1 (1985): 45–67; David Hennessee, "Gentlemanly Guilt and Masochistic Fantasy in *Great Expectations*," *Dickens Studies Annual* 34 (2004): 301–328.

4. See also Kathleen Sell, "The Narrator's Shame: Masculine Identity in *Great Expectations*," *Dickens Studies Annual* 26 (1998): 203–26.

5. Charles Dickens, *Great Expectations*. Ed. Angus Calder (1965; reprint New York: Penguin, 1986) 249. Further citations will be noted parenthetically in the text.

6. Trotter 172–73.

7. Trotter 173.

8. Trotter 173.

9. See, for example, Lyn Pucket, *Charles Dickens* (Basingstoke: Palgrave, 2002) 169.

10. John Lucas, *The Melancholy Man: A Study of Dickens's Novels* (London: Methuen, 1970) 302.

11. Sharon Marcus, *Between Women: Friendship, Desire and Marriage in Victorian England* (Princeton and Oxford: Princeton University Press, 2007) 169.

12. Marcus 178.

13. Marcus 173.

14. Marcus 178.

15. Marcus 178.

16. Marcus 167.

17. I would question for instance whether Pip really desires "to be Miss Havisham" or wishes "to occupy Estella's place as a fashionable doll, set off by jewels and lovely clothes, attracting the admiration of a wealthy woman of leisure" (168).

18. Van Ghent 135.

19. J. Hillis Miller, for example, makes the valid point that Pip's act of self-naming highlights his neglected state, but inexplicably claims that Pip hadn't been given a name in the first place. See *Charles Dickens: The World of His Novels* (Cambridge, Massachusetts: Harvard University Press, 1958) 271. Melanie Waters asserts that the sentences display the protagonist's creative misconstruction of the truth. See "Distorted Expectations: Pip and the Problems of Language," *Dickens Studies Annual* 7 (1978): 203. John O. Jordan highlights the way that the sentences establish a connection between writing and deception. See "The Medium of *Great Expectations*," *Dickens Studies Annual* 11 (1983): 85. Jeremy Tambling claims that the sentences may be viewed in a pejorative, self-disciplining light. See "Prison-Bound: Dickens and Foucault," *Essays in Criticism* 36 (1986): 19. John Reed makes a similar contention but goes even further to claim that the falseness of this act is mirrored by Pip's life. See "Dickens and Naming," *Dickens Studies Annual* 36 (2005): 190.

20. Brooks 115.

21. Anny Sadrin, *Parentage and Inheritance in the Novels of Dickens* (Cambridge: Cambridge University Press, 1994) 96.

22. Marcus 178.

23. Carolyn Brown, "*Great Expectations*: Masculinity and Modernity," *Essays and Studies* 40 (1987): 65.

24. Nicola Bradbury, *Charles Dickens' Great Expectations* (Hemel Hempstead: Harvester Wheatsheaf, 1990) 63.

25. Catherine Waters, *Dickens and the Politics of the Family* (Cambridge: Cambridge University Press, 1997) 151.

26. Christopher D. Morris, "The Bad Faith

of Pip's Bad Faith: Deconstructing *Great Expectations*," *ELH* 54.4 (1987): 943.

27. Notably, Marcus believes that the description of Pip's deceased brothers helps to reinforce "the portrait of masculinity as foreclosure" (178).

28. Max Byrd, "'Reading' in *Great Expectations*," *PMLA* 91.1 (1976): 259–60

29. Douglas 5.

30. Brown 65.

31. Miller, *Anatomy* 26.

32. Kristeva, *Powers of Horror* 2.

33. Kristeva 3.

34. Kristeva 2.

35. Kristeva 3.

36. Kristeva 3.

37. Jolene Zigarovich, "Wilkie Collins, Narrativity, and Epitaph," *Dickens Studies Annual* 36 (2005): 230.

38. Pip, characteristically, is not overly concerned with accurate reading, as Max Byrd writes: "These hyperbolic readings, these little fictions ... are in fact typical of Pip at all stages of his expectations, a boy who animates every detail of his world, a boy, as Herbert Pocket says, 'whom nature and circumstances made so romantic' (Ch. xxx)" (260). So, too, Murray Baumgarten writes: "Right from the start he reads inappropriately, out of the intensity of his need. How else can we characterize an imagination that constructs a picture of his parents from the shape of the letters on their tombstones? In this book, he serves as the hero of misreading." See "Calligraphy and Code: Writing in *Great Expectations*," *Dickens Studies Annual* 11 (1983): 61.

39. Moshe Ron, "Autobiographical Narration and Formal Closure in *Great Expectations*," *Hebrew University Studies in Literature* 5.1 (1977–78): 64.

40. Manlove 62.

41. Iain Crawford, "'Large Was His Bounty, and His Soul Sincere' — Gray's *Elegy*, Theme, and Intertextuality in *Great Expectations*," *Dickens Quarterly* 4.2 (1987): 195.

42. My opinion of this passage clearly differs from that of Max Byrd and Anny Sadrin who respectively interpret it as the metaphorical birth of Pip. See Max Byrd 260 and Anny Sadrin 96.

43. Charles R. Forker, "The Language of Hands in *Great Expectations*," *Texas Studies in Literature and Language* 3.2 (1961): 281.

44. Barry Westburg, *The Confessional Fic-*

tions of Charles Dickens (DeKalb: Northern Illinois University Press, 1977) 124.

45. Sadrin 102.

46. Westburg 124.

47. Kristeva 71.

48. Kristeva 71.

49. Kristeva 3.

50. Iris Marion Young, *Justice and the Politics of Difference* (Princeton, NJ: Princeton University Press, 1990) 143.

51. Robert A. Stein, "Pip's Poisoning Magwitch, Supposedly: The Historical Context and Its Implications for Pip's Guilt and Shame," *Philological Quarterly* 67.1 (1988): 111.

52. Ginsburg 124.

53. The term is used in an entirely different sense from the way it is used in William A. Cohen's provocative essay "Manual Conduct in *Great Expectations*," *ELH* 60.1 (1993): 217–59.

54. Gail Turley Houston, "'Pip' and 'Property': The (Re)Production of the Self in *Great Expectations*," *Studies in the Novel* 24.1 (1992): 14.

55. Forster I:16.

56. Lawrence Jay Dessner finds Pip's complaint about his sister's apron "sadly touching" in its "comic and pathetic archness" and "mock innocence" (440). The fact that the narrative is written in retrospect puts this sympathetic view into question. There is nothing particularly touching (or for that matter balanced) about a middle-aged man looking back over his life and refusing to grant his foster mother any credit for the work that she did to keep the household together. Certainly, she might have been a flawed individual but to question why she wore her apron at all is tantamount to negating all of the housework that she ever did.

57. I therefore beg to differ with Lawrene Jay Dessner, who claimed, "There is not the least hint, until the novel's close, of [Joe Gargery] having a sexual nature" (444).

58. Brenda Ayers, *Dissenting Women in Dickens's Novels: The Subversion of Domestic Ideology* (Westport, CT: Greenwood Press, 1998) 87.

59. Donald Hall, *Fixing Patriarchy: Feminism and Mid-Victorian Male Novelists* (London: Macmillan, 1996) 186.

60. Douglas 113.

61. Douglas 113.

62. Juliet John, "Sincerely Deviant Woman,"

Dickens's Villains: Melodrama, Character, Popular Culture (Oxford: Oxford University Press, 2001) 213.

63. Kristeva 4.

64. Kristeva 2.

65. Kristeva 7.

66. It is interesting to note here that in his autobiographical fragment Dickens also presents his own father as troublingly strong and weak: "Everything that I can remember of [my father's] conduct to his wife, or children, or friends, in sickness or affliction, is beyond all praise.... But, in the ease of his temper, and the straitness of his means, he appeared to have utterly lost at this time the idea of educating me at all." Qtd. Forster I: 13.

67. Jordan 85. Murray Baumgarten is in agreement with John O. Jordan: "The next to last word of Pip's letter is a pun; he means, we think, in affection, but he writes infection. The word reveals his conscious and unconscious meanings at the same time. More of him is inscribed in it than he knows" (72).

68. Morris 944.

69. Dickens was also dimly aware that his father was to some degree responsible for the injustice and pain that he suffered in his life. In the autobiographical fragment he records his first visit to see his father in Marshalsea Prison: "My father was waiting for me in the lodge, and we went up to his room (on the top story but one), and cried very much. And he told me, I remember, to take warning by the Marshalsea, and to observe that if a man had twenty pounds a year, and spent nineteen pounds nineteen shillings and sixpence, he would be happy; but that a shilling spent the other way would make him wretched. I see the fire we sat before now; with two bricks inside the rusted grate, one on each side, to prevent its burning too many coals. Some other debtor shared the room with him, who came in by and by; and as the dinner was a joint-stock repast, I was sent up to 'Captain Porter' in the room overhead, with Mr. Dickens's compliments, and I was his son, and could he, Captain P., lend me a knife and fork?" Dickens then goes on to describe Captain Porter's degraded state. Apparently, he was "in the last extremity of shabbiness" and he lived with "a very dirty lady" and two children "with shock heads of hair." Dickens states that he knew "God knows how" that the two children were his "natural children, and that the dirty lady was not married to [him]." Indeed, Dickens writes that as he returned to his father's room, he knew "all this as surely ... as the knife and fork were in my hand." See Forster I: 16–17. Dickens then is at some level aware that his father is the kind of man who can in one minute tearfully describe the woes of being a debtor but in another minute can complacently put his son in the demeaning position of having to request the loan of a knife and fork from an extremely shabby fellow prisoner of dubious moral standards.

70. This projection of emotion onto external objects is, of course, highly reminiscent of the scene in *David Copperfield* where Clara Copperfield gathers gooseberries in the Edenic garden while David stands by "bolting furtive gooseberries, and trying to look unmoved." See Chapter Three of this book (81–83).

71. Judith Weissman and Steven Cohan, "Dickens' *Great Expectations*: Pip's Arrested Development," *American Imago* 38:1 (1981): 110.

72. Qtd. Forster I: 32.

73. Qtd. Forster I: 25.

74. Qtd. Forster I: 32.

75. Tyson Stolte, "Mightier than the Sword: Aggression of the Written Word in *Great Expectations*," *Dickens Studies Annual* 35 (2005) 183.

76. Stolte 183.

77. Stolte 180.

78. Stolte 180.

79. Kristeva 3.

80. Kristeva 4.

81. See, for example: Julian Moynahan, "The Hero's Guilt: The Case of *Great Expectations*," *Essays in Criticism* 10 (1960): 60–79; Robert Barnard, "Images and Theme in *Great Expectations*," *Dickens Studies Annual* 1 (1970): 238–51; and Shuli Barzilai, "Dickens's *Great Expectations*: The Motive for Moral Masochism," *American Imago* 42:1 (1985): 45–67.

82. Jenny Gribble, "The Bible in *Great Expectations*," *Dickens Quarterly* 25.4 (2008): 235.

83. It is interesting that critics tend to unquestioningly justify or excuse Pip's lack of gratitude towards Mrs. Joe. Moshe Ron provides a typical example: "But here is a curious thing about gratitude: it may or may not be felt by the indebted person (this has to do with the law of desire), but it cannot be demanded as a right by the giver. In fact, as soon

as it is explicitly asked for, the right to gratitude is immediately and *ipso facto* forfeited and rendered null and void. I think most readers of *Great Expectations* will share Pip's feeling that he does not really owe his sister too much " (56).

84. Interestingly, Joe in his only meeting with Miss Havisham, also treats her like she doesn't exist. Perversely, he addresses only Pip and obdurately doesn't answer any of her questions. He also doesn't even thank her when she provides the handsome sum of twenty-five guineas for Pip's indentures. See pages 128–30.

85. Jeffrey Berman, *Narcissism and the Novel* (New York: New York University Press, 1990) 129–30.

86. Richard Barickman, Susan MacDonald, and Myra Stark, *Corrupt Relations: Dickens, Thackeray, Trollope, Collins, and the Victorian Sexual System* (New York: Columbia University Press, 1982) 70.

87. Bloch 6.

88. McKnight 44.

89. Houston 18.

90. Curt Hartog, "The Rape of Miss Havisham," *Studies in the Novel* 14.3 (1982) 250.

91. Brooks 119.

92. Barnard 245.

93. Ayers 90.

94. Robert R. Garnett, "The Good and the Unruly in *Great Expectations*— and Estella," *Dickens Quarterly* 16.1 (1999) 37.

95. Garnett 30.

96. Hilary M. Schor, *Dickens and the Daughter of the House* (Cambridge: Cambridge University Press, 1999) 175.

97. Ross H. Dabney, *Love and Property in the Novels of Dickens* (London: Chatto & Windus, 1967) 127–28.

Chapter Six

1. Michel Foucault, "An Interview with Michel Foucault," *Death and the Labyrinth: The World of Raymond Roussel*, trans. Charles Ruas (London: Athlon Press, 1987) 184.

2. Ruth F. Glancy, *Dickens's Christmas Books, Christmas Stories, and Other Short Fiction: An Annotated Bibliography* (New York & London: Garland Publishing, 1985) xxix.

3. Philip Hobsbaum, *A Reader's Guide to Charles Dickens* (London: Thames & Hudson, 1972) 293.

4. Leavis 372.

5. See Glancy xxix.

6. Ingham 133–44.

7. Ingham 137.

8. Ingham 141.

9. Ingham 144.

10. Charles Dickens, *Sikes and Nancy and Other Public Readings*, ed. Philip Collins (Oxford: Oxford University Press, 1983).

11. Raymund Fitzsimons, *The Charles Dickens Show: An Account of His Public Readings 1858–1870* (London: Geoffrey Bles, 1970) 146.

12. Fitzsimons 149.

13. Fitzsimons 149.

14. Fitzsimons 154.

15. Dickens, *Sikes and Nancy* 243–44.

16. *The Times*, January 8, 1869, qtd. in Philip Collins ed., *Charles Dickens: The Public Readings* (Oxford: Clarendon Press, 1975) 468.

17. *Freeman's Journal* (Dublin), January 14, 1869, qtd. in Collins, *Charles Dickens: The Public Readings* 469.

18. *Daily Telegraph*, January 6, 1869, qtd. in Collins, *Charles Dickens: The Public Readings* 468.

19. Qtd. Philip Collins ed., *Charles Dickens: The Public Readings* (Oxford: Clarendon Press, 1975) 469.

20. Qtd. Fitzsimons 161.

21. Karl Jaspers qtd. Gerald L. Bruns, *Maurice Blanchot: The Refusal of Philosophy* (Baltimore and London: Johns Hopkins University Press, 1997) 304.

22. Maurice Blanchot qtd. in Bruns 129–30.

23. Blanchot qtd. in Bruns 130.

24. In a three-hour interview, Foucault's longtime lover Daniel Defert "described at some length the importance of the idea of "limit experience" for Foucault, and also discussed how Foucault had developed the notion out of his reading of Bataille." See James Miller, *The Passion of Michel Foucault* (London: Flamingo, 1994) 398.

25. Georges Bataille, *Inner Experience*, trans. Leslie Anne Boldt (1954; Albany: State University of New York Press, 1988).

26. Bataille 3.

27. Bataille 3.

28. Bataille 3.

29. Bataille 4.

30. Bataille 3.

31. See Jacques Derrida qtd. in Leslie Anne

Boldt's "Translator's Introduction," *Inner Experience* xxiii.

32. Michel Foucault qtd. James Miller, *The Passion of Michel Foucault* 30.

33. Foucault, "Preface to Transgression," *Language, Counter-memory, Practice: Selected Essays and Interviews*, trans. Donald F. Bouchard and Sherry Simon, ed. Donald F. Bouchard (Ithaca, NY: Cornell University Press, 1977) 34.

34. Foucault, "Preface to Transgression" 35.

35. Miller 30.

36. Qtd. Miller 30.

37. Qtd. Miller 30.

38. Qtd. Miller 27.

39. Qtd. Miller 27.

40. Concerning his work on Foucault, Miller eschews its classification as biography: "*This book is not a biography, though in outline it follows the chronology of Michel Foucault's life; nor is it a comprehensive survey of his works, although it does offer an interpretation of a great many of his texts. It is, rather, a narrative account of one man's lifelong struggle to honor Nietzsche's gnomic injunction, 'to become what one is.'*" 5. (Miller's emphasis.)

41. Miller 28.

42. Miller 381. Miller's emphasis. Both the preface and the postscript of his book appear in italics.

43. Defert shared twenty-three years of his life with Foucault. See Miller 25.

44. Qtd. Miller 29.

45. Qtd. Ackroyd 1063.

46. Qtd. Raymund Fitzsimons, *The Charles Dickens Show: An Account of His Public Readings 1858–1870* (London: Geoffrey Bles, 1970) 163.

47. Qtd. Collins, *Charles Dickens: The Public Readings* 471.

48. Forster 2: 410.

49. Forster 2: 409.

50. Wilson 86.

51. Collins, *Charles Dickens: The Public Readings* 470.

52. Newsom, *Charles Dickens Revisited* 56.

53. Newsom 56.

54. Ackroyd 1039.

55. Collins, Introduction, *Sikes and Nancy and Other Public Readings* 229.

56. Fitzsimons 147.

57. Fitzsimons 149.

58. Fitzsimons 149.

59. Qtd. Fitzsimons 159.

60. Qtd. Ackroyd 1039.

61. Qtd. Fitzsimons 154.

62. Qtd. Ackroyd 1039.

63. Qtd. Fitzsimons 160.

64. Fitzsimons 160.

65. Qtd. Ackroyd 1039.

66. Forster 2: 410.

67. Collins, *Charles Dickens: The Public Readings* 470.

68. Fitzsimons 160.

69. Fitzsimons 161.

70. Fitzsimons 172.

71. Forster 2: 357.

72. Qtd. Forster 2: 358.

73. Kaplan 538.

74. Fitzsimons 173.

75. Ackroyd 1031.

76. Sylvia Manning, "Masking and Self-Revelation: Dickens's Three Autobiographies," *Dickens Studies Newsletter* 7 (1976): 72.

77. Newsom, *Charles Dickens Revisited* 56.

78. Malcolm Andrews, *Charles Dickens and His Performing Selves: Dickens and the Public Readings* (Oxford: Oxford University Press, 2006) 262.

79. Claire Tomalin, *Charles Dickens: A Life* (London: Penguin, 2011) 374.

80. Qtd. Robert Leach, *The Punch and Judy Show: History, Tradition and Meaning* (London: Batsford, 1985) 50–51.

81. Qtd. Leach 51.

82. Leach 173.

83. Robert Morse, "*Our Mutual Friend*," *Partisan Review* 16 (1949): 282.

84. Grahame Smith, *Charles Dickens: A Literary Life* (Basingstoke: Macmillan, 1996) 43.

85. Qtd. Ackroyd 1032.

86. Ackroyd 1040.

87. Molly Devon and Philip Miller, *Screw the Roses, Send Me the Thorns: The Romance and Sexual Sorcery of Sadomasochism* (Fairfield, CT: Mystic Rose, 1995) 238.

88. Devon and Miller 4.

89. Devon and Miller 2. Mindful that some might take objection to the use of the female pronoun in relation to the submissive, Devon and Miller justify this by stating that in their relationship he is the "dom" and she is the "sub" and because it is their book they will do what they want (2).

90. I owe the very valuable point about choosing to enact a murder and run the risk

of dying to Professor Virginia Blain. As Professor Blain rightfully points out, Dickens never "chooses" to be murdered — rather, he chooses to run the *risk* of dying and, while this is a gamble, it is a gamble he could win despite the odds.

91. Andrews 260.

92. Collins, *Charles Dickens: The Public Readings* 471.

93. Andrews 260.

94. Andrews 260.

95. Collins, *Charles Dickens: The Public Readings* 471.

96. Newsom, *Charles Dickens Revisited* 57.

97. Charles Dickens, *Oliver Twist*, ed. Peter Fairclough (1837–39; Harmondsworth: Penguin, 1983) 412. All references are to this edition and will be cited parenthetically in the text.

98. Kristeva, *Powers of Horror* 5.

99. Kristeva 13.

100. Kristeva 13.

101. Kristeva 13.

102. This might explain why John Kucich identifies a much stronger vein of self-negation in Dickens than in the brilliant but not so popular novelists Charlotte Bronte and George Eliot. Kucich writes: "Dickens, like Eliot and Bronte, idealized forms of desire that negate or destabilize the self, splitting it rather than completing or harmonizing it. If anything, Dickens' interest in self-negation went beyond the kind of internal doubling we find in Eliot and Bronte, which begins an infinite but mostly benign deepening of the textures and convolutions of the self. Dickens conceived self-negation as a more violent kind of desire. Of the three novelists, he seems closest to making the explicit connection between self-negating libido and death that is formu-lated in the later Freud, in Bataille, and elsewhere. For Dickens, the highest forms of human desire — whatever desire's apparent object — seek most of all to violate the coherence and integrity of the self in an absolute way, and to expend energy recklessly, in defiance of any concerns for the safety or advantage of the individual. In short, desire seeks its fulfillment outside the limits of selfhood, in the death of the individual — in a tendency that Bataille calls assenting to life up to the point of death" *Repression in Victorian Fiction: Charlotte Bronte, George Eliot, and Charles* Dickens (Berkeley: University of California Press, 1987) 204. Kucich was, of course, referring to the desire for radical self-negation that is evinced in the novels of these writers, but if we can accept Foucault's contention that the major work of a writer is, in the end, himself in the process of writing his works (or, as in Dickens's case, writing and performing his works) and that the private life of an individual and his work are interrelated, then we can extend Kucich's claim to include Dickens's own desire for radical self-negation.

103. Miller 19.

104. Miller 16.

105. Miller 29.

106. Miller 29.

107. In relation to this matter, see also Susan L. Ferguson, "Dickens's Public Readings and the Victorian Author," *Studies in English Literature, 1500–1900* 41.4 (2001): 729–49. While Ferguson believes that Dickens resisted the Foucaultian imperative that authors should reveal or display the hidden sense that pervades their work, she is nonetheless of the opinion that "the public reading performances were unquestionably part of the construction of 'Dickens' as an author in the Foucaultian sense" (745–46).

Bibliography

Primary Sources

Wherever possible, all references to and quotations from Dickens's novels are to the Penguin editions as these provide the accessibility of paperback publication.

Dickens, Charles. *A Child's History of England*. In *Holiday Romance and Other Writings for Children*. Ed. Gillian Avery. 1852–54. London: J.M. Dent, 1995.
_____. *Bleak House*. Ed. Norman Page. 1852–53. Penguin Classics. Harmondsworth: Penguin, 1985.
_____. *David Copperfield*. Ed. Trevor Blount. 1849–50. Penguin Classics. Harmondsworth: Penguin, 1985.
_____. *Dombey and Son*. Ed. Peter Fairclough. 1846–48. Penguin Classics. Harmondsworth: Penguin, 1986.
_____. *Great Expectations*. Ed. Angus Calder. 1860–61. Penguin Classics. Harmondsworth: Penguin, 1986.
_____. *Hard Times*. Ed. David Craig. 1854. Penguin Classics. Harmondsworth: Penguin, 1986.
_____. *Little Dorrit*. Ed. John Holloway. 1855–57. Penguin Classics. Harmondsworth: Penguin, 1985.
_____. *Oliver Twist*. Ed. Peter Fairclough. 1837–39. Penguin English Library. Harmondsworth: Penguin, 1983.
_____. "Sikes and Nancy." In *Sikes and Nancy and Other Public Readings*. Ed. Philip Collins. 1869. Oxford: Oxford University Press, 1983.

Secondary Sources

Abrams, M.H. *A Glossary of Literary Terms*, 5th ed. Fort Worth, TX: Holt, Rinehart and Winston, 1988.
Ackroyd, Peter. *Dickens*. London: Sinclair-Stevenson, 1990.
Allen, Michael. *Charles Dickens's Childhood*. New York: St. Martin's Press, 1988.
_____. *Charles Dickens and the Blacking Factory*. St. Leonard's: Oxford-Stockley, 2011.
Allen, Walter. *The English Novel*. 1954. Harmondsworth: Penguin, 1965.
Andrews, Malcolm. *Charles Dickens and His Performing Selves: Dickens and the Public Readings*. Oxford: Oxford University Press, 2006.

Angyal, Andras. "Disgust and Related Aversions." *The Journal of Abnormal Social Psychology* 36 (1941): 393–412.

Ashfield, Andrew, and Peter de Bolla, eds. Introduction. *The Sublime: A Reader in British Eighteenth-Century Aesthetic Theory*. Cambridge: Cambridge University Press, 1996. 1–16.

Auerbach, Nina. *Woman and the Demon: The Life of a Victorian Myth*. Cambridge, MA: Harvard University Press, 1982.

_____. "Performing Suffering: From Dickens to David." *Browning Institute Studies* 18 (1990): 15–22.

Axton, William. "The Trouble with Esther." *Modern Language Quarterly* 26 (1965): 545–57.

_____. "Esther's Nicknames: A Study in Relevance." *The Dickensian* 62 (1966): 158–63.

Ayers, Brenda. *Dissenting Women in Dickens's Novels: The Subversion of Domestic Ideology*. Westport, CT: Greenwood Press, 1998.

Barickman, Richard, Susan MacDonald, and Myra Stark. *Corrupt Relations: Dickens, Thackeray, Trollope, Collins, and the Victorian Sexual System*. New York: Columbia University Press, 1982.

Barnard, Robert. "Imagery and Theme in Great Expectations." *Dickens Studies Annual* 1 (1970): 238–51.

Barzilai, Shuli. "Dickens's *Great Expectations*: The Motive for Moral Masochism." *American Imago* 42.1 (1985): 45–67.

Basch, Françoise. *Relative Creatures: Victorian Women in Society and the Novel*. New York: Schocken Books, 1974.

Bataille, Georges. *Inner Experience*. 1952. Trans. Leslie Anne Boldt. Albany: State University of New York Press, 1988.

Baumgarten, Murray. "Calligraphy and Code: Writing in *Great Expectations*." *Dickens Studies Annual* 11 (1983): 61–72.

Berman, Jeffrey. *Narcissism and the Novel*. New York: New York University Press, 1990.

Blain, Virginia. "Double Vision and the Double Standard in *Bleak House*: A Feminist Perspective." *New Casebooks: Bleak House*. Ed. Jeremy Tambling. London: Macmillan Press, 1998. 65–86. [Published originally as "Double Vision and the Double Standard," *Literature and History* 2:1 (1985): 31–46.]

Bloch, R. Howard. "Medieval Misogyny." *Misogyny, Misandry, and Misanthropy*. Ed. R. Howard Bloch and Frances Ferguson. Berkeley: University of California Press, 1989. 1–24.

Bloom, Harold. Introduction. *Charles Dickens's David Copperfield*. New York: Chelsea House, 1987. 1–8.

Blount, Trevor. Introduction. *David Copperfield*. By Charles Dickens. Ed. Trevor Blount. London: Penguin, 1971. 13–39.

Bodenheimer, Rosemarie. "Dickens and the Writing of a Life." *Palgrave Advances in Charles Dickens Studies*. Ed. John Bowen and Robert L. Patten. Basingstoke, UK: Palgrave Macmillan, 2006. 48–68.

_____. *Knowing Dickens*. Ithaca and London: Cornell University Press, 2007.

Bowen, John. "Dickens and the Force of Writing." *Palgrave Advances in Charles Dickens Studies*. Ed. John Bowen and Robert L. Patten. Basingstoke, UK: Palgrave Macmillan, 2006. 255–72.

_____. "A Garland for *The Old Curiosity Shop*," *Dickens Studies Annual* 37 (2006): 1–16.

Bradbury, Nicola. *Charles Dickens' Great Expectations*. Hemel Hempstead, UK: Harvester Wheatsheaf, 1990.

Briganti, Chiara. "The Monstrous Actress: Esther Summerson's Spectral Name," *Dickens Studies Annual* 19 (1990): 205–30.

Brooks, Peter. "Repetition, Repression, and Return: The Plotting of *Great Expectations*." *Reading for the Plot: Design and Intention in Narrative*. Oxford: Clarendon Press, 1984. 113–42.

Brown, Carolyn. "*Great Expectations*: Masculinity and Modernity," *Essays and Studies* 40 (1987): 60–74.

Bruns, Gerald L. *Maurice Blanchot: The Refusal of Philosophy*. Baltimore and London: Johns Hopkins University Press, 1997.

Burgis, Nina. Introduction. *David Copperfield*. By Charles Dickens. Ed. Nina Burgis. Oxford: Clarendon, 1981. xv–lxii.

Burke, Edmund. *A Philosophical Enquiry into Our Ideas of the Sublime and Beautiful*. Ed. James T Boulton. London: University of Notre Dame Press, 1968.

Butler, Judith. *Gender Trouble: Feminism and the Subversion of Identity*. New York & London: Routledge, 1990.

Byrd, Max. "Reading in *Great Expectations*." *PMLA* 91.1 (1976): 259–65.

Carey, John. *The Violent Effigy: A Study of Dickens' Imagination*. 1973. London & Boston: Faber and Faber, 1979.

Chanter, Tina. "Kristeva's Politics of Change: Tracking Essentialism with the Help of a Sex/Gender Map." *Ethics, Politics, and Difference in Julia Kristeva's Writing*. Ed. Kelly Oliver. New York and London: Routledge, 1993. 179–195.

Cheadle, Brian. "Mystification and the Mystery of Origins." *Dickens Studies Annual* 25 (1996): 29–47.

Clipper, Lawrence J. "The Blacking Warehouse Again: Another View." *Dickens Studies Newsletter* 12.3 (1981): 77–80.

Cohen, William A. "Manual Conduct in Great Expectations." *ELH* 60.1 (1993): 217–59.

Collins, Philip, ed. *Dickens: The Critical Heritage*. London: Routledge, 1971.

_____. *Charles Dickens: The Public Readings*. Oxford: Clarendon Press, 1975.

_____. *Charles Dickens: David Copperfield*. London: Edward Arnold, 1977.

_____. "Dickens's Autobiographical Fragment and *David Copperfield*." *Cahiers Victoriens et Edouardiens* 20 (1984): 87–96.

Conlon, Raymond. "Bleak House's Miss Barbary: A Psychological Miniature." *Dickens Studies Newsletter* 14.3 (1983): 90–92.

Crawford, Iain. "'Large Was His Bounty, and His Soul Sincere'— Gray's *Elegy*, Theme, and Intertextuality in *Great Expectations*." *Dickens Quarterly* 4.2 (1987): 195–99.

Creed, Barbara. *The Monstrous-Feminine: Film, Feminism, Psychoanalysis*. 1993. London and New York: Routledge, 1994.

Curtis, Valerie, and Adam Biran. "Dirt, Disgust, and Disease: Is Hygiene in Our Genes?" *Perspectives in Biology and Medicine* 44.1 (2001): 17–31.

Dabney, Ross H. *Love and Property in the Novels of Dickens*. London: Chatto & Windus, 1967.

Darwin, Charles. *The Expression of the Emotions in Man and Animals*. 1872. Oxford: Oxford University Press, 1998.

Davis, Earl. *The Flint and the Flame: The Artistry of Charles Dickens*. Columbia: University of Missouri Press, 1963.

Dessner, Lawrence Jay. "*Great Expectations*: "'The Ghost of a Man's Own Father.'" *PMLA* 91.3 (1976): 436–49.

Dever, Carolyn, *Death and the Mother from Dickens to Freud: Victorian Fiction and the Anxiety of Origins*. Cambridge: Cambridge University Press, 1998.

Devon, Molly, and Philip Miller. *Screw the Roses, Send Me the Thorns: The Romance and Sexual Sorcery of Sadomasochism*. Fairfield, CT: Mystic Rose, 1995.

Douglas, Mary. *Purity and Danger: An Analysis of Concepts of Pollution and Taboo*. 1966. London: Routledge, 1978.

Drew, John M.L. *Dickens the Journalist*. Basingstoke, UK: Palgrave Macmillan, 2003.

_____. "A Twist in the Tale." *Guardian Unlimited*, October 31, 2003. 22 Jan. 2008 http://books.guardian.co.uk/departments/classics/story/0,,1075112,00.html.

Dunn, Richard J. "Esther's Role in *Bleak House*." *The Dickensian* 62 (1966): 163–66.

Easley, Keith. "Dickens and Bakhtin: Authoring in *Bleak House*," *Dickens Studies Annual* 34 (2004): 185–232.

Edwards, Simon. "*David Copperfield*: The Decomposing Self." *David Copperfield and Hard Times*. Ed. John Peck. Basingstoke and London: Macmillan, 1995. 58–80.

Eggert, Paul. "The Real Esther Summerson." *Dickens Studies Newsletter* 11.3 (1980): 74–81.

Eiger, Edwin. *The Metaphysical Novel in England and America: Dickens, Bulwer, Melville, and Hawthorne*. Berkeley: University of California Press, 1978.

_____. "David Copperfield and the Benevolent Spirit." *Dickens Studies Annual* 14 (1985): 1–15.

Federico, Annette R. "Dickens and Disgust." *Dickens Studies Annual* 29 (2000): 145–61.

Ferguson, Frances. "Sublime of Edmund Burke, or the Bathos of Experience." *Glyph: John Hopkins Textual Studies* 8 (1981): 62–78.

Ferguson, Susan L. "Dickens's Public Readings and the Victorian Author." *Studies in English Literature, 1500–1900* 41.4 (2001): 729–49.

Fitzsimons, Raymund. *The Charles Dickens Show: An Account of His Public Readings 1858–1870*. London: Geoffrey Bles, 1970.

Foley, June. "Elizabeth Dickens: Model for Fagin." *Women's Studies* 30.2 (2001): 225–35.

Forker, Charles R. "The Language of Hands in *Great Expectations*." *Texas Studies in Literature and Language* 3.2 (1961): 280–93.

Forster, John. *The Life of Charles Dickens*. 1872–74. Ed. A.J. Hoppe. Everyman's Library. 2 vols. London: Dent, 1969.

Foucault, Michel. "Preface to Transgression." *Language, Counter-memory, Practice: Selected Essays and Interviews*. Trans. Donald F. Bouchard and Sherry Simon. Ed. Donald F. Bouchard. Ithaca, NY: Cornell University Press, 1977. 29–52.

_____. "An Interview with Michel Foucault." *Death and the Labyrinth: The World of Raymond Roussel*. Trans. Charles Ruas. London: Athlone Press, 1987. 169–86.

Frank, Lawrence. "'Through a Glass Darkly': Esther Summerson and *Bleak House*," *Dickens Studies Annual* 4 (1975): 91–112.

Fraser, Nancy. "The Uses and Abuses of French Discourse Theories for Feminist Politics." *Revaluing French Feminism: Critical Essays on Difference, Agency, and Culture*. Ed. Nancy Fraser and Sandra Lee Bartky. Bloomington and Indianapolis: Indiana University Press, 1992. 177–194.

Freud, Sigmund. "Katharina." *Studies on Hysteria*. Trans. James and Alix Strachey. Ed. Angela Richards. Vol. 3. Harmondsworth: Penguin, 1986.

Furniss, Tom. *Edmund Burke's Aesthetic Ideology: Language, Gender, and Political Economy in Revolution*. Cambridge: Cambridge University Press, 1993.

Garnett, Robert R. "Why Not Sophy? Desire and Agnes in *David Copperfield*." *Dickens Quarterly* 14 (1997): 213–31.

_____. "The Good and the Unruly in *Great Expectations*— and Estella," *Dickens Quarterly* 16.1 (1999): 24–41.

Ginsburg, Michal Peled. "Dickens and the Uncanny: Repression and Displacement in *Great Expectations*." *Dickens Studies Annual* 13 (1984): 115–24.

Glancy, Ruth F. *Dickens's Christmas Books, Christmas Stories, and Other Short Fiction: An Annotated Bibliography*. New York & London: Garland Publishing, 1985.

Goldberg, Michael. *Carlyle and Dickens*. Athens: University of Georgia Press, 1972.

Goodman, Marcia Renee. "'I'll Follow the Other': Tracing the (M)other in *Bleak House*." *Dickens Studies Annual* 19 (1990): 147–67.

Gribble, Jenny. "The Bible in *Great Expectations*." *Dickens Quarterly* 25.4 (2008): 232–40.

Gross, Elizabeth. "The Body of Signification." *Abjection, Melancholia, and Love: The Work of Julia Kristeva*. Ed. John Fletcher and Andrew Benjamin. London & New York: Routledge, 1990. 80–103.

Grosz, Elizabeth. *Sexual Subversions: Three French Feminists*. Sydney: Allen & Unwin, 1989.

Hall, Donald. *Fixing Patriarchy: Feminism and Mid-Victorian Male Novelists*. London: Macmillan, 1996.

Hall, Jasmine Yong. "What's Troubling About Esther? Narrating, Policing, and Resisting Arrest in *Bleak House*." *Dickens Studies Annual* 22 (1993): 171–94.

Hanzo, Thomas A. "Paternity and the Subject in *Bleak House*." *The Fictional Father: Lacanian Readings of the Text*. Ed. Robert Con Davis. Amherst: University of Massachusetts Press, 1981. 27–47.

Hardy, Barbara. *The Moral Art of Dickens*. London: Athlone, 1970.

Harrison, John. *Love Your Disease*. London: Angus & Robertson, 1984.

Hartog, Curt. "The Rape of Miss Havisham," *Studies in the Novel* 14.3 (1982): 248–65.

Hennessee, David. "Gentlemanly Guilt and Masochistic Fantasy in *Great Expectations*." *Dickens Studies Annual* 34 (2004): 301–28.

Hibbert, Christopher. *The Making of Charles Dickens*. 1967. Harmondsworth: Penguin, 1983.

Hill, Nancy Klenk. "Woman as Saviour." *Denver Quarterly* 18.4 (1984): 94–107.

Hillis Miller, J. *Charles Dickens: The World of His Novels*. Cambridge, MA: Harvard University Press, 1958.

Hirsch, Gordon D. "The Mysteries in *Bleak House*: A Psychoanalytic Study." *Dickens Studies Annual* 4 (1975): 132–52.

_____. "A Psychoanalytic Rereading of *David Copperfield*." *The Victorian Newsletter* 58 (1980): 1–5.

Hobsbaum, Philip. *A Reader's Guide to Charles Dickens*. London: Thames & Hudson, 1972.

Hornback, Bert G. *"The Hero of My Life": Essays on Dickens*. Athens: Ohio University Press, 1981.

Houston, Gail Turley. "'Pip' and 'Property': The (Re)Production of the Self in *Great Expectations*." *Studies in the Novel* 24.1 (1992): 13–25.

_____. *Consuming Fictions: Gender, Class and Hunger in Dickens's Novels*. Carbondale and Edwardsville: Southern Illinois University Press, 1994.

Hutter, Albert D. "Reconstructive Autobiography: The Experience at Warren's Blacking." *Dickens Studies Annual* 6 (1977): 1–14.

_____. "Nation and Generation in *A Tale of Two Cities*." *PMLA* 93 (1978): 448–62.

Ingham, Patricia. *Dickens, Women and Language*. New York: Harvester Wheatsheaf, 1992.

John, Juliet. *Dickens's Villains: Melodrama, Character, Popular Culture*. Oxford: Oxford University Press, 2001. 199–234.

Johnson, Edgar. *Charles Dickens: His Tragedy and Triumph*. 2 vols. New York: Simon and Schuster, 1952.

Jolly, Diane L. "The Nature of Esther." *The Dickensian* 86.1 (1990): 29–40.

Jordan, John O. "The Medium of *Great Expectations*." *Dickens Studies Annual* 11 (1983): 73–88.

_____. "The Social Sub-text of *David Copperfield*." *Dickens Studies Annual* 14 (1985): 61–92.

Kaplan, Fred. *Dickens: A Biography*. 1988. London: Sceptre, 1989.

Korg, Jacob. Introduction. *Twentieth Century Interpretations of Bleak House*. Ed. Jacob Korg. Englewood Cliffs, NJ: Prentice-Hall, 1968. 1–20.

Kristeva, Julia. *The Powers of Horror: An Essay on Abjection*. Trans. Leon S. Roudiez. New York: Columbia University Press, 1982.

_____. *Tales of Love*. Trans. Leon Roudiez. New York: Columbia University Press, 1987.

_____. Interview with Elaine Hoffman Baruch. "Feminism and Psychoanalysis." *Julia Kristeva, Interviews*. Ed. Ross Mitchell Guberman. New York: Columbia University Press, 1996. 113–121.

Kucich, John. *Repression in Victorian Fiction: Charlotte Bronte, George Eliot, and Charles Dickens*. Berkeley: University of California Press, 1987.

Leach, Robert. *The Punch and Judy Show: History, Tradition and Meaning*. London: Batsford, 1985.

Leavis, Q.D. "How We Must Read *Great Expectations*." F.R. and Q.D. Leavis. *Dickens the Novelist*. 1970. Harmondsworth: Penguin, 1980. 360–428.

Lechte, John. *Julia Kristeva*. London and New York: Routledge, 1990.

Lindsay, Jack. *Charles Dickens*. 1950. London: Andrew Dakers, 1970.

Litvak, Leon. "What Books Did Dickens Buy and Read? Evidence from the Book Accounts with His Publishers." *The Dickensian* 94.2 (1998): 85–130.

Lougy, Robert E. "Filth, Liminality, and Abjection in Charles Dickens's *Bleak House*." *ELH* 69 (2002): 473–500.

Lucas, John. *The Melancholy Man: A Study of Dickens's Novels*. London: Methuen, 1970.

Manlove, Colin N. "Neither Here nor There: Uneasiness in *Great Expectations*." *Dickens Studies Annual* 8 (1980): 61–71.

Manning, Sylvia. "Masking and Self-Revelation: Dickens's Three Autobiographies." *Dickens Studies Newsletter* 7: 69–75.

Marcus, Sharon. *Between Women: Friendship, Desire and Marriage in Victorian England*. Princeton and Oxford: Princeton University Press, 2007. 167–90.

Marcus, Steven. *Dickens: From Pickwick to Dombey*. 1965. London: Chatto and Windus, 1971.

McKnight, Natalie J. *Suffering Mothers in Mid-Victorian Novels*. New York: St. Martin's Press, 1997.

Menninghaus, Winfried. *Disgust: The Theory and History of a Strong Sensation*. Trans. Howard Eiland and Joel Golb. Albany: State University of New York Press, 2003.

Meyers, Diana T. "The Subversion of Women's Agency in Psychoanalytic Feminism: Chodorow, Flax, Kristeva." *Revaluing French Feminism: Critical Essays on Difference, Agency, and Culture.* Ed. Nancy Fraser and Sandra Lee Bartky. Bloomington and Indianapolis: Indiana University Press, 1992. 136–161.

Michie, Helena. "'Who Is This in Pain?': Scarring, Disfigurement, and Female Identity in *Bleak House* and *Our Mutual Friend.*" *Novel* 22.1 (1989): 199–212.

Miller, D.A. "Discipline in Different Voices: Bureaucracy, Police, Family and *Bleak House.*" *Representations* 1 (1983): 59–89. Reprinted in *New Casebooks: Bleak House.* Ed. Jeremy Tambling. London: Macmillan, 1998. 87–127.

Miller, James. *The Passion of Michel Foucault.* London: Flamingo, 1994.

Miller, Susan B. *Disgust: The Gatekeeper Emotion.* Hillsdale, NJ, and London: Analytic Press, 2004.

Miller, William Ian. *The Anatomy of Disgust.* Cambridge, MA: Harvard University Press, 1997.

Moi, Toril. *Simone de Beauvoir: The Making of an Intellectual Woman.* Oxford: Blackwell, 1994.

Monod, Sylvère. *Dickens the Novelist.* Norman: University of Oklahoma Press, 1968.

Morris, Christopher D. "The Bad Faith of Pip's Bad Faith: Deconstructing *Great Expectations.*" *ELH* 54.4 (1987): 941–55.

Morse, Robert. "Our Mutual Friend." *Partisan Review* 16:3 (1949): 277–89.

Moynahan, Julian. "The Hero's Guilt: The Case of *Great Expectations.*" *Essays in Criticism* 10 (1960): 60–79.

Newsom, Robert. "The Hero's Shame." *Dickens Studies Annual* 11 (1983): 1–24.

_____. "*Villette* and *Bleak House*: Authorizing Women." *Nineteenth-Century Literature* 46.1 (1991): 54–81

_____. *Charles Dickens Revisited.* New York: Twayne, 2000.

Nord, Deborah Epstein. *Walking the Victorian Streets: Women, Representation and the City.* Ithaca and London: Cornell University Press, 1995.

Nussbaum, Martha. *Hiding from Humanity.* Princeton, NJ: Princeton University Press, 2004.

O'Connor, Steven. Review of *The Night Side of Dickens: Cannibalism, Passion, Necessity*, by Harry Stone. *The Dickensian* 91.2 (1995): 127–30.

Oliver, Kelly, *Reading Kristeva: Unraveling the Double-Bind.* Bloomington and Indianapolis: Indiana University Press, 1993.

Orwell, George. "Charles Dickens." *Collected Essays.* London: Mercury, 1961. 31–87.

Pearson, Hesketh. *Dickens: His Character, Comedy and Career.* 1949. London: Cassell, 1988.

Peltason, Timothy. "Esther's Will." *ELH* 59.3 (1992): 671–91.

Phillips, M.L., et al. "Disgust: The Forgotten Emotion of Psychiatry." *The British Journal of Psychiatry* 172 (1998): 373–75.

Poovey, Mary. *Uneven Developments: The Ideological Work of Gender in Mid-Victorian England.* London: Virago Press, 1989.

Pope-Hennessy, Una. *Charles Dickens.* 1945. London: Reprint Society, 1947.

Preston, Shale. "Dirty Davy and the Domestic Sublime." Jean-Paul Naugrette, coord., *Réussir l'épreuve de littérature: David Copperfield*, C.A.P.E.S./Agrégation Anglais, Paris: Editions Ellipses, 1996, 128–36.

_____. "Beating Foucault to the Punch: Dickens, Death, Limit Experience and the Pleasure of Killing Nancy." *Australasian Victorian Studies Journal* 4 (1998): 88–97.

_____. "True Romance? Dirty Davy and the Domestic Sublime: From the Alps to the Abject in *David Copperfield*." *Australasian Victorian Studies Journal* 3:2 (1998): 59–69.

Pucket, Lyn. *Charles Dickens*. Basingstoke, UK: Palgrave 2002.

Ray, Gordon N., ed. *The Letters and Private Papers of William Makepeace Thackeray*, Vol. 2. Cambridge, MA: Harvard University Press, 1946.

Reed, John R. "Dickens and Naming." *Dickens Studies Annual* 36 (2005): 183–97.

Ron, Moshe. "Autobiographical Narration and Formal Closure in *Great Expectations*." *Hebrew University Studies in Literature* 5.1 (1977): 37–66.

Rose, Jacqueline. "Julia Kristeva — Take Two." *Sexuality in the Field of Vision*. London: Verso, 1986. 141–64.

Rozin, Paul, and April E. Fallon. "A Perspective on Disgust." *Psychological Review* 94.1 (1987): 23–41.

Rozin, Paul, Jonathan Haidt, and Clark R. McCauley. "Disgust." *Handbook of Emotions*. Ed. M. Lewis and J.M. Haviland-Jones. 2nd ed. New York: Guilford Press, 2000. 637–53.

Sadoff, Dianne F. *Monsters of Affection: Dickens, Eliot, and Bronte on Fatherhood*. Baltimore, MD: John Hopkins University Press, 1982.

Sadrin, Anny. *Parentage and Inheritance in the Novels of Dickens*. Cambridge: Cambridge University Press, 1994.

Sartre, Jean Paul. *Being and Nothingness*. 1943. Trans. Hazel E. Barnes. London: Methuen, 1972.

Schor, Hilary M. *Dickens and the Daughter of the House*. Cambridge: Cambridge University Press, 1999.

Schroeder, Natalie E., and Ronald A. Schroeder. "Betsey Trotwood and Jane Murdstone: Dickensian Doubles." *Studies in the Novel*. 21.3 (1989): 268–78.

Sell, Kathleen. "The Narrator's Shame: Masculine Identity in *Great Expectations*." *Dickens Studies Annual* 26 (1998): 203–26.

Shelley, Mary, *Frankenstein or the Modern Prometheus*. Ed. James Kinsley and M.K. Joseph. Oxford: Oxford University Press, 1980.

Shires, Linda. "Literary Careers, Death and the Body Politics of *David Copperfield*." *Dickens Refigured: Bodies, Desires and Other Histories*. Ed. John Schad. Manchester and New York: Manchester University Press, 1996. 117–35.

Slater, Michael. *Dickens and Women*. Stanford: Stanford University Press, 1983.

Smith, Anne-Marie. *Julia Kristeva: Speaking the Unspeakable*. London & Sterling, VA: Pluto Press, 1998.

Smith, Grahame. *Charles Dickens: A Literary Life*. Basingstoke, UK: Macmillan, 1996.

Snef, Carol A. "*Bleak House*: The Need for Social Exorcism." *Dickens Studies Newsletter* 9.3 (1980): 70–73.

Spengemann, William C. *The Forms of Autobiography: Episodes in the History of a Literary Genre*. New Haven and London: Yale University Press, 1980.

Spiegel, Maura. "Managing Pain: Suffering and Reader Sympathy in *Bleak House*." *Dickens Quarterly* 12 (1995): 3–9.

Stange, G. Robert. "Expectations Well Lost; Dickens' Fable for His Time." *College English* 16.1 (1954): 9–17.

Stedman, Jane W. "Child-Wives of Dickens." *The Dickensian* 59 (1963): 112–18.

Steig, Michael. "Dickens' Excremental Vision." *Victorian Studies* 13.3 (1970): 339–354.

Steihaug, Jon-Ove. "Abject/*Informe*/Trauma: Discourses on the Body in American

Art of the Nineties." *ForArt* (1995). January 24, 2005. http://www.forart.no/stei haug/toc.html.

Stein, Robert A. "Pip's Poisoning Magwitch, Supposedly: The Historical Context and Its Implications for Pip's Guilt and Shame." *Philological Quarterly* 67.1 (1988): 103–16.

Stolte, Tyson. "Mightier Than the Sword: Aggression of the Written Word in *Great Expectations*." *Dickens Studies Annual* 35 (2005): 179–208.

Stone, Harry. "The Love Pattern in Dickens' Novels." *Dickens the Craftsman: Strategies of Presentation.* Ed. Robert B. Partlow, Jr. Carbondale and Edwardsville: Southern Illinois University Press, 1970. 1–20.

_____. "*Oliver Twist* and Fairy Tales." *Dickens Studies Newsletter* 10.2–3 (1979): 34–39.

Stone, Jennifer. "The Horrors of Power: A Critique of Julia Kristeva." *The Politics of Theory.* Proceedings of the Essex Conference in the Sociology of Literature, July 1982. Colchester: University of Essex, 1983. 38–48.

Tambling, Jeremy. "Prison-Bound: Dickens and Foucault," *Essays in Criticism* 36 (1986): 11–31.

_____. *Dickens, Violence and the Modern State: Dreams of the Scaffold.* New York: St. Martin's Press, 1995.

Thurley, Geoffrey. *The Dickens Myth: Its Genesis and Structure.* St. Lucia: University of Queensland Press, 1976.

Tick, Stanley. "The Memorializing of Mr. Dick." *Nineteenth-Century Fiction*, 24.2 (1969): 142–53.

Tomalin, Claire. *The Invisible Woman: The Story of Nelly Ternan and Charles Dickens.* 1990. London: Penguin, 1991.

_____. *Charles Dickens: A Life.* London: Penguin, 2011.

Tomkins, Silvan. *Affect, Imagery, Consciousness.* Vol. 2. New York: Springer, 1963.

Trotter, David. *Cooking with Mud: The Idea of Mess in Nineteenth-Century Art and Fiction.* Oxford: Oxford University Press, 2000.

Van Boheemen-Saaf, Christine. "'The Universe Makes an Indifferent Parent': *Bleak House* and the Victorian Family Romance." *Interpreting Lacan.* Ed. Joseph H. Smith and William Kerrigan. New Haven: Yale University Press, 1983. 225–57.

Van Ghent, Dorothy. "On *Great Expectations*." *The English Novel: Form and Function.* New York: Holt, Rinehart and Winston, 1953. 125–38.

Ward, David A. "Distorted Religion: Dickens, Dissent, and *Bleak House*." *Dickens Studies Annual* 29 (2000): 195–232.

Waters, Catherine. *Dickens and the Politics of the Family.* Cambridge: Cambridge University Press, 1997.

Watkins, Gwen. *Dickens in Search of Himself: Recurrent Themes and Characters in the Work of Charles Dickens.* Basingstoke, UK: Macmillan, 1987.

Weinstein, Philip M. *The Semantics of Desire: Changing Models of Identity from Dickens to Joyce.* Princeton, NJ: Princeton University Press, 1984.

Weissman, Judith, and Steven Cohan. "Dickens' *Great Expectations*: Pip's Arrested Development." *American Imago* 38:1 (1981): 105–26.

Welsh, Alexander. *From Copyright to Copperfield: The Identity of Dickens.* Cambridge: Cambridge University Press, 1987.

_____. *Dickens Redressed.* New Haven and London: Yale University Press, 2000.

Westburg, Barry. *The Confessional Fictions of Charles Dickens.* DeKalb: Northern Illinois University Press, 1977.

Wilson, Angus. *The World of Charles Dickens*. London: Secker and Warburg, 1970.

Wilson, Edmund. "Dickens: The Two Scrooges." *The Wound and the Bow: Seven Studies in Literature*. 1941. London: Methuen, 1961. 1–93.

Wilson, Robert Rawdon. *The Hydra's Tale: Imagining Disgust*. Edmonton: University of Alberta Press, 2002.

Wilt, Judith. "Confusion and Consciousness in Dickens's Esther." *Nineteenth-Century Fiction* 32.3 (1977): 285–309.

Woodward, Kathleen. "Anger ... and Anger: From Freud to Feminism." *Freud and the Passions*. Ed. John O'Neill. University Park: Pennsylvania State University Press, 1996. 73–95.

Woolf, Virginia. "*David Copperfield*." *Nation*. August 22, 1925. Reprinted in *Charles Dickens: Critical Assessments*. Ed. Michael Hollington. Vol. 3. East Sussex, UK: Helm Information, 1995. 81–84.

Young, Iris Marion. *Justice and the Politics of Difference*. Princeton, NJ: Princeton University Press, 1990.

Young, Melanie. "Distorted Expectations: Pip and the Problems of Language." *Dickens Studies Annual* 7 (1978): 203–220.

Zigarovich, Jolene. "Wilkie Collins, Narrativity, and Epitaph." *Dickens Studies Annual* 36 (2005): 229–64.

Index

211

www.ingramcontent.com/pod-product-compliance
Lightning Source LLC
Chambersburg PA
CBHW021426110726
47901CB00008B/2315